HER LESBIA[illegible]S: THE COMPLETE SERIES

K.F. JONES

❀ Created with Vellum

CHAPTER 1

"Are you ready?"

Amber didn't respond immediately, lost as she was in her own thoughts. The young woman had to clear her throat to get her attention.

"I'm sorry, yes," Amber said. "What's she like?"

"Have you ever met a dragon? Well, imagine you are about to, and you just broke their favourite bone china tea set," the receptionist whispered conspiratorially. The receptionist kept it up for just long enough for the colour to drain from Amber's face and then couldn't keep a straight face any longer. She giggled and flashed Amber a cheeky grin.

"You had me going there," Amber said with a sigh of relief, as she tried to calm her nerves.

"I'm sorry. You're right, I shouldn't tease you before your final interview. It was a little mean, I admit, you just look so flustered and really there is no need to be nervous. I wouldn't work for Miss Hamilton if she was horrid."

"It's alright, I'm nervous because the job sounds perfect and I really don't want to fail at the last hurdle," Amber admitted.

The receptionist nodded sympathetically. "I get it, believe me.

Working for Miss Hamilton is the best thing that ever happened to me. Just remember, she's the boss for a reason and she is always in charge. Be yourself, be honest, and I'm sure you'll be fine. You wouldn't have got to this floor of the building, if she wasn't interested in you," the young woman said. She was trying her best to be encouraging, but it didn't entirely settle Amber's nerves.

"Good luck," the receptionist whispered before she reached for the door handle and swung it wide open. She announced Amber with a loud and clear, slightly plummy voice, "Please go in and take a seat, Amber. Your interview will begin shortly." The office was empty, so Amber wasn't sure who that performance was for.

Amber took a deep breath and stepped over the threshold into Susanna Hamilton's office. She tried to control her body, to stop the trembling, but when the door shut with a barely audible click, she flinched like a frightened rabbit. Bloody hell, she was nervous!

There was good reason to be. This position would be worth fighting for. Already she had sat through three interviews with Miss Hamilton's personnel staff, and an interview with a psychologist of some sort, which had included a series of extensive multi-choice tests and a lengthy discussion of her life history. None of Amber's friends, not that she had many close friends, had ever described such an intensive interview process.

Now she was through that gauntlet and was going to meet Miss Hamilton, Amber was desperate to make a good impression. She had to stop herself biting her lower lip as the receptionist showed her to a chair in front of an enormous desk. It was the kind of desk that you bought once you'd realised that you had enough money not to worry about the exorbitant price.

Miss Hamilton was conspicuous by her absence. This did nothing to help calm Amber. Any minute now, she would stride into the office behind her, and no doubt Amber would find herself jumping out of her skin. She gritted her teeth, steeling herself for the surprise.

"Ah, Miss Hannam, pleased to meet you. I am Susanna Hamilton," a crystal clear voice said, seemingly from nowhere. Amber was a little startled by the unexpected sound, which came from her side somewhere.

Not that there was any doubt about the identity of the occupant, even if Amber hadn't known whose office this was from the name on the door, she felt sure that she'd have been picked this woman out as the owner of the company. There was just something about her that was immediately impressive.

Amber tried not to stare as she stood and turned toward the discreet door that had opened in the wall of the office to admit her future employer. Possible future employer, she corrected herself. "It's an honour to meet you, Miss Hamilton," she smiled. Amber would have gone for a firm handshake, as she imagined this powerful woman would expect, but she did not approach, she simply sat down in the large chair on the opposite side of the desk.

The business woman smiled graciously and gestured to the chair Amber had just got up from. "Please, Amber, take a seat. It's nice to meet you at last. These interviews have taken a long time, I know, but it can't be helped, I'm afraid. I'd hoped to get a shortlist sooner, but there were simply too many candidates with admirable qualities, for my team to whittle down the list any faster." Susanna sighed softly and shook her long black hair, running her fingers back through it and letting it settle behind her slim shoulders, then rolling her head as if she was stretching.

Amber felt a little strange sitting there in her jacket and trousers as Susanna was wearing a tight lycra top and a short tennis skirt. She could see a fine sheen of sweat on the other woman, who was now dabbing at her neck with a towel.

"Excuse my state, Miss Hannam, but I've been exercising in my private gym," Susanna said, indicating the half-open door from which she had entered the office. That was fancy, having a gym of any kind in your office. Amber would have been surprised to see an exercise bicycle, even in an office this large, but a whole other room dedicated to exercising at work seemed quite luxurious.

"Now, down to business, I think. If I were to hire you as my personal assistant, then I would expect you to play the game my way.

To be blunt, Miss Hannam I have no patience with shy, retiring violets who simply buckle under and do exactly what they are told and no more. When I ask an employee to do something I expect them to add, where appropriate, their imagination, flair and enthusiasm to the job in hand."

Susanna stood and walked over to a drinks cabinet. She began to pour two drinks. "Now I'd like to know what things you might expect your job to entail. Simply tell me what your expectations of the duties your position would entail are," she said as she walked over to Amber and handed her a glass.

"Well, Miss Hamilton. As a personal assistant, I would expect to be at your side or nearby all day, and to take and interpret your instructions quickly and efficiently. I imagine I would be responsible for organising your diary and generally act as a buffer between yourself and the outside world. That is your business and also your social life. Essentially I'd be there to deal with the more trivial matters, or with the things that you simply don't want to do," Amber took a sip from her whisky, which turned into more of a gulp than she'd intended. It was strong, but smooth and doubtless expensive. Not that Amber knew enough about the subject to tell. She just hoped that she had hit the nail on the head with the things expected of her.

"That seems fairly accurate - as far as it goes. But tell me, you said that you'd expect to be near me all day. Pray, what do I do if I need you at night? Where might you be?" Miss Hamilton asked.

"If it were part of the job requirements, I'm sure I could be on call and do what I could from home, or come to the office if there was something urgent," Amber replied, doing her best to sound game for a working life of long, hard hours.

"I don't want a glorified secretary, I have plenty of those. If you come and work for me, Amber, you'll be living in my house. You would need to be at my beck and call twenty-four hours a day. You will have next to not social life, because you will be working seven days a week, for long hours. The only socialising you'll get will be during your vacations, not more than the statutory minimum per year, and whatever fun you have at functions that you attend with me. I'd expect you to be awake whenever I am, which shouldn't be a problem for someone of your age, and perhaps work later than me, if you had something to arrange for me that was urgent," Susanna said, sitting down on the edge of the desk in front of Amber. She took a sip of her own whisky.

"When I say arrange, you'd have to arrange things that are usually outside business interests. Things such as social functions, any travel abroad, whether for business or pleasure. That sort of thing. Tell me, do you think you still want the job? Can you handle what I've told you," she said, locking eyes with Amber.

Amber was determined not to flinch from the piercing gaze and tried to sound confident as she replied, "Yes, I've had to arrange similar things in my previous post. I'm well qualified, but you know that. In fact, considering the previous interviews and their depth, I'd say the only thing you don't know about me at this point, is whether or not you like me in person." Amber took another sip of whisky to hide the fact that her bravado was entirely false.

Susanna laughed, "Hah. Good for you, Amber. Yes, that is, of course, accurate, I do need to know if I can get on with you. Remember, if I don't like you then I'm going to find it very annoying if I'm seeing you around all day. However, I still want to know if you are entirely suitable for the job. You see, I frankly don't trust all that interviewing by other people, but I simply don't have time to do all of it myself. The interviewers were actually an outside contracted firm, I don't have the kind of operations that supports a personnel department you see," she stood up, and beckoned for Amber to follow after her, as she walked towards a large pair of oak doors.

Astonishment was not the least thing that went through Amber's mind when she was the room beyond. A fabulously luxurious bedroom was the last thing she had expected, another office, a conference room perhaps, but a bedroom? On top of having a gym, this was decidedly strange.

"It's obvious that you'd find this a little unusual Amber, but the reason is simply that I don't like hotels. I prefer to stay here when I have to be in the city. In fact, these offices only serve as a decoy to the outside world. I don't really work from here. Not all that often. However my investments do get handled from here, as does all communication from prospective customers, contacts, the press - if they should have taken a sudden interest, and people begging for money for the latest charity," she threw the face towel on to the huge four-poster bed and made for a wardrobe.

"Now Amber, assuming I decide to hire you, it will be for a trial period only, say 3 months. You'd have to sign a contract that includes secrecy clauses to protect my private life and business details of course, but assuming all goes well that contract would be extended in three-year chunks," she started looking through the various dresses and suits in the wardrobe.

After a minute or two, Susanna frowned and pushed the lot aside in favour of the last outfit on the rail. Amber smiled privately as Susanna drew a hangar with a simple pair of black jeans and a denim shirt flopped on to it.

Susanna sat on the edge of the bed and undid her trainers, throwing them carelessly into the corner of the room. Susanna stood, turned to face the bed, and as her hands gripped the side of her skirt, Amber politely turned her head to one side. She found, however, that the mirrored walls meant that she could still see Susanna perfectly, albeit from behind.

The skirt came down and revealed a pale white bottom, firm cheeks unshaken by the action. The long legs were also firm and yet fleshy. An expensive pair of lace panties, elegant but little more than a thong, in Amber's estimation, were pulled down in one smooth movement, until they pooled around Susanna's ankles, before being flicked toward trainers with one flick of Susanna's long legs.

Susanna stood upright, thrusting her arms in the air as she slipped the sporty crop top off and over her head and shook free her long raven tresses. As she looked up, Amber dropped her gaze from the mirrors, to the carpet, trying to pretend that she had not caught those few seconds of Susanna in all her glory, naked and yet still so clearly in charge of everything around her.

"Amber, look up, and turn to face me now. You won't see anything you haven't got yourself. Turn around and pass me those jeans," Susanna said impatiently.

Doing as she was told, Amber turned and gulped at the voluptuous body before her. Silently, she handed the jeans to Susanna, who slipped them on without bothering to put on panties to cover her completely shaven sex and prevent chaffing.

"Um, don't you want any underwear under those?" Amber asked boldly.

"Oh no, I like the feel of the denim against my skin. They're a well-worn pair, so they aren't too harsh. Pass me a bra from the wardrobe though, would you?" Susanna said as she belted up the tight jeans.

Amber watched as she put on the shit over the bra that she had grabbed from the wardrobe. An uplifting bra, as it happened, although Amber had just picked a random one. The effect on Susanna's already ample bosom reminded Amber of Jane Russell in the Outlaw. Susanna did a couple of turns to check the fit in the mirrors and then sat on the edge of the bed again.

She cocked her head and looked Amber up and down. Amber stood still and tried to not fidget. Susanna frowned briefly and said, "I can't get an idea of what you really look like. That awful suit completely blurs your shape. I'm sure it was all you can afford, but I hope if you had the funds, you'd have enough taste to choose something more suitable for you. It simply won't do, though. You must take it off, Amber."

Amber gulped, and a myriad of thoughts raced through her mind in double-quick time. What was this? This wasn't at all what she had expected. Sure, she didn't mind seeing Susanna naked. In fact, once she had started to handle the surprise of the thing, it was hardly unpleasant. Susanna was gorgeous by any standard, not that older women were Amber's style. *Or any women for that matter, she thought. Why had she felt the need to qualify that thought with 'older', Amber wondered?* But exposing herself to her future boss? Surely that wasn't something she could do, even though she'd been told to?

On the other hand, Amber needed the job, and besides, Susanna just wanted to get the cheap suit out of her eyeline. She probably wanted to see what clothes might suit her new assistant better. After all, the suit was extremely pedestrian. It had been all she could afford at the time, and she didn't have enough money to replace it before this interview.

The decision made, Amber began to remove her jacket calmly and methodically. Then she reached back and began to unbutton her skirt. She looked up in surprise as she heard peals of laughter coming from Susanna. The other woman's head was thrown back, exposing her creamy swan neck, as she laughed and giggled. Amber frowned and stopped undressing. She waited for Susanna's mirth to subside.

Finally, Susanna stopped laughing and spoke, "You look ridiculous, about as sexy as a week old Haddock. Flair, imagination, style, my girl. This is what I want from you. Don't just take your clothes off, strip. Show some passion for it, some panache. Imagine that you are stripping in front of your lover, Amber. Make it slow, sexy, and prove to me that you can put on a show. Treat me as if I am your lover, Amber, and you are going to beguile me with your charms," she clapped her hands and giggled again. "I have to know that my personal assistant knows how to impress at events and knows how to use her body to her advantage. Our elegant dresses, our shoes, our hair, perfume and diamond earrings. They're weapons, Amber. Weapons in an arsenal the men we compete against, cannot match. Prove to me that you can captivate an onlooker."

No chance to turn back now, Amber thought. She had started this. If showing she had some kind of flair for amateur dramatics, or could at least prove willing, was going to get her the job, she would bloody well do it. Even if she had misread Susanna's order and thought she just wanted her to change clothes, not perform a striptease, Amber had no intention of backing down now and looking foolish, cowardly or both.

Amber turned her back on Susanna and slid her hands down her body, pushing her thumbs between her silky skin and the scratchy material of the skirt. Slowly, she eased the skirt down her legs until she was bent so far over that her fingertips could have touched the floor.

CHAPTER 2

Amber followed Susanna to the remarkably fast elevators. On the way up to the interview, they had almost made her nauseous, and she was grateful that they were at least internal elevators, and not those awful glass ones on the outside of a building.

The underground car park was dozens of floors below them, but they arrived faster than most elevators managed a handful of floors. There they got into a large and comfortable electric sedan. Amber was no car buff, but it was clearly a top of the line model, as befitted an eco-conscious businesswoman of Susanna's prominence. The windows were heavily tinted so passengers could not be seen from the outside.

An attractive young woman, dressed as a chauffeur in a black trouser suit and crisp white shirt and tie, was waiting by the car, holding the door open for Susanna. "Thank you, Roxy," Susanna said.

As Roxy closed the door after her boss got in, she flicked her head toward the rear passenger side behind the driver's seat, indicating that Amber should get in there.

The chauffeur did not follow her around the vehicle to open the door for the personal assistant as well, and Amber was grateful not to be treated like a celebrity of some kind, that it took a moment for her to get moving. Swiftly, she hurried around the car in the hopes that she could avoid looking awkward when she got in. She wasn't convinced that she managed it in the unfamiliar shoes. The dress was not the easiest to clamber into a car in, even a big one like this. From Susanna's perspective, she must have looked like a clumsy buffoon, but her rather odd new boss didn't say anything.

The car pulled smoothly away, eerily quiet due to the electric engine and out into the busy London traffic. Amber realised the blindfold was still clutched in her hands and wanting to seem eager and obedient, she wrapped it around her eyes, knotting it at the back of her head.

"Good girl," said Susanna.

Amber had briefly considered disobeying the spirit of her employer's instruction and trying to leave a corner free that she could see out of, but she had thought better of it. Susanna probably wouldn't take kindly to such deception, and after all, wasn't she entitled to protect her privacy and security?

Besides, Amber wasn't so familiar with London's roads or the surrounding counties that she'd have any idea where they were unless she saw exactly the right road signs and then looked it up later.

At first it was odd, being unable to see and thus not knowing when the car would bank left or right, accelerate or slow down. Amber found herself adjusting the way she sat to feel more comfortable. And yet, after ten minutes or so, the blindfold had other effects. Her senses didn't heighten, but she was concentrating on fewer of them, taking in smells and the subtle swish of their clothing, the faint hum of the high end climate control.

Amber had already had to hand over her phone back at the office, and it had been switched off by the receptionist and then sealed in a lockbox along with her keys, purse and even her lipstick. She'd been allowed into Susanna's presence with nothing but her clothes and shoes, and now she'd left those behind.

The receptionist had been waiting with the lockbox when they reached the car park, so at least that had gone in the boot of the car.

Clearly, though, if Susanna felt the blindfold necessary, she wasn't going to be allowed to have a phone with GPS built-in back any time soon.

Amber did her best to relax. By her side, Susanna appeared to be reading some documents, judging by the sound of it, and this left Amber some time to relax and collect her thoughts.

All Amber knew for sure about Susanna Hamilton was that she had been heir to a small inheritance and that she had built that up into an impressive investment portfolio of some kind. She also ran her own businesses, although Amber had no idea what those were.

Amber had assumed Susanna's businesses were in the City, since the job offer and all the interviews she'd done with Susanna's human resources agency had been in central London. There had been no mention that she would be expected to live outside London, assuming the house really was in the country, and not in some leafy suburb of the capital. Evidently, the job advert and application process had given Amber the whole story and London wasn't going to play a central role in her employment.

That didn't matter to Amber though, not really. She liked some aspects of living in London, but it had plenty of downsides too, not least of which was the sheer expense. The generous compensation package that had been listed with the position had been the first thing that attracted her to it, far more so than the location.

It didn't really matter to Amber what sort of business her employer ran provided it was profitable. Her work as a personal assistant wouldn't change much from one industry to the next. The controlling factor was her boss, in this case, Susanna Hamilton and she was clearly an unusual character.

Amber was not shy about her mercenary nature. There was nothing wrong with making sure you could put food on the table and pay your bills.

This job was a considerable step up from her last company, and though they hadn't gone into all the specifics such as her living at Susanna's home, it would still leave her much better off financially even if she kept the lease on her flat.

Amber would certainly do that until the probationary period was up, but if she was signed on for another three years, as the contract briefly mentioned, could she live in Susanna's house and save the money on a flat?

A storage unit for her meagre collection of belongings would be much cheaper than renting a flat, and it wasn't as if she had been living in some beautiful loft apartment of unusual size and insanely low rent. Far from it. If Amber wasn't going to have time for a social life either, she could have a tidy nest egg after three years.

But Miss Hamilton was not at all as she had expected, not by any means. Amber knew people who'd had male bosses who were rather inappropriate, but she was conflicted about where Susanna stood on that front.

Certainly, the idea of her being her personal assistant had never brought to mind the events of the hours. Amber only hoped that it really had all been some kind of bizarre obedience test.

It wasn't, on reflection, an onerous experience. Had she been expecting it, Amber wondered if it would have been a thrilling game between them. As it was, with no warning, Amber was still feeling uncertain about the whole thing.

What she hoped most fervently, was that Susanna had failed to notice her excitement at the touch of her fingers on Amber's flesh, and especially the effect that her branding iron hot tongue had had on Amber's nipple.

It would probably wouldn't be good if Susanna knew that Amber was still wet at the crotch, and her nipples were stiff as bullets. Perhaps that was because she couldn't stop thinking about it as she sat in the car, unable to see the buildings and London's citizens pass by.

Amber ached with desire, the need to be touched. With little else to think about except the woman beside her and what had transpired in the office a short while ago, Amber's thought strayed into dangerous territory. Closing her eyes beneath the blindfold, she put her head back against the leather head rest and pretended to doze, while in reality, in her minds eye she was picturing being stripped naked again.

A firm bodied figure stood in front of her, examining her most intimate secrets. Hands explored her figure, dancing over her ribs, squeezing her buttocks, stroking her nipples while hot breath splashed over her at the junction of her thighs.

Amber imagined herself staring at the ceiling, trying to count the tiles, as she had done in Susanna's office bedroom. She did not want to watch her tormentor, did not dare to disobey her instructions. Did not dare to look down at the woman.

Her tormentor's hands travelled between her thighs, palms outwards, and slowly she was forced to spread her stance, shuffling her feet further apart, leaving space between her thighs.

Then the hands left her body aching to be touched again, as the figure stood up and moved behind her. A hand felt its way onto her stomach, fingers pointing down, another alighted between her shoulder blades.

Slowly Amber was bent over as the hands pushed gently, but insistently, just below her neck, and alighted on her stomach to push her buttocks back toward her tormentor. She dipped ever further until her fingertips brushed the brushed the carpet and she could only look straight down.

Then her tormentor made her walk her hands forward until her weight was supported on them, and her feet equally.

Hot, strong fingers caressed Ambers buttocks for an age. Then without warning, while one hand held her hip, the other reached from the front to her wet pussy and spread her lips gently. Something pushed against her, into her, plunging deep inside in one movement. It wriggled inside her obscenely.

It drove her over the threshold and she climbed up and up to the highest peaks of a fierce climax. As Amber shook in the throes of her orgasm and the dextrous cock pulled out of her, she turned her head to face her lover and was met with a face of almost blinding light.

Amber blinked and mumbled something she didn't understand.

"Amber, what's the matter? Are you alright?" Susanna asked. The blindfold had come off, and she was temporarily dazzled by the light. Susanna had one hand on Amber's shoulders, the other rested in Amber's lap, clutching the blindfold tightly. Her new boss had a look of sympathetic concern etched on her face.

"Hmm? Err. Oh dear, I think I nodded off and was having a dream. More of a nightmare, really. I'm terribly sorry, I hope I didn't scream out loud or anything," Amber said, trying to cover as best she could the secret dream she'd been having. It certainly wasn't something one discussed with one's new boss.

Had she said anything out loud as she nodded off? Amber could feel her neck and chest flushing pink at the thought she might have been moaning as passionately in the car while she had her panty soaking dream, as she did in the fantasy itself as her tormentor penetrated her with what, a prehensile cock? No, it was fingers. Several strong fingers, Amber realised.

"Scream? No. Well, it wasn't quite a scream, it was too muffled, I think maybe you were trying to say something in your sleep," Susanna said. "Anyway, we're in the grounds now so no need for the blindfold at the moment."

Amber was grateful that Susanna didn't know what had caused her to start awake like that. It was one of her most cherished secrets that she did not need to be touched to achieve orgasm if she could come up with the appropriate sexy images and idea, of course. It was usually part of a dream and not a waking thing, though Amber had been lucky enough to manage that once or twice during particularly long sessions of fantasising on a lazy weekend in bed.

She knew she must have had an orgasm in her semi-conscious state and given some kind of voice to her thoughts, but it seemed as if she had got away with it. How terribly humiliating it would have been if Susanna had cottoned on to what was happening. It was a good job it was too indistinct for Susanna to hear properly, or whatever would she have thought?

At least Susanna could never guess that when in her mind she had turned to thank her strong, hunky lover it hard turned out not to be a muscly young man but a woman instead. And worse, it hadn't been just an indistinct female presence, it had been a vivid image of Susanna's face that she had seen before the light blinded her.

Shaking away the worrying implications of that thought, Amber tried to make it look as if she were studying the extensive grounds of the country house as they drove sedately along the drive.

Susanna's hand tapped the blindfold idly against her chin as she breathed the country air in, "Don't you just love that fragrance?"

"The open country?" Amber asked absently.

"Country. Yes, Amber."

CHAPTER 3

This was obviously an old estate, even to Amber's inexpert eye. She had visited enough National Trust historic estates to know that, even if she couldn't place the age. There were dozens, or perhaps hundreds of these enormous buildings still left standing across the UK. Most were in the hands of conservation organisations now, but a number were still in private hands.

They were too costly to maintain for most families. It really only took one generation who were bad at finances to bring an estate like this to its knees. That was probably how Susanna had acquired it, after the original owners had been left with no choice but to sell, unable to pay the upkeep.

The house itself was a huge mansion affair, and the grounds were fully landscaped gardens near the house with wooded wild areas and parks further away. The main road, where the gatehouse was, was not visible from the house. Amber couldn't hear anything other than the local birds and quiet crunch of the car's wheels on the gravel driveway.

The setting was positively idyllic, and it was easy to see why Susanna used this as her main place of residence and conducted business there too. If that's what the secretive woman did with this country pile, of course. Perhaps this was merely number four on her list of favourite homes, Amber giggled to herself.

Amber got out of the car and followed Susanna up to the house. Inside, Susanna took her into a study and they sat down. Amber sniffed the air cautiously as Susanna turned her head toward her shoulder to check where the bell-rope was and pulled the velvet cord. Thankfully Amber couldn't smell her own juices, despite the fact Susanna had not furnished her with new panties before they left London. She hoped that Roxy wasn't having to clean up the moist seat of the car.

Would the chauffer even report such a thing to her boss, though? What could she really say? "Miss Hamilton, I'm pretty sure your passenger had a silent orgasm in your car and made a mess of my lovely seats." Amber certainly hoped she wouldn't be crass enough to rat her out.

The doors opened silently, and a young woman stepped in. Amber could practically feel her eyelids rolling up and her eyes bulging from her head.

The maid was a pretty brunette with her hair up in a bun and wearing a French maids uniform. Or, Amber supposed, not actually a real French maids uniform but a fantasy concoction chosen to best display her commendable assets.

High-heeled patent leather court shoes, or pumps as they always called them on American TV shows, accentuated the fine lines of her calves and no doubt a well-toned bottom as well. A black teddy with a small white apron, and an indecently short mini-skirt. Bands of lace on the wrists, ankles and neck were accompanied by a white garter, stockings and an entirely unnecessary headband, served to complete the uniform.

"Sugar, this is Miss Amber Hannam, my new personal assistant," Susanna said. The French maid curtseyed deeply. "Please have a light dinner prepared for this evening. I shall be going out to visit the ponies and have a ride after I have shown Miss Hannam to her room, and I shall want a bath ready when I get back. You may go now."

Sugar curtseyed again to Susanna this time, and left without a word or a question, clearly knowing just how to satisfy her employer's needs.

"Sugar? That's a rather unusual name, isn't it?" Amber asked Susanna as she followed her up a huge sweeping staircase, "I don't think I've ever met anyone called Sugar."

Susanna chuckled, "Yes, I suppose it would be if it were the name she was given at birth, that is. Sugar is simply what I choose to call her. I give new names to all of my servants when they enter my household. I find it suits me far better than using their given names." Susanna flashed a smile at Amber and opened a pair of double doors wide with a flourish.

Ushering Amber inside the room, she said, "This will be your suite. I hope it has everything you might want. If not, you can ask this young lady, I call her Candy." Another maid, dressed identically to Sugar, appeared as if from nowhere. This one was a curvaceous blonde.

"Have a pleasant afternoon, I'm off for my ride," Susanna said as she left Amber alone in the bedroom with the new maid who promptly curtseyed at her. *That would take some getting used to, Amber thought, having these maids curtseying at her as if she was important. She wondered if she could persuade them to stop.*

Susanna popped her head back around the door a moment later, while Amber was still trying to decide what to do with herself, or about the maid who was standing awaiting some kind of instruction or request she imagined.

"I forgot, Candy, is your personal maid. I like to ensure that my executive staff are well taken care of. Have fun. Her duty is to ensure that the woman she is providing maid service for is kept completely happy. Instruct her as you see fit and Candy will do whatever is required. I'll see you at eight for dinner, Candy will make sure you are appropriately attired, she knows the dress code. Ciao!" Susanna said cheerily and with that, vanished, presumably to go and ride her ponies as she'd said.

Amber was quite taken aback by the opulence of the place and the presence of staff to look after her. The idea that a personal assistant would warrant a maid of her own was quite unreal to Amber.

Her salary was impressive, the bedroom suite was capacious and far larger than anything she'd ever lived in, and now she was to have her own French maid dressed in a uniform that could charitably be described as revealing, if not downright salacious. Amber's life was deviating rapidly from what she considered normal.

Amber wasn't quite sure what to do with her afternoon.

"What's your real name?" Amber asked kindly.

"Candy, Miss," the young woman replied immediately.

"No, I mean, what was the name you used before Miss Hamilton called you Candy?"

The young woman looked a little panicked but meekly answered, "Emily, Miss."

"Emily. Good. Well, hello, Emily, I'm Amber. Pleased to meet you. I've never met a maid before, let alone been assigned one to look after me. Can I ask what you actually do?" Amber said.

"Yes, Miss. I do all the usual cleaning, tidying up, bringing breakfast in bed if necessary, although I expect you'll be eating breakfast in the dining room most days. The bell-ropes or telephones can summon myself or Sugar if you need assistance. As I've been assigned to you as a lady's maid, I also help with more personal matters," Emily said, clearly feeling more confident on this more familiar ground.

"Like getting me dressed into a corset and ballgown?" Amber laughed.

"Certainly, Miss. Laying out clothes, brushing your hair, helping with makeup or scrubbing your back when you bathe. Simply ask, and I shall do everything I can to ensure you are satisfied," Emily replied.

"Well, that does sound like a rather pampered lifestyle for me, I must say.

"If you want it to be, Miss. We are here to serve."

"You mentioned the bath. Would I be correct that the door over there leads to a private bathroom for this remarkably luxurious suite?"

"Yes, Miss. The other doors are your walk-in wardrobe and sitting room come office."

"I have a sitting room?" Amber said, looking around at the doors on the opposite side of the room.

"Yes, Miss."

"Well, that's fancy."

Emily smiled.

"Can you run me a bath then, please? Is that alright?" Amber admitted.

"As you wish, Miss," Emily said, "I'm at your beck and call." Amber would have expected that to be highly sarcastic from anyone she was used to speaking to, but there was no hint of anything of the kind from Emily. This was going to be a serious adjustment in her daily routine.

The young woman curtseyed again and went into the bathroom. As the door opened, Amber got her first view of the room, and it was luxurious, to say the least. There was a huge wet room shower to one side, and an honest to goodness balcony through a bay window.

The bath looked more like an enormous hot tub than a normal bath. It was surrounded by a raised plinth and steps and had a secondary shower unit built-in. Amber frankly couldn't wait to try something quite so mundane as reading a book in it while drinking champagne. Well, probably cider, if she was honest. It was far more her speed.

Amber couldn't help but watch the sway of the maid's hips as she sashayed across the room to the bath. Her back and buttocks were left almost entirely uncovered by the uniform she wore, unless you counted thin straps as clothing.

It was little more than lingerie really, at the front the corsetry accentuated Emily's modest breasts and at the back, it exposed the deep cleft between her well-rounded arse cheeks, which was uncovered by panties and barely covered by the mini-skirt.

In any case, the slightest bend at the waist as the maid turned the taps on and began checking the temperature, caused the skirt to ride up at the back and expose her pussy in an entirely lewd display of womanly flesh.

Amber licked her lips unconsciously and felt a shudder pass

through her body. Surely Susanna must be sex-mad to make her staff dress like this and to conduct interviews the way she did? Certainly, this was not a normal country house by any means, although admittedly, Amber didn't actually have any experience. Maybe the rich lived like this everywhere.

The chauffeur and the two maids she'd met so were all dressed in fine clothes. There were all uniforms, but not, Amber suspected, off the peg. The outfit Emily wore didn't look to be of low quality, as you might find in a costume shop for Halloween. There could be no doubt that the intent of the expensive custom uniforms was to show off these young women's attributes in the most flattering manner.

It hadn't escaped Amber's notice that the chauffeur's trousers were a little tight across her bottom, but because they were tailored to be skin tight, not because they were a size too. Her shirt, while crisply pressed, had barely contained her bosom, which seemed to threaten to burst out at any moment.

Looking back, Amber realised that like Emily's uniform it was a tailored shirt, cut specifically for Roxy's top heavy curves. Her boobs were emphasised and seemed to be tightly confined, but the buttons weren't being stretch. It was carefully designed by an expert.

Had Roxy unbuttoned her suit jacket before her passengers got in the car, Amber imagined she would have been treated to a much clearer picture of the woman's figure, although the shirt and tie combination precluded the option of displaying a cleavage.

Amber could imagine the woman taking off her shirt to wash the car, and having a mans vest on underneath, which was bursting around the edges, revealing side-boob as it barely contained her big breasts. The vest would likely get soaked as she lathered soapy water over the vehicle, revealing dark, stiff nipples and large areolas through the sodden material.

As the naughty thoughts invaded her mind, completely unbidden, Amber slipped out of her dress and removed her shoes. Only two or three items of clothing, depending on how you counted, and she was entirely naked. Four if you counted her health monitor. She slipped that free of her wrist and placed it on the dressing table because hers was just old enough to not be waterproof.

"Your bath is ready, Miss. Depending on how full you require it before you use it," Emily called politely from the bathroom.

Amber didn't respond, she simply took a deep breath, imagining what it would feel like if she were far braver than she really was and strode, quite naked, into her bathroom.

CHAPTER 4

As Amber entered the bathroom, Emily turned around and stood up, smiling sweetly. The maid quite brazenly slid her eyes up and down Amber's body, and her face didn't betray the slightest hint of embarrassment. *What a bloody cheek the young woman had, Amber thought.*

It felt to her as if Emily's gaze had lingered on her more private areas and that she was being sized up like a piece of meat. There was a brief moment when she had a mental image of striking a pose to show off and fluttering her eyelids.

"Well, do I meet your approval?" Amber asked with as much sarcasm as she could muster, which being of fine English stock, was a good deal indeed.

"You're very pretty, Miss," Emily said, apparently oblivious to the rebuke, she offered her hand to steady Amber as she climbed into the bath.

Having a maid on hand to help her bathe was going to take some getting used to.

"Is there anything to drink?"

"Whisky, Miss?" Emily asked.

"No! I meant water or fruit juice or squash or something. I don't really drink that much, and I already had one in Miss Hamilton's office. I don't want to get tipsy on my first day or get a headache," Amber explained.

"Apple, orange or pineapple, Miss?" Emily asked as she walked into the other room.

"Apple please, Emily," Amber replied.

A moment later she heard the distinctive sound of a fridge door opening, which must be built in like in a hotel room as she hadn't seen it, opening and the chink of glasses. Then the maid appeared again with a large glass of chilled fruit juice, as ordered. Amber had expected the maid to have to go to wherever the kitchen was, not have drinks on hand, the lap of luxury didn't begin to describe this place.

The cool juice was delightfully refreshing after the long drive from London which had taken who knew how long? It was hard to keep track of time with a blindfold on. She wasn't even sure which county they were in, and it didn't seem like a good idea to ask Emily for that information.

"Miss?"

"Yes, Emily?"

"Would you mind calling me, Candy, Miss? Only Miss Hamilton really doesn't let us use our birth names. She likes us to remember we are in service to her and the names she gives us are a reminder of that," the young maid explained.

"Does she indeed? That's a little odd, but I don't want you to get in trouble, Candy."

"Thank you, Miss," Candy said with obvious relief as she took the now empty glass back from Amber and produced a soft flannel wash-cloth. "Shall I wash you, Miss?"

Amber had to use all her composure to keep a straight face and couldn't speak without the prospect of giggling, so she just bit her lip and nodded her assent, as if it were a question she had heard before. She didn't want to get Candy in trouble after all, even though this idea was making her somewhat uncomfortable. It felt rather odd to have another woman in the bathroom with her while she was actually naked.

The maid wasn't in the slightest offended at her nudity though and set about gently rubbing delightfully scented liquid soap over her back and neck with the cloth. A few moments later she was done with what she could reach and said, "Please, can you stand up, Miss?"

Amber did as she was asked and Candy efficiently soaped down the small of her back, and then up again from her calves, until she came to her buttocks. She thought the maid might stop there and ask her to use the cloth herself for the more intimate regions, but she didn't so much as blink before continuing.

The cloth ran over her buttocks and then without so much as a by your leave, one hand pulled aside one of her cheeks so the maid could clean her deep cleft. The soap was heavily infused with mint, and it left Amber's skin tingling everywhere that the lather touched and was not immediately rinsed off.

Most particularly, Amber could feel it making her rosebud feel fresh and prickly. It was not an unfamiliar sensation, as she used similar soaps at home on occasion, but it always caused a frisson of excitement. Amber was glad that she was already too wet from the bathwater for the maid to notice the effect she was sure the odd sensation was having on her.

The speed with which her back and legs were thoroughly flannelled, spoke of a lot of practice on the maid's part. How many times had she washed Susanna this way, or perhaps other staff or their employer's guests? Dare she ask such a bold question?

Amber suspected Candy and Sugar would be endless fonts of gossip if you could loosen their lips, so to speak, but something about their attitude spoke to a high level of loyalty and respect for their employer. In any case, how would one ask such a thing?

The cloth hadn't touched her for a while, and Amber broke from her reverie when she heard the soft sound of clothing hitting the floor. She half-turned as Candy walked from behind her and stepped into the huge bath in front of her, washcloth in hand.

Without a word, the happily humming young woman began to lather up her arms, then on to her legs, up to her stomach, and then finally she soaped Amber's full breasts. Only that wasn't final. She didn't leave a heartbeat between the considerable attention she paid to Amber's breasts, which caused her nipples to pucker pleasantly as she ran the slightly rough cloth across them, before descending between her legs.

The flannel of the washcloth teased at Amber's lips as Candy, without any sign of lasciviousness, became quite intimate with her womanly parts. It was all Amber could do not to cry out in shock, but it would have felt so out of place. Candy was entirely unabashed about her work, and Amber didn't wish to seem like a prude.

A moment later, or perhaps an hour, Candy put the cloth down and turned on the showerhead, rinsing her employer's new assistant down with water just hot enough to feel refreshing. Amber thought they were done, but Candy produced an expensive-looking razor and shaving foam, "Shall I tidy up, Miss?"

The implication that there was something to tidy felt mildly insulting at first and then Amber glanced down and realised that, of course, having been single for a while and not on the dating scene, a tidy was in order. Naturally, she hadn't felt the need to groom herself quite so personally for a job interview. Amber had visited a hairdresser to get a quick trim, but nothing dramatic or expensive.

There was no way since her redundancy that she could afford top London rates for an over the top hairdo, and it wasn't really in her nature to want it, anyway. Amber preferred a relaxing country break to endless manicures and the like.

Although she wasn't entirely immune to the pampering services that some people used on a regular basis. Amber had been on a spa break for a hen weekend once, and parts of that had been fantastic. The sports massage had worked wonders for her back, but other parts bored her to tears.

"Yes, please. Thank you. Yes. Thank you, Candy," she blurted, close to panic. Oh, dear. What an absolute provincial fool she must seem.

Within moments of lifting her arms above her head, her armpits were smooth and clean. Her legs took longer, of course, and Candy was never hurried, never less than careful. As she finished with her calves, the maid ran her hands up and down Ambers legs to check for stray hairs in a manner that felt rather pleasant to Amber.

After that was done, Candy tapped the inside of Amber's knees to indicate she should put her feet further apart. Amber dutifully complied. It was only a moment later, as the razor took care of her thighs, that she realised how exposed she was.

This stance parted her legs far enough that from Candy's position kneeling in the bath before her, the maid must have had a real eyeful of Amber's most intimate part.

Of course, Candy didn't say anything. She just finished her work with the razor and then stroked each thigh carefully, tidying up tiny rough patches as she went.

It took a moment for Amber to realise that Candy had laid her left hand on her lower stomach, and was gently pressing the smooth skin up, stretching it tight, and then a moment more to realise what that meant.

Amber looked down, Candy was poised with the razor above her thatch of hair. "Please stay perfectly still, Miss, I don't want to cut you," Candy said.

Amber responded with a croak that supposed to be, "Yes, of course." She lifted her eyes to the ceiling and then screwed them shut for good measure, unable to watch this beautiful and entirely nude, complete stranger perform such intimate grooming for her.

Evidently, Candy was able to understand her garbled response, because she sprayed a line of gel above the area and then worked it into a lather in Amber's hair with the practiced fingertips of the hand holding the razor. Then she neatly outlined the area, methodically trimming away the edges of Amber's bush as she hummed to herself.

This was thoroughly bizarre to Amber. She had been waxed a couple of times around her lady parts, but never shaven quite so intimately by another person, and never had she let them do more than tidy up.

Not even her last boyfriend, who had been with her for almost a year but who she hadn't allowed in her flat since breaking up with him several months ago, had ever shaved her.

Amber found herself chewing her lip and trying to think about anything that was completely non sexual as the young maid gently scraped away near her lips with the razor. Then, in a flash, the head of the razor swept over the bulk of the remaining hair and removed it.

Before Amber could protest, her bush was gone entirely. Not even the trimmed length concealing her lips remained.

It took a moment before she could speak and in that time, Candy had swept the razor over any remaining patches of shaving foam, rinsed her down with the showerhead and massaged her hand over the area to prove no hairs were remaining. All that without so much as a question about her grooming preferences! The very idea of it.

"Candy, what have you done!" Amber finally blurted.

"Miss?" Candy asked all innocent confusion.

"I thought you were going to tidy up, give me a nice neat landing strip or something, not shave my pussy completely bare!"

"It's how mistress prefers it, Miss," Candy stated. Something about her inflexion of the word mistress tickled at Amber's brain.

"How about how I prefer it?" Amber asked indignantly.

"My apologies, Miss. I did not mean to cause offence. I assumed you would be expected to follow the protocol mistress has laid down for those in service to her," Candy said.

What was the protocol Candy was talking about, Amber wondered. She was flushed with embarrassment now, but it struck her that Candy was genuinely surprised by her response and did seem to be following the norm for the household, however strange that was.

"I'm sorry, Candy. This is all just so strange to me, and I don't really know what's going on. Please ask if something similar comes up again, so I can tell you what I want," Amber said, hoping not to upset the maid.

It wasn't her fault, it was Miss Hamilton's instructions that had led to this. She had never entirely denuded her pussy like this herself, at most keeping the thatch of red hair under control.

Candy reached for a hand mirror and presented it below Amber's pussy, "It really suits you, Miss. If you don't mind me saying."

"What?" Amber muttered.

"Have a look, Miss. You have a beautiful body."

Amber reluctantly took the mirror and looked down to inspect herself. She turned the mirror this way and that, while Candy beamed up at her from behind it, clearly proud of her work. It had been well managed, Amber had to concede, and it was the best look she'd had at herself in years. Candy was right too, the little minx, Amber did have a beautiful body.

Perhaps she shouldn't have been hiding it. Perhaps her boyfriend would have been faithful if she had done this for him? No, that wasn't right. She definitely looked hot like this, even Amber had to admit, but he had been an absolutely first-class arse to her, and it had felt amazing when she finally kicked him to the curb. Whatever would she have wanted to drag that out for? Other than some rather desultory fucking, that is.

Amber coughed and handed the mirror back to the maid. "Yes, well, thank you, Candy. I suppose I do, and of course, you do as well," she said awkwardly.

"Thank you, Miss. Mistress Hamilton only has the best people in service to her," Candy said. As if that explained something. If the maid meant in terms of looks, Amber couldn't disagree. The receptionist, the chauffeur, the two maids, everyone that she knew worked for Miss Hamilton, was the picture of health and probably qualified as a genuine beauty to boot.

As she pondered this, Candy had somehow contrived to get behind her and guide her back down into the water. The maid sat down behind her, her legs either side of Amber's and began to massage the muscles of her shoulders.

It was immediately relaxing, and Amber took a deep breath, letting her head tip forward as the young woman worked strong thumbs into her flesh. It was at least as good as the massage at the spa day, although that hadn't involved a masseuse stark naked in the bath with her, of course.

Her reverie was broken when Candy casually posed a question as if it were the most normal thing in the world. "Would Miss require an orgasm before dinner?" the maid asked, slipped her hands from Amber's shoulders down her sides to rest on her stomach.

Amber felt her body stiffen. "I'm sorry. I must have misheard that," she croaked desperately trying to recall some nuance that confirmed that she had misheard the maid's question.

"Miss Hamilton left strict instruction that I was to do whatever was required to keep you happy," Candy clarified.

"Meaning what? Are you saying you have to lick my pussy if I tell you to?" Amber asked, nervously, fighting two urges that came across her. The first to turn around and run her hands over Candy's body, the second to leap out of the bath and flee.

"I'm sorry, Miss, no. Mistress Hamilton gave specific instructions that I was not allowed to use my mouth or lips to pleasure you, save for talking of course," Candy said with a giggle at her own joke. Amber let out a weak courtesy laugh, as she tried to rally from the bizarre exchange. While she considered if this was another test, like the one Susanna had given her in her interview, the maid continued.

"She said I may only use my fingers." As she explained this, Candy's fingers slid further down and brushed against the bare lips of Amber's pussy. Without her voluntary command, Amber found her legs parting a little more, giving the young woman easier access to her body.

"Oh, I see," Amber gasped as the fingers danced a question lightly over her lips.

Candy pressed herself against Amber's back, and she swore she could feel the stiff points of nipples caressing her skin. Was she imagining that, or was the young maid as turned on as she was? Hot breath played against her ear as Candy whispered, "May I have your permission to continue, Miss? I know you said I should make sure to ask. Mistress would be most upset with me if you were not satisfied with the way I served you."

"Why do you call her mistress like that, Candy?" Amber asked as her body relaxed against the embrace of the maid.

"Because she is the Mistress of the household, and we are her humble servants, Miss. I live in service to her and submit to her will in everything."

"And you like that, do you? You enjoy serving Miss Hamilton?" Amber asked. Her ability to resist the unanswered question that Candy had posed, was slowly weakening, and Amber knew it.

Was she delaying the inevitable by asking her own questions, or was she finally going to take a chance to get some information that seemed to be missing about Miss Hamilton's household?

"Yes, Miss. Of course. My time serving Miss Hamilton has been the happiest I've ever had. She is a great woman and a wonderful Mistress. I would do anything for her," Candy enthused.

"Even make me come with your fingers?" Amber asked breathlessly.

"Ah. I think I understand, Miss. Are you concerned that I am forced to do this, or lose my job?"

Amber nodded, "Yes, that's one way of looking at it."

"My service is entirely voluntary, Miss. I do not have to do anything Miss Hamilton commands, I may refuse."

"What happens if you refuse a command?"

"I would be punished, of course. If it were a reasonable command. If my limits were exceeded, Miss Hamilton would seek to help me, not punish me. She would help me understand why I should do as ordered."

"And if you still would not obey? What then?" Amber asked, utterly fascinated by this information.

"Miss Hamilton might release me from service if we could not find mutual pleasure in our relationship any more. But what you describe would be most unusual. She knows my tastes and Sugar's precisely, and she helps us stretch our limits, testing and teasing them, but she would never force us to break them. Mistress is kind and loving, though she might appear cold and unforgiving sometimes," Candy said, her fingers teasing the sensitive skin of Amber's thighs as she talked.

"If I asked you to put those fingers to work, then, would you enjoy that?"

"Yes, Miss. It is always an honour to serve those in service to the Mistress."

Amber raised an eyebrow at that. She was in service too?

"Especially those who are of higher station than a lowly maid such as myself."

The younger woman's fingers were playing havoc with her concentration, even just fluttering in the water across her inner thighs, without coming close to her aching pussy.

Amber had to let the concept of her station in Miss Hamilton's unusual household, go for another time, it sounded as if she outranked Candy in some way, but most importantly, she had clearly said she wasn't being forced to do any of this. Surely, it wasn't wrong to let the maid touch her, if Candy insisted that she would like to do this.

"You may make me come, Candy," Amber finally agreed. Inside her mind a war raged silently, one side very much in favour of experiencing what the maid was offering, and the other shocked by her lack of propriety.

"Thank you, Miss," Candy said as her fingers trailed over her skin and found the welcoming lips of Amber's pussy. Amber knew she would have been hardly less wet, had they been above water, so arousing was the feel of Candy's breasts against her back and the direction of their conversation.

As two fingers delved between her lips and the maid's thumb flirted with her clit, Amber tilted her head to one side and moaned. This was the first time another woman had touched her like this and, although she'd fantasised about this regularly, she'd never been bold enough to so much as kiss another woman. Not even at university where it was said all women were supposed to experiment as if it were some kind of course requirement for obtaining a degree.

Amber did her best to relax as much as she could in the entirely alien environment. She knew her own body well enough to be certain that the maid's ministrations would not bring her to a climax all that swiftly. Then a breath of warm air played across her ear, and Amber imagined Candy's tongue tasting her lobe, while her teeth nipped at her.

The maid's right hand was playing against her pussy, and doing an adequate job, Amber thought.

Candy's left hand fluttered up Amber's stomach and to her breasts, teasing at her nipples in time with the fingers between her lips. Amber gasped at the combination, it was really most delightful. She was feeling quite excited by it all, and it now seemed possible Candy might be able to complete her work rather sooner than Amber had anticipated.

It was only a minute or two later that Amber stiffened and Candy chuckled in her ear, "Is that the right spot, Miss?"

"Yes. Yes," Amber murmured, unable to speak clearly. "Candy. Oh, yes, just like that."

Whatever the little minx had been doing, she had hit the exact spots that Amber left until the most exciting part of her self-pleasure. Candy had identified her most secret triggers, like an expert poker player reading the tells of an amateur.

In short order, Amber found herself crying out in ecstasy, unheeding of the audience that might be in the house, as Candy urged her onward. "Come for me, Miss. Come hard. Make Miss Hamilton proud of me and my fingers," she purred in Amber's ear.

That did it. The thought of Miss Hamilton somehow tipped her over that final edge, her orgasm reached a crescendo, and she rode the waves of pleasure, bearing down on Candy's hand which didn't back off her pussy as she peaked.

Although Candy was whispering encouragement in her ear, it felt like several minutes had passed with Amber entirely insensible. The maid hadn't let her go at one orgasm, she had worked at her insistently, bringing her quickly back to a second orgasm. It was only then that she relented, allowing Amber to recover slowly from the intense pleasure she had expertly wrought in her.

Without a shadow of a doubt, Amber thought, that was the most exciting sexual experience she'd ever had, and she told her new maid so, in no uncertain terms. Candy chuckled, as she raised Miss Hannam out of the bath and patted her down with a luxurious towel.

Once she was dry, Candy pointed out the time and suggested that Miss Hannam should take a well-earned nap. "I will wake you in time to dress for dinner at eight, Miss," she assured her.

"Thank you, Candy. Really. That was amazing," Amber reiterated.

Candy leaned down and whispered in her ear, just before she dozed off, "Imagine what it would have been like if Miss Hamilton had given me permission to use my tongue."

CHAPTER 5

"Did you have a pleasant ride?" Amber asked between morsels of the light dinner of chicken and vegetables. She was dressed, she felt, much like the maids, though not in a uniform of any kind.

True to her word about helping with clothing choices, Candy had picked out a wet look halter neck dress with a zip-through front and a plunging neckline. The maid had insisted that it would look cute on Amber, but also be revealing enough to make the summer heat comfortable.

Amber had resisted the clothing option at first, but as time wore on, Candy's arguments became ever more inventive and persuasive. From Amber's point of view, so much material had been cut away from the dress and replaced with straps and laces, that there was barely anything left to cover her skin. She might almost have been wearing a micro-bikini for all the modesty this garment afforded her.

Candy noted that not only was the dress cutaway for ventilation, or so she claimed, it was also resistant to splashes or drips of food. Essentially, if Amber made a total idiot of herself, the dress could be wiped clean before Susanna noticed a stain. Amber wanted to say that it was more likely she'd drop a prawn into her cleavage in this dress, but Candy was so enthusiastic about her fashion sense she didn't have the heart to refuse it entirely.

Now she was sat in the enormous dining room, across from Susanna at one end of the table. The food was superb, and Amber would have happily devoured a second helping, but it was presented as a restaurant meal, laid out to perfection and served by Sugar and Candy. It didn't seem polite to ask for more, and she recalled that Miss Hamilton had specified a light meal.

"Yes, thank you. It was most stimulating. I love the fresh air and the challenge of controlling a wilful beast as I put it through its paces," Susanna replied. Amber had to bite her lip at that, she wasn't sure whether it was deliberate innuendo or if Miss Hamilton hadn't realised how what she'd said about horse riding could be misinterpreted.

"This food is wonderful. I would not have guessed that Sugar or Candy would be such amazing chefs," Amber said, trying to change tack.

Susanna laughed, "How delightful! No, Sugar and Candy are certainly better in the kitchen than I, but their true talents lie elsewhere. Our meals are mostly prepared by Cook."

"Oh, I haven't met him. Or her, yet," Amber said. "May I ask her name so that I know it when I do meet her?"

"Her," Susanna supplied. "The name I gave her is Pudding because as sweet and delightful as Sugar and Candy are, Pudding fills the parts other treats can't reach."

Amber began to wonder if her new employer was a fan of innuendo or utterly oblivious about her phrasing. "Thank you, it's helpful to know her name, so I know how to address her."

Again, Susanna laughed. "I'm sorry, Amber, I shall have time soon to bring you up to speed properly, but you should address her as Cook for the time being, as befits her station and yours. At least until you know each other properly."

"Yes, Miss Hamilton. Might I ask, why do the staff go by nicknames?" Amber asked.

"I was under the impression that I answered that when we arrived but the long and the short of it is, that it gives me pleasure to address them by names I give them. You will soon find that everything in my household is informed by my foibles, my taste and my pleasure. From the food to the decor, to the attire of my staff, and even the names by which they are known, my goal is for everything in my life to bring me joy," Susanna said.

"I understand," Amber said.

"Do you? I wonder. You see Amber," said Susanna, pushing her plate aside now that it was done and daintily dabbing at her lips with a napkin which was removed along with the plate the moment she'd put it down. "I am a wealthy woman, as you have probably inferred from my offices, car, staff and this house. I have been living comfortably from several businesses which provide an almost entirely passive income stream for some years now. I can afford to indulge myself in any manner which I please, within reason. I'm not buying tropical islands or personal jets, but I could hire either if I wished. I'm free in a way that most people simply cannot comprehend even in their wildest dreams."

Amber nodded, "I think I do understand, Miss Hamilton. You have money, and therefore you have power. You don't have to work, although I think you do so a lot because it's what you are used to and probably to keep from boredom. But you can afford any creature comfort you want."

"Yes, well done," Susanna replied. "I think I have chosen well with you."

"Thank you, Miss Hamilton. I do have one question, though?"

"No, Amber, you have many, but I think the question you really wanted to ask is, 'Are you going to give me a nickname too?' isn't it?" Susanna said.

Amber didn't know what to say. It was as if her new employer had simply stared into her eyes and plucked her thought from her very mind. She couldn't speak, so she simply nodded.

"As I thought. That is your last question, for the time being, young lady. Now, the answer is fairly simple. I do not intend to give you a nickname, that I require you to be known as around the household. You have an opportunity to curry favour now, by guessing correctly with one chance, why that is," Susanna said. "Think carefully but think quickly. I don't offer my favour for the slow-witted or lazy."

Amber smiled, "Yes, Miss Hamilton." What was it? What was the reason? Was it because she was part of the business side and not the household staff? She wished she'd thought to get the name of the receptionist now. She had to say something, but something Candy said earlier stopped her from blurting out her best guess.

"What happens if I get the answer wrong, Miss Hamilton?" she asked.

"If you get it wrong, especially after this blatant play for more time, there will be a small punishment to offset the possibility of earning my favour, if your answer is correct. Now, stop stalling, I don't approve of that sort of thing. What is your answer, young lady? Are you as bright as I am hedging my bets that you are by employing you?" Susanna asked with a wicked gleam in her eye.

"My answer is that it's about the nature of my role and how public it is," Amber gambled.

"Go on, that's not a full answer. Explain."

"If you gave me a nickname like the others have like, um, Cupcake, for instance," Amber said.

"Like Cupcake, for instance," Susanna nodded.

"Well, if we're at a business meeting, you might feel a little silly calling across the room for Cupcake to bring the muffins and tea in and put a new meeting in your diary," Amber said. She blushed when Miss Hamilton fixed her with a stare for a moment, wondering if she'd said something wildly offensive.

Miss Hamilton sniffed, apparently a little disappointed that her question was answered. "Yes, that's about it. I don't plan to give you a nickname that replaces Amber with something like Cupcake, because you and I shall be in public with all the boring, normal, vanilla types of people who inhabit the business world. My goal with them is to spend as little time as possible in their presence. I want to be among them just long enough to conduct business and then return here, or to another place where I feel comfortable. You may consider yourself the owner of some brownie points."

Amber grinned, despite herself, "Thank you, Miss Hamilton." Her grin vanished when she saw the look in her employer's eyes though, which reminded her somewhat of a serpent about to strike.

"However, do you remember that I told you that you had asked your last question for now?"

Amber nodded, beginning to see the dawn of the inevitable consequence.

"Then you asked what would happen if you got the question wrong, and I said you would be punished. I can see from the way your eyebrows are lifting up that you understand where this is going. You asked another question, didn't you?"

Amber simply nodded, her throat dry.

"As you will find, Amber, I am a generous employer. I am giving you an excellent salary to work for me, a place to live, the fine summer dress that you are wearing, rooms to live in, a live-in cook to provide us food, and even your own personal maid to tend to your every need," Susanna said, ticking off the positive items with her fingers as she recounted them. "Am I not, a generous employer, Amber?"

"Yes, Miss Hamilton."

"Yes, indeed. The thing is, I have my rules and my foibles Amber. When I give instructions, I expect them to be followed. For instance, I instructed Candy to tend to you earlier. Did she do a good job?"

Amber blushed profusely. "Yes."

"When I returned from my riding session, Candy told me that you were taking a little nap because you were all worn out after she gave you two rather explosive orgasms. Is that true?"

That little bitch, thought Amber! Did she really need to give Susanna the details?

"I like quick answers to my questions, Amber," Susanna pressed.

"Yes, she did," Amber agreed, her face burning hotter than she could have imagined.

"I know she used her fingers, Amber. I know she wanted to use her tongue for you, but she was obedient, as I expect everyone in my service to be. I expect you to be obedient too, Amber. If I tell you not to ask more questions, I expect you to do just that. Now, you are new to my service so obviously, I will be lenient on you."

Amber let out an audible sigh of relief at that.

"No, that doesn't mean you'll go unpunished but simply that your punishments in this first week will be lesser than those for my more experienced ladies," Susanna said. "Do you understand?"

"Yes, Miss Hamilton," Amber lied, having not really understood what was happening, at least not to the level she preferred.

"Capital. Now, put your plate to one side, and come with me. Candy. Sugar. Joins us in the drawing room once the plates are cleared.

Susanna beckoned for Amber to follow her, and without looking back, swept out of the dining room.

"Yes, Miss Hamilton," Amber replied.

CHAPTER 6

"Come, Amber. Stand here," Susanna said, pointing to a spot in the centre of a rug which lay in front of the enormous fireplace. Thankfully, given the summer heat, the fire was not raging as it would surely have blistered the skin, it was such an enormous beast.

Susanna poured herself a gin and tonic and stood by the fireplace, watching Amber, without speaking. The silence was unbearable, but Amber didn't want to break it only to find out that there was a rule about that too.

Presently, Sugar and Candy joined them. Susanna gestured to them, "Prepare the spanking bench."

Amber swallowed as the maids busied themselves with a piece of furniture that looked like an extremely expensive mahogany version of a gym bench for a complicated exercise of some kind.

There were gleaming steel rings embedded in the dark wood and leather cuffs at various points. Amber had only seen such things during her most frantic sessions of masturbation when she sought out the most exotic material to stimulate her senses and send her over the edge. The name Miss Hamilton had used revealed the purpose of the exotic furniture though.

To Amber, this was the province of Hollywood films and pornography, people didn't own such things in real life. Except, Miss Hamilton clearly did, and although she regarded it with apprehension, Amber could feel the telltale wetness between her legs that would betray her feelings.

"Amber, let me show you what I have for you in my toy cabinet," Susanna said, smirking as her new young lady blushed from neck to forehead.

Once Amber made the long journey across the room to stand beside her employer in front of an ornate cabinet, Susanna flung open the tall doors. Within hung a wide variety of implements, many of which Amber recognised to some degree but some which she couldn't have begun to guess at.

"Pick one," Susanna said simply.

"What?"

Susanna reached up and curled her fingers into the hair at the back of Amber's head. "Your safeword, is 'banana', understand? You will use it only if you need me to stop. Now, you will address me as Mistress if you are to be punished. Do you understand what I'm telling you?"

"Yes, Mistress," Amber said, the tugging at her scalp sending shivers down her spine.

"Good girl. Now, you will pick the implement I'm to discipline you with. It's part of your punishment you see. If you pick something too lenient, I might deliver more strokes, but I might not. On the other hand, if you select an implement that is more painful than I require, I will not spare you from your mistake. You must strike a balance. Over time, you might learn to gauge my mood to your advantage, but naturally, if you choose something too easy, it may not go well for you," Susanna whispered in Amber's ear, her breath hot and moist against her skin. Her grip tightened, and she moved Amber's head closer to the cabinet full of disciplinary implements.

"This one?" Amber said, pointing to a broad, flat length of stiffened leather with a simple handle.

"My, you are adventurous, aren't you? Most young ladies go for the riding crops because of the small head, but you went straight for the paddle. Good for you, Amber," said Susanna, plucking the thick black leather paddle from the cabinet. "I thought I sensed a streak of defiance in you, and now I think I have the proof. What a bold choice you have made!"

Amber blushed furiously, ashamed for no accountable reason, that she'd picked a harsher punishment for herself than Mistress Susanna had intended. The older woman released Amber's hair and then raised the paddle, bringing it down firmly on her other hand with an intimidating slap. Amber flinched, and Susanna smiled, then motioned for her to retake her position on the rug.

The two maids were standing ready beside the furniture they'd uncovered, apparently done with their preparations.

"Disrobe her," Susanna said, taking another sip of her drink and standing directly in front of Amber, where she could watch.

Sugar stood behind Amber, and undid the knot of the halter neck, as Candy slowly unzipped the dress from the top where the zipper rested between Amber's cleavage, all the way down to the bottom. It wasn't so very far. The dress ended just below the rounded cheeks of her buttocks. Sugar reached around from behind Amber, and peeled it back from her body, sliding it off her arms until it was off her entirely.

Miss Hamilton looked her up and down for what seemed like an age then flicked the paddle in a gesture toward the bench.

Sugar and Candy guided Amber to the bench and positioned her on it. Amber could scarcely believe what she was allowing to happen to her. Again, her internal monologue was warring with itself. Should she allow this or flee back to her miserable flat? Was any job worth this treatment? Would the treatment be as thrilling as her throbbing pussy seemed to imagine? Was this the culmination of some of her most outrageous fantasies?

There were pads for her to kneel on, then a broad bench which sloped away from her, and more pads for her to rest her forearms on. Once she mounted it, the maids cuffed her ankles and wrists to the bench. Her backside was left considerably higher than her shoulder blades, her rump presented perfectly for viewing.

Sugar spoke up then, "Mistress, may I put the mirror out." Susanna nodded and complimented her on her playfulness, promising to reward her later for her suggestion. Sugar beamed with pride as she moved a wide, full-length mirror so that Amber could see herself reflected in profile, ready for her new Mistress to punish her.

A moment later, the first whack of the paddle landed, jiggling Amber's buttocks and making her wince. For some reason, she instinctively resisted crying out and took three more strokes before she gave a soft whimper.

Susanna moved to the head of the bench and leaned down, kissing her softly on the cheek. "Can you take the rest of your punishment, or shall I stop?"

Amber was breathing heavily but turned toward her and replied proudly, "I can take it, Mistress."

Candy squealed in delight, and Susanna shot her a disapproving look, but as she returned to her position at the rear of the bench, the maid gave Amber a big thumbs up sign behind Mistress Susanna's back.

Candy looked proud of her, and that furthered Amber's resolve to take the full punishment, no matter what. She wouldn't be broken. In any case, it didn't sting that badly.

It took all Amber had as she processed that thought, to keep from crying out as the paddle came down on her backside again. It felt as if Susanna had driven it home significantly harder, but she wondered if her bottom was simply feeling a bit more sensitive after the first four blows.

The next time the paddle hit, Amber writhed against her bondage, but she didn't squeal or cry out. "That's six, Mistress," Sugar said. Amber didn't know the maid yet, but it sounded as if she was paying rapt attention to her punishment and enjoying every voyeuristic moment of the personal assistant getting disciplined. Perhaps she had her own sadistic streak, despite her clearly submissive role in Miss Hamilton's household.

"Will you give Amber more, Mistress?" Candy asked.

"Do you think she's had enough?" Miss Hamilton asked, perhaps rhetorically, then she was at Amber's ear again. "Have you, Amber? Have you had as much as you can take?"

Amber shook her head vigorously, "No, Mistress."

"Brave girl. Do you want more? Would you like me to punish your pink bottom some more, Amber?" Susanna asked.

Amber didn't want more, but she had no intention of saying that. She was learning to deal with the discomfort, and she felt a rebellious mood take hold of her. She was a Hannam by birth, and she could take a lot more than this woman could dish out, she was sure of it. This wasn't even a flesh wound. Her stiff upper lip would be more than adequate in the face of such mediocre punishment she told herself.

"Yes, please, Mistress. I want more. I need more. Please, will you punish me more?" Amber blurted out defiantly. As soon as the words left her lips, she wondered if she'd made a huge mistake but she wasn't going to say banana and rescind the challenge she'd made to Mistress Susanna. Amber was a Hannam through and through, and they were not cowards.

"Interesting. I must say, ladies, I'm impressed with Amber's boldness, aren't you?"

"Oh yes, Mistress. She's taking to the paddle very well," said Sugar. "I bet she could take a good dozen more."

"I think she's really tough, Mistress. I think she needs more punishment than that," said Candy, who was now kneeling by Amber's head, entirely naked. When had that happened? She'd been in her maids uniform when she came into the room.

"Sugar, would you like to touch yourself?" Miss Hamilton offered. When the maid accepted with a squeal of delight, she was ordered to stand where Amber could see her, strip naked and bring herself off in full view of them all.

Sugar's hands were soon busy with her pussy, which was as smooth as Amber's own, and she began to make soft moans of delight. Amber licked her lips. It was deliciously naughty to watch the younger woman playing with herself, even if she was only a year or so Amber's junior.

"Candy, hold her hand and keep an eye on her, in case she gets herself into trouble. I don't want a first-timer being too proud to use their safeword when they should," Susanna said.

"Yes, Mistress."

Her Mistress put a gentle hand on her ankle then, and Amber flinched at the unexpected touch. The fingers paused, then when Amber relaxed, ran up her calf, along her inner thigh, and stopped as they found their way to her lips. Miss Hamilton's fingers were deft, and Amber was as wet as she could remember being in her life.

The fingers of her Mistress slid easily into her pussy, possessing her and quickly finding that special spot that she loved to play with. The paddle might not have, but the tips of Miss Hamilton's fingers on her G-spot made her whimper. Amber's moans were the product of pure pleasure, rather than pain.

"My, my, Amber. Did you know that you are soaking wet? I barely noticed any friction when I penetrated you. Tell us all, Amber, are you enjoying your punishment? Does this turn you on?" Miss Hamilton demanded, her fingers emphasising her dominance with firm strokes that had Amber gasping for breath.

"Yes! Yes, Mistress. I love it! Please. Please, punish me," Amber panted.

"See what I mean, Candy?"

"Yes, Mistress. Amber looks so happy from here," the maid replied.

"Amber, have you ever been with a woman before?"

Amber shook her head, her voice captured by the need to moan as her Mistress worked her sensitive spot.

"Have you kissed a girl?"

"No, Mistress," Amber managed.

"Have you ever fantasised about being with a woman?"

"Yes, Mistress."

"Are you a lesbian, Amber?" Susanna asked.

Amber hesitated. Was she? Was she bisexual? If pushed, Amber might have admitted to being bi-curious until today. There was no simple answer that was correct so she went with what she could truthfully say, "I don't know Mistress."

"A question for another time. What type of women have you fantasised about? Young ladies your age, or older women?"

"Both Mistress. I've had some fantasies about both," Amber said, licking her lips and smiling awkwardly at Candy who was looking up at her with an expression that even Amber, with her limited experience, recognised as unbridled lust.

"Who was the first woman to put her tongue on your breast, Amber?" Susanna asked.

"You were Mistress," Amber replied. Candy licked her lips at that, clearly pleased with the answer.

"The first to touch your pussy and make you cum?"

"Candy, Mistress," Amber groaned.

"That's right. Not me! You didn't wait for me, did you, you little slut?" Susanna growled. Her fingers were gone from Amber's pussy in an instant, and the paddle whistled as it flew into her buttocks. Still Amber did not cry out, though she could feel tears of pain in her eyes.

As the follow-up blows landed and Sugar called out, "Twelve!" with evident glee, Amber's eyes were blurry with tears. Her hand clutched at Candy's so hard, the young maid pulled away, breaking her grasp with her own whimper, then returning her wrist to Amber's crushing grip instead. Candy wrapped her hand over Amber's. Her new friend could squeeze her arm without her worrying about her crushing any bones.

Sugar's count hit eighteen, and Miss Hamilton came forward again, one hand dipping back into Amber's sodden pussy as she licked her earlobe, "Amber Hannam, so help me, if you don't cry out, I'm going to give you the full three dozen, right now! I want to hear your suffering."

In her mind, Amber thanked her Mistress for the extra fuel she would use to resist. She did not cry out at nineteen, or twenty, or twenty-three. She would take the full three dozen.

But at twenty-four stinging slaps with that paddle, Amber felt a dam inside her break. Two dozen. That was a big number. It was like a switch being flipped in her head. Both her cheeks were stinging like the blazes. Her pussy was sopping wet, and though she resisted crying, tears of pain ran freely down her cheeks.

"Stop! Stop it, you filthy bitch! You evil cow. Leave me alone!" she cursed.

"That's it, Amber! That's what I wanted from you," Susanna yelled triumphantly.

Sugar cried out too, in absolute horror at the tirade of vulgarity that was still streaming from Amber's mouth. "You can't speak to Mistress like that, you slut!" she complained.

Then the maid began to come, and come hard, pushed over the edge at the thrilling notion of a new pet being so vulgar to her Mistress. Amber watched as Sugar shuddered and quaked with wave after wave of her orgasms as her fingers frantically worked at her pussy.

"Fuck! That hurts! What did you do to me?" Amber cried out, and finally, her watering eyes became full-blown tears, and she began to sob in great, shuddering gasps.

Susanna smiled and slipped her fingers back into her new submissive's pussy, causing the younger woman's head to lift up in a mixture of shock and excitement as she called out, "Yes, fuck me. Please, make me come!"

Amber's Mistress was only too happy to oblige, working hard at her pussy until Amber's sobbing turned into full-throated screams of ecstasy.

Susanna was relentless, forcing Amber to ride her fingers to multiple orgasms. Amber lost track of how many times she climaxed as each orgasm blended smoothly into the next. Finally, when Amber's tears stopped, and her gasps of ecstasy subsided, Susanna withdrew her fingers. Amber was left panting and gasping by the treatment.

Candy stood up, and took hold of Amber's hair, brushing it back from her face, then pulling her head up a little, to tilt it toward Susanna, who was crouching at her side. The maid knew what would happen next, that much was clear, as the position readied Amber perfectly, for Susanna to take her fingers and slip them into her new assistant's mouth.

"Clean off your cum, bitch," Susanna ordered coldly. Amber had no choice but to lick and suck her Mistresses fingers clean of her own strangely delicious juices.

"That's better, you foul-mouthed trollop. Fancy. All the filthy things you called me. Have you ever heard such a mouth on a new sub, Candy?"

Candy blushed profusely. "No, Mistress. I have not. She was very rude. Very rude indeed. I'm so sorry."

Susanna ruffled Candy's hair and then pulled her in for a prolonged kiss. "It is not your fault, my sweet. Amber just needs to learn a lot of lessons, don't you Amber? How to behave for Mistress? How to keep Mistress happy? How to set a good example for my play-things, hmm?"

"Yes, Mistress," Amber confirmed.

"Are you a lesbian, Amber?"

Amber swallowed. In less than a day, she had gone from being a single woman, who had the occasional fantasy about other women, to some kind of plaything to an older woman she barely knew.

She'd played sexual games with three women and experimented with bondage and being paddled. She had a new job and new lovers, and she longed to learn more from Miss Hamilton and her French maids.

Amber looked up at her Mistress and licked her lips. "I don't know Mistress. How do I find out?"

Susanna smiled, "Good answer, you little slut. Sugar, Candy. Let her loose and bring her up to my room."

"Shall we clean your new slut off, Mistress?" Candy asked hopefully.

"No. I want her just as she is. Amber, you can ask another question now," Susanna said.

Amber could tell immediately that there was a right question to ask, and she pondered it for a few moments until an idea hit her.

"Am I a lesbian, Mistress?"

"I don't know, Amber, but come upstairs with me, and we'll find out."

"Yes, Mistress."

SEDUCED BY HER LESBIAN BOSS

Book 2

CHAPTER 1

Amber followed her new Mistress up the stairs, meekly keeping her head bowed and remaining quiet, as she had always imagined a submissive would do. There was little choice but to improvise, since Susanna had not yet given her much guidance about how Amber should behave in the future.

The most immediately unusual part of their movement through the house was that Amber was entirely nude. Even in the privacy of her own small flat, Amber rarely even went from her bedroom to the shower without putting on a robe. It was just a habit, not to walk around naked even when there was no possibility that someone else would see her.

Doing so now, through this enormous building, gave her a frisson of pleasure that was quite unexpected. If she had been asked a few days ago about walking around her boss's house without a stitch of clothing on, Amber would have been utterly bemused at the idea. The way she was feeling about actually doing it made her wonder if she had some kind of undiscovered thing for exhibitionism.

Although everything about this situation was completely new to Amber, she had just enough exposure to the world that kinky people seemed to live in, that it didn't feel entirely alien. A few pornographic videos, feature films, and even the odd episode of TV had inspired some satisfying fantasies and eye-opening internet searches.

Of course, Amber had read some popular books when they went around her university, and that had led to her reading a fair amount of steamy romance stories that touched or even focused on BDSM relationships.

However, the thought that these works of fiction could lead to anything more than a few lurid fantasies and frenzied sessions of self-stimulation had never really occurred to Amber. It didn't seem any more likely to her that she would explore these possibilities, than that she would become an astronaut, work for a millionaire, or experiment with other women.

Not that her fantasies in any of those areas had really stopped, although the daydreams of being an astronaut were usually replaced with being whatever heroine was currently in the cinema. Becoming a world class secret agent seemed much more realistic somehow, if only because Amber had discovered that rollercoasters did not thrill her.

As sumptuous as the bedroom suite Amber had been given was, she couldn't wait to see the room Susanna used. This palatial house probably had dozens of bedrooms built for family members and visitors. Let alone the servants quarters.

A whirlwind of emotions was clouding her thoughts as she followed her boss along the corridor deeper into the house. Susanna had promised her that together they would find out if she was a lesbian, but what did that mean?

Somehow, Amber doubted that they were going to sit at a laptop and fill in online questionnaires written by click-bait copywriters, or have an in depth heart to heart discussion of the issue. No, a more practical exploration of the question seemed to be what was on the cards.

Amber had to suppress a giggle at the thought. As nerve wracking as the idea of being thrust into a sexual experiment with her new boss was, it was infinitely less unsettling than the dreaded pseudo-scientific online tests. What house did she belong in? Those tests usually showed her a gryphon logo, but Amber felt more drawn to black-feathered intelligent birds. She couldn't recall ever taking a test like that convinced her it was applying clever psychological questions to determine her thoughts and hidden preferences.

Amber hoped that whatever Susanna did have planned, it wouldn't involve another paddle being applied to her bottom. She was still smarting from her punishment in the drawing room, and it felt like she wouldn't be able to sit down without being reminded of it for a week.

When she had been uncuffed from the spanking bench, Amber had caught a glimpse of her thoroughly chastised buttocks in the full-length mirror that Sugar had positioned near the bench. She knew her cheeks were not a rosy shaded of blushing pink, but perhaps a dozen shades darker.

Amber put her arms behind her back and tentatively caressed her bottom as they walked. It felt sore and was sensitive to the touch, and she flushed with pride that she'd taken two dozen whacks of Susanna's paddle before crying out.

Susanna pushed open a set of double doors and turned to usher Amber in. Quickly, Amber brought her hands to her sides, but Susanna caught the motion and smirked, "Enjoying my handiwork, I see. Does your bottom feel hot?"

"Yes, Mistress."

Susanna nodded slowly, as if she was digesting some new and fascinating information. Amber glanced around the room but didn't see a bed. Instead, they were in another richly furnished sitting room, with armchairs and coffee tables and French windows leading onto a balcony.

As was to be expected, the suite her Mistress used was significantly larger than the seemingly enormous one Amber had been placed in.

"Good. That is exactly how it should be. Stand there, on that rug," Susanna said, pointing at a small circular rug that lay in the middle of a semi-circle of furniture in front of a large stone fireplace. The rug was entirely incongruous with the country house antique style of the rest of the room, or the carpet, and looked like it had come from a modern department store. Albeit a rather niche shop, judging by the design.

The rug bore a detailed print of an illustration which depicted a domme in fetish clothing, wielding a riding crop and standing over a submissive woman. The submissive was on her knees with her face pressed to the floor and her bottom raised high, awaiting whatever the dominant had in mind, Amber supposed. Her hands were bound behind her back with a silken cord, and her mouth was open in a pout that Amber read as pleasurable anticipation.

Amber almost felt guilty standing on the poor girl's body. The artwork was highly provocative, and she could well imagine Susanna delighting in putting her own subs atop it, knowing it would set their mind racing with all sorts of ideas.

Behind Amber, the double doors closed with a decisive click.

"Is this ok, Mistress?"

"Is what ok, Amber?" Susanna asked, still standing behind her.

"The way I'm standing. I haven't any experience with," she trailed off, unsure how to finish her sentence. "I mean to say, I haven't ever been someone's submissive. I don't know if there is a way I'm supposed to stand or sit," she said. A moment later, she remembered herself and added, "Mistress."

"I see. What a perceptive question. Allow me to respond with one of my own, Amber. Have you read any books about dominance and submission, perhaps?"

It could have been a rhetorical question in any other situation. Hadn't everyone these days? Amber couldn't recall a single female student she knew having avoided the trend of reading such material, and not just in the privacy of their bedrooms to be discussed in hushed whispers later. She had seen her contemporaries on trains and buses, devouring books with covers that left little to the imagination.

Amber's e-reader was still brimming with all sorts of romantic and erotic books. A good number of them featured some form of BDSM in the relationship. But that was all fiction, and this was real life. Her bottom was stinging in a way that certainly wasn't fictional, and nor was the sensation of wetness between her lips.

"Yes, Mistress. I've read a few."

"A few? Is that three or four, or the kind of few implied when someone says they've been eating chocolate raisins or biscuits? Hmm?"

Amber giggled. "More the raisins and biscuits type of few, Mistress."

"Good girl. I respect honesty a great deal, you know. So you've read quite a few books with kinky themes, and you're wondering if there's to be some kind of protocol when we are playing. Is that the gist of it?"

Amber nodded, "Yes, Mistress."

Suddenly, Susanna moved in, pressing herself against Amber's naked body. Her breath was hot on her ear as her hands caressed Amber's thighs, and she whispered, "Very well, my eager little slut. Mistress will position you as she prefers and you may default to this stance when told to stand somewhere."

"Thank you, Mistress," Amber said, her pussy immediately responding.

Susanna held her embrace for a moment longer, then pulled away, her hands drawing back. A slap on Amber's inner thigh indicated she should place her feet further apart. It stung with a sensation that she was surprised to find herself thinking of as delightful. "Further apart. Shoulder width," Susanna ordered.

A firm hand in the small of her back, then running up her spine, as the other hand pressed in from the front, adjusted Amber's posture until she was standing upright. Her shoulders were drawn back, and her chin set perpendicular to the floor.

Susanna tried a few positions with Amber's hands and arms, but settled on having her place her arms behind her back, with her wrists crossed at the cleft of her buttocks. Her breasts were accentuated in this position, and she felt somewhat vulnerable around her chest and her pussy, both of which were displayed for anyone to see.

Miss Hamilton walked around her a few times, making minor corrections and commenting on her stance, telling her not to wobble or shake, then stopped a few feet in front of her. Susanna looked her up and down, appraising every inch of her. Amber kept her eyes forward, like a soldier on parade. It seems like the best call.

"Yes. I find I'm rather enjoying this precocious idea of yours, Amber. If you have any thoughts, I should hear in the future, make sure that you let me know, at an appropriate moment, of course. I can tell already that you and I are going to get along famously. I'm sure we'll become firm friends, if you keep up this behaviour. We shall have simply buckets of fun together," Susanna said.

"Thank you, Mistress," Amber replied, finding the praise heightened her arousal rather unexpectedly. Was this what it meant to submit? Did it always feel this way to please a dominant, even in such a trivial manner? Was that what led people to involve themselves in this scene, the endorphin rush of being metaphorically patted on the head like a puppy that performed a trick for the first time?

"I assume you can remember this stance when needed?"

"Yes, Mistress, definitely."

"Good girl," Susanna said, reaching out and gently stroking the back of Amber's head.

That was it. *That was the rush, Amber thought*. It felt like her pussy was on fire and simultaneously flooding. Could her Mistress see the evidence of her excitement on the lips that Candy had freshly shaved?

"I must say you have a good physique, Amber. Shapely breasts, enough muscle to be fit and enough fat to give you such delightful curves. Do you get much exercise?"

"I swim now and then, do some yoga, and I try to get my step count in, Miss Hamilton."

"That is very conscientious of you. You can practise yoga with the other staff. They get together several times a week. You'll be able to use my swimming pool, of course, and I expect you to do so. I encourage everyone who works for me to keep themselves in good shape, fit and healthy through good diet and keeping active. Some of them should increase their step count as well, so I might have you schedule some walks in the grounds with them. You can take the maids for walkies, that would be fun," Susanna mused.

Amber giggled, then bit her lip to stop herself when she saw

Susanna's right eyebrow raise into an arch.

"Explain the joke?"

"I'm sorry, Mistress. When you said 'walkies' I just pictured Sugar crawling around the lawn on all fours, with a dog collar around her neck and me holding her leash, taking her for a walk," Amber hesitated, unsure if she should say the rest.

"Spit it out, girl," Susanna demanded.

"She had one of those things. I don't know what to call it. A fluffy tail that's stuck in her bottom," Amber replied.

"A butt plug, Amber. What you're imagining is a butt plug for pet play, with a tail. It could be a curly piggy tail, or a fox brush, or a dog tail. And that imagery appealed, did it?"

Amber nodded, "Yes, Mistress."

"Then when you take the girls for a walk, you will collar and leash them, and have them put in butt plugs. My rules are that they may pick the plug of their choice as long as it has a tail. And there is to be no crawling, they're to get a good, upright walk around the grounds at a brisk pace. This can't be all about your fun. Do you understand, Amber?"

"Oh, yes, Mistress. Thank you, Mistress." This was amazing. Just a couple of throwaway comments had metamorphosed into her leadings pet girls around the garden for morning constitutionals! With butt plugs in their bottoms, no less. How deliciously dirty.

Susanna had not been joking when she asked Amber to let her know about any ideas. Far from being insistent on having her own way in everything, it seemed her Mistress would accept inspiration, if only when it sparked her imagination. Inevitably, Amber found herself wondering what other peccadilloes she had read about, that Susanna would let her indulge.

"And Amber."

"Yes, Mistress?"

"You will also wear a pet play butt plug. A foxtail for you, I think," Susanna said.

Amber gulped. She had never played with her bottom in that way.

"Yes, Mistress."

CHAPTER 2

"Now, let's see about testing the valuable knowledge you've gleaned from those books of yours, shall we?" Miss Hamilton said.

"Yes, Mistress," Amber replied.

"I want you to assume the position. Don't ask me what it is, just do what you think is best. Remember, this is a test."

Isn't everything? Amber thought. The phrase, 'Assume the position' was one she had heard and read many times though, in books and in certain forums and articles online.

When she had bought her first proper erotica novel at a small newsagents shop in one of the large London train terminals, she had felt so naughty. Amber had been on the way back to university after the first Christmas break and had been browsing the shelves while she waited for her train. At first she had blushed when she saw the top shelf with a small selection of what were clearly erotica books.

The covers were much more discreet than material she'd seen online, just thorny roses, masquerade masks and the titles to identify the genre. Her hand had trembled as she reached up to take one down and of course, everyone in the shop had known what section she was perusing, and were staring at her with fierce disapproval.

That was how her anxiety shaped her perception of reality, even if intellectually she knew that the other customers were mostly trying to decide if they could face a slightly stale sandwich from the refrigerator or if they needed a cheap umbrella.

All of this could have been avoided, of course, but when Amber went up to university, she hadn't got a credit card or her own account to buy e-books. She was still attached to her childhood account, and the parentally approved books it had access to.

Not that her parents were unusually strict or censorious, or that they actually checked the content of books they did buy her. Some of Amber's teenage reading, in fantasy and science fiction and thrillers, was probably far more violent and laden with swearing than her parents had imagined from the covers. That wouldn't have been the same as her asking to buy a steamy romance novel, let alone an erotica book.

No teenager wanted to have that sort of conversation with their parents. Well, Amber had had a few friends who probably would do just that, as it happened. But not the majority of her peers, who took pretty much the same stance of not discussing anything about sex or romance with their parents unless they absolutely had to, or it was entirely mundane.

Amber always felt awkward when her less timid friends invited her over for dinner at their house and proceeded to include sex in the conversation with their mothers as if it were perfectly normal. It made her cringe inside, and of course, her blushes would make an unwanted appearance. It was tough to look mature with that sort of reaction going on.

The birds and the bees had been well handled by Amber's mother, without much fuss or bother, but they just didn't talk about anything too lurid, which suited Amber just fine, thank you very much. Buying a paperback erotica book with cash meant that all she had to do was conceal it physically to avoid any awkward moments with family.

It was too tempting to resist completely and Amber remember Oscar Wilde's quote on the subject of temptation. If he couldn't resist it, she certainly wasn't going to.

Actually buying that first book had felt so naughty, as if the shop assistant would admonish her or demand to see proof of age. Of course, the woman didn't bat an eyelid, or pass any remark about it. That didn't stop Amber's overactive blush response from making it clear to the woman that she was an erotica virgin. At least, that's how it seemed in Amber's mind at the time.

That had become a habit, buying a new book every time she was on a trip and reading it on the train, taking care to conceal the cover from the other passengers, but secretly feel a thrill at the thought of being caught. Her pussy would respond even before she'd got to the first actual sex scene, in many cases. It left her aching to touch herself, but she had only actually done so on a couple of trips, where she was in a mostly empty carriage.

Amber would usually just have to squirm and chew her lip to manage the arousal reading the books provoked until she could get somewhere private to masturbate furiously to a powerful orgasm.

It was worse when she went back home, of course, as she couldn't very well rush to her bedroom and hide herself away from her family in order to relieve that tension. On those legs of the trip, she had to wait for hours of socialising to be over before she could silently bring herself off in bed.

Her blushing behaviour had always remained though, even after her fourth or fifth purchase on a trip, Amber had found that first her chest and neck would feel warm and then her face would burn with anxious shame. It didn't stop her little ritual though, and she became quite brazen, sometimes buying two or three books at once.

Each year, she had to purge some by selling them to a second-hand bookshop before her parents picked her up from university. There was only so much space in the family car, and she didn't want to risk her erotic books being discovered. Only the books she read over and over had made it through her entire course without being sold.

That teenage habit might serve her well now, giving a much better idea than those that were not addicted to train station erotica purchases, would have had of what was being asked of her. Of course, her anxiety mind goblins were quick to point out that the books she'd read could have been wild fantasies with little basis in the reality of kink. That was so unhelpful.

Slowly, as she hoped was proper in this situation, Amber bent forward at the waist. She put her hands to her thighs and let them slide down to her knees as she bent over until her fingers wrapped around her ankles.

"Most impressive. You are a flexible little thing, aren't you? The yoga is really working for you, and for me, it seems."

"Yes, Mistress."

"I love the colour of your bottom, Amber. It really suits you. What is your safeword? Do you remember?"

"Banana, Mistress."

"Good girl. Don't forget it," Susanna said as she fetched something from the other side of the room.

Mistress Susanna crouched before her submissive and Amber looked up at her, finding an expensive-looking camera in her employer's hand.

"I want to take photos, Amber. To record your posterior, for posterity?" Susanna said with a self-satisfied grin at her own joke.

The pun might have been awful, but it was disarming. Amber smiled and nodded her consent. This wasn't the first time she'd tried posing for erotic photography, although that had all been at the behest of her ex-boyfriend and in all honesty, was mostly about his desires, not hers.

Amber had taken plenty of measures to protect her privacy before she broke up with him, including some compromising shots of him in her underwear that she'd sworn to him would never see the light of day. When she split with him, Amber had calmly explained that she would not be the victim of any petty revenge.

If she said, it turned out that her efforts had not deleted all his copies of the photos of her, then she had her own of him that he would not want to be made public. It was mutually assured destruction with dirty pictures instead of missiles.

Friends of hers had been caught out by the same trick, and it wasn't any comfort to seek legal redress when a video of your mouth wrapped around an ex's cock, or something even more graphic, was posted online. Thankfully, Amber's insurance policy had proved unnecessary, and she'd never had to use it as none of her ex-boyfriends had become monstrous cretins when they broke up.

What Susanna wanted seemed to be for her personal pleasure, of course, but Amber had a sense that her own desire to exhibit herself was also being factored in by her beautiful employer.

Given the work Susanna had done on her with the paddle earlier, it would have been easy for Amber to imagine the older woman as an unrepentant devil in a business suit. A succubus, sent to tempt young straight women and seduce them into the wickedness of a relationship as the submissive of a lesbian dominatrix. She bit her lip. *Where had that all come from, she wondered?*

Susanna began to take pictures from all angles, capturing Amber from the low down at the front first, before moving behind her. She made appreciative noises as she worked, mumbling to herself as the camera flashed. "I think you'll like these, Amber. They show off your bottom beautifully," she said when she finally stopped. Then she showed the screen on the back of the camera to Amber, to let her see just how pink her bottom was now.

"Perhaps we'll go through these and print out the best ones one day, would you like that, Amber?"

"Yes, Mistress," Amber admitted. She hadn't ever had a photo printer of her own, so had only seen her naughty pictures on computer screens, which was good in lots of ways but not quite the same.

Putting the camera down, Susanna said, "You can stand up now." Amber did so and reeled for a moment as the rush of blood hit her head.

"Unzip me," Susanna ordered, presenting her back to Amber.

Amber reached up and carefully pulled the zip down the back of Susanna's wet-look black dress. It contoured her body, showing her generous curves off well, and the zipper was under the ideal amount of strain to keep the dress tight.

Once it fell to the floor, Amber could see that Susanna was entirely naked underneath, with not so much as a garter belt. It felt as if they were on even ground in some small way, even if her aching backside was a clear reminder that they were not.

"Pick that up, fold it and put it over there," Susanna said, gesturing toward a chaise longue. "Then join me."

When Amber finished tidying up the dress, she found her employer seated on an expensive-looking brown leather couch. A large, impressive affair. Susanna was sat on the middle cushion, leaned back and patted the corner to her left side, indicating that Amber should sit there.

"Now, Amber, are you still wondering if you are a lesbian?"

Amber nodded.

"You don't have to be, to serve me, you know. Just because I am a lesbian, doesn't mean you will be no good to me, if you are not," Susanna said.

"I don't understand, Mistress. I thought you wanted me to..."

"Be my plaything?" Susanna asked with compassion.

"Yes, Mistress."

"I do, Amber. But that simply requires that you take my instructions to heart and accept my discipline. If I get a massage, does the masseuse have to be a lesbian for me to enjoy it?"

Amber shook her head.

"But if she were, might she enjoy running her hands over my back, kneading my muscles and putting oil on me?" Susanna asked.

"Yes, Mistress. I suppose she might, but it wouldn't be very professional," Amber replied.

Susanna waved that away, "Perhaps not if she acted on it, but it would be understandable for her to have feelings. Either way, I would have what I required, with or without her sexual preference. It is slightly different when I play with my friends, of course, but I think the analogy is sound."

"Yes, Mistress."

"What I'm saying Amber, is that I can enjoy your service if you still feel that you are straight, as I believe you did before you arrived this morning. Would I enjoy it more if you were bisexual or a lesbian? If you could have romantic feelings toward women? Of course, that might alter our relationship, but I would still be your boss. You will still prepare reports for me, book appointments, and get my dry cleaning done. I will still be your Mistress, whether or not my touch thrills you as it might a young lady who is lesbian or bi. Questions?" Susanna said.

"How could you enjoy it though, if I'm completely straight? What if I'm not a lesbian, or even bi?" Amber asked.

"For a dominant of my persuasion, Amber, that is a treat. A challenge if you will, and one of an especially tempting kind. All sorts of fantasies can play out within that scenario. Can I seduce the straight woman? Can I help the bi-curious or lesbian woman come out of her closet to play? Can I bring a submissive straight girl to her knees? Will she recognise my dominance?"

"You'd want a straight girl to do that? What for?" Amber puzzled.

Susanna laughed merrily, "Oh yes, Amber. Are you really so surprised?"

"Yes."

"Despite the fact that just a short while ago it was my fingers inside you, making you come?" Susanna teased.

Amber swallowed, "But you think I'm like. You think I'm a lesbian, really, don't you?"

"I do."

"But what if I'm just a straight girl? What then?"

"Amber, you can gift your submission to any dominant you please. A submissive feels a desire to serve a dominant. It's not always so sexual. Maybe you're a bad girl, Amber. Do you have wicked thoughts? Do you lie in bed at night," Mistress Susanna asked, slowly stroking Amber's knee, "touching yourself as you imagine being spanked? Have you spent countless nights reading dirty books and watching filthy girls on their knees, doing anything that's asked of them, for tiniest chance, the faintest hope that their Mistress will touch them?"

Amber looked up into Susanna's piercing eyes, meeting her steady gaze, her breath rising and falling as she considered what to say. How much of herself should she reveal to this woman who had driven strong fingers inside her no more than an hour previously? She was already nude, and used, and in her private chambers. Would revealing her secret thoughts really expose anything more intimate than she already had?

"I have had, thoughts, Mistress," Amber said, using the formal address again, feeling how it sounded in her head and on her lips, "filthy thoughts."

"About spanking? Perhaps leather?" Susanna prompted gently.

Amber shook her head. "No, yes, maybe," she said uncertainly, "I'm not sure how to describe it. I've had thoughts about being on my knees, or crawling on a floor, or bent over a piece of furniture waiting."

"Is there anyone in these thoughts? Another presence you can sense or an actual person you see clearly?"

"Sometimes, Mistress. I can almost picture them, standing over me as I kiss their feet or throwing me over their lap for a spanking," Amber explained.

"Is it a man, or a woman?"

"I'm not sure. What does that mean?"

"I'm not a psychologist, but it sounds like perfectly ordinary fantasies that revolve around your deep-rooted need to submit to someone. Do you masturbate when you have these thoughts?"

Amber nodded, turning her face to hide her shame.

"Do you understand a bit better now, my sweet thing?" Susanna asked kindly, her fingers cupping Amber's chin and tilting her head up.

"Understand, Mistress?"

"Why I might want to play with a sweet, innocent young woman such as yourself?"

"I'm not innocent, Mistress," Amber said with a sly grin.

"Perhaps to in some respects that's so. But if you truly imagine that I would not enjoy you fully, simply because you aren't unsure of your own sexuality, you may be as unworldly as a nun about some matters, Amber," Susanna said.

"But how would a straight girl truly serve you, Mistress?"

Susanna chuckled at that question again and leaned to her right, turning her head to look over Amber's shoulder as her left cheek brushed up against Amber's. "A straight, submissive young lady, much like you could serve me, quite well, Amber. Just as well as a young woman who was positively giddy at the thought of another woman's touch, in fact."

"How," Amber rasped, her throat parched.

Susanna's voice dropped to a near whisper, "An obedient straight girl could be spanked, to be sure that she knew her place. Then, with a light hand on her shoulder, or perhaps a firm command, she would drop to her knees before me. Can you picture it?"

Amber closed her eyes and nodded gently, her face still next to Susanna's. "Yes, Mistress," she confirmed, her voice a dry whisper in synchronisation with Susanna's.

"This straight sub, so eager to please that she's accepted the dominance of a powerful, lesbian domme, simply to experience the rush it, provides," Mistress Susanna continued. "I would let my knees part, and gently cup the back of her head, guiding her toward me, until her sweet tongue found its mark between my wet lips. There she would carry out her duty, serving me with her hungry mouth, eagerly worshipping my needy clit, demonstrating to me her willingness to submit to my every whim."

"Oh," Amber sighed unsteadily, her breath short from holding it without even realising it.

"The gift of her submission, just the very act of it, would have made her soaking wet by the time she was done bringing me to the orgasm I required of her," Mistress Susanna said, enunciating each word slowly and carefully as the hand on Amber's knee gently walked up her thigh, fingers dancing closer and closer to Amber's molten core.

"Do you think she'd be wet, Amber? This straight girl I had eat my pussy?" Susanna asked. "Would a straight girl who felt the need to submit want me to touch her, to feel how wet she was?"

"Yes, Mistress. A straight girl would want that, if she'd been licking you," Amber agreed.

Then Susanna's fingers danced those final steps to her wet lips, quickly sliding down the length of her slit, and slipping between her lips as they came back up toward her clit. Amber let out a needy whimper, she couldn't stop herself.

"Does that explain my interest well enough, Amber? Do you begin to understand why a wicked lesbian such as myself might like to seduce young women who may be straight after all? Why a submissive can still bring me pleasure, even if they don't want to worship my pussy because they're into women?" Susanna said, her voice louder now, demanding of an answer, her breath hot against Amber's ear as her fingers pushed slowly, ever so slowly, deeper inside the younger woman's pussy.

"Yes, Mistress. I understand. I understand why she'd want your fingers deep in her pussy. Fucking her while her thumb rubbed gentle circles across her clit," Amber agreed, her moans and soft squeals interrupting her speech throughout.

"Oh, yes, my dear. Now you begin to understand the true power of the dominant side of the relationship," Susanna purred while she pressed her thumb against Amber's clit. Amber was breathing hard, her back arched, and she chewed her lip.

"I think we can cure you of your naivete, Amber, would you like that?"

"Yes, Mistress."

"Then let me begin your education," Susanna said, working her fingers in the younger woman's sex as she spoke, "Picture our hypothetical submissive, serving a dominant and becoming excited when they do it. Even if their dominant is not of their sexual preference. The submissive goes to a play party at a club, and she is spanked by dominants of either sex. She finds the spanking painful, but stimulating in a way purely sexual contact might not be, despite only being sexually compatible with one of the dominants who plays with her."

Susanna's fingers continued to thrust slowly in and out of Amber's pussy, rubbing firmly on her G-spot in the process. The domme used the pad of her thumb, covered in Amber's own secretions, to describe tight circles on her subject's clit.

"Plenty of subs play at club nights, even when sex is not permitted. They just go to indulge in their favourite aspects of BDSM. Maybe they'll have sex when they go home, but they enjoy their playtime at the event all the same. What about a straight young man, dropping to all fours so an older gentleman can cane him in front of everyone? He has no mistress to call his own, and no romantic feelings toward me, yet as the cane leaves stripes across his buttocks, he grows hard for all to see. He is aroused by the act of submitting to a dominant, even another man. Do you see?" Mistress Susanna asked insistently.

"Yes, Mistress, I see," Amber replied slowly as her hips bucked up to meet the probing digits. "That feels so good, Mistress. Do you think I might be a lesbian all the same? The way you touch me excites me so much."

"I still do, Amber, I still do, but not just because I can get this reaction from your sweet, young pussy. Do you want to find out together?"

"Yes. Yes, please, Mistress."

"Good girl. I want you to understand, that for now, it truly doesn't matter. We can play, have fun, you can keep me happy with your servitude, and I can take pleasure in your suffering when I torment you. You'll learn about yourself and everything will be fine. Nothing is forever, and you have a three-month probationary period to impress me with your work, while you decide if this lifestyle is for you. Of course, if you do join the Sisterhood, the loyalty card has amazing member benefits," Susanna said enticingly. "I'm sure you'd enjoy trying them out."

"That does sound wonderful, Mistress," Amber conceded.

"It will feel wonderful too, so come for me, Amber. Come now for your Mistress."

Amber nodded, concentrating on the rising pleasure Susanna was causing in her pussy. It was not too long after that she cried out in ecstasy as her climax arrived in wave after wave of pleasure. Her sex clamped down repeatedly on Susanna's strong fingers.

"That was beautiful, and so noisy, Amber."

"Thank you, Mistress," Amber panted.

"You're welcome, gorgeous. Are you ready to clean up for your Mistress," Susanna whispered in her ear.

Amber nodded.

"Open wide, slut," Susanna ordered. Her wet fingers slipped from Amber's pussy and she presented them the open mouth of her submissive with a triumphant smile, but did not push them inside. Amber lifted her head, craning forward to envelop Susanna's sticky fingers and suck them clean, running her tongue around them to lick up every drop of her arousal. "Yes, that feels good, doesn't it? Don't you taste good, Amber?" Susanna asked, smiling as Amber nodded, while still sucking the proffered digits. Finally she finished her duty and pulled back, gasping for air.

"That was good, Mistress. I confess I'm still a little nervous though," Amber said.

"Oh, cupcake, I know. That's perfectly natural. If you think about it though, you could have seen this coming. We both know you've thought about this before. You've done plenty of homework, haven't you?" Susanna prompted.

"Do you mean the books I've read, Mistress?"

"Yes, but not just the erotica books. Think about all those forums you joined. The kinks and perversities you listed on your profile, the filthy videos you watched. The all point to your need to seek out the answers I can provide you," Susanna said, stroking Amber's knee as she spoke.

"My profile? I don't know what you mean," Amber said nervously.

It wasn't true, she was just buying time. Amber knew very well which profile on which website Susanna must be referring to. But it was an anonymous profile with no information that could track her down, wasn't it? *There shouldn't be any way Susanna could find it, Amber thought.*

Amber felt a guilty blush rising up her neck.

The information in that profile was like an instruction manual on how to seduce Amber. It revealed all sorts of specific niches she had fantasised about or had researched. Things that others posted that she'd clicked on to say she liked them. Comments she'd made on pictures.

If Susanna had access to all that, she might as well be having her mind read. Amber would be an open book to her. The whole time from arriving at Susanna's office for the interview, until now, flashed through her mind on instant replay.

How dare her new boss nose around in her private life!

CHAPTER 3

"You do know what I mean, Amber," Susanna chuckled.

"I really don't," Amber deflected, playing for time to think it over.

Susanna laughed. "Your profile on that naughty website, Amber. You know the one, I mean. I've seen the groups you joined, the tasteful if boring pictures you chose to upload, what you wrote in your description. I've read the list of sexual activities you've tried, and the kinks you are curious about. It's a big list, isn't it? You have such wide-ranging interests, too. I couldn't help noticing that a lot of them almost demand another woman as well."

Amber was taken aback. How had Susanna found her profile? Her face wasn't shown, and the location was deliberately vague. Surely she couldn't have seen it, but if she had, her new boss had an intimate knowledge of her darkest desires that weren't intended to be for public consumption.

There weren't any of Amber's real life friends connected to her on the site, and she hadn't seen anyone she recognised. Barely anyone had reached out to her to be online friends, and so no-one could connect her list of kinky interests with Amber herself. Except that it seemed Susanna was rather obliquely claiming to have done just that? But how could she have?

Amber shook her head, denying the possibility. "But how could you have found my profile, it's anonymous!" she blurted out, a note of panic creeping into her voice. She realised immediately that she'd just confessed to having a profile and cursed inwardly.

Susanna laid a soothing hand on her shoulder and squeezed, "It's alright, Amber, any filthy desires or dirty secrets you have, will be quite safe with me. You've signed my non-disclosure agreement after all. Do you really think I would offer you any less privacy than you are guaranteeing me?"

Amber leant forward, putting her head in her hands, resting her elbows on her knees. She took deep breaths as Susanna gently stroked her neck, trying to calm her.

"I don't understand how you found my profile," she said finally, when she'd fought back the urge to cry.

"The position you applied for had a high number of promising applications. You weren't the only one that went through the interview process. I had you all vetted thoroughly so I could be as sure as possible about anyone I ended up meeting."

"But that doesn't explain how you could have found me on that site."

"I honestly have no idea. I sub-contracted the security and background vetting out to a specialist company, as I did with headhunting and the extensive interviews you had with the human resources company. It was the Manning Detective Agency. They did an extremely thorough background check on you, I must say," Susanna explained. Then she caught the expression of horror on Amber's face. "Please don't look at me like that, Amber," Susanna admonished her.

"It's such an invasion of my privacy," Amber said.

"People of with my kind of wealth and business interests attract all sorts, Amber. Not all of them friendly and kind like you. Some are jealous, vindictive, and even violent. I have restraining orders against several people, you know. Protecting my security is paramount for me as well as that of my friends, business associates, and my other staff. I can't have someone coming in here for an interview and blabbing it all to the press because they turn out to be a prudish 'nilla," Susanna said.

Amber interrupted, "What's a 'nilla?"

"A vanilla person. Someone whose sex life is entirely mundane, with nothing at all exotic. The opposite of a BDSM player or a swinger. Vanilla like the ice cream, rather than my raspberry ripple," Susann clarified, "May I finish what I was saying?"

"Got it. I'd heard what vanilla meant but not hear it called 'nilla before. I'm sorry I interrupted, please continue," Amber said.

"I'm not the only one who has stringent and admittedly somewhat exotic requirements for those who live in my house you know. I couldn't have met with you, without knowing there was a chance you would be suitable for the job," Susanna said.

"Why not? You could have just hired me to be your assistant. I could have asked to be included in," Amber gestured, "all this. You didn't have to nose around my private business."

"I need someone who isn't going to be entirely shocked or appalled by my lifestyle. But I also need an excellent executive assistant. My process was designed to find the perfect candidate, and I think it did," Susanna offered.

"You think I'm the perfect candidate? When did you decide that?"

"Truthfully not until I told you to take off that awful suit and that appalling grey underwear you had on. How was it even still hanging together?"

"I'm pretty good with needle and thread and quite thrifty," Amber replied then waved her hand dismissively, realising the conversation was very off topic, "I can't believe you had me strip in an interview."

"Don't be ridiculous. People do it all the time."

"When? In porn films?"

"Exactly. Porn actresses and strippers do it to get jobs. Models too. Why shouldn't you?"

"I'm an assistant! It was so far over the line!"

"And yet, you took everything off without much objection," Susanna pointed out, smirking at the way Amber's mouth dropped open as if she was going to refute the comment. Then she piled on, "You did it quite sexily as well, I must say. And now, here you are."

"You tricked me," Amber protested.

"I most certainly did not! Well, not that much anyway. Why split hairs?" Susanna replied. "Models and life models strip all the time too. People who work at naturist clubs. People who work at fetish clubs too sometimes. A masseuse sees lots of naked clients. Medical staff. It's just a bit of nudity, Amber, I really think you're blowing it out of proportion," Susanna said innocently.

Amber decided to move on; clearly she wasn't making progress with that point, "It's just so sordid. A private detective digging into my sex life?"

"What sex life?" Susanna countered. "You had split up with that useless shit of a boyfriend and not before time, if you ask me,"

"I didn't."

Susanna ignored that completely, "You were spending half your free time looking at a kinky social network. You were searching for something. I submit to the prosecution that I'm the answer to all those dirty, needful, naughty little thought crimes you have been committing. Didn't you say you were curious about 'Older woman/younger woman' kinks?"

Amber gasped, turning her head away and covering her mouth. She couldn't look at Susanna when she replied, "You're not that old." It was odd. It was all she could think of.

Susanna giggled. "Why, thank you. I'm only thirty-four as it happens. I do think I've held up well."

"You have," Amber said, "very well. You're so beautiful. You're not older at all."

"Not old enough to satisfy fetish for cougar and kitten relationships then? My, Amber, how old were these women you were imagining? Should I be worried that you're going to be snatched away from me by some silver-haired MILF?" Susanna teased.

Amber shook her head, "Not much older than you. Just old enough to be a bit more experienced."

"I can assure you, I'm more than experienced enough for your needs, Amber. What is it you like then? The sex-starved soccer mom? The busy lawyer who just needs a younger woman to keep her bed warm at night and iron out the stress from her busy day? The mature college professor who has more to teach than you could imagine?" Susanna asked. Amber licked her lips.

Susanna stood up, then kneeled down on the couch facing her. Amber couldn't help but look her up and down. Her lesbian boss was older than her by almost eleven years apparently, but the quality that really sold their age gap as a turn on wasn't anything so crass as crow's feet or wrinkles.

No, it was the look of wisdom in Susanna's eyes and the way of carrying herself she had. Her innate confidence and a lascivious way of looking at Amber that told her Susanna was a woman who could teach her forbidden caresses and delights.

"How about older, but still useful lesbian businesswoman looking for a younger submissive to tease and torment? Does that work for you?"

Amber couldn't bring herself to answer. She swallowed hard and gave Susanna her best angry glare and pursed her lips. She wasn't going to play her employer's game, much though she wanted to reach out and touch her.

"These are all-natural you know?" Susanna said, jiggling her shoulders from side to side and causing her boobs to shake in a way that was reminiscent of beautiful breasts with proud, firm nipples, rather than silicone. "Not that I object to surgery when it serves a purpose, but I think these are perfectly fine for the time being, don't you?"

Amber nodded, reflexively, "They're lovely. But you're trying to change the subject."

Susanna shrugged, reaching up to play with her nipples, "You can't blame a domme for trying to lighten the mood when her assistant is being a bit dramatic. Not to mention a little judgemental."

"Did you do this with Sugar as well? Dig into her profiles and find out all her sordid little secrets?"

"Hah. Not likely. Sugar doesn't really keep secrets about herself very well. Very discreet about her Mistress and other people's business, but doesn't mind talking about herself at all."

"It's not funny."

"Ok, maybe not but no, I met Sugar at an event, and she was eager to please well before I did. I knew all about her before I had a chance to think about bringing her into my household. I got her adult life story the first evening in the pub at a munch."

"Then you put her through the same checks?"

Susanna shook her head. "I wasn't so well practised at this then, even just a couple of years ago. But sure, I did some checks. Nothing as extensive as on you, of course. It took time to get that organised about it all."

"Why not? Didn't you want to know if she liked older women?"

"Oh, I knew that at the end of the first night too. She invited herself up to my hotel room, and I found out just how agile her tongue is. But I didn't need the same rigamarole with her as I did with you. I already knew she was kinky and into women. All I needed to know was could she do the job, before I asked her about it," Susanna explained. She had let her hands drop down to her thighs now, stopping the brazen display of playing with her tits when it became apparent Amber wasn't being swayed by it.

"Wouldn't the human resources company have to do the same checks?"

Susanna shook her head and laughed. "No cupcake, she's just a maid. I'm not asking her to balance spreadsheets, prepare reports or arrange business meetings. I just needed to know she was trustworthy and not entirely dim or unqualified to hold a good conversation."

"Conversation? With that slut that you make dress up as a French maid?" Amber scoffed incredulously, "She's practically a walking sex toy!"

Susanna's expression grew dark at that. She practically pounced on Amber, shooting forward and straddling her personal assistant. Her knees were either side of Amber, and her hips pressed up against Amber's ample bosom.

Susanna towered over her in this position, although Amber was five foot six and she guessed her new boss was only a couple of inches taller than her. She felt immediately vulnerable.

Before Amber could respond, Susanna reached out her hand behind her neck, her fingers sliding into Amber's hair and taking a firm grip. Amber felt a consistent tug that forced her to tilt her head back, so she was looking up at Susanna, from just below her ample bosom.

"How dare you? How dare you, you hypocritical little bitch? What has Sugar done to you, eh?"

"Nothing!" Amber blurted out. "I'm sorry!"

"Do you think that I want ornaments? Human vibrators?"

"I don't know. I don't know what you want," Amber stammered. "I don't know what you want from me."

"You don't know what I want from you?"

"No, I don't really know why I'm here," Amber said, her voice catching in her throat. She felt like she might cry, as she had done earlier when her beautiful employer applied two dozen painful paddle whacks to her bottom.

"Then allow me to demonstrate," Susanna said. Amber's eyes went wide, as her lesbian boss came down to meet her. Their lips met, soft and warm, for just a moment. Susanna's tongue touched Amber's lips ever so gently, not pressing for access, just teasing.

Amber found herself parting her lips willingly to allow the tongue of the older woman access.

The kiss was divine, and Amber could feel her other lips responding again, preparing her for what was to come. Her mouth and tongue allowed Susanna to rule over them, devouring her with a hungry passion she'd never experienced with any man.

Susanna took the lead, which was probably to be expected, but Amber felt that she was somehow the girlfriend and that her boss was taking the role of her boyfriend. It was how she thought about the act of kissing. That one partner, the man, was in charge and was kissing the other. The girlfriend received the kiss.

It wasn't really like that with Susanna, though. Somehow, perhaps merely from long practice, her lesbian boss was able to adjust Amber's activity with subtle cues. She found herself taking a more active role, kissing Susanna back in a way she hadn't tried with any boyfriend since her first teenage flirtations. Amber had noticed they didn't like that, at least none of the boyfriends she'd had.

Susanna responded by cupping her head with both hands, and tilting back a little, settling down on her haunches to allow Amber full reign to kiss her. They played back and forth for a long time. Kissing like horny teenagers, Amber's hands caressing Susanna's back.

Amber couldn't believe how excited this older woman was making her. She knew that her profile listed an interest of hers as 'older/younger lesbian domination' and it currently suggested she was curious about it.

It felt like she should fire up her phone and change it to something else like, 'that is so fucking hot, put me on my knees now you gorgeous and powerful businesswoman'.

It seemed like Susanna was playing expertly into her private list of foibles. Wait a minute, Amber thought. That was precisely what Susanna was doing. Perhaps she was going down her own mental list of information she'd seen about Amber and playing every card she could to seduce her secretary into a lesbian affair.

Lesbian secretaries. Tick. That was another of Amber's list of kinks. Really any younger lesbian at the mercy of an older lesbian, or a straight girl getting seduced.

Amber cursed inwardly. She was letting the touch and flavour of Susanna's kiss sway her away from her fury at her for invading her privacy in such an intimate fashion.

With an effort of will, she broke the kiss. "Banana!" she blurted out.

The effect was instantaneous.

Susanna's hand flew to her mouth, and she squealed, "Oh!". Simultaneously, the slightly older woman sprang up from her kneeling position, getting off the brown leather of the couch and backing away immediately.

Amber looked at Susanna, up and down. She was just slightly older, or at least that's how she seemed but she was old enough for

Amber's overactive imagination to find the age gap added an extra something to the overall package. Thinking of Susanna as an older woman pushed Amber's buttons it seemed.

Susanna's reaction to the safeword being used was like a light switch being flipped. One moment Susanna was passionately and persuasively making her case to be forgiven for invading Amber's privacy. Or rather she was using her a tongue and lips to do so, which gave her a distinctly unfair advantage over her nubile employee. The next moment she had pulled back and Mistress Susanna was completely turned off.

"Amber! My goodness, whatever is wrong? I thought we were getting along famously," Susanna asked, her voice trembling with worry.

Amber got to her feet too, thanking providence that the couch was so expensive it had the exact right amount of give in it. Just enough to cushion you, not swallow you whole like some dilapidated wreck you might find in a grotty pub.

"Well, we're not. Just because you have a tongue like an electric eel, doesn't mean you can get into my knickers. I'm really cross with you, Susanna! How could you be so thoughtless and intrusive and just think it was alright because you kissed me?" Amber finished triumphantly, feeling she'd won a couple of good points there.

"You're not such a bad kisser yourself," Susanna smirked.

Amber felt an electric tingle run up her spine at that, but fought it off. "What?"

Susanna covered her face with her hands, "I don't know. You've got me all flustered. I can't believe you used your safeword. That never, and I mean, never, happens to me. I practically have to run safety tests to make sure my girls are playing responsibly and not putting too brave a face on it."

"That's what's bothering you? That I used my safeword?"

Susanna nodded, "It's important for me to know why. Was I kissing you too long? Was it too forward?"

"Too forward? What are you talking about?" Amber waved her hand, dismissively, "It's got nothing to do with the kiss. The kissing was lovely. It's the detective agency laying bare my dirtiest thoughts to you so you can seduce me. Don't you see how wrong that is?"

"Is it? And if I'd stumbled across your profile, then sent you a message, would that have been wrong? You put that out there for people to see, Amber," Susanne responded crossly.

"I don't care, you nosy bitch. I want to leave!" Amber shouted.

Susanna gasped, horrified to have been spoken to in such a rude fashion. She reached for the younger woman, taking her by the wrist. "How dare you speak to me that way! After all, I've done for you. If you want to leave, nothing is stopping you. I'll have my girl bring the car around as soon as you're ready to go back to London."

Then Susanna looked down at her hand on Amber's wrist and snatched it back as if she'd grabbed a hot poker. She actually blushed with shame. "I'm sorry, I shouldn't have grabbed you like that."

It was Amber's turned to be horrified, but not by the possessive grip on her arm. By Susanna's response to her furious outburst, which completely misconstrued her meaning. Desperately, she tried to rectify her mistake, "No, I'm sorry, Miss Hamilton. Really. I didn't mean back to London. I meant, leaving this room to go back to mine."

"You want to return to your room?"

"To let cooler heads prevail, yes," Amber said.

"Good idea, especially if you're going to hurl vulgarities and nasty accusations at me," Susanna fumed. "Come with me then," her lesbian boss said, taking her hand to guide her to the door.

"Banana," Amber said immediately. Susanna let go immediately.

"What's wrong?" she asked.

"I don't need or want an escort back to my room," Amber replied coolly and calmly.

"But you want to stay in my household?" Susanna asked.

"Yes, I just don't need my hand held."

"If you're staying, you need to do so by my rules. Are you willing to do that?"

"Yes."

"Then you can't keep using your safeword like that, it's not what it's for," Susanna hissed.

"Well, I'm sorry, but I'm new to this," Amber said, adding a little heel stamp for emphasis.

Susanna turned toward her, and her face bore an expression that suggested any little madam who got uppity with her would rue the day. "Yes, you are, and perhaps I underestimated your knowledge and should have given you some clarity on the issue, much earlier."

"What about?"

"Your safeword is there to stop play, mostly in an emergency when something is badly wrong. Maybe something is hurting when it shouldn't, or the pain is simply over your limits, or a rope is cutting off your circulation. It's not a way for you to tell me that you're miffed with me, or a way to avoid an uncomfortable talk. It's like a slap in the face for me, do you understand? It means I might have messed up badly and hurt you," Susanna explained. "My first thought, any good dominants first thought, when a safeword is used is what the worst-case scenario could be. It's like pulling a fire alarm. Do you understand what I'm trying to impress on you?"

"Yes, I'm sorry. What do I say if it's nothing too serious then?" Amber replied, somewhat grumpily Susanna thought, but she let it slide and followed her as the older woman led her from the room talking while they walked.

"Stop usually works. That hurts too much, or I really need the loo can we take a break works too. I always find that's good for a laugh when the action has just got really sexy and intimate."

Amber smiled apologetically, "Ok, sorry. I won't do it again."

"You can just say no, you know? I'll check what's wrong if you do."

"Understood, boss," Amber nodded.

"Of course if you say, 'No, oh please no, please don't put the vibrator on my clit, Mistress. Please stop, I can't take another orgasm.' then you are going about it the wrong way," Susannah said with a sly grin.

Amber licked her lips, "No means no, except it doesn't always, does it? I'll keep the safeword for serious things. I'm sorry, boss, you won't hear another banana from me unless it's essential. Banana."

Susanna growled theatrically as she took Amber through the door into her own bedroom, "That's not enough, Amber. While you calm down and think about your future, I'm going to cuff you to the bed. You need to start learning some disciplinary lessons. You can't expect to misbehave and not be punished at all. If you decide you don't want to be here, that's fine, but I hope you'll decide to stay and if you do, you need to make peace with the idea that in my household, young ladies are punished for disobedience and naughtiness."

"Yes, Mistress," Amber replied.

"What is it to be then, Amber? Bondage or goodbye?"

"Bondage," came the reply, without hesitation and with more than a hint of lust.

Amber got up onto the four-poster bed and waited on all fours. Susanna set about attaching padded leather cuffs, linked by leather straps, to her wrists and ankles. The straps were long enough that she had a lot of freedom of movement.

Then took a long thin steel chain, and hooked that onto one of her wrist cuffs, the other end of it was attached to one of the bedposts.

"When you said you were cuffing me to the bed, I thought you meant splayed out and tightly held down."

Susanna shook her head. "That's not safe enough for a newbie. Caution is the watchword when leaving someone in bondage, even if you're only a room or two away. You need some private time, so I don't want to have to station Candy in here to watch over you."

"Hang on, this chain is just attached with a carabiner. I could open it in a jiffy," Amber pointed out.

"Yes, but if you do that, I'll know, and there will be punishment, unless it's for a safety reason, understood?"

"Yes, Mistress," Amber pouted.

The dominatrix pointed at a velvet cord hanging from the ceiling near the top of the bed. "Bell rope. Summon help if required."

"I'm sure I'll be fine, I can even reach the bathroom from here if I need the loo."

"Thank you for reminding me," Susanna said. She strode over to the bathroom door, pulled it shut and locked it with the key that was in it when Amber had arrived. Having no clothes and no pockets, she kept it in her hand.

"What if I need the toilet? Do I ring the bell?"

Susanna laughed. "Not unless you want a spanking." Amber's boss reached under the bed and pulled out a large porcelain bowl with a lid. She put it on a nearby armchair in Amber's line of sight and pulled out a toilet roll from within, brandishing it to make sure Amber saw.

"A chamber pot? You must be joking," Amber chuckled before she saw the look on her boss's face.

"Just squat over it and do your business," Susanna replied unsympathetically.

"No, that's humiliating!" Amber blurted out, then blushed.

Susanna smiled like the Cheshire cat. "I'm glad you think so, Amber. That makes it a much more effective punishment for all your naughtiness, your vulgarity and difficult behaviour, don't you think? If you're lucky you won't need it," Susanna said with an honest to goodness smirk on her face.

Amber didn't say anything, letting the sullen look on her face express her thoughts.

"I think that takes care of everything. Use the bell-rope if you need help, or you decide you want to talk about things," Susanna said.

"You won't be asleep?" Amber asked quietly.

"If I am, Candy will wake me."

"Just to talk to me?"

"Amber, I would lose a hundred nights of sleep to talk to you. Now, be a good girl, and get your head down for Mistress so we can talk when you're ready," with that, she flicked off the light and shut the door behind her.

"Goodnight, Mistress," Amber whispered to herself.

CHAPTER 4

When Amber awoke, she had no idea of the exact time, but the curtains were open, and although the moon wasn't visible, they were so far out in the country that she could see the stars. *Still night, then, she thought.*

There had been no chance to find out where any clocks might have been in the room, so she lay there, thinking over her options, as she'd been ordered to.

As she considered everything that had happened during the day, from her initial striptease in Miss Hamilton's office to being fingered in the bath by Candy, then thoroughly paddled by Miss Hamilton, she couldn't help touching herself.

Amber reached a crescendo of pleasure, as she recalled the last few hours, particularly those sweet moments when she and Miss Hamilton had been kissing, so passionately. She didn't bother to keep quiet, her room was quite far from her boss's, and it was a big house. Amber cried out her full-throated pleasure as she recalled Miss Hamilton's breasts jiggling in front of her as she jiggled them at her assistant purely for the sake of a cheap laugh.

Her new boss was a lesbian, and she was doing everything in her power to seduce her new assistant into a lifestyle that was as hedonistic as it was luxurious. Those facts were now completely and unashamedly, out in the open. But she was also willing to play with Amber even if she were straight, as long as she was willing to submit.

Amber could well imagine the pleasures that Susanna would unlock for her if she stayed in the dominant woman's household for the long term.

Tasting her own juices on her fingers, Amber couldn't help but wonder what her boss would taste like. Would she be the same, or did different women have different flavours? They probably did.

Then she recalled their argument and her vociferous defence of her right to privacy. Amber thought about that for a while and decided she was definitely still wound up about it. A short sleep had taken the edge off her anger but not calmed her down completely.

On reflection, she could see that it wasn't as if they'd hacked her accounts, although she supposed that was a possibility. It seemed much more likely that they had been able to connect some of her vanilla accounts to the kinky ones, with publicly available information. Had she used a photo which didn't show her face but could be searched for to see if it matched other sites? Quite possibly.

What was the actual harm to her, as well, other than a currently still sore bottom? Amber had been offered a new job, with excellent pay and medical benefits, a place to stay and a professional cook to provide food. It was a dream job, and she actually enjoyed the kind of organisational challenge that a high-level personal assistant faced.

Then there were the secondary benefits and perks. Candy, her own personal maid whose fingers were available to her if she wanted to be pleasured. Sugar, who actually came across as a little cold to her, but was perhaps also fun in some undiscovered way and had been devastatingly sexy as she played the exhibitionist for their boss, masturbating vigorously right in front of Amber's face as she was paddled.

Finally, there was Miss Hamilton herself, or Mistress, as she liked to be called. If Amber could forgive her transgressions, she could be an eye-opening delight all to herself.

It didn't take all that long for her to go through her mental checklist, and when she had, she made her decision.

Amber reached for the bell-rope.

CHAPTER 5

Sugar strode into the room a few minutes later and walked over to the head of the bed so she could face Amber. The curvaceous brunette was wearing a simple sheer mini-robe which would barely contain her curves but clearly wasn't intended to. Even in the light from the hallway, Amber could make out every line and feature of the maid's voluptuous body.

"Like what you see?" the maid asked with a sneer.

Amber captured the high ground immediately, "Yes, very much. That really suits you. It's a wonder you can sleep at all, looking like that. You must have to fight the urge to touch yourself."

Sugar actually blushed; Amber would swear it. Perhaps she didn't get many compliments like that, but whatever the case, it seemed to defuse her irritable attitude.

The maid leaned over and whispered, "I don't have to fight the urge at all." Her hands slipped to the belt, and the robe fell open, then she parted her thighs, and spread her lips with the fingers of one hand. With the other, she began to tease her lips, which were slick from her arousal. "See?"

Amber bit her lip. "Yes, I can see." She threw back the thin sheet which was all that she'd needed in the hot summer weather, exposing her nudity. Amber was lying on her back, and she mirrored Sugar's actions as if they were a challenge. She began to finger herself again, grinning at Sugar.

There was no way she wanted to let her know that she was intimidated by the more experienced submissive and so she held her gaze until Sugar spoke again, matching her stroke for stroke all the while.

"Enough of this mucking about. What did you want?" Sugar said, indicating the bell-rope that Amber had pulled and refastening her robe, not that that protected her modesty in any way. While she waited for an answer, she lewdly sucked her fingers clean and Amber found herself fixated by the display of wanton lust.

With a tinge of regret, Amber ceased her own masturbation, "I want to speak to Miss Hamilton."

Sugar nodded, "Mistress said if you've calmed down and want to talk, she's ready to listen. Want me to untie you?"

"Yes, please," Amber replied gratefully. So Miss Hamilton was awake and ready to see her?

"What did you do to get in trouble, anyway? Bite something you shouldn't have?" Sugar grinned.

"No, I told her she was a bitch for spying on my dating profiles," Amber confessed.

Sugar drew in a sharp breath and sat down on the bed with a thump. The sexily dressed maid had just been in a masturbation contest with her and yet she looked thoroughly scandalised. For a moment she did nothing at all and then she resumed undoing the cuffs.

"Shut up! You never. You called Mistress a bitch? You must be completely loopy. What did she do, pitch a fit and spank you until you came?"

"No, she got really cross, especially when I used my safeword. Twice."

"Oh, my word. Stop it, will you! You can't be telling porkies around here like that, you'll get us both in trouble."

"I'm not lying. Wait, did you say spanking can make you come?"

Sugar nodded. "Not everyone, but it does me," she sighed. "I love a good hard slap on my arse. Mistress treats me sometimes, but I have a trick to get what I need if she's not in a playful mood."

"Is she ever not in a playful mood?"

"Fair point, but she's not always here. Want to know my one weird trick?" Sugar asked, dropping her voice to an unnecessary conspiratorial whisper.

Amber nodded enthusiastically. Having an orgasm just from a spanking sounded plenty intriguing.

"Make sure you get to have lunch in the kitchen with Pudding. If you tell her it wasn't cooked right, or the fillings in your sandwich didn't complement each other very well, she really takes umbrage. She'll insist on punishing you," Sugar said with a wink.

"She's allowed to punish you?"

"Well, duh, she's a higher station than us, so of course she is. As long as we've done something naughty of course," Sugar said. She noted that blank look from Amber and added, "Not found out about stations yet? It's easy. It's like a ranking system, so we know where we all are on the pecking order. Candy and me, we're the bottom and Mistress is the top. Anyone above you can play with you, or even punish you. You and Pudding are right up there, just below Mistress. Well, at least until she shakes things up again. Mistress is never fully satisfied, and she loves to keep us on our toes. Sometimes by suspending us from the dungeon ceiling so she can cane us!" Sugar giggled as she finished up her rambling comments.

Amber couldn't absorb all that in one go, but felt she should hear the end of Sugar's trick, just in case she needed it, "That's fascinating. So, Pudding will punish you for being rude about her food?"

"Oh, yeah. Pudding will punish you alright. Skirt up, knickers down, and she'll go to town. Pudding has a mean streak, and the kitchen gets quite hot. I think she gets all pent up, hot and bothered in the literal sense, and loves to get some release. She takes you in her office, and then she'll spank the crap out of you over her desk. It's lovely," Sugar said, elongating her final word for emphasis.

"Does she do anything special to make you come from it?"

Sugar giggled, "For me, it's just about the number of whacks. She takes her time does our Pudding, and she doesn't spare your skin or hers. By the time she's done, it's three times the spanking most will give you, and my bum is cherry red. I get so wet, and she's a dirty cow, so she knows it. I can come when anyone spanks me, and she brings me off good and proper all the time, just from spanking my bum. But if it doesn't tip me over the edge, then she uses her best trick and that is guaranteed to set me off. It's like a finishing move from a martial arts game!"

"Go on, what is it?" Amber pleaded, "Tell me, go on, please?"

Sugar grinned wickedly and stood up, "I think we should go and see Mistress now, don't you, little Miss didn't think I saw her playing with herself while I told my story?"

"Oh, don't be mean, Sugar. It's such a sweet name, don't you want to be sweet to me," Amber begged.

"You're not such a bad sort, after all, Amber. I'm sorry I was rude when you got here. You can punish me if you like. When Mistress lets you play with us."

"Punish you? I could spank you rotten, you know. You have been snippy with me until now."

"Promises, promises. Ok, I'll spill. So, Pudding gets you all hot and bothered with a good, hard, bum jiggling spank. She's got hands like wooden paddles you know. When I'm as excited as I think I can get, bent over her desk getting spanked, but I'm just not coming for her, that's when she flips me around. She has me park my sore bum on the desk and lay right back like this," Sugar said, sitting down on the edge of the bed and lying back to demonstrate.

The position included spreading her legs quite wide, exposing her hairless pussy nicely. Amber didn't interrupt her again, she just looked on lustily as Sugar talked.

"Then she sets to with some more spanks, not as hard. Sometimes she goes for my thighs, on the inside here, where it's sensitive," Sugar said, indicating the soft skin of her inner thighs. "But when she really wants me to scream, she brings her hand down here. Just a couple of those and I scream my head off on account of it being painful, but that always sends me right over the edge."

Amber had her hand over her mouth at that point. Sugar was gently rubbing her wet lips with the palm of her hand and biting her lip at the same time, "She actually spanks your pussy?"

Sugar nodded, "Yes, and hard too. Not as hard as my bum, but it gets tears from me sometimes, and I don't well up easily, just like you."

"Wow. I've never thought of such a thing. Is that what you want me to do to you?"

"Nah. You're all right. If Mistress lets you play with me, you can just spank me and then finish me off with your fingers if you want. You'll probably need a while to get that good, and I'm certainly not letting a newbie spank my poor cunt. Not until she knows what she's doing, anyway," Sugar cackled.

"Come on, up and at them. Let's get you over to Mistress before she punishes me till I'm crying."

"I thought you liked that though. It doesn't sound like it's a punishment for you, does it?"

"It is when she makes me stand in the corner, facing the wall and not touching myself. It's the worst kind of torture. It's evil. Don't every really upset, Mistress, my girl, you'll rue the day. She'll make your sixty minutes feel like a five-hour amateur opera," Sugar said as she helped Amber to her feet and led her out of the room.

Sugar smacked Amber's bum as she went through the doorway, "I hope you can walk back whatever you did with Mistress, Amber. I'd love it if you stuck around."

"I'm going to do my best, Sugar. My very best."

CHAPTER 6

When they reached Miss Hamilton's suite, Amber could hear the distinctive sound of a woman in the throes of passion, before Sugar even opened the doors to the sitting room. Someone was having fun and being quite noisy about it too.

Sugar ushered her in, then straight through the outer room, opening the bedroom door quietly and waving her inside. The maid remained out in the sitting room herself, shutting the bedroom door quietly behind Amber, with a quick thumbs-up and a silently mouthed, "Good luck."

The room inside was aglow with mood lighting from concealed sources, creating a warm effect like a big fire or more candles than you could light before getting bored. It was easy on the eyes, yet it was possible to see everything in the room clearly. Including the occupants of the enormously proportioned bed.

Miss Hamilton was lying on the bed, her back and head supported by a wedge of supportive foam, that Amber recognised from various adult websites as a customisable support that made all sorts of fancy sexual positions dramatically more comfortable to experiment with.

In this case, Susanna had plenty of support for her back and neck, and could easily look down the length of her body, at the young woman who was on her knees between her legs. It was Candy, Amber quickly realised, after she recognised her blonde hair.

Candy had her face buried in what Sugar had crudely called the cunt of their Mistress. That word was filthy but seemed to fit the situation rather well. Candy was moaning loudly as she worked her tongue and lips all over Miss Hamilton's pussy. She didn't seem wild or out of control but rather, ravenous. As if she were eating a long overdue meal, that consisted entirely of fattening desserts.

Susanna's eyes flicked open, and she fixed Amber with an expectant look. Her mouth was opening, and she too was giving vent to her passion. Mostly without words, but the occasional 'Fuck me, that's good' or 'That's right, eat me like you're starving, you dirty little slut.' escaped her lips.

Her Mistress was evidently relishing every moment of what Candy was doing to her, and clearly the maid was enjoying it almost as much. That didn't stop Susanna responding to Amber's presence entirely, but it did slow her down. With her left hand, she gestured at a spot nearer the head of the bed, "Stand there, like a good girl and watch Candy work me like the artist she is."

"Yes, Mistress," Amber said. She did as she was told, standing as she'd been instructed earlier, with her hands crossed in the small of her back and her feet shoulder-width apart. She could now see Candy's pink tongue as she licked and sucked their boss's swollen lips and she lapped like a cat at their boss's clit.

Amber had never seen a pussy being eaten in person like this, just on videos, and she began to notice subtleties quite quickly. The way Candy's head bobbed, provoked one type of gasp from Mistress and when her lips pursed on her clit, she often verbalised her lust, 'You naughty little minx. Yes, suck it like that, you filth bitch.'

She could also see that Candy's arms were looped under Mistresses thighs and her fingers gripped her tightly, allowing her to keep Susanna's hips from bucking up hard as her probing tongue provoked the most dramatic responses.

It was like sitting in on a masterclass in the art of cunnilingus. But

Candy's own pleasure was denied. There was nothing physically stimulating her, except for the encouragement of her Mistress and the satisfaction of giving her pleasure.

Susanna's right hand found Candy's hair and Amber was sure she was going to grind her pussy into her face and keep her there. In her place, it's what she might have wanted to do. Instead, she guided Candy's head to tilt to her right, so she faced toward Amber.

"Say hello to Amber, slut," Susanna ordered.

"Hello, Amber slut," Candy said with a cheeky grin. Her tongue lashed out, stroking up the length of her Mistress's pussy, and then teasing her clit. All the while, she kept her eyes locked with Amber's, and even though Mistress released her head as her pleasure mounted, she kept herself tilted from then on. Candy began to perform not just for the benefit of their boss, but to show off to Amber.

"If you weren't so gifted at this, Candy, and I weren't so very horny, I would stop right now and give you six of the best for that cheek. Now finish me off," Susanna instructed.

Amber was reminded that the maid had told her she was allowed to finger Amber, but not give her cunnilingus. She fervently hoped Miss Hamilton would relinquish that stranglehold soon, Candy was, after all, supposed to be her personal maid. It would be jolly unfair if Amber could never call on her for this kind of service.

Yes, Amber, she thought to herself, that's a problem that a thousand tiny violins would scream over. Had she really become that entitled about having a maid already that she was put out not to be allowed to order her to lick her pussy?

"Now, Amber, it is still well before dawn," Susanna commented between the moans of passion which Candy was drawing from her with increasing frequency. "Can I take it that you have used the time to think about our little contretemps and you are here to talk about that?"

"Yes, Mistress," Amber said. She was about to launch into more, but Susanna's hand raised to forestall it.

"Before we discuss this further, ah," Susanna managed then faded out for a few seconds as she regained control of her brain. Whatever Candy was doing, it was clearly effective.

"Yes, as I was saying before this, fucking slut nibbled my pussy lips, a technique you may wish to memorise for future reference I might add, there is something I wish to point out," Susanna stated. "You may imagine that one practitioner of the noble art of cunnilingus is much like another. That any head is good head, as the saying goes. Much like the nonsensical phrase, 'You can't judge a book by its cover' which ironically, doesn't apply to books at all and barely applies to people unless they're all naked, it is absolute rubbish. Candy here is one of the best pussy licking subs I've had the pleasure to own. With me so far?"

"Yes, Miss Hamilton. Candy certainly seems to be enjoying what she's doing as well."

"That, my girl, is the mark of a good submissive or any sexual partner. With a few exceptions, you generally want a partner who enjoys eating you out, or fingering you or whatever works for you. Her enjoyment is part of my enjoyment. The important bit is that I assigned this excellent young lady to be your personal maid for the time being. Need I emphasise the fact that if you are here to ruin my night and tell me that you want to be no part of my household, that that offer will be voided. You would never get to experience the delights of Candy's tongue and lips on your pussy. That's the stick," Susanna said, stumbling before she tried to speak again.

Candy won her game at that point though, and although Susanna tried to finish her thought, she was sent crashing into paroxysms of orgasmic pleasure. The dominant screamed, cursed, thanked and decried Candy for a slut, all in the same breathless monologue of dirty talk. Her body shook and her fingers bunched in the Egyptian cotton sheets as her legs clamped around Candy's face.

The submissive French maid didn't seem in the slightest bit bothered, but Amber imagined she was much in demand in the household and regularly experienced a vigorous thigh clamp around her head. It didn't stop her trying to keep eye contact with Amber or working her tongue at her Mistress's pussy, even as the slightly older woman rode the waves of her orgasm.

Amber considered replying to Susanna but felt it would be a stupid mistake to interrupt, especially once she realised her boss was cresting toward another climactic peak. She watched in awe as Candy triumphantly gave her a thumbs up, while Miss Hamilton came close to passing out and collapsing from the second orgasm in as many minutes.

Candy tried once more to lick at her Mistress's pussy, but Miss Hamilton shooed her away. Breathing heavily, she ordered the maid out. "That was a good game, Candy, well played. But it's time for me to talk to Amber now. Go out to my sitting room and tell Sugar that I want you to sixty-nine each other, with you on the bottom. Nice and slow of course, because neither of you has permission to come, unless I come out there and tell you otherwise," Susanna said.

"Oh, Mistress, you are wickedly sadistic to us. Orgasm denial is the worst! I hate it," Candy grumbled.

"I understand my dear, but it gives me a great deal of pleasure to deny it to you, as you very well know. Your Mistress must always think of herself and her own pleasure and not just yours. Now, scoot and go and make Sugar miserable too, won't you, dearest?" Susanna insisted.

The young maid brightened at the prospect that Sugar wasn't allowed to have an orgasm either which Amber judged must be extremely difficult if Candy was licking your pussy. She was starting to get a feel for all this, much better than she had from forums and books and she guessed that there would be a playful punishment if either or both maids, reached an orgasm.

When the doors closed, Susanna said, "The fridge is there, a nice big glass of juice for both of us, if you'd be so kind and still remember that I employed you to be at my beck and call."

Amber did as she was told while Susanna sat up in the bed and rolled her head in circles, stretching her neck muscles. The dominant woman sat cross-legged on the bed and told Amber to do the same once she'd handed her a glass of apple juice. Susanna gulped it down, and Amber could see why. The bed was damp with sweat and the arousal of her boss.

Her employer noticed her furtive glances at the state of the bed and grinned. "I never sleep in the wet patches, you know. Do you know how?"

Amber considered for a second and then said, "You want me to say you make your maids sleep there, but I think if it was that bad, you could simply go to another bedroom."

Susanna giggled and clapped her hands, "Bravo. I can see I'm going to have trouble slipping any naughty tricks past you, aren't I?"

Amber was silent for a moment.

Susanna tilted her head and sighed despondently, "I am going to have more trouble with you, aren't I, Amber? Please tell me we can put our earlier disagreement behind us and move on."

"Yes. I want to stay, Mistress. If you will allow it."

"Of course, do I sense a condition behind this change of heart?"

Amber hadn't actually got that far; she'd just determined that she would mend fences. Then an idea for something that could be to her advantage, struck her, "Yes, there is one. Sugar told me a little secret about herself, and I'd like the opportunity to find out more."

"Let me guess. Sugar told you about her spanking fetish? You'd like my permission to spank her?"

Amber smiled nervously, "Yes. Is that sort of thing ok? Sugar implied it was, but I did wonder if she was being naughty."

"Sugar and Candy are always being naughty, in one way or another. Disciplining those lower in station is something I expect and encourage all my more senior staff to do. I can't very well spank all the bottoms and gag all the mouths on my own, can I? I'll show you how to deliver a proper spanking and give you the opportunity to practise under my supervision. When you're sufficiently trained up, you may spank Sugar until she covers your lap in her cream. Deal?"

"Yes, Mistress. Thank you, Mistress," Amber said. Miss Hamilton was going to train her how to spank Sugar. That would mean her taking charge to some extent she realised, and previously she'd thought her role would be to be entirely submissive to her lesbian boss.

"Good, then let us speak no more of privacy concerns, shall we? Except to say, that there are excellent cameras throughout my property and for instance, I could watch what Sugar and Candy are up to now, or on replay as I choose. I hope you don't mind being on camera while you are here? Strictly for my pleasure, and general security, of course."

"Oh, Miss Hamilton, you are a naughty bitch," Amber replied, a moment before she was manhandled into position over her lesbian boss's lap.

"Now, that comment deserves a punishment that will have you howling, young lady."

Amber turned her head and looked up at her beautiful Mistress, licking her lips seductively.

"Bring it, Grandma!" Amber replied with a smirk.

CHAPTER 7

"How did that feel, Amber?" Susannah asked as she put down the implement she'd been wielding.

"How do you think? It fucking hurts, Mistress," Amber sobbed, tears streaming freely down her cheeks.

"Wonderful. Simply wonderful."

"Who keeps a fucking cane by their bedside table, anyway?"

Susanna chuckled, "I think you may have misunderstood something about the concept of a dominant, older."

"Slightly," Amber interjected.

A hard slap on the arse made her cry out in surprise.

"Thank you, slightly older woman. But no interruptions you cheeky little tart or I shall not hesitate to stripe you some more. Where was I? Ah, yes. You, Amber, seem to be a little confused about the nature of the relationship between a slightly older, dominant lesbian woman, and the younger ladies who serve her as her sexual submissives. Allow me to explain," Susanna said.

As she launched into a monologue, Amber felt the delightful but light touch of fingertips against her inner thighs. Presented as she was, naked with her bum in the air and laying over the lap of her equally nude Mistress, Amber's pussy became even more obscenely displayed when she inched her knees apart.

"Good girl," Susanna commented, as her fingers gained freedom of movement and she began to tease Amber's pussy lips, ever so gently. Amber moaned softly at the gentle touch of her Mistress.

"I am many things, Amber. I am a lesbian. I like the dominant role during sexual intercourse and associated playtime. I have significantly sadistic tendencies, and I derive enormous pleasure from teasing and tormenting my sexual partners. There are toys, implements, items of furniture and clothing, lubricants and erotic media all over this property. All of it, carefully placed to ensure the maximum amount of time devoted to my pleasure, as I believe I have touched on before," Susanna said as her index finger teased between Amber's lips and traversed the length of her pussy, back and forth.

"The presence of a cane, or any other implement used for corporal punishment of winsome young lasses in my boudoir, should not come as a particular surprise. How else am I to punish them for their behaviour?"

"You could tease their pussy with your fingers instead of getting to the point, Mistress."

"Bully for you, Amber. I rather despise the phrase, 'Sarcasm is the lowest form of wit' because being English myself, I rather enjoy our real national sport - delightful banter. I much prefer banter to all that playing with balls, don't you?" Susanna opined. Judging it impolitic to press the matter of her lesbian boss's appreciation of balls, Amber remained quiet.

"Silence? I'll take that as a sign that we can move from the appetisers to the main course, at last. Stand up, come on," Susanna said. "Good girl. Now, hop onto the bed, and sit there, back to the pillows, legs straight out. Yes, good."

Susanna had stood up too and now joined Amber on the bed, placing one knee either side of the (slightly) younger woman's hips and shuffling forward until she could rest her bottom on Amber's thighs.

Without hesitation, her hands cupped Amber's face, and Miss

Hamilton kissed her passionately. Her kisses moved from Amber's lips to her cheek, along her jawline and down her neck, alighting on her collarbone before she nibbled at the earlobe of her young submissive.

Their lips met again, and Susanna established her supremacy, her tongue taking control of their interlocking mouths, guiding Amber into the pattern that gave the dominant woman the most satisfaction.

They battled back and forth, to a rhythm that Susanna set, and Amber quickly learned what provoked the sounds that held the most sexual urgency from the shapely neck of her beautiful Mistress. Her most ardent sounds of desire came from her throat, and it was when Amber's tongue slipped between the lips of her Mistress that they were provoked the most.

Amber's head lolled back from the kiss, and she moaned in pleasure when her Mistress caressed her breasts, and her fingers began to toy with the freshly captured nipples of her new assistant.

Susanna used a mixture of erotic caresses and powerful pinches to excite her subject, teasing and tormenting Amber's firm nipples alternately.

Susanna kissed her again, "Do you like this, Amber?"

"Yes, Mistress, it's wonderful," Amber gasped.

"It feels good, doesn't it?"

"Yes."

"Would you miss me if I were not here?"

"Oh, yes, Mistress. Please don't go."

"I'm not going anywhere, my beautiful pet. Do you think you will update that profile of yours soon?"

"I don't know what you mean, Mistress," Amber asked between kisses and caresses that left her gasping for air.

"It says you're bi-playful at the moment if I recall. Perhaps you might prefer, bi-curious? Or maybe even bisexual." Susanna suggested.

"I think you have a good point, Mistress," Amber agreed.

"I have an argument that I think will convince you. All my tongue to build the foundations for my case," Susanna said.

Amber squealed as her Mistress broke the kiss, then gave her a quick shove to the shoulders, pushing her back into the pillows. She gazed up adoringly at her lesbian boss, hoping that they would not have to wake up to work the next day.

"I'm going to treat you like a princess, Amber. Would you like that?" Susanna asked as she shuffled back down the bed away from her submissive.

"Yes, Mistress. Of course. Will you be my slightly older Queen?" Amber asked playfully.

"Would you like that, my dear? A little roleplaying?"

Amber nodded enthusiastically as she looked up expectantly at Susanna.

"Very well, let us begin then," Susanna said solemnly. Amber took her bottom lip between her teeth and gently chewed it in a way she knew would provoke her audience.

"Welcome, oh Princess Amber, to the finest castle in all the lands, the seat of my government in our green isle, Albion," Susanna delivered, in her finest impersonation of an actress.

"Thank you, Queen Susanna. Your hospitality is second to none. I have never been a guest at a castle so beautifully decorated, or been given such personal attention by my host."

"Indeed. I take it as a point of pride that all the Princesses who have stayed here, have always given rave reviews. I aim for nothing less than full star service," Susanna said.

"How can I repay you for such exquisite hospitality, Queen Susanna?"

"Think not of repayment, Princess, merely allow me to part your legs, so that I may worship your womanhood," Susanna replied. Amber's legs spread apart, as if of their own accord and presently, Susanna lay between them, her mouth descending to meet Amber's nether lips.

"Oh. Oh. Queen Susanna. You are. Oh, my. You are the most wonderful hostess. Your conversation is so pleasant, and I love. Mmm. I do love the way the citizens of your kingdom worship their Goddess," Amber managed to improvise more responses, even as Susanna's tongue worked a magical dance around her pussy, licking between her puffy labia and then sucking at her clit.

"I am a High Priestess of the Goddess, Princess Amber, in addition to being the Queen of this fair land. For many years, I have practised the noble pursuit of cunnilingus as our Goddess demands. My tongue is the instrument of worship through which I venerate the Goddess, as her divinity is embodied by the womanhood of her subjects. My devotion to her is demonstrated by my master of the art of cunnilingus. Your pussy is the canvas that I paint on. Now, please, cry out if you must, scream worshipful words to the Goddess as your prayers, reach the heights of religious ecstasy if you can, but please do not require me to speak again until my own prayers are at an end. My worship of your womanhood deserves time and concentration, I'm sure you will agree," Susanna replied.

"Oh, Queen Susanna. I will respect your wishes. You have my utmost appreciation for the opportunity to be the vessel through which you worship the Goddess. Oh, fuck, oh fuck, yes. Thank you, Mistress, I'm coming. Please. Please continue your worship until you are entirely done, Queen Susanna," Amber shouted as she came for the first time under the tongue of her lesbian boss.

Amber had never been as playful in bed as she was with her 'Queen Susanna' and she hoped she would be forgiven for her stumbling in her improvisation.

Then again, as her Mistress brought her to a second orgasm, Amber did not hesitate to use every vulgarity she could think of to give voice to her pleasure. If her Mistress was displeased, she did not show it if anything, Amber wilted under the renewed application of tongue, lips and the gentle nibbling of sharp teeth.

By the time Amber's rising chain of orgasms was finished, she was quite exhausted.

Susanna moved up her body and pulled the bell-rope, then passionately kissed her submissive. Her face was covered in the orgasmic juices of her young companion. "Slut, I'm covered in your juices. Use your tongue to clean me!".

Amber hesitated, but Susanna took hold of her hair and forced the issue. The assistant dutifully licked her boss's face clean of all evidence of her own arousal. Susanna smiled contentedly when she was done. "So biddable. So easy to command."

Sugar arrived, in answer to the summons of the bell-rope, sweating and breathless.

“You rang, Mistress?” she asked.

“Hot flannels to clean us up, chilled water to cool us down and slake our thirst, and then, you and Candy will resume your previous positions. I have worshipped my Princess’s womanhood quite fervently so we will nap after our refreshment, and you and Candy have my permission to have as many orgasms as you wish,” Susanna ordered magnanimously.

“Thank you, Mistress,” Sugar said, turning to leave.

“No. Wait a moment. I order to you to use your fingers and tongue to give each other as many orgasms as possible before you are quite exhausted and fall asleep, and remember, I will check the video to be sure you did as instructed, Sugar,” Susanna said.

“Yes, Mistress, if you insist then we must of course, obey,” Sugar said, pouting a little and pretending that her orders might be a burden.

When they were cleaned up, watered, and refreshed and the maids were back to providing a background accompaniment on the pussy and mouth organ, Miss Hamilton lay down beside Amber. The lesbian boss spooned her personal assistant, her hands furnishing gentle caresses as they drifted off to sleep together.

Before Amber was quite ready for sleep, she had one final exchange with her employer.

“Thank you, Mistress. That was earth-shattering. I’ve never felt such pleasure.”

“That is just the beginning for us, my lovely assistant. Tomorrow, we shall have the whole day for me to train and teach you,” Susanna murmured.

“That sounds wonderful, Mistress. I hope I take well to your teaching.”

"You had better, you filthy slut. The first lesson will be cunnilingus, and I'll be your practice model."

"Oh, Mistress. That sounds wonderful. I won't let you down, I swear. I'll be the finest Novice my High Priestess has ever trained, or may the Goddess punish me for my sins."

"Good girl," Susanna mumbled. "You have only to exceed Candy's skill and devotion to prayer, to win my approval. Next time try not to be so boastful, Amber. Now go to sleep, that's an order."

As she snuggled back into her Mistress's embrace to sleep, Amber smiled dreamily to herself.

The prospect of learning to eat pussy from her Mistress was exciting for Amber, even in her drowsy state of exhaustion. Even as she drifted off to sleep, Amber could tell she had lined herself up for some painful experiences that would be a counterpoint to the pleasure of the following day's lessons.

It would all keep her Mistress happy though, she reasoned, smiling happily as she obeyed the last instruction of her lesbian boss.

"Yes, Mistress."

TRAINED BY HER LESBIAN BOSS

Book 3

CHAPTER 1

Amber was dreaming of dark and delicious temptations which involved lots of lips caressing body parts, tongues dancing against each other, and fingers moving deep inside hot, wet places. Her reaction on being woken was irritable at best as a result.

Susanna withdrew her hand from her new submissive's wetness, and smacked her firmly on the rump, "Don't be cheeky, Amber. It's time to get up. Come on, into the shower with you."

The bed jiggled as Susanna got up, and Amber tried to wriggle back under the light sheet. It was rudely, really rudely, tugged from her hand. "Stop pouting," Susanna ordered, "get up, I don't want to have to tell you again."

Reluctantly, Amber swung her legs over the side of the bed and stood up. Apparently, it was light outside already. She could tell because some monster had opened the curtains fully. The morning mist over the grounds of the estate was eerily beautiful. At least, she imagined it was. When she looked toward the balcony, Amber's first response was to cry out and shield her eyes like a vampire being exposed to the sun. "It burns! The light, it stings my eyes, Mistress!" she hissed dramatically.

"Not half as much as your backside is going to sting if you don't stop mucking about, and get in the shower with me, my girl," Susanna said.

Amber hissed again, then blinked drearily. In the shower with Mistress? The sunlight be damned, she wouldn't miss that out, even if she'd barely slept for six hours. She scuttled across the room past her Mistress, and into the huge wet-room shower in the bathroom.

Susanna strode in after her and turned on the showerheads. Plural. There were two of those enormous rain shower heads that blanketed an entire area, and the water was immediately at the perfect temperature. Amber rinsed her face quickly, tasting the sex of the night before on her lips as she washed them.

Mistress handed her a toothbrush in a blister pack and an open tube of toothpaste. "First lesson of the day, I have a strict no kissing before brushing rule. It grosses me out. As does someone using my toothbrush. Make sure it's your own you are using," Susanna said, indicating a set of holders by the sinks.

They were all made of bamboo it seemed, and each had been decorated with pyrography, reserving it for one user. Mistress herself had a rather grand affair, with lots of sections for soaps, and bathroom products dental products. There were smaller guest items, labelled Sugar, Candy, Pudding, and Amber. Amber gulped. She already had her own place here? When had that happened? Susanna must have had it made before they even met for her interview.

She set to brushing her teeth, picking her preferred toothpaste from a holder that had a good selection of open tubes. When she was done, she rinsed her mouth at the sink and went back to the shower. Mistress was rinsing her mouth in the shower and simply handed Amber her toothbrush. Amber took it, and placed it back in the appropriate holder, leaving hers behind as well.

When Amber was back in the shower, Mistress pulled her sub close, drawing her into a kiss that went on forever. Susanna pressed her up against the cold tiles as she took her mouth and plunged her fingers into Amber's welcoming pussy. Amber was soon gasping, and bucking against her Mistress's fingers, struggling to maintain the kiss as she dealt with the sensations from her pussy.

Then the pleasure rescinded as Susanna pulled back and handed her a bottle of branded mint body wash. "Lather me, all over beautiful," she commanded.

Amber squirted a generous helping of the thick green liquid into her palm before putting the bottle down. She started from behind running her hands over Miss Hamilton's shoulders, and down her arms. She was thorough, making sure every inch was tended to and using a lot more soap than was probably necessary.

It was hard, but she managed to get around to the front of Mistress's body and get her limbs well-taken care off before she had to wash her ample breasts. When she did begin to smooth her palms over them, Mistress tipped her head back and sighed.

Presently, Amber fell to her knees, and reached around behind Mistress, soaping down her, buttocks, and making sure to run her fingers through the deep cleft between her rounded cheeks. Cheekily, she little teased Susanna's puckered rosebud with the tip of one finger, just running over it to lather it, of course, not sticking a finger inside her. "That tingles nicely," Susanna said dreamily.

Amber squirted more soap onto her palms, and came to the main treat, gently lathering between Mistress's thighs, and around her pussy, before finally applying the soap to her lips, and thoroughly working it in. Susanna wasn't hesitant about indicating her pleasure at being touched so intimately, her moan of delight was audible even above all the splashing water that fell around them.

There was another head attached to a hose, and Susanna handed it to Amber, showing her how the tap turned on, then commanding her to rinse her off. Once she was clean, she ordered Amber to stand at the end not drenched by the showerheads and lather herself up.

Apparently, Mistress wasn't going to soap down her personal assistant, perhaps that was too submissive for her lesbian boss. While Amber lathered up her body, and her face, Mistress took care of her own face, with a soft flannel, and a facial wash.

Amber came back under the showerhead, and rinsed off again, starting with her face. When she was done, she turned to face her Mistress who drew her into another kiss, pushing her against the wall again, and possessing her mouth for several minutes of pleasure.

Susanna reached out for another flannel and began rubbing it roughly over Amber's breasts and paying close attention to her nipples. It was immediately apparent that this was about the sensation, not about cleaning her. Amber relished the feel of the material against her skin and gasped when Susanna switched to a long-handled exfoliator that had a brush on one side, and a loofah covered surface on the other.

Her lesbian boss used the rough loofah against the skin of her breasts, and even teased her sensitive nipples with it, before scrubbing at her bottom with the bristled reverse side. Amber was mewling like a kitten with pleasure at the sensations the brush caused, and she shivered when they ceased, and Mistress commanded, "Assume the position, slut."

Amber recalled their conversation of the day before, and quickly, she bent over at the waist, grasping her ankles with her feet spread apart to emphasise the beautiful target her bottom made. Her suspicion about what would happen next was confirmed the moment the wet loofah side of the handle impacted her bottom.

She squealed in surprise in spite of her guesswork. "Count them out, Amber," Susanna said as she brought the brush down again. "Two!" squeaked Amber. The brush came down again as Susanna said, "No, you must start the count afresh if you miss one." The improvised paddle impacted, and Amber optimistically tried, "One."

Three smacks landed in quick succession, all on the same cheek. "Wrong. You must get the rhythm correct, Amber or my satisfaction will be minimised, and whose pleasure is paramount in this household?"

"Your pleasure, Mistress."

"That's right, and who do you serve?"

"I serve you, Mistress."

"Better. Now, when I paddle you again, you will count one, and you will count each time I paddle you, immediately after. If you miss a count while you're panting like the slut we both know you are, or you allow the pain to distract you, or for any other reason, we will start the count again. Clear?"

"Yes, Mistress," Amber said dejectedly.

The exfoliating brush descended again with a meaty smack, and Amber cried out, "One."

She stumbled again at the count of five, breathless for a moment from the feeling this was arousing in her pussy, that seemed so at odds with the pain. The wet paddling, even with the softer surface of the loofah material, was a different kind of pain than the leather paddle, but her Mistress didn't soften her strikes, and the pain took some getting used to. Nevertheless, she was wet from more than just the shower.

Amber finally got it right the second full time around, managed to maintain enough control to count the full six.

"Much better. I like how you controlled your pain this time, Amber. You must not fear my implements. You must welcome them. The little death as the French call it, is not to be feared. If you embrace my discipline when you are subject to it, you may in time, like Sugar, be able to reach orgasm simply from being spanked. Do you understand?"

"Yes, Mistress."

"Would you like that, Amber? Would you like to come from being spanked?"

"Yes, Mistress, very much," Amber admitted, her face blushing as she did.

Mistress grabbed her by the hair, and pulled her upright, bringing her into another short kiss.

"Then, I will continue your training and bear that goal in mind."

"Thank you, Mistress."

"Don't thank me yet, the training will be arduous. You will need to be spanked frequently, and for extended periods until you learn to associate the pain with your pleasure, and reach a climax when pain is your main stimulus. It's a skill of the mind, not just the body, and you will practice it, over, and over again until you are sure you will never master it."

"I will master it, Mistress."

"Oh, I hope so, but before then, there are many spankings for me to deliver, and I assure you, I will relish every ounce of your suffering so don't forget about it. You may beg me to stop before you acquire Sugars skill."

"Yes, Mistress," Amber said.

CHAPTER 2

"Breakfast is served," said Sugar as she came in, pushing the door open with her foot. The gorgeous French maid was carrying a tray which she balanced with the skill of a waitress in a busy restaurant.

Amber wondered if Susanna had found her in a restaurant or perhaps working as a barista in a coffee shop. Despite the French maid uniform that she and Candy wore, neither of them were of French origin at least, as far as Amber could detect from their accents.

Sugar seemed to have the confidence in carrying the cumbersome breakfast tray that was borne of regular practice. Amber could imagine Susanna spotting her in a hospitality environment, a young, beautiful lesbian, secretly yearning for the touch of an older woman. She imagined Susanna sweeping Sugar off her feet with promises of wanton pleasures, firm discipline, and a luxurious lifestyle.

However, she'd been seduced, Sugar was now half-naked, wearing a costume that was more of an erotic homage to a real French maid's uniform that came from the fevered mind of a horny lingerie designer, than it was a serious attempt to honour the real thing.

Amber had seen many such naughty costumes, and they were always a bit cheap. Not so the ones that Susanna's maids wore. She would be surprised to find out that they were anything other than the work of a highly-skilled craftswoman. They certainly didn't come from a local adult shop.

Despite the revealing, and provocative nature of her working clothes, Sugar always seemed happy, and cheerful. She would flounce around with her bottom on full display, and her pussy lips being clearly visible every time she bent over to pick something up, without an apparent care in the world.

Sugar and Candy rarely bent at the knees to pick things up as any good health, and safety pamphlet would advise. They were much more likely to present their backs to anyone present, then bend elegantly at the waist, exposing themselves as they did so. Their flexibility was quite impressive, and Amber was pretty sure they could have put their palms flat on the floor if they chose.

Amber was sitting beside her Mistress in bed, and Sugar put the tray down on a side table, before unfolding a lap table for Susanna and placing it over her legs. The maid placed the tray on the table and then removed the two silver domes, which kept the food warm.

One plate held two slices of delicious looking brown toast, and fluffy looking scrambled eggs. There was a tiny cup of coffee, and two small glasses of orange juice, full of pulp which Amber didn't personally like, but Susanna clearly did.

The smaller dome had concealed a side plate, with two slices of wholemeal toast, freshly, buttered on it. This small plate and a glass of orange juice were passed to Amber. She looked hungrily at the meal presented to Susanna as she bit into her toast and tried to conceal a wince as she drank the bitty orange juice. Sugar waited while they finished their meals, taking the empty plate, and glass from Amber, and placing them on coasters on the side table.

Amber still felt quite hungry, so when Sugar had placed Susanna's crockery back on the tray and removed the lap tray, she said, "I'm still hungry, Mistress. Can I go down to the kitchen with Sugar to get some more please?"

Susanna turned to look at her, dabbing her mouth daintily with a napkin. "No, I think not. You want a little more sweetness on your tongue, Amber?"

Puzzled, Amber replied, "Yes, please, Mistress."

"Very well, if you wish to sate your sweet tooth, you may lick some Sugar," Susanna said.

The maid gave a little squeal of excitement.

"Yes, Mistress," Amber said.

"Sugar, swap places with Amber. Amber, move down the bed," Susanna ordered calmly, picking up her tablet, and beginning to flick through the morning newspaper.

Sugar got onto the bed where Amber had been sitting and lay back against the pillows.

"Pull your skirt up, and spread your legs dear, no need to make it difficult for Amber," Susanna commented, without apparently looking up from her financial news.

Amber was on her knees, facing Sugar, who blew her a kiss as she pulled her skirts up, revealing her bare pussy. She hesitated, wondering if Mistress would command her, but then wondering if she would be punished for delaying. She crawled forward until she was positioned between the knees of the giggling maid.

"Get on with it, Amber," Susanna prompted. Her paper rustled as she turned the page.

Amber stopped hesitating, and dipped her head between Sugar's welcoming thighs, running her tongue gently along her lips. She tried this several times, as Sugar looked down her body at her. Sugar seemed rather apathetic so she tried slipping her tongue between the maid's lips, pressing harder, and as deep as she could get.

Sugar sighed softly, without the excitement that Amber had hoped to hear. Amber wasn't experienced, but she was beginning to suspect Sugar was giving her a deliberately hard time, making it tougher than it should be to satisfy her.

There was no way Amber was going to be put off, so she reached up, and added her fingers to the mix, parting Sugar's lips, and exposing her stiff bud completely.

When her tongue pressed against Sugar's clit, and her lips formed a seal, she began to suck as she flicked at the little nub. Her thumbs held the young maid open as she licked, and sucked, and Sugar began to moan softly.

"Yes, that's better. Suck hard, Amber, that feels so good," Sugar said.

Amber nodded as she looked up at Sugar, who was smiling down contentedly at her as she moaned. She caught Susanna looking at her, and almost stopped what she was doing. She wasn't yet used to the subtleties of Susanna's facial expressions, but she could sense disapproval.

"Did I tell you to use your hands, Amber?"

"No, Mistress," Amber said, before putting her mouth back to work. She seemed to be in trouble, and she didn't want to get in more for stopping without being told to.

"That's right, I did not. The lesson you are supposed to be learning is how to give another woman pleasure with your tongue. Sugar is an expert, and I want you to learn from her since she seems particularly gifted. Sugar loves it when I go down on her, don't you sweetie?" Susanna said.

"Yes, Mistress. You're marvellous with your tongue," Sugar said.

"Thank you, darling. Isn't that nice of her, Amber? I know I'm not actually as skilled as Sugar, but of course, she loves it when her Mistress licks her pussy, because I'm her Mistress, and it's a rare treat for a submissive to be pleasured like that by her domme. I have an unfair advantage in her estimations as a result," Susanna said. "Do you understand why I'm telling you this, my gorgeous new slut?"

Amber shook her head and giggled into Sugar's pussy as the maid let out a loud groan. She shook her head again vigorously and got a similar reaction.

Susanna laughed, "See? You've discovered a new technique already, you'll have to try that another time, and see if it always works. Perhaps it's peculiar to Sugar's tastes, and perhaps not, but I have a specific reason to set you two up like this, Sugar as your teacher, and you as a new, and delightfully lusty student. Can you hazard a guess why?"

Amber thought for a moment as she licked vigorously at Sugar, who was panting harder, and faster by the second. "Please, Mistress, can she finish me off first?"

Susanna smiled charitably, "Of course, Sugar. Amber, make her come, quickly now."

Amber redoubled her efforts and was gratified when Sugar did indeed come a short while later. When the maid had finished crying out and moaning, Susanna told her she could stop licking and answer her question.

"I think you want us to learn to be as good with our tongues as we can so we can treat our Mistress as she deserves to be treated. You want the pleasure we give you to be out of this world."

"Ten out of ten. I live a luxurious lifestyle, and I use my power, and money to bring me the best that life has to offer. A young woman who has potential is a wonderful thing, but I demand that anyone who serves me acquires the greatest skill levels to ensure they can always please me. Sugar is an excellent cunnilinguist, and I hope a good teacher. You, I'm sure, will make a fine assistant, and I want you to improve upon all your skills daily, but in particular the art of pleasing women with your tongue, since that's something that I will require of you on a very regular basis."

"Thank you, Mistress. I will take my lessons very seriously," Amber said, licking her lips of Sugar's juices.

"Good. Now, Sugar, you get up and get this slut's face between my legs, I want her to try to demonstrate on me," Susanna ordered.

Sugar shot out of bed like a rocket, then climbed over Amber, reaching down, and grasping her hair, pulling her almost bodily to their Mistress. The maid pushed Amber's head down roughly, forcing her mouth against Susanna's wet pussy, and ordering her, "Lick, Mistress's pussy, you filthy slut."

It was Susanna's turn to moan as Amber's tongue began to work her pussy. "No hands, Amber. Just your tongue, and mouth. Sugar, it's time for your lessons to continue. A dozen spanks on one of Amber's cheeks to show your skill, and if you're studying properly, I expect you to make her eyes water. If you can do that, you can give her another dozen on the other cheek."

Amber whimpered into her Mistress's pussy as Sugar thanked Susanna for the opportunity to learn. As Sugar began to spank her without mercy, she tried to fight back the tears to avoid further punishment.

"Yes, Amber. You look so beautiful licking me like that while you are punished for using your fingers without my permission. I want you to know, it hurts you more than it hurts me, and I relish your suffering, it makes my pussy even wetter for you," Susanna said as Sugar spanked Amber with her right hand, holding her head down against their Mistress with her left.

Amber's eyes watered, and she resigned herself to her painful fate with some reluctance. Her ensuing pain was tempered when Susanna began to come as Sugar spanked her other cheek to a bright pink hue.

"Fuck yes, your spanking is getting so much better, Sugar. I love how pink this slut is. It made my orgasm so much sweeter."

"Thank you, Mistress. Should I practice some more?"

"Yes, make sure you spank Amber at least every two days if I don't otherwise order you to."

"Yes, Mistress," Sugar replied. "For how long should I do that?"

"Until I say otherwise, sweetie," Susanna ordered.

Sugar pulled Amber's face-up by the hair, "There, what do you say to that, Amber?"

Amber whimpered, swallowed, and took a deep breath before answering, "Thank you, Mistress."

"You're welcome, sweetheart."

CHAPTER 3

Amber was trying to concentrate on the serving tray she was carrying, and not dropping the fine china that Susanna's food had been served on, and not think about how much her bottom smarted. The spanking Sugar had given her had felt very effective, and she was sure she'd have lasting bruises from it.

The spanking had stung more than enough with each smack and gone on until her eyes were quite wet, but she'd managed to stay just the right side of not crying. If she'd actually blubbered, Amber would never have forgiven herself for giving either Susanna or Sugar the satisfaction.

"Just remember, mind your manners with Pudding. She's got a heart of gold, but the kitchen is her domain. I don't think even Mistress would challenge her on that turf," Sugar said as she waited for Amber to negotiate the final steps of the elegantly curved staircase.

"Thank you, if you hadn't said anything, I might have insulted her to her face!" Amber replied, pouring on the sarcasm as she reached terra firma at last.

Sugar cackled. "Fair enough, but around here, if you step on the wrong toes, it's not like other places you've worked. You'll really regret it if you do it in the kitchen."

"I was always told to never insult chefs, police officers or hairdressers. It's a sure way to guarantee a bad time," Amber said.

"I dunno. I've met a few policewomen that I wouldn't mind taking me to task," Sugar giggled. "Through here," she said, opening a wide swing door into the kitchen.

"Good morning, Sugar," came the immediate response as the tiny bell above the door tinkled, like in an old-fashioned shop. Amber could see what could only be Pudding, Susanna's live-in cook, standing at the sink doing the dishes.

"Morning, Pudding. It's not just me today, Mistress asked her new girl to help me bring the tray down," Sugar responded cheerily, sitting down at a robust looking, oak dining table, and pouring herself a cup of tea from the pot in the centre of the table. The tea cosy she removed from the large china pot was made with a printed material that showed women getting up to all sorts of saucy things.

Pudding shook her hands to flick off the water, and then picked up a towel to finish drying as she turned to face them. "Good morning, Amber. Lovely to meet you," she said as she walked over. "Here, let me take that," the cook said as she relieved her of the heavy tray, and placed it by the sink.

"Good morning, Pudding," Amber said. Then she wondered if that was alright, "Is it alright for me to call you Pudding too, or should I use your real name?"

Pudding smiled happily, "Pudding is my real name, Amber, while I serve in Mistress Hamilton's household. If we're ever somewhere public, you can call me Mrs Crumble though. We really only use our birth names for official purposes or when we're out amongst the vanilla people who might be boorish."

Amber nodded. "Thank you. I'll remember to call you Pudding then in future, and not worry about it. I'm afraid Miss Hamilton hasn't given me a nickname," she said.

"That's fine, you're going to be meeting all sorts of business people, and she probably doesn't want you having any confusion about which name to answer too. Now, let me have a look at you," Pudding said, looking her up, and down.

Amber was wearing a sheer black dressing gown, that barely hung below her far enough below her waistline to cover her bum. Not that the material left much to the imagination. She was used to similar garments featuring strategically placed lacy patterns to obscure more private areas and tantalise a partner with glimpses of her waist or back.

The garment Susanna had told her to pick was evidently expensive, but it hugged her curvy figure well, and her breasts and pussy must surely be plain to see. She bit her lip as both Pudding, and Sugar admired her. *Could they see her nipples clearly, she wondered? Could they see that they were taut with arousal?* They probably could she decided, and perhaps even catch a glint of the moistness between her pussy lips as she contemplated their gaze.

"Why don't you give us a twirl, Amber?" Sugar suggested. "Let Pudding see why Mistress is so infatuated with her new secretary."

Amber blushed, and spun around, doing her best to seem graceful, and wishing she'd done better with ballet classes. "Now, now, Sugar. Amber is not a secretary, she's a personal assistant, and Mistress wouldn't be happy if you tease her like that," Pudding admonished.

"Yes, Pudding," Sugar said meekly.

"Well, Amber, I can certainly see why Mistress Hamilton took a shine to you. I'm sure all this must be a bit overwhelming for your first experiences. It's like being thrown in the deep end instead of taking a gentle swimming lesson," Pudding sympathised.

Amber nodded shyly. "Yes, it is rather a steep learning curve, I must say. So much of this is new to me."

Pudding stepped forward and wrapped strong arms around her in a tight hug. "If it all gets too much or you need anything, you come to my kitchen, and I'll make it all better, okay, my lovely?" the cook said. Amber could feel Pudding's ample bosom pressed against her own.

The cook was wearing a stylised uniform that reminded Amber of the French maid's outfits that Candy and Sugar generally wore. When they weren't naked as the day they were born, of course.

From what she had seen, and could feel pressed against her as they hugged, Pudding was wearing a black under bust corset and a knee-length latex skirt. A cunningly designed apron seemed to be all that was keeping her breasts from being on display. It was made of good quality material, the kind restaurants used for chef's whites. It was obviously intended to be a proper garment for cooking in.

It was also scandalously exposing the side of her breasts, and her back was naked. Over Pudding's shoulder, Amber spied a coat rack with several sets of trousers, and chef's jackets as well as hats so clearly Pudding had the full gear available. Amber imagined that it was quite necessary for cooking a full English fry up or a roast dinner. Looking sexy was all very well until you found out how much it hurt when hot fat was spitting over your naked chest.

She guessed Pudding cooked in protective clothing then got out of it at the earliest opportunity or when she thought she might have guests. Finally, Pudding broke the hug and eased back to look at her.

"Is there anything you need this morning, gorgeous?" Pudding asked.

Amber swallowed, and blushed, but not because of the delightfully sexy older woman in front of her, but rather for the question, she had to ask her. "I only had a couple of slices of toast for breakfast. Is there anything more I could have, please, Pudding? I don't mind getting it myself, and doing the washing up, of course."

Pudding let go of her and put her hands on her hips, frowning. "Your breakfast was worked out to be more than enough for office work. You'll be getting a full meal later, and Mistress doesn't like us overeating." She seemed quite put out at the question.

"I'm sorry, I just didn't eat much yesterday, it was all such a whirlwind since my interview. Mistress had some lovely scrambled eggs, but the toast didn't really fill me up. Perhaps a bowl of cereal or a fried egg on toast?" Amber pressed. She really was hungry, she wasn't greedy, and she rarely put on more than a couple of pounds during the most indulgent of holidays.

"I'm quite offended. I worked hard to put together the right calorie count and plan out your daily meals so you can get a balanced diet within your budget, and here you are throwing it back in my face," Pudding retorted.

"Amber," hissed Sugar, "you should apologise. Pudding works hard keeping us properly fed." She sounded helpful, but the wicked glint in her eye wasn't lost on Amber as the maid beamed at from out of Pudding's eye line.

Amber's hand flew to her mouth. "Oh, I'm so terribly sorry, I didn't mean to seem rude or ungrateful, Pudding. Please, I just felt a bit more peckish than usual. Please say you'll forgive me."

This time, Sugar chimed in with something more helpful, "Mistress does have her doing more than office work too, so she's probably going to need more calories."

"What? Pudding snapped, turning her frown on Sugar.

Sugar mimed vigorously licking between a V shape she formed between her fingers. "She's been licking us both this morning for ages already. Mistress sent us down because she wanted a nap. Amber wore her out a bit. Perhaps she does need a bit more food, eh Pudding?" Sugar suggested.

"Don't be silly, Sugar. You don't burn that many calories, even having rampant sex. A little pussy licking doesn't warrant more food. That's just a slippery slope," Pudding replied crossly.

"Mmmm. It was a slippery slope when Amber was licking me. Does getting a really hard spanking on both cheeks burn calories though? Amber definitely got that from me so maybe that accounts for how peckish she is?" Sugar mused.

Pudding shook her head. "No, of course not."

Sugar shrugged. "Well, if you think she is being rude to you, perhaps you should punish her to make sure she knows her place?"

Amber wasn't surprised by this suggestion. She felt she was getting a handle on Sugar's naughtiness, and suggestive behaviour now. "Yes. Anything to wipe the slate clean, Pudding. I really didn't mean to upset you. I'm sure I can manage until lunchtime, and then maybe you could explain the diet you've planned for me one day, so I know what to expect?"

"Very well," Pudding sniffed. "You've got off on the wrong foot with me, but I'm nothing if not magnanimous. Turn around, and show me your bottom, I want to see if you really got a spanking already."

Amber replied, "Thank you, Pudding." She turned around and lifted the hem of her see-through gown up to her lower back, exposing her cheeks which still glowed red with uncomfortable heat.

"You did this, Sugar?" Pudding asked.

"Yes, Pudding."

Pudding reached out, and stroked Amber's arse slowly, almost soothingly over the tormented flesh. "It looks like you did a good job. For a beginner," the cook mused.

"Thanks, Pudding. I'm trying to learn," Sugar said happily.

Pudding reached out, across Amber's back as she was still bent over to expose her bottom. She took a firm hold of Amber's hair and pulled her back and up using it as a way to guide her. Quickly, she turned her around and had her facing head down across the kitchen table, from one end.

The cook reached her arms around Amber's waist, and swiftly undid the knot in the belt that kept at least some semblance of decency as a facade. Pudding carefully pulled the gown back off Amber's arms and hung it up on the back of the kitchen door, then returned to her subject.

Pudding pressed herself up against Amber's body, folding over her, and running her hands up to the younger woman's breasts. Amber sighed as the stronger fingers teased her flesh and caressed her nipples.

"Do you like that, Amber?" she whispered into her ear, as she nuzzled at it, nipping at the lobe, and sucking it.

"Yes, Pudding."

"You know your safe word, yes?"

"Yes, Pudding," Amber replied. That confirmed it. She was going to get a proper spanking. Amber wondered if the cook's reputation was well deserved, and decided it probably was. This was probably going to be quite a step up from what the slender Sugar had done to her. Pudding had a striking hourglass figure, but the strength in her arms had been evident in her hug, and Amber could easily imagine her spanking being much fiercer than Sugar's best effort.

"Good," the cook said, and immediately began kneading her

breasts firmly, like dough for morning bread. She squeezed, and tugged, and really worked her fingers in. Amber gasped at the uncomfortable sensations that somehow weren't entirely unpleasant.

Then she yelped, quite loudly, and hear Sugar stifle a giggle in the background. Pudding's strong fingers had alighted on her nipples, caressing them at first before pinching them really hard. The instant pressure made her cry out in pain, rather than pleasure, and yet, Amber could feel the wetness between her legs increasing. Pudding kept tormenting her for what seemed like an hour, so firm where her attentions.

Finally, she backed off and stood upright again, stretching her back, and arms like a cat. Pudding placed her left hand on Amber's lower back and pushed firmly until her belly was against the wood and her sore, but stiff nipples gently swayed against the hard grain of the oak.

Unlike Sugar, she started lightly, spanking Amber with firm, but relatively light smacks of her bare hand. She was quite rapid, however, delivering flurries of a dozen smacks quite quickly, one set to each cheek. Amber gasped, and bit her lip, moaning as the older woman delivered her punishment.

After a couple of dozen impacts on each cheek had got her bottom stinging again, Pudding called Sugar over. "Sugar. Kneel between her legs. Further forward. Good, now lick this slut's pussy while I punish her," she ordered.

Amber murmured, "Oh, fuck, yes, that feels good." Sugars tongue, and lips immediately focused on her swollen clitoris, sucking, and flickering over her nub at the same time.

Pudding spent a few seconds shifting Amber's position so that her backside was curved up high as a great target, there was enough space for Sugar to work her magic without hitting the table, and the cook had a good position for her next round.

The next sequence of spanking came harder than the first, and less predictably. Pudding was obviously using a fairly random style so that Amber couldn't anticipate the next source of pain. The unpredictable spanking accompanied Sugar's rhythmic efforts like a cunning piece of music that mixed tempos in a counterintuitive way to make something that was, nevertheless, entirely beautiful.

Amber cried out as she came, banging her hand against the table, and cursing loudly as Pudding continued to spank her, holding her firmly in place while the devilish young maid tormented her pussy with the most agile tongue imaginable. Her second orgasm ripped through her mere moments after the next, and Amber's shoulders began to heave as she found herself sobbing from the combination of pleasure, and pain.

"Please, stop. Please. I can't take any more," Amber howled as she raced toward another peak.

Pudding laughed, and Sugar made appreciative noises more suitable for someone enjoying a delicious dessert, than licking the pussy of a young woman who was being ruthlessly spanked. "Your bottom looks beautiful in this colour, we must take some pictures to show you," Pudding enthused.

"I'm begging you; I can't take any more," Amber whimpered.

Pudding laughed again, "Yes, you can, and you will. You'll learn your place in this household, you filthy little slut. I will teach you to respect my craft, and my kitchen, my girl."

"Owww. It hurts," Amber complained, as Pudding continued to spank her. "Miss Hamilton won't like that you're doing this," she claimed, seeking any angle to make it stop.

Again, Pudding laughed at her without mercy. "That's Mistress Hamilton to you, Amber. I've known her a long time, and I assure you, my girl, she'll approve of all of this when I tell her. She'll wish she was here to watch it, instead of hearing about it second hand. If you're very lucky, she'll let you have some rest before she adds her own punishments on top."

Amber began to cry, as Puddings hand, which felt almost like wood, continued to descend on her blazing hot cheeks. "Beautiful, my girl. I love it when a young slut cries over a spanking. You let it all out, sweetheart," Pudding whispered in her ear as she bent over her. Her hand continued to spank, even in that position.

Although she was still being spanked, Amber's tears began to subside as she cried herself out.

"There, doesn't that feel better?" Pudding asked as she stood up.

"Yes, Pudding," Amber managed eventually, her words broken up as her sobbing made her gasp for air, and it did. It really did. Her bottom hurt like the blazes, and her pussy was sore as she reached another climax, but the tears had been utterly cathartic.

"I'm coming!" Amber screamed as Pudding's hand finally ceased its tirade and began to stroke her sore bottom.

"Yes, sweetheart. Come for Pudding, and get this dirty maid's face nice, and wet," Pudding said encouragingly.

While Amber began to recover, lying exhausted against the table, Sugar stood up, and she could hear the cook enthusiastically kissing the maid behind her, though she was too tired to turn, and watch the show, much though she wanted to. Something cold squirted against her cheeks, and she could feel Sugar's soft hands working the cream into her beleaguered cheeks, it was pleasant, and didn't burn. Hopefully, it was some kind of restorative concoction that would reduce the bruising.

Pudding pulled her upright by her hair as Sugar continued to massage her bum. The cook turned Amber's head toward her and firmly kissed her on the mouth. Amber could taste her own pussy on Pudding's lips as she drove her tongue into her mouth and thoroughly explored her. The woman was an expert kisser as well as a skilled spanker, and Amber melted into her arms as Sugar carefully wiped off any excess cream with a small towel.

The cook broke the kiss, and hugged her tightly, rocking her gently, "There there, sweetheart. It's all over now. You were a very good girl; I shall tell Mistress you took your punishment like a champion. Yes, I will, indeed."

Amber swallowed, "Thank you, Pudding. I'm sorry."

"Aren't you sweet?" Pudding cooed. "Are you still hungry darling? It's okay if you are," Pudding said, pulling back from the hug. The cook cupped Amber's chin in one hand and gently lifted her up so she could look her in the eye. Amber nodded slightly.

"Then come with me into my office," Pudding said, taking her by the hand. Amber followed meekly and waited while the cook pulled some cutlery out of a drawer, and then grabbed a jar from a cupboard.

They went to the far side of the kitchen, and Pudding called out over her shoulder, "Sugar, clean up any of the mess, and finish the dishes, there's a dear."

"Yes, Pudding," Sugar replied. There wasn't a trace of resentment in the maid's voice, and Amber could see why. Despite her apparent fondness for being spanked by the cook, she wasn't looking for a punishment to follow on from Amber's so the sarcasm, and impish behaviour had to take a back seat.

Cook's office was a large room off a side corridor. The whole layout was typical of country houses Amber had visited for school trips or with family, and friends. The place was a warren of pantries, storage rooms, servants' quarters, and rooms reserved for the senior staff like the butler, housekeeper, and head cook. It would have been heaving with servants when it was built, and whatever sexual deviance they got up to, almost certainly wouldn't have been carried out on the kitchen table.

Pudding removed the lid of the jar with a twist of her strong arms. It gave a loud pop as the air pressure equalised. Then she set the jar, and a spoon down on a side table, next to a large, reclining armchair of a slightly old-fashioned design.

Amber waited patiently, as Pudding busied herself about the room. The cook took off her apron, revealing her black, leather corset, and her quite honestly amazing breasts. They were large, and well-formed, with small, pert nipples that looked hard as bullets. Amber couldn't help licking her lips and watched in awe as Pudding unzipped her latex skirt and placed it carefully with the apron over the back of another chair.

Half-naked now, with a carefully shaven pussy on display, and just the corset around her middle, which she clearly didn't need for any practical purposes, given the rest of her figure, Pudding sat down in the recliner.

"Come here, Amber," she said as she leaned back. "Kneel on this footstool," she ordered imperiously.

"Yes, Pudding," Amber replied. She got down on the footstool and watched as Pudding picked up the jar.

"Do you like cherry jam, Amber?" Pudding asked.

"I think so, I haven't had it in a while," Amber said with a shrug.

Pudding nodded with a mischievous smile on her face and scooped a big dollop out of the jar with her spoon. The older woman proceeded to apply the jam to her pussy lips, smearing a good-sized blob of the sticky stuff all along the length of her hairless slit. She covered her labia, squashing the thick jam against her skin, and making a mess. She even pushed the rounded back of the spoon a little way between her lips to make sure the dark red jam was everywhere.

The cook beckoned Amber forward, and reached out with her left hand, taking a grip of the hair at the back of her head. "Open wide, slut," Pudding said, and promptly placed the spoon in Amber's mouth. "Clean it off."

Amber sucked the tasty jam of the spoon, and savoured the mixture of pussy juice, and cherries, as she licked the cutlery clean. "Good girl," Pudding cooed. "Now, clean my pussy, and make sure I come hard while you do it."

Amber went to town, like the starving animal she was. The meal was unusual yet delicious, and Amber had never had an opportunity to so thoroughly thank a cook for the meal they'd made her.

Pudding seemed to appreciate her compliments.

CHAPTER 4

"What is that on your face?" Susanna asked the moment Amber walked back into the master bedroom.

Amber reached up, and touched her face, finding a sticky smudge of cherry jam near the corner of her mouth. She wiped it with her finger and sucked it clean. "Cherry jam, Mistress."

Susanna raised an eyebrow, "Why do you have jam on your face?"

"Pudding was punishing me, and then she smeared jam over her pussy and made me lick her clean," Amber said, deciding that honesty was the best policy in this situation.

"Why was it necessary for Pudding to punish you, Amber?"

"It wasn't really, Mistress. I just asked if I could have a little more to eat, and she took it badly," Amber protested.

"I see, and how were you punished for your rudeness, Amber?"

"She spanked me, Mistress," Amber replied.

"Show me," Susanna said, motioning for her to come closer.

Amber walked to the side of the bed, and turned around, bending forward at the waist before pulling the shirt nightgown up to over her hips.

Susanna reached out and stroked her cheeks. "Pudding is such a wonderful spanker, isn't she? She's left quite the impression on your cheeks. You're a wonderful shade of rosy pink, my dear."

"Yes, Mistress."

Susanna stood up, took hold of Amber by the wrist, and guided her to the bathroom, and into the shower.

"Take off the gown, and give it to me," Susanna ordered impatiently as she took off her own nightdress. Once their nightwear was safely hung up, Susanna joined her submissive in the shower and turned on the powerful jets of water.

Susanna had picked up a face flannel and put a generous helping of liquid soap on it. "Close your eyes," she ordered, a split second before she began to scrub at Amber's messy face with the rough flannel. One hand-wound into Amber's hair while the other thoroughly scrubbed at every inch of Amber's face, and neck, even behind the ears. When she was done with that, Susanna rinsed her sub's face.

"Up against the wall, spread your legs, palms on the wall. I'm going to make sure you're clean as a whistle you messy girl," Susanna said. True to her word, she began to use the flannel roughly on every inch of Amber's skin. The material swept back, and forth across her, and she could practically feel the layers of dead skin being exfoliated.

Amber's mistress switched to a new flannel before tackling her legs, and a third when she turned her around and pushed her back against the wall, to tackle her front. Susanna seemed particularly attentive when it came to Amber's breasts, working with great vigour to make sure not a spot was missed. The rough material of the flannel created delightful friction as Susanna held Amber's breast with one hand while rubbing the cloth back, and forth across the nipple with the other.

Amber found herself moaning passionately as her Mistress tormented her nipples, but it didn't put Susanna off her task. She was single-minded, and methodical, systematically attacking Amber's skin with as much soap, and as many flannels as she felt like using. Amber couldn't remember the last time she'd felt quite so clean, and her skin was quite pink all over.

The time spent on her legs was relaxing, and then Susanna finally got to her pussy. Mistress took a bar of hard, tea tree, and mint soap, and worked up a lather on Amber's inner thighs, and around her pussy. When she was done with that, Susanna took a firm grip on the soap, and introduced it between Amber's pussy lips, working it up, and down, rubbing against Amber's clit without holding back.

Once Amber was lathered up, Mistress put the soap back in the tray, and worked Amber's pussy, and clit with her fingers. The mint content of the soap was quite high, and Amber could feel it tingling away between her tender cheeks where Susanna had vigorously rubbed it in, and of course, all over her pussy.

She could feel an orgasm building and bit her lip, to stop the moans that were escaping her lips. Susanna took up the flannel again at that point and used it to work the lather between Amber's legs. Her orgasm subsided and washed away as the sensations shifted from pure pleasure to rough abrasion.

"Would you like Mistress to make you come, dear?"

"Yes. Please, Mistress."

"Bad girls don't get orgasms for making themselves dirty, Amber," Susanna replied, taking her sub's face in her hands, and kissing her passionately. "You're here to do as you're told, and please me. Get on your knees, slut."

Amber whimpered as the chance of coming under Susanna's fingers vanished before her eyes, but she dutifully got down on her knees. Susanna shifted to lean up against the wall, taking hold of a couple of handles which Amber had first assumed were there for the benefit of people with mobility problems, but now realised were present in such abundance mostly to support sexual antics in the bathroom.

Her lesbian boss sighed contentedly when Amber's tongue teased between her lips as the water cascaded down Susanna's head, and shoulders, over her chest, and splashed over her submissive assistant. Amber was about to reach out, and add her fingers to her work, but remember the reaction her Mistress had had earlier when she was supposed to be licking Sugar.

Instead, she crossed her wrists in the small of her back to avoid the temptation to use them and pushed her face firmly against her Mistress's pussy. Using only her tongue, and lips was tricky, but it focused her mind, and she concentrated on listening to the sounds Susanna made, against the backdrop of the falling water.

Amber found that trying to look up at her Mistress, as was her usual habit when giving oral sex, was useless in this environment. With the way that Susanna was leaning against the wall of the shower, the water just splashed into her eyes uncomfortably. Closing her eyes was the best way to give head to her Mistress now, and it further focused her senses.

With her eyes shut, she could only use touch, and taste, and hearing to guide her, and Amber soon discovered that she could try out different techniques, and ways of moving her lips, and tongue or how hard to make the suction while getting immediate feedback. Each time Amber tried something new, if she didn't note an immediate, audible response, she would revert back to the last thing she'd been doing.

Amber could then build Susanna back up again, before trying another way of pleasuring her. Each attempt brought her closer to finding the perfect way to eat her Mistress's pussy. She kept up this routine, as long as she could. It was rather impressive that the hot water didn't run out as Susanna seemed to be in no hurry to finish the shower.

The cut-off point wasn't running out of hot water, Amber found, it was finding the right technique to send Susanna over the edge. This time, the cue that it was working wasn't just audible, but physical. Susanna cried out, "Fuck, yes!", and then grabbed Amber's hair, forcing her hard against her pussy.

Amber's Mistress ground her sweet cunt against her sub's mouth, and ripped an orgasm from her, while the younger woman maintained the rhythm she'd found. Moments later Susanna verbalised her climax with a stream of expletives so filthy, Amber wouldn't even have used them as a teenager.

Finally, Mistress let go of her head and even gently pushed her young assistant away from her pussy. “Enough. I think the practice is doing you good, Amber, you seem to be learning new skills apace. Well done,” Susanna said, softly patting her on the head. “Now, let’s rinse off, and go, and get dry before our skin prunes up.”

“Yes, Mistress,” Amber replied, smiling up adoringly at her boss.

CHAPTER 5

Susanna mandated a brief nap after their shower, and when the alarm woke them twenty minutes later, she rang the bells to summon Candy, and Sugar to the room.

The maids appeared promptly and curtseyed as they entered the room. "How may we be of service, Mistress?" Candy asked.

"I'm sure Sugar told you that I'm training Amber today?"

"Yes, Mistress, she did. Sugar said Amber is getting better all the time," Candy agreed.

"Yes, but she still has a way to go until she's as good at her personal duties as Sugar, or yourself. To that end, I want both of you naked now so you can help her practice her skills," Susanna ordered.

"Yes, Mistress," the girls chorused, stripping off their skimpy maid outfits with an economy of movement that impressed Amber. More haste, less speed after all, and the girls managed to get naked, and have their clothes neatly stacked on a chair with surprising alacrity. She almost gave them a round of applause, and only the thought of another punishment spanking kept her from clapping.

Amber was sitting cross-legged next to her Mistress, watching the show. "Get on the bed, Candy, I want you lying down on your back, feet on the floor," Susanna said to her new recruit. "Amber, get on top of her, I want you to sixty-nine my naughty little maid for me, do you understand?"

"I do, Mistress," Amber said. How exciting. She'd never done a sixty-nine because none of her boyfriends had ever seen the appeal.

While the girls arranged themselves, Sugar waited patiently for her Mistress to give her a task. She didn't have to wait long. "Sugar, you get up here next to me," Susanna said, patting the bed beside her.

"Yes, Mistress," Sugar replied. Amber was looking over her shoulder and saw the maid lean in close to Susanna so Mistress could whisper something in her ear. The maid giggled, and covered her mouth with her hand, glancing at Amber slyly, and winking. Amber wondered what the pair were up to, something painful probably. It didn't matter though, she had Candy's glorious pussy waiting below her.

"You may begin, Amber," Susanna ordered. The maid below her took hold of her hips, and lowered Amber's wet pussy until she had it just where she wanted it, low enough to be comfortable, and grant her tongue easy access, but not so low that Candy would suffocate.

Once Candy's tongue buried itself between her lips, Amber dipped her own head. She rested most of her weight on her left arm and used the fingers of her right hand to part Candy's lips, before seeking out her clit with lips, and tongue.

"Sugar, you get to work too now, please," Susanna said.

Amber tensed up a little when she said that, anticipating a firm spanking or perhaps a paddle, but nothing like that happened. Instead, she felt the weight shift behind her as Sugar moved position on the mattress. Perhaps she was going to go down on Mistress?

When Sugar's hands parted her, buttocks though she had to struggle to concentrate on what she was doing, rather than trying to puzzle out what the maid had been ordered to do. A moment later, she felt Sugar's gloriously agile tongue against her pussy lips. Surely there wasn't room for two girls to eat her pussy at once, thought Amber.

Sugars tongue didn't stop at her lips though, it ran upward slowly, wetly, until it reached the most taboo of places, and suddenly Sugar was tonguing her rosebud. Amber could tell she was blushing. No-one had ever eaten her arse before, and she immediately regretted that fact.

Between Candy's tongue flicking at her clit while she sucked on her like a vacuum cleaner, and Sugar's probing wetly into her arsehole, she was in a state of pure ecstasy. Or perhaps that should be, impure ecstasy since this was clearly not an activity that could be considered in any way decent.

Amber imagined a Victorian governess entering the room and gasping in horror to the housekeeper who had discovered the girls in bed together, 'Why look at that, Mrs Martingale. The new ward of the Master and Mistress is sandwiched between these two maids! Is Sugar applying her tongue to Amber's anus?'. The housekeeper would reply, 'Yes, I do believe she is. The filthy beasts. Once they are done, we must punish them, most severely.'

There wasn't time to play out her fantasy though, and she needed all her concentration to make sure she was using every ounce of her new skills on Candy's delicious pussy. The orgasm that tore through her a mere handful of minutes after the double-tongued action started up did nothing to help her with her goal, of course.

Try as she might, Amber wasn't able to get Candy to come at all until she'd had three orgasms herself. She kept eating Candy's sweetly spicy pussy until the maid had a second orgasm, by which time she'd come herself again. Only then did Susanna speak up, "Good girls. Let's switch things up a bit, shall we? Amber, get over here and put your tongue to work on my pussy. Sugar, and Candy, torment Amber with some vibrators. If you can make her come twice before I come once, you can introduce her to the tawse or the school cane."

Those words created a flurry of movement. Amber wasn't quite sure what a tawse was, but doubtless, if it was being offered as an alternative to a cane, it wasn't going to be as mild as a spanking. She disentangled herself as quickly as she could, and practically dived on her Mistress's pussy, using the best technique she'd identified in the shower as her opening move.

One of the maids had a powerful vibrator slid deep inside Amber and turned up to the max before Susanna had even started to moan as Amber licked her. It felt as if she would easily win at first, but then a second vibrator was turned on and applied to her clit directly. That was somewhat difficult to fight.

In the end, it came down to luck more than willpower to resist coming herself or the skill to make Susanna come. Susanna cried out, "Amber wins!". A mere heartbeat later, Amber lost her fight to retain control and began to cry out into Susanna's pussy as she struggled to keep licking. Mistress grabbed her head with both hands, pulling her in tight, and clamping her shuddering thighs around her ears, riding Amber's face, and tongue to a second orgasm, before pushing her away, and collapsing back into the pillows as the waves of pleasure rushed through her body.

When Susanna came back into focus, she dismissed all three of them, saying she would work until the evening meal, and they were to bring her a light lunch before then.

Candy took Amber's wrist and gently led her from the room. Once they had shut the doors behind them, she pushed Amber up against the wall and kissed her passionately. Sugar didn't want to be left out, and they ended up in a three-way kissing contest.

The girls kissed each other, tasting their pussies, and their Mistress on each other's lips. Sugar tasted different at first, and it was then that Amber blushingly recalled what she'd been doing to her a while ago. She wondered if she should be ashamed, then giggled at the thought before kissing Sugar deeply again.

The doors to Susanna's room opened wide with an audible rush of air. Mistress Hamilton did not look entirely happy.

"I said that I need to work, and you sluts are out here making noise. Unless you want tears before lunchtime, I suggest you make yourself scarce so I can tend to my business interests," Mistress said with a scowl.

Sugar grabbed both of them and dragged them away, "Sorry, Mistress. Let us know what you want for lunch, and when."

Susanna grunted a response, and stomped back into her room, slamming the doors behind her.

Candy saw the look on Amber's face when they were well away from Mistress's suite of rooms and smiled at her. "Don't worry, her bark is worse than her bite."

"Rubbish. She's got a really painful bite, and actual rooms just for torturing people," Sugar scoffed.

"Torture rooms? Like a dungeon?"

Candy grinned and wagged an admonishing finger at Sugar. "Now, now, Sugar. You know we mustn't go filling Amber's head with all sorts of scary thoughts about Mistress's colourful rooms of pain!" she said theatrically.

"Silly me. You're right, of course. I don't watch to get stretched on the rack," Sugar said.

"Too right," Candy concurred, "once was enough for me!"

Amber's eyes were wide with horror. "You must be joking?"

Candy tapped the side of her nose with one finger.

"That's for us to know, and you to find out," teased Sugar, and the two maids skipped off down the hallway.

Amber stood stock still for a moment, wondering if the girls were winding her up or not. When she looked up again, they were skipping off around a corner.

"Hey, wait for me!" she called out, jogging after them.

CHAPTER 6

Amber didn't see Mistress again until the evening meal, as Candy took her the simple salad that Pudding prepared. She'd tried pressing the maids, and even Pudding for information about the existence of a dungeon room, but was blanked at every turn. In the end, Pudding rolled her eyes and threatened a spanking if the giggling maids, and Amber didn't make themselves scarce. Sugar wanted to stay, of course, but the others dragged her away.

"Do you two need a hand with any of the cleaning?" Amber asked?

Candy shook her head, "No, we're fine. Mistress has a company come in once a month and do a thorough clean. We only have to look after her private rooms, and a few of the most used rooms a little. She says she has far better things for us to do than spend all our time cleaning. I read that this place had fourteen maids in its heyday, so there's no way, Sugar, and I could keep pace. When the company comes in, we get an extra day off. They're a kink-friendly business, but Mistress doesn't like to share the space with them anyway, so we all go out."

"Yeah, I hate cleaning days," Sugar grumbled.

"But you get a day off," Amber said.

"Yes, exactly. I'd much rather be here, on my knees, where I belong," Sugar said.

"Oh, stop whining, Sugar," Candy giggled. "Honestly, you'd think she never got any pussy the way she goes on about cleaning days. Tell her what we did on the last cleaning day excursion, Sugar," Candy demanded.

Sugar stuck her tongue out at Candy, then sighed. "Fine, we went to a daytime munch," the maid said.

Amber thought for a moment, the term seemed familiar, but she couldn't quite place it. "I'm sorry, I don't know what that means."

Candy filled in, "It's a social gathering in a pub or in this case a coffee shop, for kinky people to get together, and talk shop or socialise with like-minded people. It's all very vanilla, no different than any other group of hobbyists getting together to chat about horse riding or comics or films or whatever, but that wasn't the bit I wanted Sugar to tell you about, and she knows it."

Sugar sighed dramatically. "Okay, okay. After the munch we went to a house party," Sugar said, but was interrupted by Candy.

"After we'd called Mistress for permission, of course," Candy said.

"Yes, that goes without saying," Sugar said, looking at Amber. "Actually, maybe it doesn't. If you're on leave or a day off, Mistress doesn't mind what vanilla things you do. Go to the cinema, out for food with friends, go shopping, all that's fine."

"But don't go to parties or go, and have sexy times with anyone, she doesn't allow that," Candy said.

"Well, unless you ask, and she's in a good mood," Sugar said.

"Yes. Never without her permission. Remember that rule, and you'll be fine," Candy agreed.

"Anyway, we went back to the house party, and Mistress called the host on us."

"Really? Why? What happened?" Amber asked, her mind buzzing with questions.

"She gave us to the host to use for the afternoon," Sugar said.

Amber looked at her, wondering if she meant what she thought she meant. Candy nudged her friend.

Sugar grinned wickedly. "We got stripped naked in front of a whole room full of lesbians, and then the toys came out. There were paddles and crops, and lovely canes. Then the strapons came out, and we got fucked silly, didn't we Candy?"

Candy nodded. "We certainly did. I ate so much pussy that afternoon that my jaw ached all weekend."

Amber swallowed. "Wow. That sounds. I mean," she stumbled, flustered by the idea of it all. Being shared like that, handed out to another Mistress.

"Hot?" Sugar prompted.

"Fucking hot? Pussy flooding, hip tremblingly, clit explodingly, earth-shatteringly, hot?" Candy added.

Amber nodded. "Yes. What she said."

"Stick around, you'll have plenty of fun with Mistress in charge," Sugar said, sagely.

Amber thought about their conversation all through dinner. It kept her wet the whole time.

After dinner was finished, Susanna marched her upstairs again to continue her training she said. Amber thought that meant another marathon session of pussy licking, but in fact, she got given a tour of some of the toy cabinets in Susanna's suite.

Susanna took the time to explain to her how the various cuffs worked, and which were suitable for what type of play. She put a leather hood on Amber which obscured much of her vision and left only her mouth available. There was a zip that could be used to completely cover over the mouth and air holes for the nose. It still felt a little claustrophobic, and Amber was glad that Mistress did not make her wear it too long on her first time.

When Susanna applied the 'least painful' nipple clamps she had, Amber felt tears flood her eyes. Mistress kissed them away, and teased her nipples, tugging gently on the clamps. "Do you like that?" she asked.

Amber vigorously shook her head. She found the clamps intensely painful. "No, Mistress. It really hurts."

"Do you need to use your safe word?" Mistress asked her, a note of concern in her voice.

"No, Mistress," Amber replied. Susanna smiled like the Cheshire cat.

Her Mistress leaned forward, curling her left hand around Amber's hooded head, and bringing her lips to her left ear. She took hold of Amber's hand and guided it between her legs. "Good, it makes me wet just thinking about you suffering, Amber. Watching a sub endure pain for her Mistress, turns me on so much. Can you feel it?" Susanna said as she pressed Amber's fingertips to her sodden pussy.

"Yes, Mistress. I'm," Amber hesitated, "I'm glad I make you happy."

"Oh, you do, sweetness. I'm very proud of you, my brave little slut," Susanna said, sliding her fingers down to touch Amber's lips. "You feel wet too, Amber. Very wet."

Mistress pushed her back on the bed, tweaking the clamps again until Amber cried out in pain, which only made her laugh in delight. "So beautiful in your torment," Susanna said, then moved up the bed, turning around, and straddling Amber's face.

Amber took the hint as Susanna's pussy descended, and stuck her tongue out ready to service her Mistress as required. "That's a good girl. So eager for her Mistress's pussy," Susanna said. "From this position, I can reach those lovely nipples too," she advised, before resuming her torment.

Mistress played like that with her until she came over Amber's face, then finally removed the clamps, and set them to one side. Laying back against the pillows, she allowed Amber to eat her out at her leisure. "You can use your fingers as well, sweetheart. I think you've earned it. Yes, that's good, just like that you horny little slut."

Amber lapped happily at her Mistress as she explored her with her fingers as well. As she worked at her pussy, Mistress began talking to her about submission, and domination, and other aspects of BDSM. Susanna asked questions and allowed her to answer them, correcting gaps in Amber's limited knowledge, and teaching her about all sorts of fascinating things.

"Have you done any horse riding, Amber?"

Amber looked up from her assigned task, "No, Mistress. Once or twice for birthday parties, but I never took lessons."

"I see. Well, tomorrow I want to show you my stables, and we can maybe have a race. Would you like that?"

"I'm not sure I'm a good enough rider to race anyone, Mistress," Amber admitted, "but it sounds fun."

Susanna laughed. "Oh, silly me. I didn't mean as riders, that would be horribly irresponsible if you haven't any experience. No, we'll use a pony, and trap for the racing, and it's not a sprint. My animals do the real work, and they know what they're doing, you mostly have to sit back, and enjoy yourself. Does that sound appealing?"

"Yes, Mistress," Amber said before burying her tongue back in Susanna's pussy. Mistress sighed contentedly and didn't speak for several minutes as she allowed her assistant to bring her to her first orgasm before bedtime.

Amber wondered when she would be required to do any of the actual work she'd been employed to do but certainly wasn't unhappy with her present duties. She was having the time of her life, and Susanna, her maids, and her cook were broadening her mind, and experiences in ways she'd never dreamed off. Amber was happier than she'd ever been.

"Wonderful. I think you'll love my ponies." Susanna said.

Amber assumed the comment was rhetorical, so she simply kept licking, and gazing at her Mistress lovingly as Susanna stroked her hair.

"My friends tell me they're some of the finest ponies in the country you know, and many of them are undeniably experts in the field," Susanna commented. "Yes, I think we'll have a lot of fun tomorrow."

It was an hour later that Susanna drew Amber up, and cuddled up to her young submissive, spooning her.

"Good girl. You've improved a lot today, I'm very proud of you. Now, get some sleep, we have another big day tomorrow," Susanna said, kissing Amber, and running her hands over her breasts, and stomach possessively as she talked.

"Yes, Mistress."

RACED BY HER LESBIAN BOSS

Book 4

CHAPTER 1

"Yes. Yes, that fits perfectly," Susanna said as she circled Amber, tugging a hem here, adjusting a lapel there.

"Does it? I've never worn this sort of outfit before."

"Not even when you went riding?"

"That was only a couple of times, and it was more of a tracksuit and trainers type of thing. It didn't compare to this," Amber replied, gesturing with her hands down the length of her body at the costume she was wearing. A costume or a uniform? She wasn't quite sure.

"How do the jodhpurs feel?"

"They're a bit tight. Are they too small?"

"Mmmm," Susanna murmured, running her hand down Amber's back and over the taut material stretched over her buttocks. Amber shivered and bit her lip. "No, I think they're fine. Try moving in them."

"Moving?"

"Yes, walk around a bit, see if you can bend over and touch your toes, that sort of thing," Susanna purred.

"Yes, Mistress," Amber answered. She did her best impression of a catwalk model, striding across the massive bedroom and turning on the ball of her foot before walking back. The thigh-length riding boots were fairly easy to walk in, despite the heels. She wasn't sure if they were quite right for riding, but they looked fantastic and accentuated her calves beautifully.

When she reached her mistress, she pulled up short and turned once more. Amber bent at the waist, reaching down and grasping her ankles. "How's that?"

"Provocative," Susanna said. "A perfect fit, in my not so humble opinion. The jacket too. Here's your helmet, and your carriage whip, use it sparingly and don't let me catch you with your helmet off while we're racing. Safety first."

"Of course, Mistress."

"Come on, it's time for breakfast and don't you dare get any marmalade on that jacket."

"Yes, Mistress."

"Are we going to race now, Mistress?" Amber asked as she carefully folded the napkin she'd used to dab her lips clean of marmalade and toast crumbs. It had been an unusually light breakfast for her so perhaps Susanna had asked Pudding to keep it small as they would be exercising.

Susanna, however, shook her head, "No, you're going to come to the office with me. It's time you started working for your keep." Mistress stood up and smiled before heading to the door, "After all, you are my personal assistant, and that is a real job, not just fun and games, you know."

"Of course, Mistress," Amber replied as she followed behind.

"Good. You are here to carry out tasks so that I don't have to. You're not just here to be a source of amusement, no matter how sweetly you squeal when I punish you or how appealing I find your tears."

Amber took a gamble that this was rhetorical and remained silent as they made their way across the mansion to Susanna's office suite.

Susanna stopped in the spacious room outside her office and pointed to a desk in the corner. "This is yours. I despise clean desk policies, so keep your desk as you see fit as long as it's actually clean and anything on it is to do with work. You have a room upstairs, so you don't need personal items here."

The desk had a wooden top but was otherwise quite modern, and more to the point, it was raised to about chest height. It was a standing desk.

Susanna handed her a business card, "This is your username and password for the computer. You'll need to change the password, and I presume I don't need to tell you that you shouldn't write it down and leave it lying around? Candy and Sugar are little minxes, and if I find you've been subjected to their pranks, it will be you that is punished the most severely."

"Yes, Mistress," Amber nodded. "Are there password restrictions?"

"Yes, on the back of the card. Once you are logged in, you can use our password manager to handle other accounts you need access to. I think you have access to everything I need you to, but if not, let me know. I have an IT girl who can come and deal with any technical problems you might have."

"Thank you, Mistress."

"The desk is adjusted with these buttons. It's electric, so it's not hard. I assume you're familiar with how to correctly set up your desk for the best ergonomics but if not, look for an online guide. I cannot abide young ladies who make themselves unavailable because they don't look after their health," Susanna said with a somewhat testy tone, given that Amber herself hadn't made this particular mistake yet.

"I understand, Mistress. I'll make sure the desk is adjusted properly," Amber confirmed.

"Good. As you can see, it is a standing desk. I expect you to use it in the standing position unless I tell you otherwise. It promotes good health and strong legs. If you really cannot bear it, I may let you lower it for a while, but you'll soon learn to stand all day. For the Victorians, it was the norm you know," Susanna said as if the Victorians were somehow virtuous and to be diligently replicated in every thought and deed. Amber knew that despite any accomplishments they were also, by modern standards, a bunch of horrible buggers.

"Yes, Mistress," was all she said, though."

"Now, as to your work I have a simple series of tasks for you today, " Susanna continued. "They're all listed in the task management software on your PC. I am having a party next weekend which was organised before your references came through. There are some follow-up tasks for you to carry out, mostly to do with checking that everything is ready, sending out email reminders and the like. If you have any major problems, come into my office and speak to me. Otherwise, you can use the messaging system you'll find on your desktop so you don't interrupt my workflow. Questions?"

"Umm, no," Amber replied, "I think I have everything, Mistress."

"Really? I sense otherwise. Out with it girl, I don't have time for you to be coy," Susanna snapped.

"Well, it was just."

"Just what, spit it out for heaven's sake, Amber!"

Amber coughed, "Every day so far you've. Umm. You've enjoyed me. In the morning, after we woke up, but not today. Have I displeased you, Mistress?"

Susanna raised an eyebrow. "I see. You're upset that I haven't fucked you today?"

Amber blushed. "No. I don't mean. Not like that anyway. Umm. I mean, I was just surprised, is all," Amber stumbled, wilting somewhat under the exceptionally stern look Susanna was giving her. It felt like an industrial laser was aimed at the midpoint between her eyebrows.

Her Mistress didn't respond, she just turned and pulled open the double doors to her private office, "Come in, and shut the doors after yourself." Amber swiftly did as she was told.

"Stand there," Susanna said, motioning to a spot in front of her massive mahogany desk. Once Amber was in place, she slid into position behind her, reached around her, undid her belt and unbuttoned her jodhpurs. With a quick tug, Susanna pulled the tight trousers down below her bum.

"Bend over, place your forearms on the desk for support, either side of this cushion, and your forehead on the cushion. I don't want you getting a mark on your forehead," Susanna said, placing a small seat cushion on the edge of the desk.

Amber was thoroughly exposed once she had complied. Her buttocks were bare, and Susanna didn't take long to pull her lacy thong down to join her jodhpurs around her thighs, leaving her pussy lips open to viewing as well.

The fingertips that Susanna used to stroke her lips were soon slick with Amber's mounting excitement, and they plunged into her with barely any resistance. Amber gasped, despite the fact that Susanna's intrusion had been predictable once she was told to bend over like that.

In moments, Susanna had found her G-spot and was vigorously working it under her soft-skinned but unyielding fingers. Amber could barely contain her mounting pleasure, her quick breathing and low moans filled the office.

"Is this what you expected of me, slut?" Susanna growled.

Amber could only nod, unable to form words. "You think you're entitled to this sort of treatment, do you?"

Sensing a trap, Amber shook her head and regained enough composure to mumble, "No, Mistress."

"Liar. That's exactly what my kindness each day has led you to assume is your due. Are you close? Are you going to come soon?"

"Yes, Mistress," Amber groaned. The motion ceased, and Susanna's fingers withdrew from her aching pussy, only to be thrust rudely into her mouth.

"Suck them clean, slut," came the order which Amber greedily obeyed as her mounting arousal betrayed her and was routed from the field. Her breathing slowed as she sucked the musky fingers that Susanna had pushed into her mouth.

Then the fingers were entangled in her hair, and Amber found herself strongly encouraged to waddle around the desk, her legs still restricted by the jodhpurs around her thighs. "Kneel," Susanna ordered as undid her own belt and let her jodhpurs drop down to her knees.

Her Mistress sat down on the expensive office chair, parting her legs as much as the trousers would allow. The knee-length riding boots prevented them from dropping to her ankles. Amber found her face forced uncomfortably between Susanna's thighs where it was clamped in position. She was lucky that her nose was at a sufficient angle or she'd have been unable to breathe properly as she took up her duty.

"Look at me," Susanna snapped, as her thighs pressed against Amber's cheeks and her fist gripped her hair painfully. Amber looked up as best she could given the awkward position. "You do not determine when and where I play with you. You do not decide when I want to use your tongue or allow you pleasure. You most certainly do not make demands on my time. I am the one who decides, who determines, who demands. You are the submissive. You will do as you are told, or you will rue the day you disobeyed me. When you serve me well, I may grant you freedoms and pleasures you long for, but I will do so on my own advice. Comfortable down there?"

Amber could barely move her head, so firmly was she gripped, but she managed just enough to indicate that she was not. "Good!" Susanna remarked as she reached her orgasm and smeared her lips all over Amber's face, covering her in her arousal before letting go.

Amber winced as the pressure on her ears and the tug against her hair was relinquished, falling back gasping for air.

Susanna stood and patted herself down with a wipe she produced from her drawer. "Get up, slut. Go and wash your face and put your makeup in order, then come back ready to work hard."

Frustrated and filthy, Amber nevertheless did as she was told and retired to make herself look presentable again.

When she returned to the suite, the doors to Susanna's office were emphatically closed, and she got her head down and concentrated on the party planning tasks. Amber didn't dare disturb her Mistress further, not even with more apologies she felt compelled to give.

A couple of hours later, the doors opened, and Susanna emerged.

"Off to the races then," she said without another word on the morning's events.

Amber followed meekly, at the side of her Mistress but a half-step behind.

CHAPTER 2

The gravel of the courtyard crunched underfoot as they walked briskly toward the stables. There were quite a large number of outbuildings around the estate that Amber had seen, but many were in relative disrepair and seemingly unused.

When they approached the stable block though, it was clear the old brick building had been renovated in recent years. Amber couldn't date it, but the brick showed it's age, though it had clearly been repointed in recent years. More telling where the huge wooden doors, presumably designed for carriages. One wing had been converted into more modern garages, and Amber idly wondered what cars Susanna kept. No doubt, they were all expensive.

The building was at least two stories high, with a hayloft hatch and a winch at one end. Skylights in the opposite end of the roof suggested that section had been converted for office or living space in the loft area at least. They entered through a human-sized door at the end near the winch, but not under it. No-one wanted a hay bale dropped on their head when they were getting in or out. There were thick yellow lines under the winch, a nod to modern health and safety concerns which suggested it was still in use.

The internal proportions were quite cavernous, and Amber could immediately see several sections which were to hold large, four-horse carriages to their right, facing the courtyard the stables shared with the main house.

To the left were the stalls for the horses, the doors to them were split into two sections, with the lower one being slightly taller. The upper doors were open and held in place by a simple wooden latch. Above two of the stalls was a large, polished wooden sign bearing what Amber presumed was the name of the animal.

"Amber, why don't you introduce yourself to Pepper?" Susanna said, handing her two-quarters of a freshly sliced and juicy apple. "Give her a treat, and you'll soon win her over. Don't worry, she's not a biter. My ponies are very well trained. I'll be racing with Ginger today."

Amber took the apple and approached the stall. That they were ponies and not horses explained why she couldn't see their heads poking over the partial door. She still couldn't see the pony as she reached the door, but she heard a soft rustle of hay. Was it lying down?

"Go on in, my ponies are perfectly safe, Amber," Susanna said as she opened the door and stepped into Ginger's stall. "There you go, you silly creature, I've brought you a snack." There was a distinct crunch as the apple Susanna had was gobbled up.

Amber looked back at the door, lifted the latch and stepped into the stall. "I've got a treat for you, Pepper," she managed to get out before her eyes adjusted to the shadow. "Fuck me," she exclaimed under her breath.

Pepper stamped her foot softly but firmly and whinnied around the bit in her mouth. The hoof made a clopping sound against the floor of the stall, muffled by the hay.

Susanna's pony advanced on the dumbstruck personal assistant and dipped her head, using her lips to scoop up a chunk of apple and crunching it happily as Amber watched.

Living up to her name, Pepper had a fiery mane and a brightness to her eyes the spoke of intelligence and spirit. Her legs were long, elegant and firmly muscled. Her ears were pricked up and alert, and she was already prepared for racing it seemed, wearing a bridle and harness with a bit in her mouth. No sooner had she finished her first treat, than she dipped her head to snatch the second.

Amber simply looked the young woman up and down. Pepper was breathtaking to behold, a genuine beauty. The leather of her harness accentuated her lean body, which was a testament to her level of exercise and yet she'd retained delightful curves in all the places that Amber would have wished her too.

"Well," came the voice from the neighbouring stall, "what do you think of Pepper? She's a fine pony, isn't she?"

Amber cleared her throat. "I'm no expert, but she appears very fine to me indeed, and she looks ready to race her heart out." Pepper whinnied, and her eyes sparkled at Amber. She stamped her foot again twice in quick succession.

"That means yes, in case you were wondering," Susanna called out. "Lead her out of the front of the stall when you're done checking her out, and we'll get them hitched up to the traps."

"Yes, Mistress," Amber called out absently. Slowly she approached Pepper, and whispered, "You're beautiful, Pepper. May I... may I touch you?" Her question was slightly hesitant. She wasn't sure quite how to communicate with the ponygirl. Two quick soft stamps for yes were her answer though so Amber reached out and stroked the flank of the young woman who would be her pony for the day. Pepper's skin was smooth and chill in the stable air, but she didn't flinch away. She wasn't nervous.

Amber kept eye contact with her as she drew her hand up to the other woman's chest, cupping her breast and running a thumb over a nipple which grew rapidly erect. Pepper didn't seem to object to the attention at all. Her nipples were pierced with simple silver bars, held in place by balls at either end. Though she longed to place her mouth on Pepper's aroused breast, she guessed Susanna wasn't going to allow her more than a brief time to admire her pony before she wanted to race them.

Reluctantly, Amber took up the reins and unlatched the door that led into a small grassy area, ringed in by a fence. Susanna was almost done getting Ginger into position with a small, one person trap. When she was done, she came over to see how Amber was progressing.

Amber looked at her helplessly, "I'm really not sure what to do here."

Susanna smiled. "We're just here to have fun, Amber. Ginger and Pepper need regular exercise and play to keep them fit, healthy and happy. Here, let me show you how you harness them to the trap, so they're safe and comfortable."

True to her word, Susanna showed her once, then removed Pepper from the trap and made Amber do it herself, once with pointers and the second time on her own. It wasn't complicated, but Susanna was very careful to stress all the safety protocols to avoid injury.

"Now, check that her tail is nicely in place, we don't want it to fall out."

Amber crouched behind Pepper and inspected the swishy tail. It was attached to a butt plug that was plunged into Pepper's bottom. Moving the hair aside, she made a show of inspecting it. First, she applied a little pressure to check if it was fully inserted, then she attempted to withdraw it, and move it left to right. Pepper made soft whinnying sounds as she did so, but the plug stayed firmly in her arse.

"It seems secure, Mistress."

"Excellent. Now, the last check is to ensure your pony is hot to trot as it were," Susanna said, demonstrating as she reached between Ginger's thighs and got a strong whinny and foot stamp from her. "Like so."

Amber followed suit, "Are you going to win this race for me, Pepper?" The woman's pussy was invitingly wet with her arousal, swallowing Amber's fingers with ease. Peper's eyes flashed, and she stamped her foot twice quickly as Amber whispered encouragement.

Turning back to Susanna, Amber held up her fingers, glistening with Pepper's juices. She slid them into her mouth and sucked them clean. "I think Pepper is more than hot to trot, Mistress."

Susanna laughed. "It's around the lake once. The ponies know the route, and I suggest only light encouragement with your carriage whip until you know what you're doing. Across the buttocks only. Do a slow circuit of the paddock so you can get used to it and then we'll go down to the lake."

Amber nodded her understanding as she climbed into the lightweight trap and Pepper took up the handles, tilting it back and moving off at a slow walk.

"The prize is an orgasm," Susanna called out as they set off down to the small lake.

"I'll take that bet, Mistress," Amber replied boldly.

CHAPTER 3

"Pick up the pace, Ginger!" Susanna cried as she cracked the whip in the air above her. Ginger was probably doing her best, Amber thought. There was no way she was going to be able to catch up with Pepper now though.

They were already in sight of the fork in the track they'd started the race at, and Pepper showed no signs of flagging. The lake wasn't enormous but pulling a trap with a person in it around a rather rudimentary track wasn't that easy. Amber could easily see why Pepper's thighs were so impressively muscled, strong and lean if she was regularly pulling Susanna around this track.

"You too, Pepper!" Amber said, cracking her own whip. Pepper neighed, but when Amber finished her practice sweeps and let the whip contact first her left and then her right buttock, she squealed past her gag.

Her pony stumbled, and Amber thought she might stop entirely, but after a moment, she collected herself and ran on, gradually increasing her space. Pepper pulled over the finish line with at least a hundred yards between her and her rival ponygirl. The trap came to a slow halt as Pepper's pace slowed and she finally halted.

Amber could hear the ponygirl gulping in big lungfuls of air. She'd really pushed herself for her driver, and her flanks were covered in sweat.

Susanna and Ginger pulled up alongside them, and her Mistress dismounted, coming over to Amber's trap. "Well done, you beat us, fair and square."

"Thank you, Mistress."

"How did you manage that, when you've never raced a ponygirl before, hmm?"

"Beginner's luck, Mistress," Amber demurred.

"Really? I notice you gave her a couple of good marks here, " Susanna said, running her hand over Pepper's bottom, feeling the bruised scarlet flesh. "That's an astonishing learning curve you've got there. They're just right. These look lovely, Pepper." The ponygirl whinnied appreciatively.

Amber got down from her trap and Pepper was finally able to relax, squatting down to carefully put the arms of the single-person trap down. She stood on the other side of Pepper and reached out, stroking the ponygirl's welted skin. Had she really caused that? Pepper yelped and turned her head to give her a reproachful look.

"I think Pepper thinks she was going to win without the added inducement," Susanna said, walking around the girl to whisper in Amber's ear. "You should get out of the trap and check your ponygirl as soon as you finish, to make sure they're ok. Now, check to see if she's responding as you'd hope to the welts you gave her."

Amber wasn't sure what her Mistress meant by that and Susanna raised an eyebrow at her before nodding an acknowledgement that her protege was confused. Mistress took hold of her right hand and guided her to Pepper's flank, sliding Amber's fingers over the moist skin and down between her thighs.

Susanna's breath was hot against her ear as she whispered, "Is she wet? Excited? Aroused? Does she lust for the touch of your fingers or the kiss of your whip?" Her teeth nibbled gently at Amber's earlobe, and her lips drew together around it to bring gentle suction to her.

With her fingers between Pepper's legs, she explored the ponygirl's smoothly shaved sex. Her lips were as wet as her perspiration drenched chest. Pepper shuddered and gamely attempted to whinny, but it came out as half a moan, and it was all Amber could do not to giggle.

"Guide her head by her mane, let her see you taste her arousal," Susanna whispered.

Amber reached out and took hold of Pepper's hair, which was plaited in a long tail. Of course, it was. She made the girl look at her and smiled as she lifted her fingers from their exploration of Pepper's pussy and sucked them clean. Pepper's eyes flashed with fire, and Amber grinned.

Their Mistress came forward then and looked at Pepper seriously. "Now, Pepper. Did Amber really win because she had beginner's luck?" Pepper tossed her head from side to side, giving a remarkably negative sounding neigh and stamping her foot three times for no. Amber cursed inside.

"Amber, remove her bit gag, please," Susanna ordered her, waiting for the rubber bar to be unstrapped from the ponygirl's face.

"Pepper, you may speak. Tell me how Amber won," Susanna demanded. The ponygirl glanced at Amber and then shook her head and stamped her foot three times. Amber's eyes widened. This surely wasn't going to go well for Pepper. She was risking the wrath of their Mistress.

"Come along then girls, we're going back to the stables," Mistress Susanna said finally, having glared at the pair of them. She led Ginger away, walking beside her holding her reins and Amber followed suit, beside Pepper.

The walk from the lakeside back to the stables didn't take long but all the way Amber wondered what would happen next as traipsed through the grass.

They put the traps away, and the girl's bits and bridles were cleaned in a large butler's sink, dried down and hung up in the tack room. Susanna then took them to a room that bore a brass plaque which read, "Training and Discipline".

"Amber, strap Pepper down over that punishment bench, and make sure she's properly restrained," Susanna ordered, pointing at a piece of furniture. The punishment bench resembled a gymnastics vaulting horse that had been crossed with a piece of modern gym equipment. It was padded and covered with glossy black leather, and festooned with buckles, rings, belts and straps clearly intended to restrain a human.

At first glance, Amber wasn't entirely sure she was interpreting the design correctly, but she breathed a mental sigh of relief when Pepper meekly mounted the bench. As the ponygirl got into position, Amber's understanding of how the bench was intended to be used proved remarkably accurate. A long pad either side of the body of the bench provided a place for the submissive's knees and another pair further along the bench allowed Pepper to rest her forearms.

Rather than being flat though, the knee and forearm rests were below the height of the bench, and so Pepper was held in position as if she was on all fours, with her torso supported. There was a subtle incline to the bench, so her head was slightly lower down than her buttocks.

Amber set about using the thick leather cuffs to restrain Pepper's wrists and ankles, before adding the straps which restrained her near the elbows and knees as well. Pepper whinnied and struggled against the restraints, proving that she couldn't free herself. Amber looked at her boss, who had mounted a wooden platform which raised the wooden throne she now occupied, above the floor by a good few inches.

Her boss, scrutinised her work, finally nodding, "Is she ready for punishment, Amber?" she asked. As she spoke, she casually ran her fingers through the hair of her pony, Ginger, who was kneeling beside the throne of her Mistress.

"Yes, Mistress," Amber replied, hoping that she hadn't missed any restraints.

"Is her tail still secure?" Susanna asked.

Amber reached out and took hold of the tail that sprouted from Pepper's pert bottom, near the root where the long hairs were attached to the silicon butt plug that filled the ponygirls arse. She tugged at it gently, finding the plug was still held firmly and wasn't going to come loose with a light pull. Pepper shuddered and groaned as the plug insert in her bottom was wiggled from side to side.

"Pepper's tail is secure, Mistress," Amber reported.

"Are the lips of her sex wet?"

Amber stepped to the side and bent at the waist to get a better look, "I think so, Mistress."

Susanna shook her head. "Not good enough. Kneel behind her, Amber. Use your tongue to confirm Pepper's state."

Amber obliged her Mistress without complaint, it was hardly a chore to use her tongue on the comely ponygirl, after all. Pepper was indeed wet before Amber's tongue slipped between then the lips of her pussy, and began lapping at her. She wondered how long she was supposed to do this before updating her Mistress, trying to glance to the side as she ate Pepper's pussy, but finding her Mistress's throne was positioned to the left of her, but also just far enough behind her that she couldn't see her without leaving her assigned task to turn a bit.

"Well? Is she fully aroused?" Susanna asked.

Amber pulled back and turned at the waist to face Mistress Susanna. "Yes, Mistress. I can confirm Pepper is in a clear state of arousal. Her lips are wet and delicious."

"Good, then she is ready to be punished. Stand up and come here."

"Yes, Mistress."

"Now, with which implements should Pepper be punished, hmm?"

Amber shrugged. "I'm not sure, Mistress. Which would you prefer?"

"Are you not, Amber? You must learn to make such choices on your own, and this seems like a good opportunity for you to practice your skills. Her punishment is due to be delivered, and you will give it, won't you, Amber?" Susanna replied.

Amber bowed her head, nodding agreement, "Yes, Mistress. As you wish."

"That's right. Pepper failed to truthfully answer my question, and now I expect you to induce her to do so. Do you think you can do that?"

If Pepper confessed how Amber had won and what she had promised the ponygirl, Amber knew her inducement would be revealed to their Mistress, and it seemed likely she'd be punished as well. On the other hand, if she failed to extract the truth from her, Amber could picture the situation being reversed. It would be Amber who was strapped to the bench and Pepper would be the one punisher her to correct her cunning behaviour.

It was a classic situation of being caught between a spanking bench and a hard paddle, Amber knew. Whatever she did, would likely result in punishment for her and Pepper both.

Amber swallowed hard and did her best to sound upbeat when she replied, "I'm sure that with your expert tutelage, Mistress, I could extract the truth you require from your submissive."

"This is a test for you, Amber, so I shall only guide you if I feel it is strictly necessary to do so," Susanna said. Gesturing to a rack of implements, she asked, "These are your tools. Which do you think will elicit the truth most expeditiously. Make your choice and begin Pepper's punishment. Quickly girl."

Amber hurried across the room and began to investigate the rack of impact play equipment that her Mistress had indicated. It was a beautifully crafted wooden rack, with abundant slots, hooks and rests for a wide variety of items that would thrill any sadist to use or any masochist to be the recipient of.

Honestly, she felt spoilt for choice. There were canes, small floggers, elegant carriage whips, a handful of tawses, several wooden rules of desk and classroom length, a selection of paddles made of wood or leather, or sometimes both. Some had words stitched into them or metal studs on one side.

Amber rejected the riding crops and the floggers, which she imagined Pepper would be able to tolerate quite admirably. Instead, she imagined how she might feel and the things that Susanna had already done to her. What would make her resistance to questioning crumble, and her secrets spill from her lips?

The tawse seemed likely to provide an impact that would soon bring Pepper to the point that she could no longer bear to stay silent.

Amber knew it must be painful as Susanna had offered Sugar and Candy the chance to torment her with a tawse or a school cane if she had failed a challenge. She had won, so hadn't yet experienced the tawse for herself, as such she wasn't sure it was wise to apply it to Pepper's beautiful cheeks.

Chewing her lip and sensing a growing impatience from her Mistress, Amber made her choice. She took hold of a handle and slowly withdrew a long, bamboo cane with a curved handle. This was no rough cane such as a gardener might use to support a plant, but a carefully selected and shaped tool of corporal punishment. It was thick enough to impact her palm audibly when she swished it down into her left hand but thin enough to sting.

Amber gave it a few practice swishes, like a youngster playing with a wooden sword, and it made an evil noise as it cut through the air. Pepper performed her part admirably, whinnying and testing her restraints as if she was afraid of the cane.

"Begin!" Susanna snapped, clearly impatient to watch Amber work.

The first stroke landed on Pepper's buttocks, lower than Amber had meant it to, a few seconds later. It was harder than she had intended and the line it scored just above the creases where Pepper's buttocks met her thighs, was close to scarlet.

Pepper's response was audible and shrill, but Amber knew better than to panic by now. Amber carefully lined up her next shot, and this time, her aim was true. The cane landed across both buttocks, causing another yelp from Pepper which was far more human than pony-like and a less lurid mark appeared.

Concentrating hard, Amber began to count out strokes of the cane, since Pepper was a pony and couldn't very well count them aloud for the woman who was dominating her, at the behest of their Mistress.

With each stroke, she struggled to maintain an even tempo, amount of force and keep her aim in check. The lines she left across the pony's buttocks crossed more often than Amber wanted them to, but she soon found herself able to distribute them down toward Pepper's thighs and up toward her back. They weren't perfectly parallel stripes as she imagined she wanted them to be, but she was rather chuffed that she didn't land any more strokes too far down or above the area, she was trying to aim for.

Amber would have liked to deliver a pattern that resembled lined paper for handwriting in terms of spacing and neatness. She felt a sense of achievement that her lines were as they were, but they crossed one another and made more of a deep pink rectangular splotch than a precisely lined up series of marks.

The effect on the previously pristine flesh of the young submissive's shapely bottom was wonderfully appealing. Amber wondered what that bottom would look like if she could divide it up with neat perpendicular stripes and hoped she'd one day get to find out. As her own feelings of satisfaction and arousal from submitting to Susanna deepened, she was also finding the thought of disciplining other young women, increasingly appealing.

By the time she was at fifteen strokes, it was apparent that Susanna wasn't going to stop her at some traditional number such as six of the best or a dozen hard strokes. She sensed that if she kept the strokes as they were, she could thoroughly redden Pepper's cheeks, without raising prominent welts. Reaching out, she confirmed that Pepper's bottom was as hot as the glowing skin seemed to suggest. Pepper shuddered at her touch.

"Will you talk, Pepper?" Amber asked, hopefully.

Pepper tossed her mane from side to side, refusing to break character.

Amber smiled to herself and licked her lips. For Pepper's sake, she knew the ponygirl should talk. But the act of punishing her was making her wet, even though she anticipated that breaking the girl would most likely result in her own punishment.

If Pepper had agreed to answer right then, she would not be able to deliver the next strokes of the cane, which had the girl whimpering in a most human fashion. As it was, she continued to discipline the stalwart ponygirl, with hard, even strokes. Amber found her brow creased as she concentrated intently on landing each stroke as close to her target as possible.

Pepper was vocally but wordlessly protesting each time the thing length of bamboo left an impression on her prominently displayed cheeks. Although she was stood to one side of the submissive, Amber could still see the telltale moisture on her lips that made them glisten enticingly even as the caning reddened her cheeks.

The state of her pussy was reliable confirmation of Pepper's continued state of arousal. Likewise, her breathing matched the pattern of a woman in a state of arousal, rather than in discomfort. While Pepper didn't sound close to orgasm, Amber was sure that Pudding would have been able to produce that result from the pony-girl, with the application of discipline. Pepper clearly had a taste for such games.

Mistress Susanna stood up and made her way to the other side of the bench, watching Amber's progress as she beat the unfortunate ponygirl.

"Your accuracy is coming along nicely, Amber. I don't think Pepper here is going to give in when you are pulling your strikes as much as you are though. Why don't you bring it up a notch, eh? Lay it on a little harder, see if you can bring tears to her eyes, hmm?" Susanna advised.

Pepper thrashed uselessly at her bindings, but Amber planted her left hand firmly at the base of her spine and held the wriggling submissive in place. The ponygirl was powerless to resist. The only way she could get out of this was to break character as a pony and beg for mercy as a human.

"Yes, Mistress. As you command," Amber said. She chewed her lip as she took aim once more and let rip with six strokes of the cane.

Pepper howled, and Ginger gasped in shock. Then Pepper gamely whinnied again, and Amber knew she hadn't won yet. Susanna nodded at her, and Amber continued with the punishment at the new level encouraged by her boss. Pepper took it well, Amber thought, indeed, despite the audible distress she gave voice to, her buttocks shifted, straining up to meet the kiss of Amber's bamboo. The slut was enjoying her own suffering. Pepper wasn't merely aroused, she was eager for more.

Amber was only too happy to oblige. She would not have thought it even a fortnight ago, but the act of disciplining this willing young woman was intensely satisfying to her. She wished she had another submissive kneeling before her right now, worshipping her pussy with a slippery tongue as she caned Pepper.

"You will answer, Mistress Susanna, Pepper, or I swear you will be unable to sit for a week," Amber boasted.

Pepper shook her head slowly, and Susanna smiled as Amber altered her aim and landed the next six stripes just below her target area. The fresh patch of skin was barely marked from the occasional errant stroke, and by the fifth landing on the sensitive area, Pepper had tears streaming freely down her cheeks.

Susanna moved to the head of the punishment horse and took a firm grip of Pepper's mane of hair, plaited to resemble a pony, as was only fitting. The Mistress of the house crouched a little, tilting her submissive's head back and up, and locking eyes with her even as Amber continued to cane her.

"Will you talk now, Pepper? Reveal your secrets, and this punishment will end. You don't have to suffer like this. You have stayed in character well, my dear, and I am very proud of you for doing so. It thrills me to watch you suffer for me like this, to bravely play your role as a ponygirl and refuse to talk. And yet I think you are close to the edge and must talk soon, no?" Susanna asked.

Pepper tried to shake her head but nodded slightly, finally appearing to give in. Amber stopped, and Susanna raised an eyebrow. "I didn't tell you to stop caning this slut, did I, Amber? Continue until I tell you otherwise. Pepper, stick your bottom up as high as you can for Amber, there's a good girl."

Pepper gave a throaty whimper of anguish but obediently did as she was told and Amber marvelled at the control that Susanna had over her. The ponygirl presented her tormented cheeks as best she could, a most enticing target for her to discipline. Once she had, Amber did as her Mistress commanded as well.

"Did you make an extra effort to win the race for Amber, Pepper?"

"Yes, Mistress," the ponygirl cried out between sobs and strokes of Amber's cane.

"Did she ask you to do so?"

"Yes, Mistress."

"Did you she offer you some kind of bribe or inducement to outshine Ginger?" Susanna asked.

"Yes, Mistress she did."

"What did she promise you?" Susanna said, smiling as Amber's cane elicited another wail of shock from Pepper.

"She... she promised me pleasure, Mistress. She promised to sneak out one night and bring me off with her tongue if I could beat Ginger," Pepper wailed.

"Did she now? Is this true, Amber?" Susanna asked.

"Yes, Mistress."

Susanna stood up and clapped her hands triumphantly. "Excellent, you may stop disciplining her now, Amber. About your choice of implement..." Susanna began.

"Yes, Mistress?" Amber asked.

"You chose... wisely."

"Thank you, Mistress," Amber said, gratefully returning the cane to the rack after wiping it down with a cloth.

"Now, help my reposition the bench," Susanna demanded. Together, she and Amber turned the bench ninety degrees so that Pepper was facing the throne.

Once she was happy with the new positioning, Susanna alighted her throne again, slouching a little so that she could spread her knees apart. Beckoning to Ginger, she casually gave her an order, "Loosen my jodhpurs and lick me to orgasm, Ginger."

The ponygirl did just that with practised ease and a lustful grin in her eyes. She sighed contentedly as her tongue worked between her lips.

"Isn't she a good girl, Amber?" Susanna asked as Ginger tongued her vigorously.

"Yes, Mistress. I'm sure all the ladies you choose soon learn to be good girls," Amber replied.

"In most cases, that is true. Some still seek to defy me or by cheeky though, don't they, Amber?"

"No doubt, Mistress."

"Speaking of which, you may make up for your borderline unsportsmanlike behaviour by removing your clothing and laying down with your head under Ginger's hips. I'm sure Ginger would like an orgasm from your wicked tongue, and Pepper will learn a lesson from watching her receive the pleasure she was promised, don't you think?" Susanna said.

Amber nodded and began to strip. "As you wish, Mistress."

Ginger lifted her head for a fraction of a second to add, "Yes, Mistress. Thank you, Mistress."

Pepper did not speak.

Within moments the tableau was set. Mistress Susanna reigned on her throne, while her ponygirl Ginger gleefully licked her pussy for all she was worth. Amber lay on her back, while Ginger's hips were lowered until she was almost sitting on her face, and her tongue was buried in the young submissive's pussy.

Susanna ordered Amber to improve the show for the still bound Pepper, by spreading her knees apart and playing with her own pussy. Unlike Ginger, however, she was denied the satisfaction of her own orgasm and threatened with most harsh punishments if she did cum without the permission of her Mistress.

Poor Pepper had merely to look on while Amber rode the waves of each orgasm, almost to the peak before their Mistress ruined it with a harsh word or a flick of her carriage whip, skillfully skirting over Ginger's buttocks, to sting Amber's thighs.

Amber could hear the muffled screams she gave at this, even as her eyes stung with salty tears and her tongue worked hard at Ginger's delicious lips.

Although Pepper and Amber had won the race, Ginger and Mistress Susanna felt the most satisfaction at the end of their ponygirl session.

When finally their Mistress was satiated, she showed Amber how to hose down the ponygirls, in a shower room specially set up for them, then towel them off and send back to their stalls.

With Amber still entirely nude, they made their way back to the house, the assistant following a half-step behind her imperious boss, in awe of the older woman who now controlled her life.

"Mistress, may I ask about Ginger and Pepper?"

"Ask what?"

Taking that response as implied permission, Amber pushed on. "When we got to the stables, they were already dressed up. Do they spend all their time like that?"

"Hmm. Do you mean 24 hours a day, 7 days a week? No. I know some people who find that a thrill but we experimented with their roleplaying as ponygirls and settled on a system that satisfies us all. I have a buzzer I can ring from the house that notifies them when I'm visiting, and a clock can give them a countdown if need be. That way they can get in character before I arrive," Susanna replied.

"Who dresses them up?"

"They dress each other."

"Can I ask what they do when you aren't here to play with them? What do they do when you're in the City, or you just don't have the time or inclination?"

Susanna stopped and turned to face Amber. "They have their own work to do, Amber. Just as you do. They keep the stables in order, obviously but they both have graphic and web design skills they use to support my companies. There is a bedroom they share above the stables, well, a small flat with a bathroom and kitchen and the work from there. Anything else?"

"No, Mistress. Thank you for explaining it," Amber said, then paused for a moment. She cocked her head and went on, "Except. Do they wait for you for all their pleasure, or do they play with each other or Candy and Sugar, Mistress?"

Her boss sighed dramatically, and in a blur of motion, she moved in close with Amber, causing her to backpedal swiftly until she found herself pushed up against a wall that she thought belonged to the kitchen garden.

Susanna halted any further conversation with a deep, possessive kiss, her tongue slipping between Amber's lips. Her Mistress gripped her wrists and moved Amber's arms above her head, as she claimed her mouth. Her jodhpurs and blouse felt rough against Amber's naked skin as Susanna made it clear she was in charge.

Amber felt like a toy or a doll, posed and played with, as Susanna captured both her crossed wrists with her strong right hand, continuing to passionately lay kisses over her neck and breasts.

Without speaking, Susanna stroked her left hand over Amber's breasts, stroking and pinching her nipples, then ran it down between them, over her firm belly and between her legs. The questing fingers of her Mistress soon buried themselves between her wet lips and Amber gasped loudly as she felt her body respond.

It was mere moments before Susanna had drawn an explosive orgasm from Amber, one that left her panting hard with the heat and swiftness of the act. As quickly as her boss had taken control of her, she let go of Amber's wrists, and the young assistant sank to her knees in a post-orgasmic daze.

Susanna roughly grabbed her hair, and tilted her head up, staring down at Amber with her most imperious expression. "You all await my pleasure. Every hour, of every day. Ponygirls, maids, cooks and personal assistants. You serve my whims, cook my food, provide my pleasures and endure my discipline. All for the chance to please your Mistress. Do you know why?"

"No, Mistress," Amber breathed.

"Because your lusts run parallel to my own and it excites you to find out when they will next intersect. You all want my attention, my permission to behave as you do, you crave my orders to use your tongues and fingers to please each other, don't you, Amber?"

"Yes."

"Did it thrill you when I made you eat Ginger's pussy?"

"Yes."

"Make you wet when you caned Pepper?"

"Yes."

"Shock you when I pushed you against that wall?"

"Yes."

"Excite you when I thrust my fingers into your pussy and took you roughly?"

"Yes, Mistress."

Susanna hauled her back to her feet by her hair and Amber winced, as she was held against the wall again. "Do you think Ginger and Pepper play with each other while I am not present?" she asked in a throaty whisper, her cheek pressed against Amber's and her breath hot on her ear.

Amber shook her head, cautiously, "No, Mistress."

"No?"

Amber reconsidered. "Not unless you order it, Mistress. They are here to serve at your pleasure."

"Good answer," Susanna said. "Do you intend to go through with your promise to sneak out and pleasure Pepper?"

Swallowing hard, Amber shook her head. "No, Mistress."

"Why not?"

"Because I serve your pleasure, not hers," Amber answered hopefully, "or mine."

"Hah," Susanna scoffed. "Do you really, minx?"

"Yes, Mistress," Amber claimed.

"That's right. You do. You're lucky I don't punish you properly for making a promise you aren't entitled to keep, minx," Susanna growled.

"Yes, Mistress. I'm sorry, Mistress. I won't do it again," Amber promised.

Susanna laughed. "I don't believe all that, but if you do, I won't likely give you a free pass again. You understand what I'm saying?"

Amber nodded. "If I promise things like that again, you'll punish me, spanking me so hard I'll come from that alone and then make me lick your pussy for hours to apologise."

At that, Susanna chuckled. "I'm not sure how much of a punishment that would be for you, Amber but I'll bear your idea in mind."

"Yes, Mistress."

"As for your promise today, I expect you to honour it, of course."

Amber nodded but didn't speak, waiting for her Mistress to clarify her instruction, as she sensed she would.

"You will go to the stables tomorrow night, after I have finished with you, and spend the rest of the night pleasuring Pepper and Ginger in the way they see fit. You will submit to them as if they were me, and if they wish, they may punish you. I expect you will have an uncomfortable and exhausting night satisfying those two and they'll use you like the slut you so clearly are until none of you can stay awake. What do you say to that, Amber?" Susanna asked, one eyebrow raised in anticipation of a cheeky response.

Amber licked her lips and dropped to her knees before her Mistress, bowing her head until her forehead almost touched the ground. "I serve at the pleasure of my Mistress. Always and with pride," she said.

"As it should be."

CHAPTER 4

"Show me what you've done so far," Susanna said, looking over Amber's shoulder at her monitors.

"I've been working through the guest list and checking which ones have confirmed," Amber replied, demonstrating on the screen that she'd been ticking off the responses.

"Has everyone responded to the original invitation?"

"No, Mistress. These ones I've highlighted in yellow haven't replied yet that I can find."

"Six is too many, compose an email to them, and show it to me to check it before you send it. Ask them to respond by the end of the day tomorrow. If anyone still hasn't responded, we'll phone them, and I'll speak to them in person."

"Yes, Mistress. I should be done with this shortly. What should I do next?"

"Check on the deliveries we're expecting, if it's been shipped to us, confirm it's arrived. If it's arriving on the day, call the supplier and check if there are any problems. I've had too many soirees fall flat because the champagne or chocolate coated strawberries or cake didn't arrive," Susanna said.

Amber made notes as her boss talked and then glanced up at her to see if anything else was coming. Susanna had the off-centre gaze of someone who was sifting through their mind trying to remember something, so she waited patiently.

"Also, check up on Pudding. She's not doing all the catering, but she might need ingredients, or fresh produce or something. For the party to go well, it's crucial that Pudding is in a good mood and not feeling the effects of stress. She does fret so, and if there's a problem, she won't ask for help until she's failed to solve it, which just leads to whole stress. Then it becomes a thing. And I hate things," Susanna said, visibly shuddering at the thought of it. Amber bit her lip and turned her face away to hide her amusement.

With a little cough, she squeaked a reply, "Yes, Mistress."

"Good, let me know if you have any questions."

Amber nodded and began checking for responses from the guests as Susanna returned to her office.

It took less than an hour to confirm that almost everyone invited had already responded. A few noted special requirements such as dietary restrictions or allergies they wanted to notify them of. Fortunately, most were minor, but Amber made sure to take special note of the potentially dangerous allergies so that she could check the menu for peanuts and the like.

The email to ask the three outstanding guests if they could confirm whether or not they would be attending the weekend took a little longer. Amber wasn't quite sure how to approach it. It seems Mistress Susanna wanted these people to come to the event and expected that they would, but the fact they hadn't responded suggested they weren't the most organised of friends or colleagues.

Since Amber didn't know the purpose of the party, she wasn't sure if it was a business problem or a social problem if these people didn't come. Either way, she drafted and redrafted the email several times, trying to strike a balance between asking and insisting that the guests respond. Eventually, she had to send it to Susanna to be checked and hope she'd done an excellent job.

Once she had done that she began to go through the list of orders that Susanna had given her. Alcohol and soft drinks certainly weren't going to be a problem. Amber sincerely hoped that her boss was restocking the mansion's pantry because these deliveries contained enough booze to render the entire guest list insensible.

Given the number of people on the list whose names bore such formal honorifics as Lady, Dame and Madam, Amber didn't think they were going to have an undignified weekend of drunken debauchery. All she could really glean from the guest list was that they were all-powerful women, and they were bringing one or two people with them. Those people were only identified by an initial and their surname. They could be staff or family members or spouses for all Amber knew.

There wasn't time for her to dig into their backgrounds online and see if she could identify anyone though, and for the tasks she'd been given, it didn't matter anyway. Regardless of this being a business or a social event, Amber needed to do her best to ensure it went off without a hitch.

Her boss, Susanna, might tolerate a small problem, but Mistress Susanna would exact her revenge for sure if anything went wrong because of a mistake Amber made. Just the thought of what that would entail for such a public failure, made Amber squirm uncomfortably in her expensive office chair. She shook her head to clear it of diverting thoughts and got back to work.

Amber had made a couple of preemptive phone calls to suppliers before a notification popped up that Susanna had replied to her email. The response was brief, a couple of minor tweaks her boss requested and Amber was ready to send it. She filled in the recipient's email addresses and sent the mail.

Then it was time to finish off the supplier checks, which didn't take long. Finally, she was ready to tick off the last task on her list, and there was plenty of time before the end of a typical working day.

Amber stood up and stretched her back and neck.

Then with a cheerful grin, she went to the kitchen to speak to Pudding.

"Five bags of self-raising flour?"

"Umm. Yes, we've got those."

"Three bags of raisins and two of sultanas?" Pudding asked, crossing out the flour.

"Yes," Amber replied, pulling them out of the box the groceries had been delivered in.

"Wonderful. That's everything I needed then," Pudding said a little gruffly.

"It seems so. Is there anything else I can do to help?"

Pudding sighed. "No, not unless you're a qualified sous chef."

Amber laughed. "No, I'm afraid not. Anything that doesn't involve cooking?"

"No I'm just anxious about the event," Pudding said, looking up at Amber, "Mistress Susanna's parties always make me tense. I can't help worrying that I might get something wrong and ruin the event."

"Maybe a shoulder rub if you're feeling tense?" Amber suggested.

Pudding shook her head. "That doesn't work with me. I don't think Mistress sent you here to give me the kind of stress relief I enjoy."

Amber giggled. "I think she wants you to be relaxed for the weekend. Maybe she wouldn't mind if I gave you some pleasure."

"It sounds more like you want to put that wicked tongue of yours to good use than you want to help me," Pudding said. "That isn't my favourite way to relax anyway."

"No? I thought that relaxed everyone," Amber teased.

"It does, I suppose. But what really helps me find peace is a nice pair of rosy cheeks and a pretty girl bawling her eyes out over my lap."

"You'd find it more relaxing to just spank me?" Amber asked incredulously.

Pudding laughed at that. "Oh, after the spanking, the oral sex. I wouldn't let an opportunity to press my lips to your sweet mouth pass me by."

"You do seem awfully stressed about the party, perhaps you should ask Mistress to borrow me?" Amber said with a giggle.

Pudding cocked her head and stood up, beckoning to Amber,

"Alright minx, come with me." She led Amber into her suite and picked up a phone, dialling the intercom.

Amber found her chest tightening in anticipation. In truth she'd just been teasing Pudding, intending to report back to her boss that the cook wasn't in the best of moods. She hadn't meant to volunteer for a vigorous spanking to finish off her workday.

It came as no surprise when Pudding said, "Mistress, I wondered if I might beg the use of Amber for a while?"

Pudding nodded and passed the phone handset to Amber with an anticipatory gleam in her eye, "Mistress wants a word."

"Mistress?"

"Amber, what have you been up to?"

"Just doing as you asked and checking that Pudding has everything she needs for the weekend, Mistress," Amber replied.

"And does she?"

"No, I don't think so," Amber said.

"Does she want to spank you? Good and hard?"

"Yes, Mistress."

"I'm sure she'd put your tongue to good use after that," Susanna replied, "while the tears streamed down your cheeks, I imagine."

"I believe that is her plan, Mistress."

"Does the prospect excite you, Amber?" Susanna asked.

"Yes, Mistress, it does," Amber admitted.

"I see, then who am I to stand in the way of Pudding getting some much-needed stress relief. You'll do as she says. I want you back up here at a quarter to five at the latest though," Susanna said, "now pass the phone back to Pudding, there's a good little slut."

Amber handed the phone over to Pudding whose face lit up as she listened to their Mistress.

"Thank you, Mistress. I'm sure I'll feel much more relaxed about the weekend soon," Pudding said. The cook listened to the response and then obediently replied, "Yes, of course. As you wish, Mistress."

Pudding put the phone down but not in the cradle. The cook wasn't hanging up, she just rested the handset on the desk, the line for Mistress Susanna's office was still open so she could hear everything. Amber considered that, chewing her lip for a moment, while Pudding watched her.

"Are you ready, Amber?" Pudding finally asked.

"Yes, Pudding."

"Then why don't you take off all your clothes so I can appreciate your beautiful young body."

Amber nodded and began slowly, teasingly, stripping off her clothes.

Pudding shook her head, "No, don't flirt with me. I want you naked now."

"Yes, Pudding," Amber said, hurrying her unbuttoning up. She was nude and turning slowly at Puddings command in a few moments, showing off her body for the cook.

"You are a beautiful young woman, Amber. I'm going to enjoy you. Thank you for volunteering to help me wind down. I suppose that might make another woman go easy on you, but I will be looking to see your cheeks moist with tears," Pudding said. "I enjoy spanking a younger woman, but I simply adore hearing them weeping and wailing. It's so exciting. If you want a shred of comfort in that, perhaps it would help to be reminded that my preferred instrument is my own palm and not a cane or whip. Now, why don't you come here and put yourself over my knee so I can begin?"

Amber bent herself over Pudding's lap, her knees resting on the velvet upholstery of the chaise longue Pudding favoured. There was no preamble, beyond what Pudding had already said. She simply began to spank Amber, and she didn't offer the young woman any build up from a light smack to a fierce impact.

Instead, Pudding went straight for a hard spanking from the first. Her left hand was in the small of Amber's back, holding her in place even before Pudding's right hand made Amber cry out in pain and begin to wriggle.

"You can struggle if you want, Amber but I'm not letting go. If it were really too much for you, you'd use your safeword," Pudding stated flatly.

When the prospect of getting a spanking this late in the afternoon had first been mooted, Amber had imagined a long session of carefully progressive impact play, building her slowly toward a climactic outpouring of tears. Instead, she could immediately feel her eyes watering. Pudding was taking her frustrations out on her bottom, and she could picture it in her mind's eye, glowing hot and deep red.

Her cheeks were warming up rapidly, and Pudding was setting a fearsome tempo, like a metronome set to a hundred beats per minute. The thought made Amber let forth an involuntary giggle, which was immediately interrupted by the next smack.

"Do you think this is funny?" Pudding demanded, "You offered yourself up for a spanking, and you're getting a good firm going over, and you find something amusing in this?"

Amber gasped, as Pudding stopped for a moment, taking a firm grip on her hair and tilting her head up. "Well? Answer me, girl!" the cook demanded.

"No, Pudding. It's not funny."

"Then, why did you laugh?" Pudding demanded, punctuating each word with another smack.

"I'm sorry," Amber managed. "Your spanks are so fast and rhythmical I couldn't help thinking they could be set to a high tempo metronome."

"Well," Pudding huffed, "that's not necessarily a bad idea now you mention it. A metronome might be a good training tool for spanking girls like you. But there's nothing funny about this punishment you're getting."

Pudding followed that statement up with another round of spanking and Amber couldn't help the words that came spilling out of her mouth a few moments later. "You're not punishing me, though. You just needed to relax, and spanking girls does that for you. I haven't done anything wrong."

"You cheeky little minx!" Pudding cried. "You're just like Candy and Sugar, always denying that you're naughty girls, acting as if you're all sweetness and light. Do you think I don't know you're always getting up to mischief you naughty girl?" Pudding gave her six more spanks. "What do you say to that?"

"I swear, I've done nothing to be punished for. You can spank me if it gets you off, but I've been good, I promise!" Amber protested.

"You little fibber. I don't believe you. I bet you can't get through the morning without doing something naughty. Shall I ask Mistress hmm?" Pudding asked.

Amber shook her head, as her spanking resumed, biting her lip to keep from squealing as Pudding's firm hand punished her bottom.

"I thought not. How gullible do you imagine I am, eh? If Mistress didn't think you needed a punishment, she'd hardly have let me have you, would she?"

Amber wasn't convinced of that, and though she immediately regretted it, she blurted out a denial, "Mistress loves my suffering just as much as you do. That's why she's listening on the phone, so she can hear me getting spanked and enjoy it. She doesn't care if I've done anything wrong, she just needs an excuse to play her games with us."

Pudding gasped in horror. "How dare you! The Mistress would never make up an excuse just to have you, or Candy or Sugar or the ponies punished. Mistress Susanna isn't like that. She's a very fair woman, and she looks after you all, despite your sluttish ways. I don't know what you did, but the fact I'm punishing you for it means you must have done something naughty."

Amber couldn't get out another word as Pudding delivered the next round of spanking. She was too busy howling and squeezing her eyes shut to hold back the tears, with limited success. When Pudding let up the pace to take a few deep breaths, Amber found her body wracked with sobs and her chest heaving as she hauled in great lungfuls of her.

"Yes. You should cry, for saying such unkind things about my Mistress, Amber. You might protest your innocence, my girl, but I know what's really in your heart."

"What's that?" Amber snivelled defiantly.

"You know whatever it was that you did to deserve another punishment from me, though you might deny it. You wanted to be punished for it too, didn't you?"

"No!"

"You offered yourself up as a sacrificial lamb, my dear," Pudding cooed softly.

Amber shook her head. "Don't shake your head, I can tell you wanted to be chastised, it's obvious to me, Amber."

"It's not true," Amber claimed, as tears streamed down her cheeks. Her denial didn't ring true to her, and she didn't think for a minute that Pudding was convinced either.

"Really? Am I mistaken?" Pudding remarked doubtfully. Another smack landed on her cheeks, and Amber blurted, "Yes!"

Pudding's hand didn't leave her cheeks when it landed the next time. Instead, it slipped down the curve of her burning bottom and between her thighs. Amber didn't protest or try to squeeze her legs together. Instead, she parted her thighs to admit the cook's questing fingers which smoothly plunged between her wet lips.

Amber uttered an entirely different type of noise as Pudding's expert fingers parter her sopping wet lips and took charge of her aroused clit.

"In my experience, Amber, a girl who is this wet, is getting exactly what she wanted in her heart, even if she denies it. Would you like to come?" Pudding asked.

"Yes, please, Pudding," Amber admitted, sagging in defeat.

Pudding chuckled, and her fingers performed an intricate dance which had her panting in lust in short order. Amber was soon floating on the edge of a much-needed orgasm, her bottom still fiery from Pudding's disciplinary efforts.

"Admit you deserved this punishment, Amber."

Amber shook her head.

"Admit it, and I'll let you come," Pudding insisted.

Amber shook her head again, but Pudding's fingers held her on the edge of her climax, even when she tried to move her hips to send herself over the edge. The wily cook was playing her like a familiar musical instrument, keeping her in precisely the state she wanted.

"Admit you were naughty, Amber and you can have what you want," Pudding offered.

Amber couldn't take any more of the cook's teasing and gave in, "Yes, I admit it. I deserved my punishment."

"Yes, you did. You're just as naughty as the maids aren't you?"

"Yes, Pudding," Amber groaned, although she wasn't sure that was true. She was pretty sure she had a lot more to learn about being naughty before she could match Candy and Sugar.

"Are you sorry for telling lies about Mistress?"

"Yes, I'm sorry," Amber admitted, this time with the conviction of the truthful. If Mistress Susanna disciplined her or had the staff do so, it was because she needed it. In any case, even if she hadn't bribed Pepper against the spirit of the race, Amber couldn't deny the effect that Pudding's spanking of her bottom had produced.

"Then come for me, you eager little minx," Pudding said, her fingers dancing to a different beat over Amber's aching clit. In a few seconds, she pushed Amber over the cliff into a tremendous orgasm that had her crying out in ecstasy.

Pudding kept her fingers working as Amber rode the wave of repeated orgasms that she demanded from the younger woman. When it was finally done, the cook pushed her off her knee, and Amber found herself on the floor. The older woman reached out with her left hand and took a firm grip of Amber's hair, roughly manhandling her into position. Amber was dragged around, and her head tilted up to look at Pudding, even while she was still coming down from her intense climax.

Without preamble, Amber found her mouth filled with the wet fingers of Pudding's right hand, slick with her own juices and heady with her musk. "Suck my fingers clean. I know you filthy young things love that," Pudding ordered, her eyes flashing with lust as Amber readily complied.

When she was done, Pudding stood up and shrugged quickly out of her dress. Under the simple flowery garment, she wore a set of lingerie that was a stark contrast with the dress that would have looked right at home on the apocryphal 1950's housewife.

Stockings and suspenders were teamed with bra and panties, all matching and all designed to provocatively frame her body and invoke lust in the lucky observer.

"Take off my panties, Amber," Pudding ordered, and the younger woman did as she was told, shuffling forward on her knees and hooking her thumbs into either side of the underwear.

Amber licked her lips as Pudding's pussy was exposed to her gaze and felt a pang of longing as she had to look down and wait for the disciplinarian to step out of the silky panties. Once she had them in her hand, her eyes slid back up Pudding's shapely legs, to the inviting spot the panties had concealed. Amber drank in the sexy view for a brief moment.

It was a struggle to tear her eyes away from Pudding's delightfully bare pussy and the enticing glimmer of arousal that she could see, but Amber just about managed it. On hands and knees, she crossed the room and carefully placed the panties on a large footstool. Naked as she was, that would have given Pudding a great view of her reddened bottom.

That was simply a side benefit of her action, though. The reason she had taken such care was that Pudding's lingerie wasn't a set of garments that should be strewn about the floor, during a rush to get frisky. They were expensive items that needed to be cared for. Even if Amber were inclined to treat a partner's lingerie with casual disinterest, she knew that if the set belonged to her, it would be a treasured item of her wardrobe. Presumably, they were a favourite of Pudding's as she couldn't imagine the cook wearing undergarments like this every day.

Pudding seemed to approve of her care and attention. "Good girl. Now, crawl back over here, and kneel before me."

Slowly, to draw it out, Amber slinked back across the floor, not leaving her hands and knees. She took care to sway her hips and dip her chest low enough that her nipples brushed the carpet.

"Mmm. So you do know how you should behave after all," Pudding said as Amber reached the spot she had indicated and drew herself up on her knees, with her hands behind her, wrists crossed in the small of her back and chest thrust up.

"I'm trying to learn, Pudding," Amber said earnestly, looking down at the cook's expensive, kitten heeled shoes as seemed the most respectful pose to adopt.

"I'm glad to hear it," Pudding replied, stepping forward and slipping a hand into Amber's hair to tilt her head back. She planted her feet either side of Amber's hips and pulled the younger woman's head firmly up between her thighs.

Amber's tongue found Pudding's wet lips, and she was pleased to hear the cook breathe out a sigh of untrammelled lust as she went to work.

"My oh my, you have been learning, haven't you? Is it true that you had never been with a woman until you came into Mistress Susanna's service?" Pudding asked, relenting for a moment on the firm pressure that held Amber's face against her pussy.

Amber took a deep breath and licked her lips, "Yes, Pudding. It's true. I've been missing out on so much."

"Yes, you certainly have been. What a tragedy it is that it took until now for you to experience all that women have to offer you," Pudding lamented. "I'm glad that you now serve our Mistress, Amber. Your tongue is so willing, and you take your punishments well. I'm quite sure that Mistress Susanna is enjoying you a great deal. I do hope you are able to carry out your work duties well. It's frustrating when Mistress has to let a promising girl go because she can eat pussy well but can't manage her actual job."

Amber nodded a fraction in agreement as her tongue continued to lap hungrily at Pudding's delicious pussy. The older woman tasted different from the other staff that Mistress Susanna had ordered her to pleasure. Idly she wondered if there was an equivalent to a wine tasting for pussies. Could an expert tell who she was licking while blindfolded, perhaps?

"Yes, that's really very good for such a short time for you to learn how to eat pussy, my dear. I must commend you on your diligence," Pudding managed to say between moans and deep breaths. Amber's mouth twitched at the corners in a half-smile as she continued to please the cook.

"Oh, yes. Very good indeed. Should you encounter any difficulties in your work, do let me know if I can help, Amber. I worked in a similar field for a while before I found my calling as a cook, and I've worked in enough kitchens and catering jobs to know all about efficiency and productivity. And, of course, self-discipline as well as giving discipline," Pudding chuckled. "Mmmm. I would much rather help you in your free time than allow you to fail to meet the high standards that Mistress sets. Just ask if you think I can help you, I'm positive we can't afford to lose your tongue for want of some skills a personal assistant needs."

Pudding allowed Amber a moment of respite to reply, "Thank you, Pudding. That's a lovely offer, I'll be sure to take you up on it if need be."

"Good. I'm sure that you'll rise to the challenges Mistress sets you and she's an incredibly generous boss. Mistress Susanna takes such good care of us, and the benefits of working for her are amazing," Pudding replied. The older woman had taken Amber's head between her hands now and began to grind her pussy against the submissive's tongue, as she let rip with throaty exhortations to make her come.

Amber was enthusiastic about doing just that. The filthy things that came out of Pudding's mouth as she licked at her seemed entirely at odds with the woman's usual demeanour but turned her on massively. Knowing that Mistress was probably listening to every word added no small frisson of pleasure.

Was Mistress Susanna heading toward her own crescendo, leaned back in her office chair and rubbing at her clit with fingers that were slick with arousal? Would she come at the same time as Pudding, as she heard her cook use her personal assistant's mouth?

The thought of that made Amber wish she could touch herself, but this moment wasn't about her. It was about serving Pudding's needs and through her, serving their Mistress. The spanking had really hurt, and her tormented cheeks rested painfully against her heels as she knelt between the cook's thighs, working her tongue hard and fast against her nub.

It was all worth it, the pain, the embarrassment of being shared like this. Every doubt and moment of anxiety was washed away by the desire to serve her Mistress, and bring pleasure to Pudding so that the party would be a huge success. Amber needed to please Susanna, with every fibre of her being and it was no hardship to do so as the sexual plaything of her boss's cook. Nor, she remembered, would it be a bad thing to serve the ponygirls later. Or the maids if Mistress should choose it.

As Pudding finally began to climax, and her juices ran freely down Amber's chin, she knew that she had found her true calling as Mistress Susanna's lesbian personal assistant.

Amber wondered what else lay in store for her that evening as Pudding pulled her to her feet, and ordered her to pick up her clothes. The clock on the desk showed that they were out of time and the cook shooed her away, bidding her return to their Mistress as she picked up the headset and said, "Thank you, Mistress. That was just what I needed. Amber is on her way to you now."

Pudding flashed a grateful smile at the naked young woman as she hurried from the room.

Amber scurried through the house, naked and anointed with the scent of sex, keen to reach Mistress Susanna's office before her time ran out.

Mistress Susanna must have heard the door to the outer office open because she called out from her own office before they had even shut behind Amber.

"Amber, get in here now, I have need of you," Mistress called out.

Amber knew she was in a state and hesitated for a second before throwing her bundle of clothing on her chair and stepping up to the doors. She would have preferred to clean up, but it wasn't as if Mistress didn't know what she'd been doing just a minute or two ago. If Mistress Susanna wanted her to come in now, making herself look presentable probably wasn't an option.

Amber took a deep breath, straightened up and put her shoulders back, pushing her bosom up, and opened the double doors wide.

"You called, Mistress?" she announced, as she stepped into the office and closed the doors behind her, doing her best to forget the state she was in.

Amber had to turn away from the desk to see her Mistress, who had taken up a position on one of the expensive leather sofas.

Susanna was entirely naked, one foot resting on a plus stool. A stylish and expensive looking phone that would have been at home in the 1920s was on a side table next to her. The handset was off the hook, resting on the table, much as Pudding's had been downstairs, only with a much more expensive phone.

Amber bit her lip as she imagined Pudding listening eagerly on the other end of the line. It was just as delicious a thought as the reverse had been. Was the cook going to hear her punished again, Amber wondered?

"Yes. I want to use your tongue. I do hope Pudding hasn't worn you out. She hasn't, has she?" Mistress Susanna asked, raising a quizzical eyebrow.

Amber shook her head, "No, Mistress. I'm getting quite used to it now."

Susanna nodded, her fingers continuing to work at her pussy. She lifted her other hand and pointed at the floor, swirling her finger around in a circle. "Show me what Pudding has done to you," she ordered.

Amber nodded and came a few steps closer, standing near the footstool so that her Mistress could get a good view. She began to turn on the spot, slowly and smoothly, performing a complete revolution and then carrying on until her back was to her Mistress.

To show off her bottom, Amber planted her feet apart, and slowly bent at the waist, leaning forward and pushing her buttocks up as she slid her hands down her thighs until they rested just below her knees.

In this pose, her body was displayed in a particularly lewd fashion, with her pussy and her puckered hole both clearly displayed for her Mistress, who made appreciative sounds. A few moments later, the noise of a digital camera made it clear that Susanna was recording the state of her bottom for posterity.

"Did Pudding hurt your bottom, Amber? You've gone a nice dark shade of pink," Susanna asked.

"Yes, Mistress."

"And you cried, didn't you?"

"Yes, Mistress."

"Did it hurt too much? Was it excruciatingly painful?"

"No, not too much, although it was painful, Mistress," Amber agreed.

"How did you feel about it?"

"I felt. I mean, I was proud, Mistress. To know I was helping Pudding relax and serving you," Amber explained.

"That's good. I want you to be proud of your submission, Amber. If you are suffering for me, I want you to know that it serves a purpose. I don't want you to think I would punish you for no reason," Mistress Susanna said. Amber could hear the faint sound of her Mistress playing with her pussy, the soft, wet noises just audible in the quiet spaces between her remarks.

"I understand, Mistress."

"Good girl."

"Mistress?"

"Yes, Amber? What is it?"

Amber licked her lips and cleared her throat, trying to find the words.

"Spit it out, beautiful. What's on your mind?" Susanna asked forcefully.

"If you wanted to punish me. To hurt me or, make me cry. I mean. If you wanted to spank me or something, but I hadn't done anything wrong. Well. You can do that, Mistress. If it would please you. I'm yours. I want to make you happy, even if I must suffer to do it," Amber stammered.

"Are you asking to be punished for something, Amber?"

Amber shook her head, "No, Mistress."

"Come over here and kneel down young lady," Susanna said. Amber stood up, wobbling a little as the blood rushed to her head. She blinked a few times and shook her head to clear her vision, then turned around and fell to her knees next to the sofa, where her Mistress was pointing.

"What are you telling me, Amber."

Amber swallowed. "That if it gives you pleasure to cane me or flog me, you should, Mistress. You don't have to have an infraction to mind if you want to punish me. I think I," Amber paused and corrected herself, "no, I mean, I know that I like it."

"You like the pain?"

"Not that, Mistress. Not really. I like that you like my pain. I like that you are pleased when I'm obedient. It's exciting," Amber blushed.

"Did you feel the same way about Pudding liking your suffering?" Susanna asked.

"A little, Mistress but mostly it was nice because I knew you wanted it," Amber said. She looked up at Mistress with a sly smile, "And knowing you were listening on the phone was really sexy too."

"I thought you might like that, you naughty little exhibitionist," Susanna laughed. "I'm glad to hear you are so eager to please me, Amber," her Mistress said, sitting up and cupping Amber's chin with fingers wet from her nether lips.

Mistress Susanna leaned forward, and ran her tongue from Amber's jawline, up the trail of salt left by her tears. "Your suffering is delicious, my sweet. Your bottom looks so beautiful. Pudding did a fabulous job on you, and I found listening to you receive such firm discipline wonderfully arousing," Susanna took hold of Amber's hand and guided her assistant's fingers to her wet lips, her eyes never leaving hers. Amber's Mistress kissed her and leaned back, "You can feel how wet I am. That was just from hearing you cry out as Pudding's hand gave your bottom those sweet caresses that you crave so much. How does that make you feel?"

Amber smiled and slipped two fingers deep inside her Mistress, risking not having permission to do so and enjoying the mild surprise on the older woman's face, "I'm happy to be of service, Mistress. If my pain brings you pleasure, I am your willing victim."

Mistress Susanna growled throatily, "I'm so pleased to hear it, you little minx. Do you mean things like this?" Amber gasped as her stiff nipple was pinched and twisted at the same time, giving a little whimper as the pain subsided.

"Yes, Mistress. You're so wet. I hope my pain continues to please you."

"Amber, you are developing so well, I'm proud of your progress. Enough talking. I want my sly tongued slut to please me before dinner," Mistress Susanna said, grabbing Amber's head and roughly pulling her down until her face was buried in her pussy.

"Make me cum, like a good assistant," Susanna ordered.

"Yes, Mistress," Amber said, though the words were muffled by her boss's lips.

CHAPTER 5

"Girls, get on the bed and sixty-nine, please. I want you to warm up for Amber and me," Susanna ordered Candy and Sugar. After dinner had been served and a little conversation had passed, Susanna had announced that she had a training session in mind for the evening's amusement.

Amber was still unsure of what it would entail, but they had come up to Mistress Susanna's bedroom, with the maids in tow and she had been ordered to strip them of all their clothing while their Mistress watched.

Susanna and Amber's clothes had followed suit, with Amber disrobing herself and then her Mistress. Her bottom was really quite sore, and Susanna had spent several minutes stroking it and laughing as even light spanks caused Amber to whimper.

Mistress had then taken several more photos of her rosy cheeks, and shown them to Amber on a tablet so she could see how her bottom was still changing colour after Pudding's spanking. She announced her intention to take more photos over the next day or two, so they would have a record of how Amber bruised.

For comparison, Susanna showed Amber some photos of Candy and Sugar, in the same pose, as their bottoms went from their untouched state to coral pink, to maroon and then through the stages of light bruises until they healed up. It was clear that reminiscing over the pictures excited their Mistress, and Amber found herself admiring them as well.

Now all four of them were completely naked with Candy and Sugar enthusiastically entwined in a pussy eating contest. Both of them seemed to be winning, or perhaps losing, Amber thought, depending on one's perspective.

Susanna offered her a harness and helped her step into it. It looked expensive and was surprisingly bulky. The straps were made of leather but padded on the inside, and unlike some she'd seen, the excess length was tidied up with an arrangement of poppers to stop it flapping around. All in all, it was very well thought out.

When Amber had seen strap-on harnesses in videos, they'd often seemed awkward but wearing this one didn't feel that way, even when Susanna showed her the dildos it would be paired with.

"We're going to practice fucking them. Would you like to fuck Candy or Sugar, Amber? This is a treat for you so you can choose."

It didn't really matter to Amber, so she quickly said, "Sugar, please, Mistress."

"Which of these would you like to use?" Susanna said, gesturing at a cupboard she'd opened that concealed a breathtaking array of silicone toys.

Amber looked at them for a while, reaching out to touch a few hesitantly. It was hard to decide. A slim, smooth purple one perhaps? Maybe the significantly larger than seemed plausible one that was otherwise a remarkably realistic imitation of a real cock, down to the colouring of the head and the swollen veins along the shaft.

"I'm really not sure. Which would you recommend, Mistress? For a beginner?" Amber asked.

"This one, if the person you are going to fuck is a beginner themself," Susanna replied, stroking the tip of one of several that were smooth and purple. It was surprisingly small. "It's easy to get carried away and pick a toy that's far too big for a new couple to handle. Particularly if you are going to fuck them in the arse," Susanna said.

Amber swallowed nervously, and Susanna laughed. "Don't worry, there are no hungry bottomed male subs here, thankfully. You'll be thrusting into Sugar's hungry pussy, Amber so it'll be a lot easier. Less warmup and less lubricant. We'll leave fucking arses until you've got a good handle on the rhythm and the technique."

"Oh, good, glad to hear it. So should I pick something medium-sized then, Mistress?" Amber asked, eyeing the extensive collection of silicone.

Susanna nodded. "Yes, about six inches is an ideal length, and it doesn't have to be incredibly thick either, they're a bit firmer than the average real cock, and of course, they never go down. It's better to start with something that is modest and work your way up once you know what you are doing. That leaves the big choice between something smooth like these, the ones that try to be realistic and the exotic shaped ones that have ribs and ridges and lumps and bumps for their pleasure. Oh, and the double-ended models or ones with vibrators of course, but again, we'll leave those for another day. This evening is about learning to fuck a girl and make her come hard, not about how you can get off on it too."

"Would this one be ok?" Amber said, touching her fingertip to a deep purple dildo, that looked about six inches long to her. It was shaped like a real cock complete with a big pair of balls but with some rather wild ridges on the shaft that were based on fantasy rather than human anatomy.

"Yes, not too big or exotic. I wouldn't recommend it if Sugar was new to this, but since she's not, you should be able to fuck her brains out with that. Won't that be nice, Sugar?" Susanna said.

The maid lifted her head from between Candy's thighs and replied, "Yes, Mistress. I can't wait." Sugar winked at Amber and with a lewd abandon, dipped her head back between Candy's thighs.

Susanna watched the wanton display of her maids for a moment before coming back to the present moment and smiling at Amber. "I don't think we'll need lubricant, but we'll use it anyway so you can practice. I'm sure the girls are more than wet enough now. Help me on with my harness, will you dear?"

Amber did as she was told and learned more about how the harness was adjusted. It was easier to see what was going on with another person. Once the harnesses were ready, Susanna selected a large and remarkably realistic looking silicone cock and showed Amber how it fitted into her harness. Then Amber attached her pick to her own harness.

Susanna picked up a paddle and applied it with vigour to Sugar who had the misfortune of being the top girl in the sixty-nine. Or, Amber thought, perhaps the fortune if she liked being paddled. Either way, her cheeks were rosy pink by the time the maids had obeyed their Mistress and licked each other to rather loud orgasms.

Mistress Susanna passed Amber the paddle to put away and ordered the girls onto all fours. Amber got up behind Sugar and looked to her Mistress for instructions.

Susanna had got on the bed in front of Candy and Amber thinking she'd done something wrong made ready to move beside her.

"No dear, you stay behind Sugar and get some lube onto that cock head. I'm going to have Candy demonstrate another way to get a little lube on a strap-on," Susanna said, before offering up the head of her dildo to Candy's welcoming mouth.

The pretty young maid began to fellate the silicone with the lusty abandon both girls employed with all their sexual play. Amber wondered if the girl had ever sucked a real cock, or if she'd learned to be so exuberant purely with Susanna's collection. It certainly looked like she knew what she was doing, as she attacked the dildo with all the tricks that Amber would have tried to use on a guy, just a few short months ago. If she really, really liked him, that is.

"Mistress, why do that?"

"Because I can't feel it, you mean?"

"Yes, Mistress."

"I would say that for many most dominant women, it's about the power and the imagery of it. Candy is sucking a rubber cock, like a good little slut, for her domme. Maybe it's a little about humiliation, maybe it's a demonstration of her submission. It varies from domme to domme. Sometimes it's service to the submissive, giving them something they enjoy for their own needs. If I was using a double-ender I could maybe get a little pleasure from it bu,t I prefer fucking a girl for that," Susanna explained as she let Candy work back and forth on the shaft. "Now, make sure that lube is smeared over the head nicely. That's right. You can line it up with Sugar's pussy now and slowly work it in. I suggest holding the dildo with one hand to guide it, the aiming is more tricky than you think."

Amber did as she was instructed and with slippery fingers, guided the cock into Sugar's welcoming lips. Susanna wasn't wrong about it being tricky. Amber had trouble pushing with her hips and getting the dildo to slide into Sugar, despite how aroused and wet the girl was.

"Try slipping your fingers into her first. Get inside her, then work back and forth a bit, then straighten your fingers up and thrust in and out. You'll be able to work out what angle is right then, it's hard to visualise it for newbies, and if you can't get the cock in her, it's probably because you're pushing the dildo at the wrong angle. Does that make sense?" Susanna asked as she pulled out of Candy's mouth with a plop and moved around the bed.

Amber nodded thoughtfully and found that Sugar was much more easily penetrated with her fingers. Doing as she was advised, she played with the maid for a few moments before getting her fingers straight and then establishing the angle she needed to penetrate the pussy before her with something straight.

"That's good. Can you see what I mean? You need to remember the way the girl you are going to fuck is positioned, of course. Perhaps you've got them bent over the back of a sofa, or on a spanking bench, or they have longer legs than you, and you might need a pillow to kneel on. Maybe you've got their bum up high, but your hand is on their neck, holding the side of their face down in a muddy paddock. Each position they're in affects the position you need to fuck them," Susanna explained congenially.

Her second attempt was much more effective. With a little adjustment of Sugar's hips and switching to kneeling on just one knee, Amber was able to slowly push the dildo into the excited young maid.

Sugar moaned appreciatively as the silicone toy entered her. Amber felt like she had more precise control now.

"That's better, now watch this," Susanna said, taking hold of Candy's hips with both hands and resting the tip of the heavy cock against her lips. Amber wondered how many times she'd have to do this before she could aim one of these things that accurately.

With one slow push, Susanna buried the thick dildo to the hilt in Candy's hungry pussy. The maid let out a passionate groan. "Mmm. That feels wonderful, Mistress," Candy said breathlessly.

Susanna began to draw her hips back and then just before the tip reached her lips, she slowly and smoothly thrust her hips forward again, burying the strap-on in her submissive maid.

"Now, you try. Nice and slow. Pull back until you think you're about halfway out, then slowly back in," Susanna said.

"Yes, Mistress," Amber replied as she began to withdraw the purple silicone from Sugar. She thought she had it just right and was about to change directions, but then the head of the dildo flopped out.

Beside her, Susanna was casually thrusting back and forth, slowly and deliberately. She reached out and patted Amber on the shoulder, "It's ok, sweetie. Get it back in and try again."

Her next attempt was much more satisfying, she managed to build up a bit of a rhythm and slowly fucked Sugar for a dozen or so cycles before she got a bit excited and tried to speed up. That was when the dildo flopped out again, and Susanna laughed.

"Again! Fuck on, fuck off!" her boss said. Sugar and Candy laughed at the reference, and Amber felt her cheeks flushing with embarrassment. Being naked wasn't bothering her, or engaging in lesbian strap-on play with three other women but being made fun off got to her.

Gritting her teeth, she gripped Sugar by the hips and tried to line up the head of the dildo with her pussy. It took longer than she'd hoped, but she finally got it pressed between Sugar's lips. Then she adjusted the maid's knees, bringing her backside down just a bit. That was better.

Amber began to fuck the maid again, and this time, it felt much more comfortable. The dildo slid home with ease, and she didn't pull back far enough for it to pop free. Sugar was soon moaning and groaning with evident delight, and Amber was thrilled with her success.

Grinning wickedly at her, Susanna mouthed, "Watch this."

Reaching forward, Mistress Susanna took a bunch of Candy's hair in her hand and pulled firmly back, lifting the maid's head up as she began to roughly thrust the thick cock back and forth. Candy was mumbling something that was too indistinct to catch, but Amber nevertheless had the distinct impression it was both filthy and approving.

It was hot to watch her Mistress fucking the maid so roughly, and even hotter seeing how much Candy was enjoying having her hair pulled and used as a way to control her and fuck her harder. Amber had to concentrate hard not to go wild fucking her own maid. She was determined not to fumble the cock again.

Amber slapped Sugar's arse, "Why aren't you moaning like that, you little slut?"

"Oh, please, miss. It's nice, really it is," Sugar said.

"I want you to come from it, Sugar, like Candy is," Amber grumbled as Candy grew increasingly excited.

"Yes, miss. I'll do my best," Sugar sighed. Amber frowned as she concentrated and tried to up the pace.

"Fuck me, Mistress, fuck me! Oh. You're fucking me so hard. Sugar, you need it like this. It feels so fucking good. I'm coming!" Candy cried out as she began to climax.

"Lucky cow," Sugar replied, watching her enviously. "Amber needs more practice so she can fuck me good and hard, Mistress."

"Don't be cheeky, Sugar," Susanna said as she pulled out of Candy who contentedly collapsed on the bed, making happy noises.

Susanna moved behind Amber, her strap-on held upright and pressing against her assistant's bottom as she pressed herself up against the younger woman, and wrapped her left arm around her waist. "Let me help you, darling," she whispered in Amber's ear. "Follow my lead."

With that, Susanna took charge of the rhythm of Amber's fucking motion. She pressed her forward with her hips, then guided her back with the hand around her waist. Her right hand brushed up her side and cupped Amber's breast, the fingers playing with her nipple. Mistress Susanna's lips found Amber's neck, and she kissed her softly as she coached one submissive to fuck the other.

Once Susanna had synchronised their movements, she began to speed up the motion. "See baby, you do it like this. Faster," Susanna said before thrusting her hips forward vigorously, causing Sugar to gasp in surprise, "and harder. Just keep it going. Ramp it up slowly. Don't try and pull back too far, short, swift strokes are fine. You'll be able to fuck her with much more length when you get some more practice. For now, let's keep it to short strokes and really get some slapping up against her bottom going, hmm?"

True to her word, Susanna had them thrusting fast and hard until Sugar came a few minutes later. "What do you say, Sugar?" Susanna prompted.

"Thank you, Mistress, and thank you, Amber. That was lovely," Sugar mumbled happily.

"Thank you, Mistress," Amber said as Susanna let go of her, and began to unbuckle her harness.

Her Mistress looked up and frowned, "Come on, get your harness off. We've made them come, now it's their turn to give us pleasure. Girls, on your backs now."

The maids grumbled a bit but rolled onto their backs when Susanna slapped their bottoms and told them to hurry up.

Copying Susanna, Amber moved forward and lowered herself onto Sugar's face, soon feeling the young maid's tongue lapping at her needy clit.

Amber was soon throwing her head back and sighing contentedly as Sugar worshipped her pussy. Susanna reached out and pulled her into a kiss, fondling her breasts as they rode the maids face. That explained why she'd made them lie on the bed head to head, rather than side by side, thought Amber.

"Ride her, Amber. Make her satisfy you. Don't wait for it, take your pleasure from her mouth," Susanna breathed in her ear. Amber looked down to see that her Mistress had one hand twined in Candy's hair and was positively grinding her sex against the maid's flushed face.

"Fuck her mouth with your pussy, Amber. She's a slut just like you are. She'll respond to it," Susanna whispered, smiling triumphantly when Amber obeyed and began copying her motions.

Sugar moaned into her pussy as she worked her tongue over Amber's sex.

Susanna glanced down at Sugar's face, "See, what did I tell you? Sugar loves to be ridden like this, don't you sweetie?"

Sugar said something that sounded agreeable but was muffled by the wet lips pressed hard against her mouth.

"Candy too. I've trained them both to enjoy the finer things in life," Susanna said. "Just as I'm going to train you."

"Yes, Mistress. She's really going to town," Amber said.

"Feels good, doesn't it? To take control of them and take what you want?"

"It does, yes. Sugar is so gifted with her tongue, Mistress," Amber replied, stumbling over her words as she began to come hard, shuddering and shaking over the maids face. Her thighs trembled as her orgasm ripped through her. "Sugar, that was glorious," she sighed.

Susanna reached for her again and kissed her deeply as she rode Candy's face to her own orgasm.

They collapsed on the bed, leaving the maids licking their lips and dozing contentedly.

"Did you enjoy your orgasm?" Susanna asked.

"Yes, Mistress, it was perfect."

"Don't forget you're spending tomorrow evening serving at the pleasure of my ponies though," Susanna pointed out.

"I hadn't forgotten, Mistress. I'm looking forward to it," Amber replied happily.

"Are you indeed?" Susanna said, with obvious amusement.

"Yes, Mistress."

"Interesting. You do understand that Pepper and Ginger are probably going to torment you and they're unlikely to let you come, don't you?" Susanna said with a laugh.

"Yes, Mistress but that's alright," Amber said.

"How so?"

"Well, I won the race, so I'm due to collect my prize of an orgasm anyway, right?"

Susanna sat up with a start. "Are you perfectly serious, young lady?" she snapped.

Amber sat up and shrugged, "I thought that was the deal."

"But you cheated!" Susanna protested.

"Cheating is a bit of a strong word. I just offered some encouragement and Pepper raced her little socks off," Amber pointed out.

"So you think you're due a prize?"

"Yes I do," Amber said confidently.

That was when Susanna pounced. She flipped Amber onto her back, making her shriek in surprise.

With a growl, Susanna claimed her mouth, kissing her passionately. Then she began working her way down Amber's body, kissing her neck, the swell of her breasts and then nibbling and sucking hungrily at her pert nipples.

The trail of kisses passed down her chest and over her stomach, and then Susanna slipped her arms under Amber's knees and hauled her legs up, pushing them back toward her shoulder. Her Mistress rolled her up, so her knees ended up on either side of her head, then placed her mouth on Amber's pussy, her tongue dipping between her wet lips and her mouth hungrily sucking on her clit.

Amber purred in delight.

"I'll give you your prize, you cheeky little slut. I'm going to give you the best orgasm of your life," Susanna boasted. Amber bit her lip and moaned as her Mistress put her tongue to work. She writhed under the agile tongue of her Mistress for quite a few moments before she was able to get enough of a grip on herself to lift her head and reply.

"Yes, Mistress."

SHARED BY HER LESBIAN BOSS

Book 5

CHAPTER 1

"Are you ready, Amber?"

"Yes, Mistress," Amber confirmed, lifting her head from the pillow to answer. She was naked, and on her knees, face down in the pillows. Her nipples were pressed to the bedsheet, the light friction of the Egyptian cotton stimulating the erect buds.

A slap descended on her bottom. "Not for this, cheeky girl. For the party tomorrow!" Susanna chided.

"Oh, yes, I suppose so, Mistress," Amber said.

"You suppose so? You mean, you don't know?"

"Well, the invitations were quite vague, but I got the impression the guests you invited are all business contacts, and this is an event you regularly host which is why the invitations didn't need details beyond the time and date. I know that all the deliveries you asked me to check on were received and all the guests you invited did confirm they were coming in the end, so I'm sure all that is ready. Sugar, Candy and Pudding haven't said anything about any problems with their preparations, so I assume they're all ready to carry out their roles. I'm sure the evening will go well for you, Mistress," Amber explained.

"Of course, it didn't occur to me that you didn't know about my soirees. You're right, I've invited some of my business contacts, but I've also invited some friends that I don't have business relationships with. Most of my guests are successful people as it happens, but that wasn't why they got invited. Only people I actually like make the list.

"Is it a social occasion then, Mistress?"

"That's the way we think of these events, yes. There's no rule against conducting business though, and I'm always looking for new business relationships and investment opportunities. My guests can do as they please, as long as everyone is happy," Susanna replied as she prowled into position behind Amber.

"I understand, Mistress," Amber said.

Susanna paused, "They can't go in the stables though, of course. There are a couple of guests who are new to the group so if you see them wandering in that direction, be a dear and head them off."

"Yes, Mistress. I'll make sure no-one accidentally disturbs Pepper and Ginger.

"Good," Susanna said, as her hand reached down between Amber's thighs and strong fingers quested for her lips. "You really are ready, aren't you, my dear?"

"Mmm, yes, Mistress," Amber said, pushing herself up and back at Susanna's touch.

After the briefest brush against the outer lips of Amber's sex, Susanna plunged the sizeable dildo she had selected for her harness home in one expert and smooth stroke.

Amber yelped in surprise and approval, her utterances quickly becoming thick with passion. Her guttural groans inflamed her Mistress to thrust harder and faster with each stroke.

It wasn't long before Amber's crescendo was approaching, and the volume of her voice rose in time with it. Susanna changed her pace, slowing right down until the happy noises Amber was making subsided. She continued for a few minutes like that and then suddenly increased the power of her thrusting again.

Once more, Amber's excitement rose, and she felt the approach of a powerful climax, but Susanna denied her again, letting her calm down before bringing her up a third time.

Amber mumbled incoherently, her frustration evident as she realised her Mistress was teasing her with quite deliberate and expert skill. She tried staying silent, biting her lip and concealing her rising excitement, but Susanna always seemed to know when she was close.

After what seemed like an age of torment, Susanna pulled the thick dildo out and took hold of her subs head by the hair, dragging Amber around until the silicone cock waved in front of her face.

"Clean it up, slut," Susanna ordered.

Amber didn't hesitate, she ran her tongue along the length of the toy, lapping up her own juices and making appreciative noises for Susanna's benefit. Then she took the tip in her mouth and began to suck it, bobbing her head up and down as much of the length as she could manage. If Susanna was going to tease her so mercilessly, she would put on a show and see if she could turn the tables.

Her blowjob skills had not been spectacular but had always been popular with her boyfriends, and she used every visually appealing technique she could remember. When Susanna's fingers twined in her hair and began to guide her head, Amber knew she had her rapt attention.

Eventually, though, Susanna pulled back and undid the harness. Amber eagerly awaited the chance to use her tongue to please her Mistress more directly, but her boss ordered her to go to sleep.

Susanna wrapped her soft-skinned limbs around her submissive, spooning her as they drifted off.

"Get a good night of sleep, Amber. Tomorrow will be a busy day," Susanna murmured as Amber's eyes grew heavy.

"Yes, Mistress."

CHAPTER 2

"It's beautiful, Mistress. It looks expensive," Amber said, admiring the black maxi dress Susanna had chosen for her. The wrap front had a plunging neckline that flattered her cleavage wonderfully, and the strappy back matched it. The thigh split gave tantalising glimpses of her recently waxed legs.

"It wasn't cheap, I must say. The sequins give it a wonderful sheen, don't they? Do you like it, my dear?" Susanna asked.

"Oh, yes. Very much," Amber replied, turning to her Mistress with a coy smile. "Does it suit me?"

"It certainly does. I'm sure you'll be turning quite a few heads this afternoon."

"It's going to be quite a fancy do, if I'm dressed like this, and you're wearing that suit," Amber commented.

Susanna turned gracefully on the spot, showing off her outfit. The sequinned jacket was buttoned up, but just enough cleavage was revealed above the blouse, Susanna wore to draw the eye. The leather trousers had sequin accents and laced sides to give a hint of the legs beneath them. Amber thought it a nice touch that their outfits echoed each other, and their matching shoes completed the effect.

"What do you think?" Susanna asked playfully.

Amber licked her lips and drank in the sight of her Mistress, her gaze travelling from the shapely ankles, up her legs and over the swell of her bosom to her dark cherry red lipstick and then those captivating eyes. She grinned and lifted her hands, clawing them in imitation of a cat, "Rawr!"

Susanna laughed, "I'll take that as a sign that you approve."

"Yes, Mistress. You look business-like but sexy at the same time. I can't wait for the party to be over so I can unwrap you and have you all to myself," Amber replied.

"Is that what you think is going to happen?"

"I imagine you'll have me unwrap myself first, but a girl can hope," Amber said with a shrug.

"It's good to have dreams. Now, young lady, my guests will be arriving shortly. Let's go downstairs so we can welcome them," Susanna said, offering her arm. "Come with me, my pet. Accompany your Mistress, so I can show you off."

Amber slipped her arm into the crook of Susanna's, and they walked downstairs side by side.

They waited in one of the large reception rooms, and Amber served chilled fruit juices from the bar for herself and her Mistress while they sat and watched the clock.

When the first guest rang the doorbell, Amber shot to her feet and almost spilt her drink, much to Susanna's amusement. Amber took her Mistress's arm again and accompanied her to the front door.

By the time they entered the hallway, the door was already being opened. As if by magic, a maid had appeared to welcome the guests. Candy was handling the door, and Sugar appeared a moment later to take the guests coats.

Both maids were wearing much more conservative uniforms than they did day to day, Amber noted. The revealing cuts and mini-skirts were gone, and there was nothing obviously risque about their clothes today.

Roxy, Susanna's chauffeur, stepped in first, showing two women in after her. Amber could see more waiting on the porch.

"Baroness Imogen Carruthers and her companion, Charlotte,"

Roxy announced flamboyantly as if presenting people to an old-fashioned ball.

Susanna whispered in Amber's ear, "I must welcome the guests, so please take the coat of the baroness and her companion and the other guests. Sugar and Candy will go and hang them up."

Amber nodded and scurried forward, "Your coat, my Lady," she prompted the Baroness once she was standing behind her. The weather was clement and wearing a coat at all seemed unnecessary, but Amber reached out as the baroness began to remove the coat, helping to slide it down her arms and passing it off to Sugar.

The baroness wasn't tall and had a broad-shouldered figure. She had a pixie cut of dark hair and platinum highlights and wore a finely tailored tweed suit, like a model from a country lifestyle magazine. Baroness Carruthers even had a silver-topped black cane, which seemed to be an accessory rather than an aid to walking.

Amber moved behind the baroness's companion, whatever that meant, and helped lift her full-length cashmere coat up and off her shoulders. Charlotte was shorter than the baroness, perhaps 5'3" if that. As the coat came away, Amber found herself taking a sharp intake of breath.

Charlotte was completely nude under the coat, aside from the black kitten-heeled shoes and the straps that wound up her calves. As she tried not to gape, open-mouthed, Susanna stepped forward and gently took the Baroness's hand. The women performed a side to side air kiss that usually irritated Amber, but she was too distracted by the effort required to avoid staring at the cleft between Charlotte's cheeks or her cute dimples and hourglass figure, to care.

"Good afternoon, Imogen. I'm so pleased you were both able to come. Doesn't Charlotte look lovely today? Are those new shoes?"

"Aye, supposedly they emphasise her calves and buttocks, but mostly they don't make too much noise, and they're comfortable for long periods when she's standing up," the baroness remarked.

"I applaud your practicality, Imogen. So many people forget the finer details like that, what use is a girl who is too sore to stand up?" Susanna said. "We're in the ballroom today," she continued, gesturing down the hallway toward Pudding who was waiting to show people in through the large double doors.

"Thank you, Susanna," Imogen said as she made for the ballroom. Amber couldn't help staring at Charlotte's swaying bottom as she followed after the older woman. Was that a glint of metal that Amber could see as the young woman's bottom moved?

"You're practically drooling, my dear," Susanna whispered in her ear as Roxy fetched the next guest to announce.

"Sorry, Mistress," Amber said, pressing her lips together and turning back to face the front door. "So umm. It's that kind of party then?" she ventured cautiously.

"Of course. I conduct most of my business meetings in the conference rooms in London," Susanna confirmed.

"Yes, Mistress," Amber said meekly. She didn't want to get in trouble, but it was quite clear that she hadn't just been mistaken in assuming that this was a business event. There was a lot more going on than a simple social occasion, Amber realised.

"Dame Cartwright and her companions, Holly and Ivy," Roxy announced, catching Amber's eye and giving her a big wink. Amber felt herself blushing a little and smiled back, hoping the chauffeur didn't notice before she stepped forward to help the Dame out of her coat.

Amber wasn't sure about the style of clothing the tall, imperious looking woman was wearing, a knee-length black leather skirt, white blouse and black jacket didn't really scream a theme to her, at least from behind.

When she took Holly and Ivy's coats and found they were dressed as naughty schoolgirls, she realised that Dame Cartwright was a sexy headmistress. The two girls were of university age at least but were dressed in uniforms. They had kitten-heeled shoes, knee-length white socks, plaid skirts, white blouses and neckties on. Both girls were about 5'4" tall, and their Mistress probably had a good six inches on them,

As Holly and Ivy were introduced to Susanna, Amber got enough of a look to see that the girl's blouses were stretched tightly over their buxom bosoms. The buttons were straining at the material, and ample cleavage was on display. They both wore glasses with thick black rims and had pigtails and bright red lipstick. Holly was a blonde and Ivy a brunette. Amber longed to bury her face in their gorgeous chests and tug at their blouses until the buttons popped off and their heavy breasts sprang free of their constraints.

Instead, she had to content herself with passing the coats to Sugar.

"Emma, so lovely to see you again. Are you still pining for the life of an army colonel or have Holly and Ivy got your mind on other things."

Dame Cartwright boomed out her response in the clear cadence of an army officer, "They are quite exhausting, Susanna. There's no end to their mischief, and they take every ounce of my attention to keep them in line."

"They can't be as much to handle as a class of new recruits, I'm sure?" Susanna remarked.

"Can't they? I think they're worse if anything. Don't let their size fool you. They may be petite, but they're more than a handful," the Dame cautioned.

"You've come to the right place if you need help with them or inventive suggestions, so I'm sure you'll have a wonderful evening," Susanna said, motioning toward the ballroom.

"Oh, I'm sure I will. Someone is bound to be able to give me a pointer that will help," Dame Cartwright said, before leading her girls into the main room.

"Mistress Cauldwell and her companion Diamond," Roxy announced next.

Taking Mistress Cauldwell's coat, she discovered a black latex mini-dress with a plunge that went all the way to the woman's navel and was held fastened by thin chains locked with small heart-shaped padlocks. Regardless, her bosom was barely constrained by the garment and her hips curved generously. The dress had almost no back so everything that wasn't covered by Mistress Cauldwell's long, black and red hair, was tantalisingly exposed.

Diamond was dressed in latex lingerie that left everything covered, but little to Amber's imagination. Both women were heavily tattooed, but with obviously high-quality artwork and taste. Once Diamond's coat was removed, Mistress Cauldwell clipped a leash to the collar around her neck. Amber noted that ankle cuffs and wrist cuffs were an integral part of Diamond's clothing for the afternoon.

Mistress Susanna welcomed the pair, as she had done with the other, glancing at but not speaking to the submissive who apparently didn't warrant a direct conversation, then they were off, spirited into the ballroom.

"Mistress Vanessa Steele and her companion, Jasmine."

"Vanessa, it's been far too long," Susanna said.

"Yes, I'm sorry I've missed a few of your events. My sub took a long term job abroad so that relationship ended. It was a while before a new girl caught my fancy. Jasmine, curtsey for Mistress Susanna," Steele said.

Jasmine, who wore a bondage harness made of leather and seemed to mostly consist of straps and buckles, politely curtseyed to Mistress Susanna, her eyes firmly glued to the floor. Her outfit complimented Mistress Steele's leather corset, trousers and belt that was home to several implements for disciplining her sub.

"Pleased to meet you, Jasmine," Susanna said, acknowledging the sub with a smile and a subtle nod. "Is this her first time at an event like this?"

"Yes, I've been enjoying training her up for it," Vanessa said.

"My new girl, Amber, is also new to the scene. I'm sure this evening will open their eyes to a whole new world," Susanna suggested.

"I'm looking forward to putting Jasmine through her paces in public. She's perhaps a little headstrong, but for me, that makes it all the sweeter when she falls to her knees and submits to my rule," Vanessa said.

"I look forward to seeing her do just that," Susanna replied as Vanessa led her sub toward the ballroom. "I think you'll like this next guest, Amber."

"Yes, Mistress."

CHAPTER 3

Roxy cleared her throat and announced the last couple, "Mistress Yolanda and her companion Zoe."

The final couple struck Amber as rather gothic, even before she removed their pure black coats. Yolanda wore a corset which flattered her figure from her waistline to her cleavage, and a skirt made of leather and lace. Her submissive, Zoe, had a red and black underbust corset on and no blouse.

Zoe's perfect breasts were on display and tipped with pierced nipples that drew Amber's rapt attention so strongly that she barely took in the pale beauty's short gladiator skirt, made of strips of black leather that revealed tantalising glimpses of the girl's body as she moved.

"Yolanda, welcome back to my humble abode," Susanna said.

Yolanda laughed, "It's like a bloody castle, Susanna and far from humble. Most of my friends would kill to live here."

"But not you?"

"Sure, if you ever feel like going over my knee for regular spankings, I'd be delighted to take charge of your estate," Yolanda replied cheekily.

"While I'm sure your spankings are lovely, my dear, I couldn't give up being in charge," Susanna replied.

"Not even temporarily?"

Susanna smiled. "Perhaps. Is that why you come to my parties? In the hopes of giving me a spanking?" Mistress Susanna teased.

Yolanda laughed, "The thought has endless appeal, but you're fishing for compliments, Susanna. You know your parties are the best around, such beautiful surroundings and so many delightful temptations."

"I do try to make my home welcoming."

"Yes, I always feel wanted when I'm here. So does Zoe, I know," Yolanda said, gesturing toward Amber, who looked up at the Mistress's with a guilty expression. "Your new girl is gorgeous, and she can't take her eyes of Zoe's tits, can she?" Yolanda said smugly.

Susanna shook her head, "Amber is a work in progress, I'm afraid. Amber, it's rude to stare. My apologies Yolanda, you must excuse her. I acquired Amber only very recently, and this is her first party."

"It's not a problem, you'd think she'd never seen a pair of boobs before though," Yolanda chuckled huskily, "from the way she's been admiring them."

"Well, one can hardly blame her. I've rarely seen a more exquisitely shaped pair than your Zoe possesses", Susanna said.

"Her tits are close to perfect, aren't they? Of course, she does have the luxury of being young and firm. Zoe will be nineteen next month," Yolanda explained.

"Congratulations. Amber is twenty-three, but you're right, she had never seen boobs used in anger before she came here."

Yolanda looked positively scandalised, "You're pulling my leg. Are you telling me you popped her cherry?"

Amber blushed profusely as the two dommes discussed her virginity so openly. She could feel Zoe giving her curious glances as the women talked.

"With women, at least. Amber hadn't done much more than have a few stray thoughts until I found her," Susanna said, with a hint of obvious pride.

"You lucky thing, it's been years since I got to taste a virgin," Yolanda mused. "Happy days. When I met Zoe about four months ago, she was already well broken in, weren't you, my pet?"

"Yes, Mistress Yolanda," Zoe agreed, her cheeks flushing red.

"I love it when they blush," Yoland said, "it's so sweet and innocent. It's amusing because the things that Zoe can do with that tongue of hers are far from innocent."

Yolanda turned to face Susanna and whispered with a conspiratorial stage whisper, that everyone could hear, "I'm giving serious consideration to collaring her, provided she continues to be a good girl,"

"Really? That's wonderful news. I'm happy for you both," Susanna, catching Amber's eye and her confused expression. "You look puzzled, Amber, what is it?"

"I was wondering why putting a collar on was something to consider," Amber said. Presumably, it had some significance, but she had no idea what.

"My, my. She really is green, isn't she?" Yolanda said.

"Oh, yes. Amber has a lot to learn."

"May I?" Yolanda asked, continuing when Susanna nodded her approval. "There's a world of difference between me putting a collar around Zoe's neck so I can use a leash to control her, or indulge in some pet play or the like and collaring her. In our little community, when we say that we're going to 'collar' someone, what we're talking about is a relationship commitment. If I offer my collar to Zoe and she accepts it, it's a little like an engagement. We even get together to have a little collaring party with friends, just like an engagement party. Does that cover it?" Yolanda checked with Susanna.

"Yes, I think so. Does that satisfy your curiosity, Amber?"

Amber nodded, "Yes, thank you, Mistress. I mean, Mistresses."

The explanation given, Susanna returned to her conversation with her friend, "I see you've had her pierced since we last met," Susanna remarked. "I love the little bat wings on the studs. That's very 'you', Yolanda."

"Oh yes, you've got to have bats or skulls or vampire fangs in my little niche of the world," Yoland chuckled. "I asked her to have it done to see if she was coming along as well as I hoped."

"And I'm guessing, Zoe passed your test with flying colours," Susanna prompted.

"Absolutely. I have a lovely video of her getting pierced. Tell, Mistress Susanna if it hurt you, Zoe."

"It did, Mistress. It hurt a lot, Mistress Susanna," Zoe replied, chewing her lip wistfully as if remembering the experience fondly.

"But she let them do the second one," Susanna said to Yolanda.

"Yes, I'm very proud of her. Zoe took it like a champ. She cried and winced a fair bit, but she didn't try and wimp out of it, did you, darling?"

"No, Mistress."

"They let you film it in the piercing shop?"

Yolanda shook her head, "No, I have a friend, Amaranth, who works in one, but she's quite the sadist. She has a reputation for doing it painlessly in the shop and really knows her stuff. I've used Amaranth for years, and she's done some of my tattoos too. I got her to come over, and we had a little dinner party. Just us, my piercer's sub and a few other friends. Then Zoe got all of her piercings while we all watched and enjoyed the show."

"How wonderful."

"It was. I suspect Zoe's piercings are what was intriguing your sub," Yolanda said shrewdly.

"Is Mistress Yolanda correct, Amber? Were you admiring Zoe's beautiful piercings?"

Amber nodded. "Yes, Mistress. I haven't seen piercings like that up close before."

"You haven't seen them up close now, either," Yolanda smirked.

"Perhaps she should?" Susanna chuckled.

"Zoe, push your chest out, so Amber can really see you show those tits off," Yolanda ordered, before leaning in to whisper something in Susanna's ear.

Susanna smiled. "Amber, come here," she ordered, pointing to a spot beside her.

When Amber was close up against her, Susanna put her lips to her sub's ear, "I need to know if you will consent to what I want from you, today. I want to share you with my friends, as I see fit, with my guests. You have a choice to make. Will you continue to serve me, even if I share you with others, or is this too much for you today?"

Amber swallowed hard and licked her lips, before replying clearly and loudly, "I will serve as you wish, Mistress."

"Good girl. Yolanda, please be my guests. You may direct her as if she were your own for the idea you suggested," Susanna said.

"Smashing," Yolanda said, putting her hand on the back of Amber's head and sweeping her toward Zoe. In a moment, Amber had a close-up view of Zoe's bosom.

"Do you like what you see, Amber?" she purred in Amber's ear.

"Yes, Mistress Yolanda."

"They're delicious, aren't they? So stiff with need. Would you like to lick them?"

Amber nodded. "Yes, please, Mistress."

Yolanda smiled, "You may lick, suck and kiss Zoe's nipples for a short while. Be gentle and kind, I don't want her to suffer at your mouth. Her pain is reserved for my amusement."

Dipping her head, Amber brought her lips to Zoe's pierced doing as she was permitted. She gently probed the erect nubbin with her tongue, delighting in the audible response from the other submissive. Then she tried sucking it gently, playing with the bat-shaped piercing bar that ran horizontally through the coral pink flesh.

"I think Amber likes that," Yolanda commented.

"I think they both seem to," Susanna replied.

"Do you think Amber wants her own piercings? If you want her done, I'm sure Amaranth would do a great job."

"I'm sure she would, I shall discuss it with Amber at some point, but for now, I think I've pushed her far enough."

"Any time you want an introduction just let me know. I can send you the video of Zoe getting pierced if you would like to watch it together with Amber," Yolanda offered.

"Perhaps we will. I would like to see Amber's reaction at least," Susanna mused.

"I think you'd enjoy it. After all Zoe's piercings were done, the night wasn't over," Yolanda said.

"All her piercings?"

Yolanda grinned, "Oh, yes. It's not just her nipples we had done. Her clit hood too. That really brought on the tears but now she loves it, as do I. Zoe totally can't cope with that kind of pain, but it doesn't stop her from enjoying serving me."

"Good for you, how did the rest of the night go?" Susanna enquired.

"Oh you know, just your regular six-way all-girl orgy," Yolanda said with a shrug. "Of course, after Amaranth had gone to so much trouble to come to my house to pierce my beautiful little sub, I had to play the gracious host."

"Well, naturally. Where would civil society be without the basic niceties of hospitality being observed?"

"I assume it would fall apart. Zoe thanked Amaranth with her tongue for quite some time though, so I think the obligations of a host were discharged admirably. Amaranth certainly seemed to be happy," Yolanda said.

"As is only right. Zoe seems to be benefiting greatly from her work, after all."

Yolanda grinned, "Yup. If we let Amber go any longer, the dirty little bitch will be coming all over your hallway." Mistress Yolanda stepped forward and pulled Amber's head away. "That's enough, greedy girls. Anyway, Susanna, Zoe thanked Amaranth, and her sub and my other guests all night. She's been thanking me every day since."

"I would expect nothing less," Susanna said, wiping Amber's sticky mouth with a tissue before she kissed her deeply.

"I think Amaranth would fit right in at your little soirees you know. No pressure, of course, but I'd love to make the introduction," Yolanda suggested.

"Subject to the usual background checks, of course, I'm sure that wouldn't be a problem. If you can email me your friend's details, I'll get that started, and as long as she's cleared, we could all meet up for afternoon tea," Susanna said.

"Great, I'll send you Amaranth's info when I get home. Even if you don't have this girl pierced, I'm sure you'll love her just as much as I do," Yolanda said confidently. "Now, I think we'll go and wait in the ballroom until the others get here."

As Yolanda and her sub walked off, Susanna pulled Amber in for another long kiss, her hands roaming down over Amber's elegant dress. "I cannot wait to get this off you," Susanna growled, nibbling at her sub's ear.

"That sounds good, Mistress," Amber moaned, as strong fingers squeezed her bottom.

"Did you enjoy playing with Zoe?"

"Yes, Mistress."

"Remember your safeword, but I hope you don't use it today. I want you to impress my friends. I can't help being quite proud of how much you've grown in such a short time," Susanna said.

"I'll do my best to impress them, Mistress," Amber said.

"Good, now let's smarten up a little bit. I think I can hear Roxy returning up the drive with the rest of the guests."

Amber stepped back and turned to see the car approaching the turning circle. What would the rest of the guests be like, she wondered.

CHAPTER 4

It hadn't been all that long since Roxy had left after announcing Mistress Yoland and Zoe. Amber was puzzled about how the chauffeur had already managed to pick up more guests, "Mistress, how did they get here so quickly? Didn't she have to go to pick them up from their hotels or something?"

Susanna laughed. "No, we tried that, but it was frustrating. When I got the old gatehouse cleared out, we started to use it as a staging post. The guests arrive and veer off to the car park that's near the gatehouse. Then they can get changed and ready for the party. Roxy brings them to the main house in one of the bigger cars. That way, they arrive at the house fairly quickly, and there aren't lots of stragglers. If you let people turn up on their own, half the people arrive mid-orgy, and that can be a bit tedious."

"Orgy? Wow. To think I thought this was going to be a business event until I took that first coat," Amber said.

"I did wonder. That's why I kept you away from the details, once I got the idea you thought this was some kind of business schmoozing dinner party, I told everyone to play up to that," Susanna said, grinning wickedly.

"Well, I failed that test, didn't I?" Amber said grumpily.

Susanna gave her a friendly fist bump to the shoulder, "It was just a bit of a practical joke, no harm done. Sugar and Candy have been having terrible trouble keeping a straight face."

"I might have known they'd enjoy keeping me in the dark," Amber grumbled.

Susanna imitated Sugar's voice, "Ohhh, the caterers don't like it when people go in the dining hall and disturb things."

"That sounded perfectly sensible to me!" Amber protested.

"That does happen actually, they like to know they can get the job done and not be criticised for something the hosts changed like moving the tables and mucking up the seating chart. But in this case, it was because we wanted to set-up the ballroom for the party, not for catering," Susanna said.

"But I saw their vans, and they were unloading lots of boxes and stuff. They had half a dozen people lugging stuff around," Amber said. The doors were pushed open again, and the new guests arrived.

"You'll see," was all Susanna said before Roxy announced the first person.

Amber had to stew as she removed coats and passed them to the maids, admiring each new guest's sense of style. The dominants certainly liked to dress up, and each had their own unique look, albeit with certain themes running through their outfits.

A lot of the fetish clothing that the guests and their submissives wore was custom-made. There was leather, lace, PVC and latex in abundance and, of course, a lot of collars, cuffs and buckles. Amber had never seen the like of it, even having lived in Susanna's mansion for a while now.

Amber marvelled at how beautiful and varied the ladies attending were. Susanna's friends ranged from the classically beautiful like Zoe, who could easily have been a model, to the Baroness who was butch through and through. The Baroness had set Amber's mind racing, and her non-traditional style hadn't felt out of place at all or been off-putting.

One of the dommes had arrived dressed as a pirate queen, thankfully sans parrot, but she did have two comely sailor wenches, dressed like something out of a swashbuckling film. Another had two girls who wore cat ears and once they took off their coats, revealed cat-tails attached to butt plugs, just like Pepper and Ginger wore.

They had dropped to all fours when their Mistress attached clips to their collars, and they'd assumed their personas as kittens. Then they'd crawled across the hard floor of the hallway into the bathroom, their Mistress following after them holding gripping their fine leather leashes in one fist. Amber didn't like to ask if it was a bit out of character for a kitten to accept a collar and leash and if that wasn't more like a dog.

"Roxy, is that everyone?" Susanna asked, frowning slightly.

"Yes, Mistress. Everyone who was at the guest house."

"Amber, check the list for me."

Amber picked up the clipboard from a nearby table and ticked off the names one by one. "Mistress Chevalier is the only one missing, Mistress."

Susanna rolled her eyes. "Of course, she would be," she sighed.

"Mistress, do you think she'll be very late?" Amber asked.

"Probably not, she's just a bit disorganised with this sort of thing. She has a tendency to lose track of time. It's not deliberate."

"Should we wait for her, Mistress?" Roxy asked.

"We'll give her another ten minutes. I should probably have called her myself this morning to chivvy her along," Susanna admitted. "Sugar, Candy, go and start serving drinks and make sure the rest of the guests are happy. Please tell them we may be a few minutes. Pudding you can get back the kitchen if you need to."

The rest of the staff dispersed, leaving Roxy and Amber with Mistress Susanna.

"Is there anything we can do for you, while we wait?" Roxy asked.

"Hmmm. Would you like to kiss Amber, perhaps?" Susanna replied.

"If it would please you, Mistress," Roxy said, advancing on Amber. "Come here, slut," the chauffeur said gruffly, pulling Amber in and taking her mouth, much as Mistress Susanna did when she wanted to claim her.

Amber felt herself wilting in Roxy's grip. She was strong and held tight to her, as Amber's knees went weak, shaking from the sensation that was so like being kissed by her boss. Roxy was hungry, animalistic and passionate. Amber could hear Mistress Susanna behind her, giving words of encouragement. Not to Amber though, she was prompting Roxy, telling her to control Amber, to own her lips and tongue, to savour the moment.

"Yes, this is definitely better than checking my phone for social media updates," Susanna mused. "You two look good together. Perhaps I should have made this happen sooner."

"You should have," Roxy replied, taking a break from her exploration of Amber's tongue. "This slut is delightful."

Amber was shocked. Not at being described as a slut but a woman she was attracted to, but by the overly familiar way that Roxy was speaking to Susanna. It seemed disrespectful, in a way that she, Candy, Sugar or Pudding wouldn't have dared.

Roxy seemed to have a different dynamic with their Mistress than Amber or the maids did, and that made her immediately curious about their relationship.

"Isn't she though? I seem to remember a certain scepticism on your part when Amber first arrived," Susanna replied.

Roxy shrugged and kissed Amber again for a moment, before replying. "I can't be right all the time. You've done an excellent job with her. To think, she was a virgin less than a month ago, and now she's at her first all-girl orgy. Mistress, you are a genius with new girls," Roxy said.

"Flattery will get you everywhere, Roxy."

"I certainly hope so."

"I think I hear a vehicle approaching so we'll have to resume this another time, but can I take it that you'd be keen to have a more involved play session with Amber, Roxy?"

Roxy wiped her mouth and nodded. Then she did something that surprised Amber, given their interaction so far. The chauffeur dropped to her knees, crawling over to the chair that Susanna had sat in, she looked up at their domme from between her legs.

"Yes, Mistress. I would like to serve at your pleasure alongside Amber, whenever you wish me to do so," Roxy confirmed, her voice thick with lust.

Susanna reached down and gently cupped Roxy's face in one hand, "I'm sure that can be arranged, my darling. Perhaps next week we can find enough time to fulfil your needs, hmm?"

"Thank you, Mistress," Roxy said, her head bowing as she kissed Susanna's outstretched hand subserviently.

"Good girl. Now, stand up, it's time for us to welcome my last guest," Susanna ordered.

CHAPTER 5

Amber watched as the mud-splattered Land Rover pulled around the turning circle and disappeared out of view toward the tradesman's entrance. It was towing a large horsebox.

"Is that her?" Amber asked.

"Yeah, that's Mistress Chevalier, alright," Roxy with resignation.

"Come on, we may as well go and meet her at the side door," Susanna said, hurrying off with an exasperated look on her face.

"I'm guessing that's not her real name unless the horsebox is a gigantic coincidence."

"No, she's quite horsey, but her real name is Xanthippe Jade Marshall," Roxy whispered as they followed after Susanna.

"What?" Amber hissed back.

"I'm not kidding."

"Xanthippe?"

"Named after the wife of Socrates. Most of us call her Mistress Chevalier, of course," Roxy said. "She goes by Jade among our betters."

"I'm not surprised."

"Enough chatter you two," Susanna ordered before opening the door and going out into the yard.

Mistress Chevalier had already parked and was about to open the rear of the horsebox.

"What ho!" she called out when she saw Susanna.

"You're late, Jade," Susanna said crossly.

"Sorry, I was working on a particularly tricky commission and time got away from me. You know me, I'd forget to eat if someone didn't tell me it was lunchtime," the ruddy-faced replied.

"Really, Jade. There are lots of calendars and reminder apps and all sorts of ways to be organised these days. Everyone has had to wait for you."

Jade had the good grace to look sheepish. "Sorry old bean didn't mind to cause you grief. I do have something I think you'll want to see, though. Can I get some help with this?" the jodhpur wearing woman asked.

Susanna gestured, and Roxy stepped forward to help lower the door, which became a ramp. Amber was glad that she hadn't been picked as she didn't have a clue about this sort of thing.

"Who's the new girl?" Jade asked over her shoulder.

"Her name is Amber, she's my personal assistant," Susanna answered.

"Do you like ponies, Amber?" Jade asked.

Amber shrugged. "I don't really know much about horses."

Jade guffawed at that, in the kind of hearty way that genuine country gentlewomen had about them. "No, not horses, you silly girl. Ponies. Haven't you met Ginger and Pepper yet? Really, Susanna, you shouldn't keep your girls so isolated in that big house. You are a terror for forgetting to introduce people."

"I'm forgetful? Oh, you've got some nerve Jade Marshall," Susanna grumbled.

"Come on up, Amber. Don't worry, just hitch up your skirts, so they don't snag. It's perfectly clean in here," Jade called from within the horsebox.

Amber glanced at Susanna for permission, then made her way up the ramp.

"Amber, meet my new pony, Victoria. Vicky for short. Isn't she a sight to behold?" Jade said proudly.

Victoria was indeed a sight to behold. She was at least six feet tall and had a long plait of platinum blonde hair trailing down her back. Her feet were encased in knee-length hoof boots, which imitated the shape of a horse's hoof, by having her almost on tiptoes.

A complicated leather harness wrapped around her body, with straps passing between her legs, and over and under her shoulders. Her large breasts were mostly unobstructed but did have large bar piercings through her nipples and black leather straps over and under them, emphasising their size and shape.

Vicky's head was encased in a harness with a rubber bit gag between her teeth and blinders on, as well as a bridle hanging down behind her head. A prominent tail was jutting from between her cheeks, and Amber could only imagine the butt plug that was buried in Vicky's bottom.

All of this was similar to the kind of tack and harness she'd seen Mistress Susanna use on her ponygirls, Pepper and Ginger. There was one difference, and it was big. Not only was Amber tall, but her stomach showed if not a full six-pack, the clear indications of strong muscle and low body fat. Her thighs were thick and muscular, and her shoulders were similarly rounded with muscle.

Vicky wasn't the most extreme female bodybuilder that Amber had ever seen, in pictures at least. She was softer and less lean than the professionals, but Amazonian would have been an apt description.

"What do you think?" Jade asked excitedly.

"I'm no expert, Mistress Chevalier but Vicky seems like a lovely pony. She's very impressive," Amber replied, trying not to say the wrong thing.

"I call her a Shire Pony, because she's such a fine physical specimen and I can work her as hard as I like," Mistress Chevalier said, as she led the young woman down the ramp.

"What do you think, Susanna?" Mistress Chevalier asked, expectantly.

Susanna's eyes widened in surprise when she saw the huge ponygirl, but she soon got herself under control and approached to get a closer look. Her hand reached out, but she stopped herself before she touched the pony and looked at Jade to ask for permission, "May I?"

"Of course. Vicky loves to be touched, don't you, my pet?" Jade said, stroking the shoulder of the much taller woman.

Vicky stamped her foot in confirmation and whinnied. Susanna reached out and stroked the woman's shoulder, then down her side, all the day to her strong thigh. Vicky shivered in response to the light touch.

"She's amazing, Jade. Is she quick?"

"Oh yes, she's got quite some pace on her, and she can pull hard, of course," Jade agreed.

"Does she respond well to the whip? She looks pretty tough," Susanna asked.

Mistress Chevalier chuckled, a dirty sound if Amber had ever heard one. "Want to find out?"

Susanna blinked. "I meant, in a race."

Vicky's domme shook her head gently, passing Susanna a riding crop. "Yes, but I'll only answer if you test her mettle yourself."

"We should probably get inside."

"Probably, but lighten up a little, Susanna. If we go inside now, everyone will want to play with Vicky, don't you think?"

"I'm sure she's going to turn heads, she's rather special," Susanna agreed.

"Yes, she is. Believe me, I'm happy to have found her. Now, are you going to crop her bottom and see how she responds or are you going to be a spoilsport?" Jade teased.

Susanna shot Jade a dark glance and Amber realised she was chewing her lip, hoping to see the crop in action and what Vicky's response might be to it. "Jade, you are quite simply, impossible," Susanna hissed. But her objection didn't stop her counting out all six strikes of the crop she applied to Vicky's left buttock.

Amber swallowed, her throat dry as Vicky whimpered. The pony might not have responded how Susanna or Jade would like, but Amber could certainly feel her own mounting arousal as she watched Vicky receive her discipline.

Susanna reached out with her left hand, flattening her fingers against Vicky's strong stomach. Then she turned her head to face Jade, who merely grinned lasciviously as Susanna's hand quested down over the smooth flesh of Vicky's abdomen.

When her Mistress licked her lips, with just the tip of her tongue, and Vicky whinnied, Amber felt her arousal spike. A moment later, Susanna lifted her fingers and inspected the glistening moisture that coated them. Susanna lifted her right hand, crop clenched in her fist, and uncurled her index finger to beckon Amber forward.

Amber moved to her Mistress's side, and soon Susanna's wet fingers were sucked between her lips. The taste of Vicky's arousal filled her mouth as she greedily sucked her boss's fingers clean.

"Now that, is sexy," Mistress Chevalier breathed. "What do you think, Susanna?"

"I think Vicky likes the whip, a lot."

Jade nodded. "Yes, yes, she does. Instant wetness. It does help her pace as well since you asked. She's a great all-rounder."

"Good. Glad to hear it. Congratulations. Now, shall we join the party?"

"I have my stuff to unpack still," Jade reminded Susanna.

Susanna sighed. "Of course. I wish you'd come earlier. Amber, Roxy, Mistress Chevalier has some of her products that are going to need taking inside so she can display them. Some of the ladies might want to make purchases."

Turning to Amber, Susanna gave her an appraising look. "I love that dress on you, and there's a certain appeal to seeing you filthy, covered in mud with a torn dress but that's not the theme for today, and it's an expensive indulgence. You can strip off now, Amber and serve Mistress Chevalier in the nude, which I'm sure everyone else will enjoy."

Amber began to strip off without a word, blushing as Mistress Chevalier wolf-whistled and applauded loudly. She carefully took the dress inside and made sure it was safely stowed away where it wouldn't get dirty. Amber took her expensive shoes off as well, and returned to the horsebox entirely nude, as ordered.

"There you go, Jade. Please try and be quick with this, I want you at the party before we start properly. I'll send Sugar and Candy to help too," Susanna said.

"Thanks, Susanna. I appreciate it, just a few more loyal customers would be a big help. I'm sorry, I was late. I promise I'll make it up to you," Mistress Chevalier said.

"Good, because if you do it again, I'll give you such a spanking!" Susanna said, then stuck her tongue out at Jade and turned to leave.

Jade laughed, "Darling, you can bend me over and spank me any time you want."

Susanna stopped dead in her tracks and took a deep breath. "Noted," she said before she hurried off.

"Oh dear, Mistress Chevalier, I think you're going to get it good and hard later," Roxy opined.

"I do hope so, dear. Oh, don't look so scandalised. I may have a preference for topping girls like you but doesn't mean I don't like a good hard spanking now and then. Especially in front of my peers," Mistress Chevalier said with a hearty wink. Roxy laughed.

With that, they set about emptying the ponygirl tack that Mistress Chevalier explained were her business. She specialised in high-end leather goods and other equipment for people into pony play and similar things. Her boxes of goods were full of riding crops, bridles, body harnesses, bit gags and more delightful things.

By the time they were done, Amber was glistening with perspiration. Mistress Chevalier looked her up and down as she took deep breaths to catch up, clearing enjoying what she was looking at. "You look scrumptious after a little light exercise, Amber. I could lick you all over and eat you right up. Have you tried pony racing?" she asked.

"Yes. I raced Mistress earlier in the week, and Pepper and I won," Amber said sheepishly.

"I sense a but coming?"

"I got in trouble for it."

"You got in trouble just for winning? That's not like Susanna," Jade pointed out.

"No, for telling Pepper I'd give her an orgasm if she could win. Apparently, that wasn't in the spirit of the thing, but I didn't know that" Amber said.

"You loved your punishment though, I'll bet," Jade commented, chuckling when Amber's blushing confirmed her guess. "Anyway, I didn't mean racing with you as the driver. I meant you'd look gorgeous if you worked up a good sweat pulling a trap."

"Agreed," Roxy interjected. Vicky whinnied and stamped her foot to add her endorsement.

"Thank you, that's very kind," Amber said.

"Not a bit of it, I'm just a filthy old mare who loves to see a young filly hot and sweaty," Jade said.

"But you're not old," Amber protested.

"Kind of you to say so, and it was just a figure of speech. I'm the oldest here, but I keep myself in good shape. Well, until you compare me to someone like Vicky of course, who spends a ludicrous amount of time on her health and fitness. Not that I don't appreciate that, of course, it looks great on her and giving her enough exercise to break a sweat gets me all the exercise I need," Jade said with a dirty laugh.

"You seem to be in much better shape than me, Mistress Chevalier," Amber pointed out. "You didn't get out of breath moving this stuff."

"You work in an office, I'm making and moving leather all day. If Susanna wants you to get some more exercise though, I'm sure Vicky and I would be happy to help," Jade said, earnestly, before giving another delightfully filthy laugh.

"I live to serve, Mistress Susanna," Amber replied, coyly.

"Translation, I hope Mistress Susanna shares me with you, Mistress Chevalier," Roxy scoffed.

"That sounds fun," Mistress Chevalier said. "Come on, we've done enough. Let's go and get the party started, shall we?"

"Yes, Mistress," chorused Roxy and Amber, with an agreeable whinny from Vicky.

CHAPTER 6

When Amber had last wandered into the ballroom, it had been a largely empty room, the only things that drew the eye were on the wall. A grand fireplace against one wall and even two smaller ones and paintings. There were paintings everywhere. They were all old and looked like they'd come with the house, just like the wood panelling and polished oak floor.

The change since she'd last been here was immediately noticeable. For the most part, it was the additional furniture which drew the eye. Around the edges of the room, Chesterfield style leather seating had been placed. There were right-angled sofas in each corner big enough for a group to sit on, and big 3-seater straight sofas along the long walls, with a handful of chaise longues as well.

Near each of the main seats, a footstool had been placed, and each of those was several feet long, big enough to lay down on if your feet were on the floor. It was all a rich oxblood red, the creases of the leather darkening to an almost black colour.

A series of huge and thick black rugs had been used to carpet most of the floor, protecting the well-polished oak from the feet of the furniture and presumably, the knees of any submissives ordered to them. One area was free of rugs because it had been covered instead with thick exercise mats that interlocked like a jigsaw puzzle.

Next to them was an area that had been covered in plastic sheeting, because what looked like a large inflatable paddling pool had been placed there. There was a table by it, covered with thick towels and bottles of baby oil, which Amber really wanted to see in use. Oiled up submissives wrestling each other? That had to be something she'd get to see, it just had to be.

Then there was another ring of furniture, but not in the classic vein of a country house. These items were more modern, constructed from heavy, wood stained black, wrought iron and shining steel. Where these items were upholstered, they'd been covered in the same oxblood leather as the Chesterfield sofas.

The inner ring was all far more specialist than the outer ring. There were three St Andrew's crosses, used for restrained a submissive upright and spreadeagled for play or punishment. They were joined by several spanking benches and a matching pillory, a modern take on a medieval favourite. Amber licked her lips as she imagined her head and wrists being clamped in one of those, while her body was on display and accessible to the room full of dominant women and their submissives. She shivered in anticipation of what might happen.

There were two cages, currently unoccupied, one a low style a submissive would need to be on all fours to occupy that had a coffee table on top, the other a tall one with cuffs dangling from the top bars to allow a girl to be displayed standing upright.

A hefty looking frame supported an arrangement of straps and padded supports that Amber recognised as a sex swing from a bawdy comedy film she'd gone to see with friends. Next to it, was a boxy-looking leather chair which seemed innocent at first glance, until you see the thick leather wrist and ankle straps on the arms and legs that could restrain a subject for interrogation.

It was no wonder Mistress Susanna had hired the furniture for the party, rather than owning it outright. Not that Amber thought she couldn't afford it, but it would hardly be practical to store this much furniture without having a dedicated room for it.

Mistress Susanna's guests were distributed around the room, lounging on sofas with their subs at their feet or standing, sipping wine and stroking the head of a submissive who was kneeling beside them.

In the centre of the room, a shallow stage had been assembled. Low enough to step on to easily and high enough to make the occupants easy to see. Mistress Susanna stood up there, waiting as her guests chatted.

"Ah, I see our final guest has officially arrived," Susanna said, her voice cutting through the conversation around her, which soon faded away. "Good, now we can begin. Amber, please join me on stage."

Mistress Susanna gestured around her, "Welcome to my humble abode, one and all. For those of you who don't know, or are new to these events and for anyone who might have forgotten, I must go over some ground rules."

"There are buffet tables in the dining room next door, and plenty of drink options and nibbles. I ask that everyone remain sober for the whole event, and I regret that if anyone is intoxicated, they'll have to leave. Please be respectful of the furniture, in particular the items outside of this room. Much of it is as old as the house and quite valuable," Susanna said, pointing at a marble-topped side table near one of the hearths.

"The group safeword for this evening is 'Cotswold', but please remember to be mindful of any other strange words a submissive may blurt out that could be their normal safeword. If in doubt, as you already know, pause your play and check. The kitchen is strictly off-limits. Pudding is an excellent cook, and none of us wants her disturbed or our evening meal will not be up to her high standards," Susanna said, "not to mention the spanking she would give a transgressor would leave them unable to stand for a week!" The audience was clearly familiar with Pudding's cooking and her predilection for turning bottoms hot pink.

"As you can see, I have provided an excellent selection of furniture for you to use, as well as a collection of instruments and toys. On the table by the hallway door is a bowl with some keys in it. These unlock bedrooms upstairs, which you may use at your discretion. If you want privacy, you may lock the door, and put the 'Do not disturb' sign on it, but an unlocked room is in open invitation to other guests that you would like more company, for play or voyeurism. Please don't hog the rooms all night if you must use them."

Amber looked around the room while Susanna talked, watching how the guests responded to the speech. Plenty of them caught her gaze as she looked at them, and she could feel other eyes on her, admiring her nakedness. She straightened her back a bit and pulled her shoulders back, making sure her figure was displayed well and enjoying the twinkling in the eyes of the guests as they sized her up like a piece of meat.

"I want to encourage you all to avoid the bedrooms, and instead, play in public in here, so that we can all enjoy the sights and sounds of each other's pleasure," Susanna said, "or pain. I think that covers everything."

"Who's the new girl, Susanna," Mistress Cauldwell asked.

"Of course, silly me. Everyone, this is Amber, my new personal assistant," Susanna explained.

"Is she one of us, or a submissive?" Mistress Cauldwell asked.

"As you might guess from her state of undress, Amber is also one of my submissives," Susanna confirmed.

"Are you sure? She doesn't look very deferential to me. She looks quite proud and defiant," Mistress Cauldwell said, "Diamond here is kneeling and ready to serve." The domme used the leash wrapped around her fist to destabilise Diamond's position and pull her off balance. The girl fell to the rug beneath her, and when the leash was relaxed, resumed her kneeling position without complaint, despite the fire that Amber saw flashing in her eyes.

"I'm quite sure," Susanna said. "What is it you all want, a demonstration of Amber's submission to my will?"

Amber wondered if it was improved or if it was pre-arranged but either way, her Mistress was clearly enjoying putting on a show. The audience was enjoying themselves too calling out encouragement and agreeing with Mistress Cauldwell.

"Kneel before me, Amber," Susanna ordered. When she did so, her Mistress called out to the crowd, "Is this what you? To be entertained?"

"Yes!" came the response. "More!" the ladies shouted.

"Amber, who do you serve?"

"I serve you, Mistress."

"A month ago, had you been with a woman before?"

"No, Mistress."

"Had you been spanked? Or caned?"

"No, Mistress."

"Turn to face the audience, and touch yourself," Susanna ordered.

Amber shuffled around and spread her knees apart, obediently slipping a hand between her thighs to stroke her wet lips.

"If I told you to lick my pussy in front of my guests, would you, Amber?" Susanna asked.

"Yes, Mistress. I would love to," Amber gasped.

Susanna crouched close behind Amber, tugging her head back and kissing her neck, slipping a hand around and pinching her nipple hard until Amber couldn't help but cry out. "Amber, if I told you to walk across the room, and drop to your knees before one of my guests, then worship their pussy until they come, would you do it?"

"For you, anything, Mistress!" Amber cried out.

"Stop touching yourself and lick your fingers clean, slowly," Susanna ordered. Amber was frustrated from being denied a climax but did as she was told and supported her Mistress as well as she could. She made her display of submission as wanton as possible, licking and sucking her fingers wetly and with evident pleasure. The audience watched her with rapt attention and evident approval.

"Ladies, Amber was completely new to the scene when I found her and I've been training her hard for weeks. I am the only dominant who has had the pleasure of her. Should I share her with you? Would anyone like that?" Susanna asked.

The response was a huge cheer and a chorus of agreement.

"The vote is clear, and I shall abide by your wishes, as the gracious host that I am. Now, who shall I choose to have the services of my latest girl, I wonder?" Susanna pondered, looking out at the assembled dommes. "Perhaps our most august members, the Baroness or Dame Cartwright would like a turn? Or perhaps you would like to sample Amber yourself, Mistress Cauldwell."

"Everyone in here wants her, Susanna," Baroness Carruthers replied.

"Of course we do, make your choice so we can all have some fun," Dame Cartwright echoed with a hearty laugh.

Susanna pretended to ponder the decision for just a few moments longer, teasing the crowd expertly. Amber was bursting to know who she would be given too as well. Between her thighs, her arousal was keenly felt, and she could imagine that spending time with any of the dominant women in the room would be nothing short of amazing.

Finally, when the tension was unbearable, Susanna announced her choice, "Mistress Chevalier, despite your tardiness, would you accept the offer of being the second domme to break in my newest acquisition?"

Mistress Chevalier looked quite taken aback, coughing on the sausage roll she had been happily eating, and thumping her chest to clear her throat. "Me?" she asked with obvious disbelief.

"Yes, Jade. You. I would like to offer you the full services of Amber for the afternoon. Does that sound good?" Susanna asked.

"Umm. Well, I'm flattered, and yes, it does sound good. Thank you," Mistress Chevalier replied. "I do need to finish setting up a few things first, though."

Susanna shook her head, "No, that's alright, take Amber with you, I'm sure she can help you with that, as well as any other needs you might have. Ladies, as a special treat, Mistress Chevalier has brought along some of her wares to show off. As you probably know, Jade is a highly regarding saddler and harness maker who provides leather goods to the ponygirl community, in particular. She also makes many items for more general play and takes custom orders. I can personally recommend her services as a leatherworker. Later on, when the goods are set up in the other room, you'll be able to take a good look and purchases or place orders as you see fit."

The news was met with a good deal of approval, and Amber noticed that Mistress Chevalier looked quite relieved at the positive response. leather goods and speciality items for you to look at and either purchase or place

"Enjoy Amber, Jade, she's rather good at taking orders, as you'll soon discover."

"I'm sure we'll get along famously, Susanna. Would you be able to look after Vicky while I'm otherwise engaged?" Mistress Chevalier asked.

"I'd be delighted to."

"Please, use her as you see fit. She too is good at taking orders," Mistress Chevalier replied, "and she's happy to be on display. Victoria is something of a show pony, you see."

"I'll make sure to give everyone something to appreciate then, Jade. Thank you. Run along with Mistress Chevalier now, Amber and make me proud," Mistress Susanna said.

"Yes, Mistress," Amber said as she stood up and followed the Mistress from the room.

CHAPTER 7

Amber was hot and sweaty again by the time she'd finished unpacking the boxes and moving the tables around and laying out Mistress Chevalier's products. The whips and paddles were easily dealt with, but the saddles and some small items of furniture and display stands were more cumbersome.

Mistress Chevalier barely lifted a finger to help her; instead, she sat back and gave instructions as Amber did the physical work. The older woman was having the time of her life, sometimes making her move a heavy saddle several times before she liked the position.

Amber had asked what type of horses the saddles were for and been roundly mocked. The saddles were designed purely for human ponies, to be worn when they were on all ours and allowing them to be ridden. They were far lighter than horse saddles, and not all subs could support their Mistress and move much. Mistress Chevalier said it was more about roleplay, although she had found that Vicky was so unusually strong, she could easily crawl around the room, carrying her domme on her back.

"I'll say it again, Amber. You look beautiful with your skin shining with sweat. Come here, sit on my lap so I can get a closer look,"

Mistress Chevalier said. “Straddle me,” she ordered, having Amber positioned face to face with her, on the footstool, she was perched on.

Once she was in position, Mistress Chevalier stroked her hands up Amber’s thighs, up her ribcage and then cupped her damp breasts in her palms. “You are truly stunning,” the domme said before she dipped her head and licked a line up between Amber’s breasts, then over to her left nipple. She licked and sucked there for a while, before tasting her other nipple.

“You’re delicious. I could definitely eat you all up,” Jade confirmed.

“Thank you, Mistress. That feels so good,” Amber replied.

“I suppose I still have some skills, despite being so old,” Jade laughed.

Amber shook her head, “You’re not old, Mistress Chevalier. You’re beautiful and sexy.”

“Well, that’s very kind of you to say dear, but I’m sure a young slip of a thing would have been much more excited at the prospect of being shared with one of Susanna’s other friends,” Mistress Chevalier demurred. “There are far younger, prettier dommes than me here today.”

“Not at all. I don’t wish to speak out of turn, but you seem much more approachable and, well, fun than some of the other guests,” Amber said.

Mistress Chevalier laughed heartily at that. “Oh, I do, do I?”

“Yes, you do,” Amber agreed firmly.

“Perhaps my pleasures aren’t to your taste, though. I’m surprised that Susanna hasn’t had you in harness yet. Do you not relish the thought of being a pony for your Mistress?”

Amber shrugged. “I haven’t been here long, Mistress. There hasn’t been much time to think about it, or to try it.”

“You’ll have plenty of time with Susanna I’m sure. I cannot imagine her giving up a submissive so thoroughly delightful and easy on the eye,” Mistress Chevalier said.

“Thank you, Mistress. Would you like me to serve you in some way?” Amber asked, her tongue subconsciously licking her lip, “I will do as I’m told, of course.”

"I'm sure that would be lovely, but I wouldn't want to cross any boundaries you have," Mistress Chevalier said.

Amber giggled. "Is there something really naughty you'd like me to do? It's ok to tell me, if there is," she teased.

"Minx. I'm not sure how naughty the things I like would seem to you, but I don't want to shock you, all the same," Mistress Chevalier said.

"I'm sure you won't, Mistress. Would you like to ask me about something, and see what I think?" Amber suggested.

"Fine. Since you insist. How do you respond to pain?"

"Quite well, I suppose. I've been brought to tears and managed to cope with that since I got here," Amber said proudly.

The dominant had a little half-smile at that comment. "Have you indeed? That's interesting. What I really wondered though was whether pain had you getting wet in places your tears didn't run?"

Amber dipped her head and stared into Mistress Chevalier's eyes, "It has done, yes. Would that please you?"

Mistress Chevalier didn't reply, she reached up and pulled Amber down into a long kiss, her hands exploring the younger woman's body all the while. When the kiss finally broke, the dommes mouth dipped to Amber's right nipple, and her fingers found the left.

Slowly at first, Amber's world blossomed with pleasurable sensations as the older domme licked and sucked at one nipple while stroking and teasing the other with her fingers. Then the gentle manipulations grew firmer, more insistent. The teeth nipped at her sensitive flesh, and the fingers pinched and tugged. Amber gave a low moan, and that spurred Mistress Chevalier on.

The fingers on her left nipple shifted, taking a good grip and then combining a tight pinch, with a twisting and tugging motion. Amber's head tipped back, and she squealed, loud enough that she half-expected someone to come running. Mistress Chevalier chuckled triumphantly, her amusement muffled by the wet nipple in her mouth, which she proceeded to bite hard, causing another burst of pain.

A hand slid down between Amber's thighs, and the strong fingers of someone who worked with her hands delved between her sopping wet lips, quickly finding her clit. Amber felt the wave of pleasure begin to swell as her swollen clitoris was expertly played with, then she felt the sting of tears filling her eyes when Mistress Chevalier pinched her sensitive nub as well.

"You're sopping wet, you naughty girl," Mistress Chevalier said. "Come for me, Amber. Come from my gift of pain."

Amber wanted to resist, as the domme manipulated her nipples and clit with her mouth and tongue, but it was far from easy. Gradually she felt her passion rising, despite the intense pain she was being tormented with.

"Are you fighting it, you hot little bitch?" Mistress Chevalier growled.

"Yes, Mistress," Amber groaned, holding her release back with all her willpower.

"You won't win. You're too much of a slut not to give in to your filthy thoughts," Mistress Chevalier insisted, between bites of her nipples and pinches of her clitoris. "You'll get off on the pain despite yourself, I can tell. Girls like you get so wet when you torment them, and they come like fountains."

"No. I won't, Mistress," Amber claimed boldly, but was soon disproven as she rushed over the peak of her first climax and straight into a second, shuddering and gasping and calling out Mistress's name, "Jade, oh, Jade!"

Wet fingers were pushed into her mouth a moment later for her to suck clean and she tasted herself on Mistress Chevalier's fingers. A sharp slap landed on her thigh, "That's for being disrespectful and not using the title I've earned."

"I'm sorry, Mistress. I meant no disrespect, I promise," Amber moaned.

"I warned you that you couldn't resist my touch," the older domme said, before pulling her head down and passionately kissing her, tasting Amber's pussy from her lips. "I've been playing these games since I was your age. I started serving older women when I was a fresh young university student, and I've never stopped playing since. Once I would have been the one serving the pleasures of a woman twice my age. Then I changed roles, and now the sluts serve me. Worshipping me. I've had more pussy than you can dream of so when I tell you to come, you're going to come, my girl, whether you want to resist or not."

Defeated, sweaty and used, Amber nodded. "Yes, Mistress. I'm sorry for fighting."

Mistress Chevalier laughed, "Don't be, my girl. Do you think I'd have taken on Vicky, with her great big muscles and such long legs, if I didn't relish a challenge?"

"Did I make you happy, Mistress?" Amber asked.

"Why don't you feel me and find out?" Mistress Chevalier suggested, then took hold of her hand and pressed it into her lap. Amber gasped. Below the material of the dominant woman's jodhpurs was a distinctly unladylike bulge. The woman chuckled at her reaction and pulled her in tight, "Get it out."

Fumbling blindly, with their torso pressed together and little room for her to move her hand, Amber sought the buttons of the jodhpurs even as she whimpered at the thought of it. The cock she had felt was swelling, as she tried to free it. Amber felt confused, disoriented by the unexpectedly phallic contents of Mistress Chevalier's riding trousers, but when the woman gave her more room, easing back on the hug, she was able to open the buttons and release the stiffening member within.

"Good girl," Mistress Chevalier said, pushing her roughly off her lap and to the fall.

Amber fell back and looked up, startled by the move. Jutting from Mistress Chevalier's lap was a large, purple and crimson cock. The silicone was detailed, with veins on the shaft and a big mushroom head. Mistress Chevalier's hand was resting on a bulb strapped in place at her side, and a thin tube disappeared toward her crotch. It was inflatable, which was a relief to realise.

"That gave you a shock, didn't it?" Mistress Chevalier laughed.

Amber blushed, then giggled. "Yes, Mistress. I didn't know what to think."

"Have I lost you entirely, or are we still playing?"

Amber took a deep breath, "We're still playing, Mistress. Until Mistress Susanna takes me back."

"Good girl, then up, and on your knees, and give my big boy a good suck, won't you? Make it nice and whorish for me," Mistress Chevalier ordered confidently.

Amber found the cock buried in her mouth, as deep as she could take it. The swollen girth stretched her jaw, and the head came close to choking her. All the while Mistress Chevalier called her vulgar names and demanded that she redouble her efforts. Amber could feel her inner thighs were getting coated in dribbles of her arousal.

"Enough, on all fours so I can fuck you, Amber," Mistress Chevalier ordered.

The cock buried in her to the hilt made her whimper and moan. The domme was not gentle or slow, riding the submissive she'd been loaned hard and fast, and making her gasp and mumble with excitement.

"Come hard for me, slut. Come now or I swear I will spank you so hard that you won't be able to sit down for a week!" Mistress Chevalier demanded it. "Don't fight it, girl. Come for me, Amber!"

This time, Amber did as she was told. Giving in to the insistent urging in her loins, the need the strapon created in her to climax. She cried out as Mistress Chevalier rode her hard, collapsing into the rug as her orgasm washed over her.

Amber was still gasping, trying to recover her breath when Mistress Chevalier stood up, grabbed her by the hair and hauled her around, forcing the thick length back into her mouth. She sucked and licked at it, putting on a show of cleaning the fake cock for her Mistress.

"Good girl," Mistress Chevalier said when she'd had had her fill of making Amber do that. With a speed which spoke of practice, the domme unbuckled the strapon harness and sat down in a Queen Anne armchair. Amber was impressed when the older woman lifted her legs, and draped them over the high arms of the chair, spreading her legs wide and displaying her pussy.

Sensing that Amber was impressed, "Yoga and years of horse

riding. They're a great combination for improving flexibility. Eat me, slut." The domme laughed and pointed at her glistening pussy with an exaggerated motion.

Amber dove right in, her face already wet with saliva from fellating the silicone cock that lay discarded on the floor. Mistress Chevalier tasted delicious, and she devoured her hungrily.

Soon the domme was sighing and taking deep, contented breaths. "It's hard to believe that you're so new to this. Susanna and her girls are clearly doing an excellent job training you. My compliments on your tongue, girl."

When Amber, too busy to speak her reply, lifted a hand and gave Mistress Chevalier a big thumbs up, the older woman laughed heartily and reached out to cup her head. The domme mashed her sub's face into her pussy as she licked, gently rolling her hips too and grinding herself against the younger woman's face.

"Oh yes, an excellent job indeed," she repeated.

"I'm glad to hear it," Mistress Susanna said.

CHAPTER 8

"Has she made you come, yet?" Mistress Susanna asked.

"Not yet."

"Really? You've been beavering away in here for quite some time. Amber, I must say I'm disappointed with you," Susanna said from somewhere behind her kneeling sub.

Amber's eyes lifted, and she could see Mistress Chevalier's amused smirk as she twisted the situation. She tried to lift her head to explain the situation. That she had only been giving her Mistress's friend head for a few minutes, and the rest of the time she'd been helping set up the stall and getting tormented herself.

Clearly, that wasn't on the card because Mistress Chevalier clamped her thighs together and tightened her grip on Amber's hair, keeping her face firmly pressed against her hungry pussy.

"She seems to be doing her best, but I clearly haven't been able to impress my need on her in the right way," Mistress Chevalier remarked, sounding rather bored with the efforts Amber was making to make her climax, which were entirely earnest.

"Perhaps I could help encourage her for you? I came in to find out what all the noise was about, expecting you to be half-unconscious from her ministrations."

"Oh no, that was Amber, not me. I thought a little reward might help focus her mind. Sadly her tongue, while agile doesn't seem quite dedicated enough," Mistress Chevalier said, winking at Amber.

"I wonder what might do the trick?" Susanna replied.

"There are plenty of great things to try on that table," her friend said.

"Oh, yes, there certainly are. I sense a sales pitch. What beautiful paddles," Susanna said excitedly.

"I do my best," Mistress Chevalier said, smiling down at Amber, who was also doing her best to make the woman come in the hope she might get out of what was about to happen.

"I'm spoilt for choice. Perhaps this nice looking tawse? Or a bamboo paddle?"

"Amber told me that you haven't tried her out as a pony yet," Mistress Chevalier prompted.

"No, not yet. I've thought about it, but there's only so much time in the day, and Amber is so new to the lifestyle. She has a lot to learn, although I honestly thought she was better with her tongue by now," Susann said. She sounded genuinely disappointed, and Amber couldn't help but feel hurt. What Mistress Chevalier was doing was so cruel. She was making Susanna doubt her commitment to serving her Mistress. Making her think her sub wasn't performing well enough and all the while, she was smirking and gloating as Amber's heart was torn in two by the doubt of her Mistress.

"If you'd like to introduce her to some elements of pony play, you could try that horsehair flogger there. The one with the green handle," Mistress Chevalier suggested.

"An excellent choice, the handle is charming, though I'm not sure the colour is ideal," Susanna commented, as she leaned down and pulled Amber's hips back, thus forcing her to all fours. Mistress Chevalier slid down the cushion to a more horizontal position, so Amber wasn't freed from her pussy.

"It's a novel style, popular with youngsters. I can't tell you how many young punks, Goths and anime fans have seen my toys in that vein and offered themselves up to," Mistress Chevalier bragged. "I can do it in any colour of course, but that one does glow in the dark."

Susanna laughed, and the stinging explosion of pain on Amber's buttocks made her scream into Mistress Chevalier's pussy.

"She doesn't like that, does she?" Mistress Chevalier said, gleefully.

"No, but Amber loves to suffer for me, don't you, my dear?" Amber breathed hard through her nose but was finally able to lift her hand and give another thumbs up.

"See? She can take her punishment so well, Jade." Mistress Susanna said.

"That's always good news," Mistress Chevalier said. "I find I have to be very careful using that style of flogger on the university students I meet at conventions. They act like their women of the world and claim to be up for it, but not many have been properly broken in by an experienced domme."

"So, true," Susanna agreed as she delivered two more swishes of the stingy flogger. Amber felt tears well up.

"Keep going, you're making her eyes water," Mistress Chevalier encouraged.

"Of course," Susanna said, delivering more discipline. "Would you like to see her really cry?"

"Tempting but I'd prefer to see you take her to the edge, and maybe one day you'll let me enjoy her tears at my hand?"

"Of course, I'm sure I can complete her punishment without taking her over the line," Susann said, delivering the next few blows at less speed. They still stung, but Amber didn't have to fight the welling up of tears, she could master her reaction to the pain better. "Did you fuck her with this strapon?"

"Yes, she loved it. In her pussy and her mouth too."

"I'm glad she's doing something right. There, all done, Amber," Susanna said, dropping to her knees and using her tongue to soothe Amber's bottom.

"My oh my, Susana. That is hotter than you can imagine," Mistress Chevalier said.

Susanna crawled forward and watched Amber's efforts as she licked at the sopping wet pussy before her. Finally, with Susanna looking on, Mistress Chevalier came hard, shuddering and crying out. Her hands let go of Amber's head and flew to her face. Amber could see her biting her knuckle with excitement as she rode the wave of her orgasm.

Before Amber could speak, Mistress Susanna gripped her head and pulled her into a sloppy and passionate kiss, claiming her mouth with her tongue. Amber was left gasping and flushed.

"That wasn't a bad finish," Mistress Chevalier said.

"She's lying, Mistress!" Amber blurted out. "I'd barely started eating Mistress Chevalier's pussy before you came in. She took her pleasure from me by tormenting my nipples and pussy and making me come, then she fucked me with that thing. I didn't let you down. I was trying really hard to please her. I would never want to disappoint you like that." The two dommes let her rant until she ran out of words and then exchanged a look, before Mistress Chevalier laughed at her, while Susanna passionately kissed her again, on the lips and then all over her face, her hands teasing Amber's breasts.

"You silly girl, of course, you haven't disappointed me. It was just a game we were playing for our pleasure. I'm sorry sweetheart, I thought you knew we were roleplaying," Susanna finally managed to say, looking a little contrite, but not nearly enough for Amber's mood.

"Mistress Chevalier, how did you find my Amber's skills as a cunnilinguist?"

"Top notch, Mistress Susanna. I'd be happy to have her give me head any day of the week, and sixteen times on Sunday," Mistress Chevalier said seriously.

"Sixteen? Only sixteen?" Mistress Susanna teased.

Mistress Chevalier threw her hands up in the air grumpily and then began to pull up her jodhpurs. "Yes, Sundays are usually when I'm at some craft fair or fetish event, marketing my goods. I only have time for half the number of orgasms I usually demand," she said, heaping on the overly theatrical performance like an actor on a television soap.

Mistress Susanna stared blankly at her for a moment, and then both dommes collapsed in a fit of giggles. "Sixteen times!" Mistress Susanna managed, gasping for breath. "Dear me, I can barely breathe."

Amber sat back on her haunches and crossed her arms grumpily, a dark frown taking over her face.

Mistress Chevalier laughed. "Oh no, the subby looks pissed off, Susanna. You're going to pay for this later!" she laughed.

"I'm sure she'll get over it, won't you, my sweetness?" Susanna said. Amber didn't answer.

"Did you enjoy Vicky?"

"Oh yes, she's delightful and so strong," Susanna said.

"Isn't she though? Honestly, I have daydreamed about collaring her," Mistress Chevalier stage whispered conspiratorially.

"I can't say as I blame you, and that does seem to be going around. Yolanda announced earlier she's thinking of collaring Zoe you know," Susanna said.

"Great. Maybe we could have a group ceremony," Mistress Chevalier said. "If you have anyone to collar, we could make it a group thing, perhaps?"

Susanna smiled, "Perhaps, and even if we don't, you should give serious consideration to collaring Vicky before she loses faith that you will. I don't think you'll be happy if that tongue of hers is stolen away by some more giving doom. But for now, we have plenty of fun to have today. I was wondering if you'd like to go and visit Ginger and Pepper, Jade?"

"Are they in your stables? I've never seen your stables you know, I've just met Ginger and Pepper in the grounds or at events you brought them to," Mistress Chevalier pointed out.

"Yes. I thought you might like to see my modest facilities, Amber can take you over to see them. Then when you've said hello, you could bring them back to the party, and we can have them serve drinks. How does that sound?" Susanna suggested.

"Aren't you taking Amber back now?" Mistress Chevalier asked with evident surprise.

"No, I think you should use her for the afternoon at least if you're enjoying her. If you'd like to play with Ginger and Pepper before bringing them in, please feel free to, but if you can keep it fairly short, I'd appreciate it. We want you back at the party with us so we can all have fun together," Mistress Susanna said.

"That's lovely, thank you so much. Amber is a delight to play with. I think we should probably get your ponies in quickly though, so we can join in the fun," Mistress Chevalier said.

"We should have another pony play day soon. Then we can concentrate on your favourite things," Susanna said.

"That would be fun. Perhaps you could even try racing Amber?"

"Maybe. I'm not sure if she is pony material."

"She did rather warm to that horsehair flogger," Mistress Chevalier pointed out.

"True. Perhaps a discussion for another day though. I'll leave you to it. Amber, be good for Mistress Chevalier," Susanna cautioned.

"Yes, Mistress."

CHAPTER 9

"Can I see the rest?" Mistress Chevalier asked as Pepper used her lips to pick up sugar cubes from her outstretched hand and munch the sweet brown sugar down happily.

"The rest? There's really just the tack and playroom, the showers, the stalls and the apartment upstairs where Ginger and Pepper sleep. I think you've seen everything," Amber replied.

"Are you sure? Do you think we have time?"

Amber shrugged. "Mistress wanted me to keep you happy. I'll follow your lead, Mistress Chevalier. We haven't been that long though."

"Good. Let's have a look at the other stalls then," Mistress Chevalier said.

Amber followed as the domme inspected the stalls down from Pepper and Ginger. There were four more in this part of the stable, and only one was in the same good condition as the stalls that Pepper and Ginger played their roles in when called upon.

The other three had seen better days and would need renovation before they'd be appealing to play in. The doors had been cleaned up a bit so that as you approached Pepper's stall, they looked well maintained, but it was just a facade.

"I knew Susanna had done some of the work, but I didn't realise how dilapidated the place was before she bought it. Do you know what's through here?" she asked, heading toward the door at the end of the row of stalls.

"No, I haven't spent much time here outside of the main house. I suppose we could ask Pepper and Ginger, but I think they don't like to break character," Amber said.

The door opened into a much larger stable area, but it was full of muck and cobwebs and clearly hadn't been refurbished at all.

"That's about right, pony and pet play works best if you can keep it up for a while. I don't know anyone who bothers trying to do it 24x7, but with a party going on, it wouldn't be kind to ask them to talk about renovations," Mistress Chevalier agreed. "Look at all this space. There are twelve stalls in this room, and a floor above us."

"I think there are two floors above us, thinking about the windows you can see outside."

"Gosh. I still can't believe how well Susanna has done for herself. She's worked hard as long as I've known here, but some of her businesses really took off. Of course, she got this place for a song at the time. The major cost was all the renovation. I wonder if she's going to renovate more of this?"

"I don't know, Mistress. Mistress Susanna hasn't mentioned anything, but I haven't known her that long."

"It makes my workshop and little paddock seem pitiful by comparison. I really must get a bit more serious about my business. I could never afford something like this, but a little stable and extending my workshop would be lovely," Mistress Chevalier mused.

"Maybe Mistress Susanna could help you find investors or help you market your goods?" Amber suggested.

"That's a kind thought, but she's already letting me bring my wares here so I can try and drum up more business. I'm not sure what I could do with investment anyway. If I had a bigger workshop and more storage, it'd help me be a little more efficient. Even so, there's still a limit to how many harnesses or what have you, that I can make, you see?" Mistress Chevalier explained.

"Perhaps you could get to the point where you could employ some help? You could train someone up to do the basic work for you, maybe?" Amber said.

"That would be nice. Ponyplay is a bit of a niche market, but lots more people are playing with leather goods these days. Maybe I could do more things like paddles and floggers," Mistress Chevalier said.

Amber nodded enthusiastically, "See? Maybe Mistress Susanna would be able to give some better suggestions? I don't know much about business, but she does."

"I can tell you really like helping people, don't you?"

Amber nodded, "I suppose I have. You seem nice, and if you could reach more customers, you'd be in a lot better positions.

"That sounds nice. I do like being in a superior position," Mistress Chevalier replied with a big wink.

"I noticed that," Amber giggled. "It seems to be a lot more popular than I'd have guessed before I applied for my job. I didn't realise so many women liked this stuff."

"Not as many as I'd like but almost enough. I bet you didn't know what you were in for at all, did you?" Mistress Chevalier grinned.

"Being stripped naked, spanked and taught to lick pussy?"

"Yes, it sounds like all that came as something as a surprise. Don't worry, not everyone realises that they are into BDSM without a little push. It's nothing to be embarrassed about," Mistress Chevalier said. "Susanna is very lucky to be able to employ such exciting ladies."

"That's another reason to kick your business into a new gear," Amber pointed out. "You could have a little team of your own too. You could start with one of those girls who like your toys. A little anime fan, maybe?"

"Maybe. Or a cosplay girl who makes her own costumes? That way you could find someone whose crafty like you?"

"I do like being crafty," Mistress Chevalier said. "It would be nice to have another girl at my beck and call. Vicky isn't available all the time, she has a job to go to."

"If I can do anything to help you, do let me know," Amber said.

"One or two things do come to mind, but perhaps we should rejoin the party?"

Amber giggled again. "Yes, probably, but that's up to you, not me. You're the Mistress," Amber teased.

"Oh dear, I'm in charge, aren't I? What a pity," Mistress Chevalier said. Quick as a flash, she closed the distance, and span Amber around, pushing her up against the door of one of the stalls. "You're wet again, aren't you, Amber?" she asked, her breath hot against Amber's ear.

"Yes, Mistress," Amber confessed, as Mistress Chevalier's left hand stroked her breast and her right plunged between her legs.

"You'd like it if I played with this hot little pussy now, wouldn't you?"

"Yes, Mistress. Please," Amber begged.

Mistress Chevalier's strong fingers plunged between her lips and into her pussy, her thumb grazing Amber's swollen clit. "You love that, don't you, slut?"

"Yes, Mistress."

"You girls are all the same, with your eager, tight little pussies. You love having someone take control of you. Having someone teach you how to behave. You'd be on our knees all the time, worshipping my pussy, if you could, wouldn't you?"

Amber nodded and mumbled, "Yes, Mistress." Her body responded to the expert caresses from the domme.

"I know you would dear," Mistress Chevalier agreed, pulling her hands back and leading Amber out to where Pepper and Ginger were waiting. "Now, let's finish getting the ponies ready and get inside shall we?"

"Yes, Mistress," Amber said, the disappointment evident in her voice.

"Awww don't be glum, chum. I promise once we're inside, I'll make good use of you if your Mistress allows it. You'll get what you need."

"You promise? Really?" Amber said with rising excitement.

"I think you and I are going to be good friends, Amber," Mistress

Chevalier said. "I promise to use your hot, young body to put on a great show for everyone. I swear it on my riding crop!"

"Well, that does sound like a cast-iron promise," Amber said with a grin.

"From me? You can take that to the bank."

CHAPTER 10

The ballroom was a riot of imagery that seared itself into Amber's brain for weeks to come. Everywhere she looked, young women were submitting to the dommes that Mistress Susanna had invited.

Mistress Chevalier hugged her from behind, her fingers roving over Amber's body possessively and her mouth hot against her neck as they surveyed the room from the doorway.

"Let's take a tour, shall we, sexy?" Mistress Chevalier asked, nibbling at her ear. They began to walk around through the exhibition of debauchery, voyeuristically appreciating each scene, stopping to watch some and slowing to a stroll for others.

One of the first things they saw was Dame Cartwright and Baroness Carruthers enjoying a display of hand to hand combat.

Holly and Ivy had put their schoolgirl uniforms to one side, and they were wrestling, naked in and covered in shiny oil in the paddling pool. They struggled to remain on top of each other, slipping and sliding around. One would appear to have the upper hand, then would lose her stance and fall to her side with a shriek of laughter.

Each time one of the girls laughed, Dame Cartwright would flick out a long bamboo school cane, lashing their buttocks and making them howl as she admonished them for not taking it seriously. They watched a few tumbles and then Holly planted her sex on Ivy's face and sat on it until Ivy tapped out.

"Make her come then, Ivy," Dame Cartwright ordered, her hand slipping into her tight black skirt and down between her legs as she watched. "You can begin round three after you're done."

Baroness Carruthers had applauded when Holly scored her point and licked her lips lasciviously as she caught sight of her friend masturbating. Slowly, she turned back to face the two subs she had been playing with. Both were now naked and covered in baby oil. Amber wondered if they'd started in the paddling pool.

The Baroness had apparently taken charge of Vicky for the time being, and Mistress Chevalier's well-muscled submissive was sat on the wrestling mats, with her legs wrapped around Charlotte's upper back, ankles crossed and holding her in place. Vicky was holding Charlotte's head with both hands, keeping it tightly pressed to her pussy as the Baroness's submissive serviced her.

"I guess that means Vicky won," Amber said with a giggle.

"Vicky is very tasty, perhaps Charlotte won?" Mistress Chevalier suggested. "Look at the treatment she's getting from her Mistress," Mistress Chevalier said, walking Amber to the side for a better view.

The Baroness had a hand, slick with glistening lubricant, almost to the knuckles on all five digits. Amber gasped and whispered in Mistress Chevalier's ear, "Is she going to?"

Mistress Chevalier gave her an appraising look, then nibbled at her ear, "Is she going to go deeper? Why don't you get down closer for a proper look?"

With that, Mistress Chevalier reached down and gave Amber a fierce, stinging smack across the back of her thighs, causing her to wince in pain and her knees to buckle as the domme expertly dropped her to the floor. She was in control of Amber's descent and by the time she was done, Amber was on her knees near, Charlotte's broad bottom, bent forward, with her hair roughly gripped by Mistress Chevalier's strong fingers.

The scent of Charlotte's arousal was heady, and the slick

squelching noises that Baroness Carruthers fingers made as they withdrew and then pushed back in, were bordering on the obscene. Charlotte was making happy moans as she licked at Vicky, who added to the noise with delighted animalistic noises.

"Have you ever seen this done, Amber?" the Baroness asked.

"No, Baroness," Amber replied, entranced by the way the woman's fingers spread Charlotte's pink lips open.

"Watch closely then," the Baroness demanded as she concentrated on edging her fingers deeper and deeper inside her sub. Charlotte must have been extremely excited because it didn't take much longer until the knuckles passed the threshold of her lips, and the Baroness's hand was swallowed to the wrist.

"Beautiful, isn't it?" Mistress Chevalier said.

"Yes, Mistress," Amber replied as Charlotte began to come and the Baroness's eyes flashed in triumph.

As she was hauled to her feet by the hair, Mistress Chevalier remarked, "I'll remember to tell Susanna how much you admired it, so she can arrange for the Baroness to fist you too, you little slut."

Then they were off again, to see what else was happening. Mistress Chevalier and Amber passed the pirate queen as she flogged one of her serving wenches, who was strapped to a St Andrews Cross. The second wench she'd brought with her was crouched between her widespread legs, eating her pussy as she fondled her own breast and fingered herself.

The cat lady, as Amber had mentally tagged her, was reclining on a chaise longue and enjoying having one kitten worship her feet, as the other put her tongue to use between her legs. The dominant woman opened heavy-lidded eyes as they paused to watch and favoured Amber with a greatly exaggerated wink.

"I think she likes you, Amber," Mistress Chevalier chortled as she pulled the submissive on to the next show.

Mistress Cauldwell was playing with her own submissive, Diamond, who was strapped down to an adjustable spanking bench, her latex panties and bra discarded. The stockings and suspenders were still in place. Diamond was struggling to make her cries of anguish heard past the large ball gag that had been tightly strapped around her mouth.

The cause of her distress was the long, black paddle-like implement which Mistress Cauldwell was slapping against her exposed sex. Her mons Venus was hot pink already, contrasting with the tanned skin of a careful sunbather.

Diamond's legs were strapped to thigh pads and spread as wide as possible, to expose her sex in the most humiliating and vulnerable way imaginable. The bench was curved upward, forcing Diamond's back to arch, and leaving her head lower than her body. It looked uncomfortable in more ways than one.

Amber was fascinated by the way the thick length of leather would impact poor Diamond's prominent mound and then curl down to slap against her labia with a wet smack. Diamond was thrashing against the straps, but her obvious state of arousal betrayed how much she was enjoying the harsh treatment.

"My compliments, Megan," Mistress Chevalier said, "you've created a thoroughly delightful scene."

"Thank you, Jade," Mistress Cauldwell replied. "What do you think of it, Amber? Does our little session delight you as well?"

Amber swallowed hard, "It's quite, umm, intense, Mistress Cauldwell. Is Diamond enjoying it?"

"I believe she is, in the relevant sense anyway. Feel free to touch her and find out," the domme offered generously.

Amber was hesitant to get involved, but Mistress Chevalier stopped holding her hand, and instead, took hold of Ambers left hand with her right, lifting it up and resting it on Diamond's breast. "Feel her nipple. Can you see how stiff it is, how she reacts to your touch?" Mistress Chevalier asked.

"Yes, Mistress. Diamond's nipple feels like it's made of the stuff," she gasped.

"That might convince some people Diamond is enjoying it, but your sub is welcome to taste her pussy, if she still has any qualms," Mistress Cauldwell suggested.

"Are you still concerned about Diamond's pleasure, Amber?"

Mistress Chevalier asked. Amber looked at the two mistresses and hoped she understood the game.

"Yes, Mistress," she replied.

A moment later and Mistress Chevalier was pressing Amber's face hard into Diamond's swollen, sopping lips. "Get your tongue in there, make sure you taste every inch so you can be sure she's turned on, you dirty little slut!" Mistress Chevalier ordered.

Amber could see the length Diamond's body as she licked and sucked at the hot, swollen flesh, and she made eye contact with Mistress Cauldwell who was watching her as if she were a piece of indulgent chocolate cake she was planning to eat.

With growing excitement, Mistress Cauldwell was admiring Amber's pussy eating skills, as she demonstrated them on the tormented submissive's aching pussy. The domme put down her leather strap, hanging it from a hook screwed into the bench, before using both hands to slowly hitch her figure-hugging latex skirt up and over her shapely thighs, until her pussy was exposed too.

As her hands travelled up her body, freeing her admirably large bosom from constraints, Amber got to see the glint of metal in the cleft between her legs as she mounted Diamond's face and demanded her satisfaction. Mistress Cauldwell's slender, tanned fingers found her own pierce nipples and began to play with them.

When Mistress Cauldwell beckoned to Mistress Chevalier, she came forward with excitement, and began to tongue and suck at one of those big perky nipples, like a calf hungry for milk. Mistress Cauldwell let out a contented sigh as she began to ride her submissive's face to orgasm.

Amber did her best to get Diamond there as well and was pleased to see a flash of fire in Mistress's Cauldwell's eyes as her submissive screamed her passion into her pussy, even as she tried to bring her Mistress off.

When the sun-worshipping lovers had had their fill, the two dommes kissed for a while, before Mistress Chevalier said farewell and pulled Amber away, her mouth still wet with Diamond's juices.

When Amber went to wipe it away, the domme forbade it and told her to stay messy for now. Amber blushed profusely at the mere thought of it and was sure the skin of her chest and neck would burn to a crisp from the embarrassment by the time they encountered their next stop on the tour of the ballroom.

Pudding was kneeling beside the exquisite bottom of Jasmine, giving her a thorough spanking. The cook was in a corset and elegant elbow-length gloves, as well as thigh-length books. If Amber hadn't known she was submissive to Mistress Susanna, she would have thought her every bit the dominant.

Jasmine, still in her strappy bondage harness, was on all fours because her face was buried in the pussy of her domme, Mistress Steele. Despite the attentions of her submissive, the domme looked more excited by the pain Pudding was gleefully inflicting on the girl.

"Don't spare the horses, Pudding," Mistress Steel exhorted with a hungry look on her face, as her hand kept Jasmine's head firmly secured against her.

"Yes, Mistress," Pudding agreed.

Mistress Chevalier fondled Amber's backside, even dipping her fingers lightly into the cleft of her buttocks but ultimately, moved them on from the scenario without comment or interrupting the players.

They passed by a few dommes whose names Amber hadn't recalled, playing with subs who were locked in the two big cages. One was on all fours in the coffee table cage, a big vibrator stuffed obscenely in her pussy and a dildo in her mouth that was held to the floor of the cage with a suction cup. The sub was sucking on it obscenely as the dommes around her made lewd comments and reached in to tease her flesh with cruel pinches and slaps.

The sub in the standing cage wasn't faring much better. Although the submissive was standing, she was also manacled by wrist and ankle, spreadeagled and tightly bound. Another sub was crammed in the cage at her feet, teasing her with a powerful sounding wand-style vibrator. The dommes commanding them were threatening the standing sub with terrible punishments if she came without permission.

Mistress Chevalier smiled but swiftly moved them on to where Mistress Yolanda was conducting a session with her sub, Zoe. The sex swing was getting a good test of its stability and strength with this pair. Yolanda was slow-fucking Zoe with a strapon, much to the freshly pierced subs delight.

"Isn't this party marvellous, Yoland?" Mistress Chevalier asked.

Mistress Yoland didn't stop thrusting into her young sub, "It's fantastic. Zoe is beyond excited, aren't you sexy?"

"Fuck, yes! Fuck me harder, Mistress," Zoe begged.

"You're welcome to join us if you'd like?" Mistress Yoland offered generously, "Maybe Amber would like a close-up of Zoe's hood piercing?"

"I think that would be eye-opening for her, but I'm rather keen to give her a thorough workout myself," Mistress Chevalier said. "I'm so horny after seeing all this."

"I know what you mean, this has to be the best party that Susanna has organised yet," Mistress Yolanda agreed. "I'm sure we can play another time. Maybe you and I could have fun while we watch Zoe and Amber?"

"That's definitely something I'm up for if Susanna will lend me Amber, or if you'd like to play with Vicky."

"Maybe you and Vicky and Susanna and Amber should come and try out my new play space one day, I'd love to have some guests," Yolanda suggested.

"Sounds fab, we'll sort something out soon, I promise," Mistress Chevalier said as they left the gothic beauty fucking her nubile submissive with wild abandon.

"So, are you enjoying your first lesbian orgy?" Mistress Chevalier asked.

"Yes, Mistress. Very much. Is it always like this?" Amber asked.

"Not always quite as impressive or in such nice surroundings, but I've been to a lot of exciting events in a similar vein. There are always lots of pretty young women, like yourself, who want to learn about pleasure and pain from old girls like me," Mistress Chevalier said.

"It sounds like you've had a wonderful life, Mistress," Amber said enviously.

"There have been some good times, this is certainly one of them. I've had my share of troubles, but the future is bright, especially for the younger generation. Honestly, it wasn't my generation that had to fight for the most important rights either but I do envy you young things your freedoms," Mistress Chevalier said.

"Oh, is that why you like restricting them so much?" Amber joked.

"It may have been," Mistress Chevalier replied with a knowing wink, "All joking aside, I don't actually know what got me into this, more's the pity. We could talk about that all night, and still not agree on a reason for it. I do know I have lots of thoroughly pleasurable tricks to use on a willing victim like you."

"That sounds fun," Amber said.

"Would you like me to show you some of my tricks now?" Mistress Chevalier asked, pulling Amber in close and kissing her neck, before nibbling at her ear. Her hands roved all over Amber's body as she continued to kiss her deeply. It was a while before they came up for air, and Amber felt too breathless to respond at first.

"Yes, please, Mistress," Amber finally replied.

CHAPTER 11

Amber wasn't sure what Mistress Chevalier had planned but knew that she'd recruited Mistress Susanna to her cause. After a few moments of animated whispering between the two excited dominants, the interrogation chair had been moved to the stage for all to see.

Mistress Chevalier had carefully strapped her down to the chair, which used thick, padded-leather ankle and wrist cuffs. The seat had space for Amber's thighs, but large cutouts in strategic places made her surprisingly accessible.

Another strap from the frame that formed the high back of the chair, went around Amber's forehead and prevented her from so much as turning her head. There was no back-rest to the chair, the frame went up in an arch by her shoulders, and peaked where the headrest was. Her back was left entirely exposed, open to any implement that might be used against it.

The addition of a blindfold, and finally even big can style headphones playing ambient music, left Amber entirely in her own world. It wasn't long before she felt a certain amount of trepidation. Every now and then, Mistress Chevalier would reach out, and roughly pinch her nipple, or slap her thigh.

Or at least, she assumed it was Mistress Chevalier tormenting her. It could have been any of the women present. The buzz of a vibrator against her trembling knee, made Amber think she would soon receive pleasure as the wielder would slowly drag it up her leg until it was pressed between her thighs.

That wasn't what happened though. Sensation returned in the form of a sharp stinging across Amber's back, from some kind of whip. Amber couldn't hear herself properly over the music from headphones which were doubtless noise-cancelling for extra solitude. She was sure she screamed at the sudden pain though.

A soft dry tongue was placed against her pussy then. It was not a human tongue, Amber realised, from the lack of moisture or wriggling movement, but a tongue of leather. Softly it tapped against her lips, not hard enough to hurt, but slowly and teasingly.

Amber's imagination filled in the rest. One of the dommes was going to give her the pussy spanking she probably deserved for being such a slut. It would be agonising and they would laugh and delight in her suffering.

Fingers danced the length of the cleft between her cheeks, and then two pairs of hands helped spread her buttocks apart. She wondered which of the many women present was holding her wide like that, to reveal her puckered hole.

When the fingers returned, they were damp with lubricant and began to work themselves deep inside her. Amber felt shame as she realised there was little resistance to the intrusion, not because she was gaping open unnaturally, but because she was surprisingly relaxed in her state of arousal. Her sphincter wasn't tight with anxiety but allowed the slowly thrusting digits to coat her with thick, cool, jelly.

A broad-based butt plug, which Amber imagined to be the largest she had yet received, was pushed slowly, ever so slowly, into her welcoming arse. Then it was jiggled, and tugged, pushed a little deeper, as the dommes tested it's fit. Amber could feel the excitement, leaving a thin trail of liquid down her thighs. She imagined the excited onlookers pointing at the juices dripping from her pussy and commenting on how much of a slut she was.

For a while, a long rubber bit gag was forced into her mouth, and it pulled her cheeks back uncomfortably, considerably lessening her ability to cry out. That was right after both her nipples were pinched quite fiercely and she screamed again.

The pain was intense, and she thrashed against the chair while it subsided to the point she could control her response. The pressure remained, and then Amber realised a weight hung from her nipples, a length of cold metal draped over her torso. It had to be a set of clamps and a chain between them.

Soft kisses made a bizarre counterpoint to her suffering. There was a flurry of them, against her inner thighs, down her spine, on her feet, her face, and breasts. Where there was exposed flesh, soft, warm lips were pressed against her and tongues were lightly brought into play.

Amber was left alone for a while, and all she could feel was the faintest breeze of people moving around her, and the shaking of the stage as people moved across it. She could no longer picture what might be going on. Who was helping with her torment? The kisses had come from at least four people at once, and it could easily have been more. Were mistresses still fucking their subs as they watched the performance with vague interest?

Or were they all sitting quietly, completely engrossed in the events on the stage? The thought of being watched like that didn't temper Amber's arousal, but rather inflame it.

Her need to have something dramatic happen, whether it be pleasurable or painful, grew with every passing moment until finally her straps were unbuckled.

Strong hands took hold of Amber by her upper arms, helping her to her feet. Whoever it was, supported and guided her, marching her across the stage. Amber was still blindfolded, gagged and had headphones on, she stumbled a little, but they didn't let her fall.

A firm body pressed against her from behind, and her captors held her arms up high. Hands stroked up her sides, and she smelled the nearby scent of baby oil, as the fingers reached her breasts, and danced over the clamps that still tormented them.

Amber knew she was whimpering, though she couldn't be sure if it was from pain, excitement or fear at this point. The hands ended up behind her neck, strong fingers interlaced in a full-nelson that held her tightly in place. Her back pressed against Vicky's surgically enhanced breasts, the woman's nipples were as stiff as bullets. It had to be Vicky, only she was tall, strong and firm enough, combined with the scent of baby oil.

Sound rushed back to her as the headphones were removed. Someone was talking, but she didn't know who.

"Amber Hannam, you have been charged with wanton and slovenly behaviour and in addition, the tempting of good women into your sinful embrace. How do you plead?" an unknown official said.

Amber took a moment to catch up, and the question was repeated. "How do you plead?"

"Not guilty! I have done nothing wrong!" she cried out.

"We have your confession. The entire court heard it when you were in the chair."

"Lies, you tortured me. You can't hold me to anything I said to ease my suffering. I have done nothing wrong, only that which my Mistress ordered," Amber replied, getting into the swing of things and wondering where this would go.

"It is your Mistress who has brought you to this court for judgement, Amber," the voice answered. Amber thought it was most likely Jade, but since the woman was putting on a rather hammy theatrical voice, she couldn't be sure. The key to roleplaying an improvised scenario, she'd once heard an actor say, was to always say yes. Not literally, but to go with the flow of other people's input and dialogue, rather than argue with it.

"No! Why would my Mistress betray me? I have only ever served at her command," Amber wailed with as much hurt as she could manage.

"Do you deny the charges?"

"Yes!"

"You did not attempt to pervert the course of a competition by offering inducements to the ponygirl, Pepper? Inducements of a sexual nature," the interrogator asked.

Amber hung her head, "Yes, I did, but it was only supposed to be fun."

"Was it only supposed to be fun when you wantonly applied your tongue to the task of alleviating the distress that the servant known as Diamond, was experiencing, after receiving a lawful punishment?" the prosecutor asked, concluding, "I warn you, that Mistress Cauldwell has already testified that having used lawful disciplinary measures against Diamond's intimate person, you did everything in your power to turn her against her employer."

"You're twisting what happened. I was ordered to lick Diamond's pussy, for the amusement of her mistress," Amber protested.

"Ladies of the jury, can you see what we have to deal with here?" the prosecutor said. "It seems clear that Amber Hannam is a slut. A wanton temptress who uses her voluptuous, youthful body, to corrupt innocent young women. Her actions have proven that she is so skilled in the arts of seduction, that she can even cause the most respected of women to abandon their good senses."

"Are there more examples the prosecution wishes to give?"

"Certainly M'Lady. Why, only today, I saw Miss Hannam offering her body to several gentlewomen in exchange for favours of a sexual nature."

"Shameless!" someone cried out.

"Ladies, please hand your decision to the bailiff," another voice called out, cutting through the discussion among the jury.

After a heartbeat, the judge solemnly intoned, "Amber Hanna, it is the verdict of this jury that you are guilty of all charges mentioned in court today, and more besides I'll warrant. It is not appropriate for a judge to act as a witness in a trial, but now that the verdict has been handed down I can add my own comments. I witnessed this slut, having enticed a gentlewoman of this town to dally with her, to her own pleasure, refuse to properly worship the Mistress to whom she was assigned. Miss Hannam left her Mistress without relief for some good while, and I had to intercede myself, disciplining her with a flogger until she fulfilled one of the few duties her tongue is useful for."

The judge waited while the court returned to quiet after this terrible secret was revealed. It seemed to Amber that this wasn't all above board as trials went, but perhaps it was a fair cop. She could hardly completely deny all the instances that they might bring up.

"Your honour," she spoke up, "I confess. I'm guilty. Of all these things and more. Please, have mercy on my poor body. I don't want to be transported to Australia. I beg you, your honour. I will take any punishment you deem suitable to atone for my behaviour."

"Silence in court!" the bailiff holding Amber tightly called out.

"It is too late for you to earn favour through confession, Amber Hannam. You stand condemned as a wanton slut, a young woman who tempts and teases, offering herself up to all and sundry for her own gain. You are a succubus in the midst of our community, and I fear if we do not deal with you harshly, you will continue to disrupt our lives. You will be placed in the pillory, until such time as I see fit to release you, there to serve your sentence with your body. You will pay for your crime, with the same body with which you have committed it and may the women of the town have mercy on your flesh, for I assure you, I will not," the judge said before banging the gavel.

Two people took her arms again, and the wrestling hold was released. Vicky and the other two women positioned Amber and then removed her blindfold. Blinking furiously as her eyes filled with tears from the sudden light, Amber was finally able to make out the room.

Mistress Susanna was seated on one of the Queen Anne high backed armchairs that had been brought on stage so that she could act as the judge. Mistress Chevalier had been her prosecutor and now advanced on the shivering nude submissive, to carry out her punishment.

Amber was forced into the pillory. Her wrists and neck were placed in the bottom curve of the cutouts the pillory had for them, then measured. Some additional sections were latched in place, to bring the large holes down to the correct size for her neck and wrists. A useful innovation that no doubt a lot of people would have been thrilled to see when the town's still punished people like this. Then the clamp was closed over her neck and wrists. Mistress Chevalier slipped fingers between her skin and the padding to check the fit and nodded with satisfaction.

For a moment, Amber worried they might actually throw rotten fruit at her and had to bite her lip hard to stop from laughing, which she didn't think would be smart at this juncture.

Amber's ankles were swiftly shackled to the floor with heavy metal cuffs, and short chains to hold her feet just where they were wanted. The frame of the pillory had a sliding mechanism, and the height was adjusted to perfectly fit the current occupant.

Sugar lifted Amber's head up by the hair, so she was forced to look in front, where Candy was standing by a table, covered with a cloth. Sugar leaned in, and kissed Amber's neck hungrily before whispering in her ear, "As ordered by the court here are the instruments of your punishment." Sugar waved her hand as Candy drew back the cloth.

"Begin," Susanna ordered, from the chair she lounged in, which was just within view if Amber turned her head to the left and offered an excellent view of both sides of the pillory. "Sugar, Candy, attend me."

There was no time to appreciate the atmosphere or the visuals provided by the audience of women whose submissives were preparing to please them. Mistress Chevalier began without choosing an implement, as Sugar had suggested. The sting of her palm against Amber's tender buttock drew a whimper of pain.

Amber took deep breaths, and steadied her feet, preparing for what was to come, knowing it would become increasingly severe as Mistress Chevalier worked her way along the table. She took the spanking well, keeping the tears from her eyes and managing to control any outbursts.

Roxy stepped forward, leaned down and kissed Amber firmly on the mouth, to general murmurs and comments of approval. Then she straightened up, smiling wickedly at the bemused occupant of the pillory and moving to the table of torture, as Amber has begun thinking of it.

The chauffeur drummed her fingers over the table as she the length of it, touching each tool briefly and glancing back at Amber as if trying to make a decision about which implement to choose. Finally, she selected one and passed it over the pillory to Mistress Chevalier. The paddle brought Amber to the next level of resistance, she scrunched her toes, bit her lip, tried to find her happy place, anything and everything to avoid crying out.

When Roxy put it back on the table and picked out a riding crop, which was soon put to good use on Amber's inner thighs. The swishing blows were not as hard as she'd been spanked and paddled, but they didn't need to be. The sensitive skin of her thighs produced stinging sensations that Amber couldn't ignore.

"Barely a whimper from this one, ladies," Mistress Chevalier remarked. "What a trooper she is, eh? Mistress Susanna, you have found yourself a real treasure here."

"I'm so glad you all approve," Mistress Susanna commented, her voice sounding slightly off-kilter. Amber glanced to her side and could see Sugar kissing their Mistress on the neck, and Candy working away between her legs. Mistress Susanna caught her looking and smiled wickedly, blowing her a kiss. "Roxy, why don't you pass Mistress Chevalier that lovely rattan cane?"

This instruction produced gasps of mock horror and filthy laughter from around the room. Amber could tell these women didn't think she could hold out against it. When she saw the cane Roxy had picked up, she had her own doubts. It was long, with a crooked handle and looked quite heavy.

Mistress Chevalier swished it around menacingly and then struck without warning. Amber gritted her teeth and resisted crying out, squeezing her eyes shut as the second swipe landed across her hot bottom. Turning her head, she saw Mistress Susanna smiling at her. Then she mouthed something as the third strike landed.

Again, Mistress Susanna mouthed a sentence and Amber understood this time. When the fourth strike landed, she let forth her response. Her sudden cry of pain silenced the hall for a few seconds before Mistress Chevalier landed her followup, and Amber cried out piteously again. That pleased the audience, and the dominant women watching their friend's new submissive caned so harshly, let out an encouraging cheer.

Amber shot them a reproachful look, but it didn't help. Her suffering merely amused them and hoping that they might be sympathetic to her plight wasn't going to get her anyway.

There was no point holding back any longer, trying to be brave for her Mistress, to impress anyone. As the next two stripes bit into her buttocks, Amber let her tears flow freely, and her voice became a vent for all her pain.

Mistress Chevalier moved to the front of the pillory, and crouched, taking Ambers mouth and covering it with her own, her tongue plunged deep inside the submissive girl and claimed her. Amber responded as if her own Mistress was kissing her and not a proxy with temporary control over her body.

Finally, Mistress Chevalier stood and approached Mistress Susanna, "Your honour," she said, bowing before her with a flourish. "Is Amber's punishment complete, or do you wish to see something else?"

Mistress Susanna stood up, "Thank you, Mistress Chevalier, for such an enjoyable scenario. I think I can speak for all of us when I saw that was most satisfying. I had intended to take Amber back at some point, but I do think you have more than earned the right to continue you using her as you see fit. I only have one request, I would like to see her fucked with the strapon you used earlier in private if you wouldn't mind putting on a bit more of a show."

"Of course. Vicky, fetch my toy and harness me," Mistress Chevalier ordered. It wasn't long before the dommes were crowded around Amber's rear, watching Mistress Chevalier pound the strapon into her aching pussy and enjoying the sound of her lusty moans.

Mistress Susanna gave free permission for the women to touch and toy with her, provided Mistress Chevalier did not object. Amber's body became a plaything for the dommes, as they pinched, spanked, fingered and stroked her. All the while, Mistress Chevalier fucked her powerfully with her favourite strapon.

When the domme's legs began to tire, Amber breathed a sigh of relief. Until the Baroness stepped forward, an oddly bulbous, luminous orange strapon jutting from her thighs.

"May I play?" the Baroness asked.

Dame Cartwright also stepped forward, in her headmistress gear, and holding a long ruler. "I'd like to play too, if I may?"

Mistress Susanna and Mistress Chevalier both gave their blessing, and indeed, Amber heard, strong encouragement to their desires.

Her mouth was soon occupied with the silicone cock of the Baroness, and her breasts became the property of Holly and Ivy, as they fondled them and suckled on her hard nipples. Meanwhile, the Dame used her long ruler to turn a lower section of Amber's bottom scarlet. Dame Cartwright was a firm spanker, counting out her strokes with each swipe.

The Baroness soon tired of her mouth and moved back to fuck Amber's pussy instead. Dame Cartwright moved to the front, ordering Ivy to her knees next to the pillory. The mistress raised her foot and placed it on her sub's shoulder, and due to her height, Amber was able to nuzzle at her pussy, if not do a sterling job.

When they were done with her, Dame Cartwright had not been able to reach a climax but rectified that by laying back on one of the chaises longues. Ivy was tasked with eating her Mistress's well-stimulated pussy, and Holly was given the honour of straddling her face, to be the recipient of her domme's tongue.

Amber thought she'd surely be released then, but the Baroness had other ideas. A footstool was positioned in front of the pillory, and the height of the clamp section was lowered until Amber was forced to drop to all fours. The Baroness presented her pussy for Amber to worship and like the slut everyone expected her to be, she dove in happily.

Mistress Chevalier was not done with her, either, it seemed. She collected several willing dommes and lined them up on a cushion behind Amber. Soon her pussy was being repeatedly claimed by a train of Mistresses, and she lost herself to wave after wave of powerful orgasms, even as her tongue satisfied the Baroness multiple times.

When the dommes finally had their fill of alternating between fucking Amber's pussy and using her mouth to make them come, Mistress Chevalier finally released her and used a damp cloth to clean her up a little.

"I think it's time for me to reclaim my girl, Jade. If that's alright with you?"

"Of course, Mistress Susanna. I should think she needs some rest after such a long day. Amber, thank you for being such a good sport," Mistress Chevalier said.

"Thank you for taking such good care of me, and using me so well, Mistress Chevalier," Amber replied as she melted into a hug with Mistress Susanna.

"You are most welcome, my sexy young friend," Mistress Chevalier replied.

"Thank you, too, Mistress," Amber said, gazing up at Susanna adoringly.

CHAPTER 12

Susanna relaxed with Amber on a large sofa. Mistress Chevalier and her sub, Vicky were entwined on the other end. The maids had fetched them all chilled fruit juice to quench their thirst while they took a break.

Eventually, Susanna looked down at her sub, and made her an offer, "Now, Amber. I feel you are due a reward of some kind for your much-appreciated efforts today. Is there anything you would like?"

Amber pondered the question for a while before cautiously asking, "Is it permitted to ask Mistress Chevalier for something?"

"Certainly, but I shall warn you, if you offend her she'll probably spank you again, and I'll let her."

"Yes, Mistress. Thank you. Mistress Chevalier, would you do me the honour of letting me play with Vicky for a while, so that you and Mistress Susanna can watch us?"

Mistress Chevalier grinned wickedly, "Of course, but I think which of you in charge of this little show, should be decided in the paddling pool, don't you?"

"That's hardly fair, Vicky is sure to win with her muscles," Susanna replied. Then she looked at Vicky hungrily and continued, "I agree. Vicky, please be careful with my sub, you might easily break her. But once you've won, please know that I have no objection to you humiliating her, riding her face, spanking her or anything of the sort. Indeed, I'm sure it would be amusing to watch you demand your pleasure from her, whatever your personal preferences are."

Amber swallowed hard as Vicky turned toward her with a predatory look in her eyes, and politely rumbled her response, "Don't worry, you little slut. You have made my Mistress very happy today, I won't injure you."

"Thank you, that's kind of you, Vicky," Amber said as they wall walked off to the paddling pool and the huge sub grabbed a big bottle of baby oil, and squeezed it all over Amber's body. Vicky leaned down as she began to spread the oil over Amber's body, kissing her hard on the mouth.

Vicky's hands found Amber's breasts and coated them with baby oil as their mistresses took to a nearby sofa to watch. "I won't injure you, Amber. But I'd love to hear you say, 'Cotswold' for me," Vicky said loudly.

Mistress Susanna laughed, "I think Amber may have bitten off more than she can chew, don't you, Mistress Chevalier?"

"I'm sure Vicky will be kind to her."

Amber let forth a startled yelp, as Vicky's powerful fingers clamped down on her nipples with vice-like security, and she tugged her forward. "I won't injure you, but I'm going to make you scream in more ways than one, pretty little slut," Vicky laughed.

Vicky's strong fingers gripped Amber's shoulders and forced her to her knees, clamping her head against her pussy. "Lick me, bitch," she growled.

Amber's nipples were still smarting, and she felt thoroughly chastened by the sudden control that Vicky had gained over her, which wasn't what she'd been hoping for. Her cheeks flushed scarlet with shame as she complied with Vicky's demand and began to tongue her vigorously. Amber's hands found her breasts and massaged the sore nipples briefly, before inexorably sliding down her stomach and between her legs.

Mistress Chevalier noticed that the young submissive had begun to masturbate, as Vicky ground her pussy into her opponents face, and pointed it out to Susanna, who laughed along with her.

For Amber, the evening did not get any less challenging. After each orgasm she gave Vicky, the Amazonian woman would push her back roughly, and Amber would end up sprawled on the other side of the pool thanks to their baby oil coating.

One of their Mistresses would say, "Ding, ding!" as if starting a boxing match, and then Vicky would decide to either win immediately or draw it out, letting Amber see some hope of a victory, only to dash it at the last moment and subjugate the younger and significantly smaller woman.

Vicky heaped humiliation on Amber, bringing her to tears by spanking her over her knee or leaving her coughing and spluttering for air after pinning her to the ground and riding her tongue and lips like a sex toy, or even flipping her upside down and clamping her mouth to Amber's pussy, and licking her to a powerful orgasm.

That last bout wasn't so bad, of course, but it was still embarrassing to be so thoroughly controlled, not through choice, rather through pure physical superiority.

Then Mistress Susanna had an idea and tossed in a positively enormous silicone dildo, that came to rest between the girls before the next match was started. A harness followed.

Vicky looked at the thing and cracked her knuckles, "I'll go easy on you, if you turn around now, and drop to all fours, like a good little slut."

Amber almost did it, almost gave in entirely. But then she saw the look on Vicky's face and dove for the weapon, lifting it triumphantly.

A second later, Vicky's powerful hand was on her neck, and she was face down, arse up in the slippery paddling pool, getting spanked hard for challenging Mistress Chevalier's champion. Vicky made her strap the harness on her, and fit the big cock, then kiss the tip respectfully before coating it with oil.

"Well?" Vicky said, expectantly, when Amber was done.

"It's better to lose with some dignity, Amber," Mistress Susanna chimed in.

Amber swallowed hard and bowed her head. Then she admitted to herself that she had been defeated, and turned around, putting her face back to the lining of the paddling pool, and carefully raising herself up on her knees to get her bottom as high as possible for the big woman.

Vicky's left hand gripped her waist, hard to counter the slippery oil, and her right forefinger pressed firmly against the butt plug that was still in Amber's arse. Amber gasped in surprise and groaned with humiliation when Vicky tugged gently on the butt plug.

"No, please," she begged the victor. "Please don't," Amber whimpered plaintively. Perhaps Vicky would grant her mercy and fuck her aching pussy?

"No mercy!" Mistress Susanna called out, laughing cruelly.

"Oh, you are mean sometimes, Susanna," Mistress Chevalier said sympathetically. Then she too burst out laughing. "Fuck her, Vicky."

Vicky didn't yank the butt plug out, which might have been kinder. Instead, she teased Amber with it, pulling it back until the wide base was almost free, and then shoving it back in and making Amber yelp. The cruel teasing only made her pussy wetter, and her otherwise useless hand found her pussy, plunging fingers inside herself. No-one stopped her, although the filthy comments about her slutty behaviour proved they had noticed.

The butt plug finally came free with a pop, and Amber felt the big head of the cock stretch her even wider, and Vicky pushed it expertly into her arse. Amber cried out as an orgasm ripped through her, and when the slow-motion of Vicky fucking her began to steadily build pace, she could not help but cry out some more.

Amber was thoroughly exhausted by the time Vicky had given up on fucking her, unstrapping the harness from her loins and leaving the silicone monster buried in Amber's aching arse.

Vicky stood up and towered over her. "Ready?"

"Please, Vicky, no more? I beg you," Amber pleaded.

"If you want this to stop, begging won't help," Vicky said, slapping her meaty hand down hard on Amber's backside and making her tear up again. "I won't stop until you tell me what I want to hear."

"What's that?" Amber said, yelping as Vicky brought her hand down again. The big woman kept going for a while, with big meaty slaps that made Amber swear like a sailor.

"You're pushing your arse up to meet me, Amber."

"Am I?" Amber groaned, as innocently as she could manage.

"Yes. You are! You filthy little slut. You'll regret that, if you don't tell me what you know I want to hear," Vicky said, flinging the strapon down by Amber's head for emphasis. Then she delivered a few more spine-tingling smacks for good measure.

"Ok, ok," Amber cried. "Cotswold. Is that what you want?"

Vicky stopped what she was doing. "Better."

Amber was pulled up from the ground and into a warm embrace. Vicky whispered into her ear, "Are you alright, slut?"

Amber whimpered as the big woman hugged her, "Yes. I'll be fine. Thank you, Vicky."

"Good. You used your safeword, so I have to stop. But I'm not really finished with you. Would you like to play some more? I promise I'll be nicer, now I've beaten you," Vicky purred seductively.

Amber was amazed. "You want to keep going."

"Yeah, baby. As long as our Mistresses will let us. Can you take it? What do you say?" Vicky kissed Amber's neck, and she felt herself weakening.

"Yes, I say yes. Do your worst," Amber replied.

"You can always use your safeword again, but I'm not after it this time," Vicky pointed out.

"I hope I won't need it."

Vicky pushed her back to the floor, and Amber squealed in surprise.

"Enough cuddling and sweet talk, slut. Put your mouth where it belongs, and do a good job, then maybe I'll let you go," Vicky offered.

Amber looked up at Vicky from the floor defiantly and said something rude.

Vicky grinned and flung herself at the smaller sub, wrestling her into a prone position. "You'll do as you're told, my girl, or I'll strap that back on, and fuck you twice as hard," Vicky boasted, gesturing to the silicone cock and harness.

Amber went limp, utterly defeated again. The big woman shifted her knees to a new position, and smiled down triumphantly at Amber, looming above her like a conquering Empress. Amber accepted her fate, and Vicky read the submission in her eyes.

Without another word, the victor straddled Amber's head, a knee on either side and began to descend at a frustratingly unhurried speed. Amber watched as the might woman filled her vision.

"Oh boy," was all she could say before her mouth was otherwise occupied for some time.

CHAPTER 13

It was gone three am before Amber finally crawled into bed, and Susanna cuddled up behind her.

"Did you have a good day, Mistress?" she asked.

"Yes, it was wonderful, Amber. Thank you for being such a welcoming host to all my guests," Susanna replied.

They lay like that for a while, and Amber thought she dozed off for a bit, or perhaps she just closed her eyes for a moment. She rolled over to face Susanna and saw her domme was restless too.

"Mistress, I have an idea I wanted to tell you about."

"If it involves me spanking you, or something like it, I'm afraid it'll have to wait until morning," Susanna said, leaning forward and kissing her sub.

"No, it's a business idea. Is it ok if I explain it?"

Susanna smiled. "Certainly, but if I fall asleep while you do, don't take it personally. I haven't been so exhausted in years."

"Well, Mistress Chevalier has a bit of a business problem," Amber began.

"Yes, she doesn't have a great head for it," Susanna agreed.

"Her space is limited, she doesn't have room for a shop on site, and she doesn't even have a stable to use with Vicky," Amber said.

"Don't beat around the bush, go ahead."

"You have a great big stable, but it needs renovating, and you've got other buildings that are vacant too. What if we got the stables spruced up, cleared out some space, and expanded the upstairs flats. Mistress Chevalier could use the stables for her pony, set up a workshop in the outbuildings, and a small shop, and live in a new flat." Amber suggested.

"That sounds great for Mistress Chevalier but expensive for me. What do I get out of it?" Susanna murmured sleepily.

"It wouldn't have to be expensive, we could do as much of the clearing up and basic work as possible ourselves. You pay a big premium having builders do that sort of thing for you when it's unskilled labour."

"What do you know about that?"

"I have friends who worked in building trades," Amber said.

"Right, so renovating more of the buildings wouldn't cost as much if we planned it well. Still, what's the actual upside you see for me? I don't make business decisions without a clear goal," Susanna pointed out gently.

"You would have an expert on pony play on site all the time. Pepper and Ginger would have more people to take care of their needs, and you wouldn't worry about them if you were away. You could get any custom leatherwork done that you wanted, within reason," Amber said.

"I hope that's not it. I'm quite happy with how Pepper and Ginger live and I'm sure I can get my leather needs met without needing to do any building work," Susanna pointed out.

"In addition, Mistress Chevalier would pay you rent and having her shop on the grounds would bring more kinky ladies to visit, which I think you'd enjoy. Your property would be more valuable with another flat, and I'm guessing you have planning permission to renovate it all anyway. You could rent out your stables for ponyplay events too, like a holiday letting for kinky people."

"You're getting warmer. Anything else to interest me?"

"If you had Mistress Chevalier as your Stable Mistress, you could have more ponies. I think you'd like more girls in there, wouldn't you?"

Susanna raised an eyebrow and sat up a bit. "You're encouraging me to split my time with you even more?"

"I think I could still persuade you to spend lots of time with me," Amber said confidently. "Plus, I think you'd enjoy having easy access to Vicky or any other girls Mistress Chevalier knows.

"You seem sure of yourself all of a sudden," Susanna replied. "But you're right, Vicky is appealing, and I would certainly tumble her again if I had the chance.

Amber boldly slipped two fingers inside her Mistress, which soon shifted the discussion. "I am feeling more confident, Mistress. That's your influence. I think you like me enough that you'd want my touch, even if you had a dozen more girls to tend to your needs."

Susanna's hand clamped down over Amber's, and she growled, "Make me come while you explain the rest of your idea, slut and you might have a deal."

So Amber did just that.

CHAPTER 14

"Good morning, Susanna," Mistress Chevalier said. "Thank you for the overnight stay."

"Good morning, Jade. Did you and Vicky enjoy yourselves?" Susanna asked, smiling at the tall, powerful submissive woman that Mistress Chevalier had arrived with.

Vicky was no longer dressed in her ponygirl outfit but in a long, sheer chemise. She was kneeling in front of the sofa on which Mistress Chevalier sat, drinking her tea. The chemise offered tantalising glimpses of her muscular form and large, rounded breasts. Amber had to concentrate hard not to gape at the appealing cleavage that Vicky had on display.

Mistress Chevalier reached out and stroked the back of Vicky's head, causing the submissive woman to tilt her head and assume a dreamlike expression. "Yes, Vicky is wonderfully sore all over. She whimpered a lot this morning when I took her. I loved seeing that you'd all made such good use of her."

"I'm glad to hear you're both happy. Vicky was a very popular girl, yesterday, and such an obedient one too," Susanna commented.

"I get the impression that we aren't in here on our own to talk about how enjoyable Vicky is as a plaything though."

Susanna smiled, "Amber had an idea that she suggested to me. I thought it was quite promising, so I suggested that she be the one to propose it to you."

Mistress Chevalier raised an eyebrow. "Amber had an idea, did she? I'm all ears."

"After we spoke in the stables, I had a much better idea. Well, I thought it might be, and then I talked it over with Mistress this morning, and she agreed."

"I see. This is a business idea, I assume?" Mistress Chevalier said, frowning.

"Yes but let me explain it before you decide," Amber said.

Mistress Chevalier nodded and allowed Amber to go through the ideas. She asked some questions and seemed happy enough with the answers.

"That does sound good. Are you really on board with this, Susanna? My rental term is up in just over two months, and I'd hate to reject signing up again, and for this to fall through."

"Don't worry, I won't leave you high and dry. If you're up for it in principle, I'll have a contract proposal over to you by Tuesday, and you can let me know if you need any amendments. I'll make sure your rental agreement protects us both in the event you take a strong disliking to me," Susanna said.

"I think it's more likely you'd get annoyed with me," Mistress Chevalier said.

"Not at all. I would never treat you badly," Susanna said. "Not even if we had a disagreement over something. You're one of my favourite people. Otherwise, I wouldn't be going along with this investment in the property. Unless your business has a sudden boom, I won't cover my costs of renovating the buildings. It's a good idea to get it done but not urgent. The estate is too big for us, though, so it would be nice to have more people here, and a few more visitors."

"Would it be a problem if Vicky moved in with me?" Mistress Chevalier asked. Vicky gasped, startled by the remark and her head whipped round to stare lovingly at her domme.

"Of course, if we move quickly, we might be able to get a second flat finished before you move in. If not, we do have spare bedrooms in the house you could use. I'm sure Vicky would be very welcome about the estate," Susanna said.

"Wonderful. Now, how do you see the pecking order working? Two dominant women in the same location and you want me to take charge of two of your subs on a day to day basis," Mistress Chevalier said, leaving the thought hanging.

"I recall you saying yesterday that I could bend you over and spank you any time I wanted," Susanna said with a sly smile.

"Would you like that to be our dynamic, then? For me to be your submissive, but dominant to the girls when needed?" Mistress Chevalier asked, calmly sipping her tea while she waited for Susanna to respond.

"You would describe yourself as a switch, would you not, Jade?" Susanna said presently.

"I mostly take the dominant role these days, but I do still enjoy offering my submission to some people. Every now and then," Jade replied.

"Then how about this, we are both dommes, and when it's required, helpful or enjoyable, I will share my girls with you. I will ask them to submit to your pleasure, just as they do to mine. I imagine they will all be comfortable with that arrangement. I will also, from time to time, ask you to submit to me. Generally, you will agree to do so, while I have no intention of submitting to you, or anyone else," Susanna stated.

"I could enjoy that," Mistress Chevalier said. "I would, in turn, offer any sub I had for your use at times, provided they were similarly agreeable. Vicky, would you agree to submit to Mistress Susanna if I asked it of you?"

Vicky was still looking at her Mistress adoringly since she'd suggested that she move in at the stables with her Mistress. She nodded eagerly in reply but did not speak.

"Does that settle it then?"

"Yes, I think we have an agreement in principle."

Mistress Chevalier smiled and replied, "Here's to a beautiful tenancy, kid!" She lifted her tea and chinked her cup against Susanna's to seal the deal. "I'm pretty sure that only works with alcohol, but I'm sure we can cope. Everyone is still here, having breakfast. Would you like to tell them, perhaps?"

"That you're moving into my outbuildings?"

Mistress Chevalier laughed, "No, though that too. I thought you might enjoy telling them that you were going to be in charge of me now and then. I'm sure some of them would love the thought of me being spanked by you."

"They would probably prefer the sight of you being spanked," Susanna pointed out.

Mistress Chevalier exclaimed in a theatrical voice, "But, Mistress Susanna, surely you wouldn't take down my panties and spank me hard in front of all our friends?" Her hand flew to her mouth, covering it in horror at the thought of it.

"Indeed I would, for a woman who deserves a firm spanking should accept that it might need to be carried out under the watchful eye of her peers," Susanna replied. "Amber, please go to the conservatory and ask the ladies taking breakfast to join us in the ballroom. I have important news for them to hear!"

Amber managed to round up all the dommes and their various subs and persuade them to finish up their breakfasts and come to the ballroom to hear what Susanna had to say to them. There was a little grumbling from some who hadn't quite finished their breakfasts, and more when Amber had to refuse to tell them what they were being summoned to hear. It took all her patience not to blurt it out excitedly.

Finally, everyone filed into the ballroom, Amber bringing up the rear to make sure there weren't any stragglers. Susanna was standing on the stage in the centre of the room, with Vicky kneeling next to Mistress Chevalier beside her.

Sugar, Candy, Roxy, Pudding, Pepper and Ginger had all been called to the room to listen as well and were politely standing at the back, behind Mistress Susanna's friends. Amber tiptoed over to stand with them.

"Ladies, I have a little announcement to make in a moment, but first, let me thank you all for coming and making this such a wonderful get together. It's always a pleasure to play host to our little gatherings, and I hope you all enjoyed yourselves as much as I did," Susanna said. The ladies favoured her with a polite round of applause and polite remarks before she went on.

"As you all know, Mistress Chevalier is a fixture in the pony play community, both as an acknowledged pony training expert and as a source of equipment, clothing and tools. What you may not know is that her current workshop premises are somewhat cramped which limits the number and type of projects she can work on at once and excludes the possibility of hiring staff to help run the business," Susann said.

"It's worth the wait though," Baroness Carruthers commented, "the best leather gear I've ever paid good money for."

"I agree. My own girls were wearing Mistress Chevalier's work yesterday. Amber has suggested an idea which we all think will help Mistress Chevalier grow her business, and make my estate much more vibrant in the near future. We will be continuing the development of my stable buildings, adding new flats, at least another dozen stalls for ponies and perhaps most importantly, a workshop and shop space for Mistress Chevalier," Susanna explained.

The audience chatted amongst themselves, excitedly for a few moments before Susanna's calming hand motions quieted them. "Ladies, if I may continue. In addition, Jade will take up a position as my Stable Mistress. We will hold more pony events for those who are interested, and I hope more events like this weekend."

That drew a resounding cheer from all assembled.

"So Mistress Chevalier is going to join your stable of girls, eh, Susanna?" Mistress Yolanda asked.

A few of the dommes chorused, "Ohhh!" Then they fell about giggling and laughing.

"No, Yolanda, she's not going to be one of my stable of girls, as you put it," Susanna replied sarcastically.

"Too right, I'm far too bossy for that," Mistress Chevalier agreed.

"Of course, Mistress Chevalier will have to live under my rules, and in my house, tardiness is not permitted," Susanna said.

"She was late yesterday, it took ages before we could get started," Mistress Yolanda pointed out.

"Yes, it did, and that is part of why I've decreed that Jade should get a good spanking before she comes to live here."

"Good idea," Baroness Carruthers said.

"About time, I'd say," Dame Cartwright agreed.

"Yes, it's long overdue!" Madam Cauldwell chimed in.

"No! Please, Mistress Susanna, I beg of you. Don't promise me a better place to live and work, and then require me to submit to this!" Mistress Chevalier protested.

"You beg? Is that how you beg for my forgiveness, Jade? Shouldn't you be on your knees if you're begging me?"

"Yes, get on your knees!" Mistress Yolanda agreed boisterously.

Jade muttered under her breath, but she dropped to one knee, "Oh great Mistress Susanna, please, forgive me for my tardiness."

"What do you think, ladies? Is that a sufficient apology?"

Some said no, but most recommended a punishment.

Susanna shook her head sadly. "It seems the ladies have spoken, Jade. If you want to join us here, you're going to get a spanking today. Now. In front of everyone."

"Please, no, don't."

"Stand here and bend over!" Susanna snapped. Mistress Chevalier stood up, looking defiant but stood where she was told and bent over, putting her hands on her knees.

"On the bare!" someone called out when they saw Jade's trousered bottom, and others added their agreement. "Yes, on the bare!"

"Yes, I think that's best, don't you, Jade?" Mistress Susanna replied.

"No, it's not. Strip her naked. A slut shouldn't keep her dignity when she's being punished, should she ladies?" the Baroness urged gleefully. The assembled ladies were easily swayed. They were baying for Mistress Chevalier to be punished properly, to see her humiliated as they would with a recalcitrant sub.

"Well, Jade? Are you going to take your own clothes off, or shall I have you stripped? I think I'll have enough volunteers."

"You wouldn't dare!" Jade said.

Susanna shook her head. "Enough. Ladies, strip her if you will."

With glee, several of the dommes got up on the stage and manhandled Jade. Two held her arms tight, while a third unbuttoned her blouse and jodhpurs. Then they pulled her trousers down around her ankles, and the shit off her back. Her underwear followed, and though she struggled, she didn't use her safeword or protest.

Soon, the tardy domme was left entirely nude.

"What shall it be, the pillory or a bench?" Susanna asked, counting the votes. "The bench it is then. Strap her down."

Susanna didn't bother with any preamble, once Jade was in position, she stepped forward and began to spank her with great big smacks that made her plump bottom jiggle and echoed around the room. Jade cursed like a sailor, as each blow connected with her big wobbly bottom, which was soon turning shades of bright pink.

"Ow. You bitch, Susanna!" Mistress Chevalier cursed, struggling against her bonds.

Susanna laughed. "Bitch, am I, Jade? I think that's earned you another two dozen, don't you?"

"Do your worst, I can take it!" Jade growled defiantly.

Susanna resumed spanking, laughing when Jade howled loudly each time her hand connected with her cheeks. "Jade is such a noisy slut! I think we need to keep her quiet," Susanna mused as her palm rhythmically pounded against the older woman's backside. "Vicky, kneel in front of her and shut her filthy mouth with your kisses, there's a good girl," Susanna ordered.

The muscular sub seemed happy with her orders and immediately complied, cupping Jade's head in her big hand and slipping her tongue into her domme's mouth. Jade still yelped and moaned as she was spanked, but Vicky muffled her quite effectively.

"Amber, kneel down behind her," Susanna said. When Amber had positioned herself, she asked, "Is she wet, Amber? Tell us all, if Jade is the slut she seems to be? Can you see signs that she's enjoying her punishment?"

Amber licked her lips, "Mistress Chevalier is really wet. She looks very aroused, Mistress."

"Let's see how my new Stable Mistress handles being punished while she orgasms, shall we?" Susanna suggested. "Amber, put your tongue to use."

Amber gratefully complied, burying her tongue immediately in Mistress Chevalier's wet folds, seeking out her clit as Susanna's hand descended again and again just above her head.

The tone and timbre of Mistress Chevalier's protests changed noticeably once Amber applied her lips and tongue to her task.

It was a source of considerable pride to Amber that she was able to make the experienced lesbian come so hard and so quickly, while she was being spanked. She masturbated to the memory quite frequently over the following months, even while being spanked herself.

When Susanna had finished, she pulled Amber up and kissed her, hungrily licking away the evidence of the multiple orgasms her sub had given Mistress Chevalier. "Good girl," she whispered in Amber's ear. As always, a thrill of pleasure coursed through Amber's body at the words. The approval of her mistress was a tangible reward to her now.

Susanna pushed Amber's shoulder down firmly, returning her to her knees, where she knew she belonged. She beckoned Sugar to her side, kissed her deeply, then whispered something in her ear, sending the maid scurrying from the room on an errand. Then she turned to the crowd to address them.

"To celebrate this happy occasion, when Mistress Chevalier agreed to enter my service so that we all might benefit from her skills as an artisan, and that I can improve my estate, I extend an offer for this gathering to continue until tomorrow evening. Who would like to stay?"

Amber was happy to see that everyone present was keen to stay another day, that meant a lot more chances to play with the guests.

Sugar returned in a hurry and handed Mistress Susanna the big purple strapon that Mistress Chevalier had used on Amber the previous afternoon. Sugar and Amber were instructed to help fit it to their domme, and when she was ready, Susanna got behind Mistress Chevalier and plunged the strapon deep into her.

"Vicky, come and watch your Mistress get fucked," Susanna ordered, summoning the ponygirl to her side to sit, entranced by the sight of the thick silicone cock filling her Mistress's wet pussy. "Thank you, Mistress Susanna," Vicky said gratefully.

"Would you like having your pussy licked, Vicky?" Susanna asked.

Amber was happy to oblige when Vicky said yes, and Susanna indicated that the task was her. She wriggled between Vicky's legs on her back, and the bodybuilding woman mounted her face with a satisfied sigh. Amber tongued her happily as the woman rode her face and watched her Mistress get fucked.

"What next? Sugar, apply your tongue to Amber's pussy. Candy, I want your tongue between my cheeks as I fuck Jade. If anyone wants to play with Sugar while she pleasures Amber, please feel free," Susanna said.

"I'd like to fuck Sugar," Baroness Carruthers said, as her sub, Charlotte, began to undress her so she could get into her strapon harness and join the party on the stage.

"Excellent! Please, ladies, this is a party. Enjoy yourselves!" Susanna said. After a second, clothes started to come off, submissives were bound to furniture, the sound of bottoms being punished and tongues being used for the purpose of pussy worship filled the room.

Amber found herself passed around like a box of luxury chocolates. Each dominant who received her unwrapped a different treat, before passing her on. Before a break for lunch was called, Amber had been taken in all holes, sometimes two at once. Her buttocks were as shockingly crimson as Mistress Chevalier's and her nipples were sensitive from the amount of licking and nibbling she'd enjoyed.

After lunch, Amber found herself lying back on one of the corner sofas. Mistress Susanna and Mistress Chevalier were on either side of her, fondling her breasts and plunging their fingers into her pussy together, as they chatted. Her thighs rested on Vicky's strong shoulders as she knelt on the floor. The ponygirl was using her tongue to pleasure Amber when their Mistress's fingers were elsewhere.

The powerful combination of sensations had Amber in an almost insensible state, as she reached climaxes one after another.

Mistress Chevalier lifted her head from another bout of nipple sucking and nibbling and grinned at Susanna. "My bum still hurts, you know."

"And don't you forget it, Mistress Chevalier," Susanna replied.

"I shall dream of returning the favour one day," Mistress Chevalier said.

"Keep dreaming."

"Do you think you'll try Amber out as a pony? I think she'd be wonderful, though I doubt she'd beat my Vicky," Mistress Chevalier asked.

Amber lifted her head from the cushions and protested, "Hey! I could beat, Vicky!"

"Don't interrupt, Amber," Mistress Susanna admonished her, roughly twisting her nipple and laughing as Amber yelped at the rough treatment before her head lolled back again as Vicky's tongue plunged back between her lips.

"I think it's certainly worth trying her out when the new stables are ready. Would you be interested in helping put Amber through some trials?" Susanna asked.

"I'd beat, Vicky," Amber mumbled. Then her head snapped up, and she screamed. "She bit me! Vicky bit me," she complained.

Vicky lifted her head and grinned wickedly, "Amber would never beat me, not in oil wrestling, and not in a pony race. She's too soft. Delicious, but soft."

"I am not. I bet I could take more strokes of the cane than you," Amber claimed.

"You can't even control your orgasms," Vicky said.

"I can control them," Amber boasted.

"Prove her wrong then, Vicky," Mistress Chevalier ordered, and her sub stopped talking and got back to worshipping Amber's pussy.

"How about we hold some pony trials then. Would you join us, Mistress Chevalier?" Susanna said.

"Vicky and I are in."

"Amber, would you like to try out as a pony?" Susann asked.

Amber's head collapsed back to the cushions again, as Vicky's tongue quickly proved her point. Amber was riding the wave of her second orgasm before she could muster the self-control to respond to her Mistress, who was patiently waiting.

"Yes, Mistress."

DRIVEN BY HER LESBIAN BOSS

Book 6

CHAPTER 1

"You missed a bit," Mistress Susanna said, pointing with her left hand as she sipped her tea with her right.

Amber looked at the spot on the wall and ran her roller over it a few times, the whitewash splashing into the cracks, and little sprays of it splattering everywhere. She wondered if she'd have made the same suggestion again, in hindsight.

"Is that better, Mistress? This whitewash is messy stuff," Amber said.

"It's not whitewash, my girl. It's masonry paint, far tougher for cleaning," Mistress Chevalier corrected her.

"Fine, is the masonry paint now covering the bit I missed, Mistresses," Amber said with an audible sigh.

Vicky gasped, but didn't stop her own smooth action with the paint roller she held. Ginger giggled, but very quietly.

"Yes, you got it and don't be so cheeky, Amber," Mistress Susanna said.

"I'm sorry, Mistress," Amber replied.

Mistress Susanna nodded curtly and set her tea down, picking up a piece of chalk and adding a tally mark to Amber's column. Amber winced. That was another punishment she was due. At least she was still behind Pepper.

When they'd begun the preparation work on the stable buildings, Amber had envisioned it being much easier. After all, a little planning and some negotiation with the builders had allowed them to keep the cost of the professional work down, if Susanna and her staff could manage to do some of the simpler elements of the labour.

The building that hadn't been refurbished yet was filthy and full of junk of one form or another. First, they'd had to clean out old straw and muck, clean up decades of dirt and pull out rotten stable doors and woodwork. Much of what they'd had to take out was disposed of fairly easily. Some in skips, some on bonfires and some to a scrap metal dealer.

They'd found a number of things that needed to be restored because they were antique. Some beautiful cast iron boot scrapers, for instance, that were currently with a professional restorer to bring them back to their former glory.

Today was the last thing they were doing for at least a while before the contractors moved in. Just a couple of coats of whitewash, or rather, masonry paint, before they were done. Mistress Susanna and Mistress Chevalier sat in old, wooden farmhouse chairs watching the girls work.

Susanna's ponygirls, Ginger and Pepper were helping and Mistress Chevalier's ponygirl, Vicky was there too. At some point or other, all of Susanna's staff of submissive lesbians had pitched in to tidy up, but now it was just them.

Pudding couldn't help all the time if they all still wanted good meals, for instance. Roxy was off driving people around for Susanna's business, a task she clearly didn't relish. The maids were doing their bit keeping the main house tidy, or rather the private areas for which they alone were responsible.

That left Amber and the ponygirls, the warm spring air, painting the stable walls with rollers and brushes. It might end up being painted over by professionals, which made it a little frustrating, but if it went well, it could save a lot of time and money.

The girls were all naked, which Mistress Susanna had ordered to ensure they didn't get their clothes dirty. Or at least, that was what she'd said, with a twinkle in her eyes that suggested to Amber that their Mistress wasn't averse to making them work in the nude for her pleasure. Mistress Chevalier had seemed to think it was a good idea too.

Ginger and Pepper had been keen that they should wear their tails while they worked and had asked if they could. Mistress Susanna had immediately refused, saying she didn't want the paint getting on the 'hair' that made up the tails as it wouldn't be easy to wash off.

Mistress Chevalier had found a compromise that Ginger, Pepper and Vicky were keen to accept. A few silicone butt plugs with curly tails had been produced and were soon inserted in the ponygirls. They weren't for ponies, but for little pigs, but they were equally filling.

Amber tried politely to decline wearing one as well, but Susanna had ordered her to be plugged the same as the others. When Amber tried to back away, Susanna ordered her seized and held down. Vicky had taken great pleasure in holding her still, while Ginger and Pepper slowly lubricated her bottom and finally filled it with a plug. It felt much larger than the ones that the others had more willingly bent over to receive.

"Ow. That's so big," Amber had protested, with a rather whiny tone.

"That's what you get when you're bratty, my girl," Mistress Chevalier said.

"Yes, it certainly is. If you behave yourself, you'll get the same treatment as the good girls," Mistress Susanna had agreed, without sympathy.

"It's only an inch or so more circumference and you took it easily enough, don't pout so much," Mistress Chevalier had said, before Amber was ordered to get to work.

Amber moved back to the section she had been working on before she was told she'd missed a patch, and dipped her roller back in the tray, before lifting it up toward the ceiling and beginning a long roll down the wall. The refreshed roller spattered and dripped quite a bit, because she'd let it pick up too much paint.

"Hey! Mind what you're doing," Ginger protested, as the paint speckles splashed against her skin.

"Yeah, watch it Amber, you're getting it everywhere," Pepper agreed, wiping at the mess on her arm.

"It's just paint, it'll come off in the shower," Amber said with a heavy sigh.

"Oh, ok then, if it'll come off in the shower, that's alright," Ginger said with the kind of withering sarcasm that only the English can summon. Ginger picked up one of the smaller brushes, dipped it in her paint tray, and then flicked it at Amber, splattering the cold white paint across her breasts and belly.

"Oi!", Amber squealed, shaking her long handled roller above Ginger's head, causing yet more paint to be splashed around over the girls.

Pepper squealed as she was splashed again and got her revenge by running her roller up Amber's thigh, leaving a big white streak up her leg.

Ginger tried to flick her brush again, but this time her aim was off, and the paint splattered over Vicky's muscular back and bottom. The tall, athletic woman rounded on the rest of them and growled. At the party Susanna held a few weeks ago, Amber had heard several of the women refer to Vicky as 'The Amazonian' and the nickname wasn't inaccurate. Vicky was tall but also had the kind of figure that came from bodybuilding or weightlifting. There were defined muscles pretty much everywhere you looked, and Amber knew from experience that wrestling her was a losing proposition.

Vicky advanced on Ginger and pinned her quickly against the wet paint on the wall, before swatting her on the bottom with a large paintbrush. "Watch what you're doing!" Vicky rumbled as she punished the smaller woman.

Ginger wriggled, but Vicky kept her against the wall with no apparent effort. Amber could see her breasts were squashed against the wet paint, but despite Ginger's verbal protests, her mouth was curled in a lusty smile as she enjoyed being overpowered by the larger ponygirl.

"Enough!" Mistress Chevalier called out finally, as Pepper and Amber tried to get more paint on each other.

"Break it up, girls. There's work to do today," Mistress Susanna demanded. "Now!" she barked when the squabbling girls didn't immediately obey.

Finally, the girls calmed down and put their tools down.

"To the showers, now!" Mistress Susanna said sternly.

The two dominants marched them off to the shower room, and lined them up against the wall where they were made to wait, while the two dominants left the room. Vicky looked at the shower heads expectantly, but Pepper shook her head dejectedly.

"No such luck," Ginger whispered. "We won't get the showers for this."

Amber frowned, wondering what was going on. Clearly Susanna wanted them clean again, so presumably soap and a shower was just the ticket?

When Susanna and Jade came back, they were hauling a garden hose reel which Jade played out behind her. A bright yellow pressure nozzle was attached to one end, and Mistress Susanna looked cross.

"Face the wall, you filthy girls," Mistress Susanna ordered.

Everyone turned around and then the hose splashed against the wall. Amber squealed at the cold water splashing off the surrounding wall, and she wasn't the only one who flinched. The flow was adjusted from a narrow jet to a wide spray mode that was more like a powerful shower.

Then the water was played across their shoulders, back and forth, as Susanna got them all wet, and not in the way any of the submissives generally preferred. The water was cold. It was a sunny day, which was a mercy but it was still only spring so the mains water wasn't anywhere near lukewarm though thankfully it wasn't as icy as it would have been in the winter.

The girls were all shivering in short order as the water washed over them, and Susanna moved back and forth over them, making sure all the paint was washed off. Then it was time to turn around.

"Wash your faces," Susanna ordered, and while they did that with the cold water that dripped down their bodies, she ran the hose over their breasts, pummelling their tender flesh and washing away the drops of paint. As the girls squealed and yelped at the cold water which made their skin produce goose-bumps, Susanna adjusted the flow back to a narrow jet which she used to target the worst areas, like Amber's well painted thigh.

When it was at last done, and each girl was inspected, before being given one more rinse off with the spray setting, they were allowed to move into the locker area, where large fluffy towels allowed them to get dry and a bit warmer.

They weren't given much time, and Amber was the last to dry off. She was still quite damp when they were all ordered back to work, chastened and feeling far less boisterous.

Amber heard Mistress Susanna saying something on the phone, and then the dominants returned to their chairs.

"I don't want to see any more displays like that, you naughty sluts," Mistress Susanna said. "I want this done before it gets dark so get cracking."

A short while later, Amber was feeling warm again as she methodically painted the walls and all the girls cooperated with each other this time.

Then Sugar and Candy arrived, and her concentration was dealt a blow as she heard Mistress Chevalier and Mistress Susanna remove their trousers and sit down to have the submissive maids pleasure them. The wet sounds of passion behind them were a distraction Amber could do without. A warm glow started between her legs as she imagined being involved with the fun, either on her knees, or being worshipped by Sugar or Candy.

By the time they finished with their painting, and were allowed to turn around and see what was happening, Sugar and Candy, still in their revealing and wildly impractical, French maid uniforms, were just as hot and sweaty from their work, as Amber, Ginger, Pepper and Vicky were from the painting.

Amber coughed politely, "I think we're finished, Mistress."

Susanna looked up and shuddered as she tightened her grip on Candy's hair, inspecting the work. Apparently satisfied, if not by the approach of what Amber thought would be her third orgasm, at least by the painting, she nodded.

"Very well, go and wash off the brushes and rollers, put everything away, and you can all go back to the house to get ready for dinner," Mistress Susanna ordered.

"Yes, Mistress," the girls chorused.

CHAPTER 2

"Now, Amber, can you name all these items correctly?" Mistress Chevalier asked.

Amber looked at the assortment presented on the table in the newly finished stable building. The last of the contractors had left the day before, and Mistress Susanna hadn't wasted any time in bringing her out this morning for her first training session.

"Bridle, reins, boots obviously, body harness, and a bit gag? Then there are the ears, a tail, and blinders," Amber replied, touching each item as she named them. Having had next to no riding experience as a kid, Amber was happy with her performance.

Mistress Chevalier had given her some reading material as homework to study up on while the contractors were in, so it wasn't a work of any particular genius, but she was happy that she got everything right.

"Good. It's important that you learn the terminology so you can get dressed yourself, and help other girls get dressed, too," Mistress Chevalier said.

"We'll dress you this time, you can consider this a taster session. Often, the submissives present themselves attired properly for our pleasure," Mistress Susanna added.

"Yes, that's a popular way to do it. I enjoy scenes where I get Vicky ready, strip her down naked, put her in her tack and harness, and then give her rub downs and hair brushing after a scene. You must learn how to satisfy whichever dominant you're playing with, and their particular needs, of course," Mistress Chevalier said.

Amber nodded as the two older women instructed her, trying to absorb what they were saying, in case there were tests later. The taste she'd developed for the sweet caress of the cane didn't mean she wanted to experience it so regularly that failure held no fear for her.

It seemed better to do as well as she could, and then be punished or pleasured with Mistress Susanna's impact toys, as her domme felt necessary. Being cheeky or lax, just took the experience into the zone of true punishment, to be borne not revelled in.

"Yes, Mistress," Amber said when they'd finished talking.

The harness and bridle came first, then the ears and blinders. The boots were next, big, hoof-like platform heels that made her stand almost on tiptoes. They made a satisfying clopping noise against the floor of the tack room.

"Bend over that spanking bench, Amber," Mistress Susanna said calmly.

At first, Amber wondered if she was to be punished for something, but then Mistress Susanna fetched several butt plugs which had long tails hanging from them. Amber swallowed hard, as her domme matched the colours to her hair to make her choice.

"What do you think, Amber? Does this one look like it would suit you? The colour is the closest I have to your hair. If you do well, I'll get you something custom made, of course," Mistress Susanna purred enticingly.

"It does look quite big, Mistress," Amber pointed out.

"Yes, but that will help it stay in. It's such a drag when a new girl drops her tail out of her bottom. When you've been doing your exercises for long enough, that won't be a problem. You'll be able to grip it tightly for me, all day if I require," Mistress Susanna said.

"Yes, Mistress."

"What do you think, Mistress Chevalier? Is this too big for our new pony?"

The Stable Mistress came forward and inspected the butt plug in front of Amber, stroking the length and squeezing the girth. "I think she'll be able to take this with no problem. Perhaps she'll squeal a bit, but I'd be surprised if she doesn't cream up in a hurry when you put it in her. It's just this wide bit, Amber, that presents a challenge, but once it's pushed slowly and firmly into your bottom, your tight little rosebud will close behind it and you'll get used to it," Mistress Chevalier explained, as Amber's cheeks flushed at the thought of the impending intrusion.

"Would you mind doing the honours, Jade, while I tend to the bit gag?" Mistress Susanna asked.

"Happily," Mistress Chevalier replied, taking the plug behind Amber.

"Now, this gag goes in your mouth," Mistress Susanna explained, as strong fingers coated Amber's tight hole with lubricant and began to slide slowly inside her, slowly coating her ring with the cool gel.

Amber whimpered, but made an effort to relax as much as she could, to admit the intruding digits of Mistress Chevalier.

"When it's in, it'll be attached to your reins, and we can gently tug on it to make you turn your head and direct you. Do you understand, Amber?"

Amber nodded and her eyes went wide as a second finger plunged deep inside her. The squelching noises coming from her bottom echoed around the room, and she knew her chest and neck had a rising crimson flush. Amber also knew that Mistress Susanna was enjoying her sense of shame at being on display like this. It certainly wasn't going to elicit sympathy from her boss.

"Good girl. One stamp of your hoofs for yes, two for no, three for your safeword if something is too much. Got it," Mistress Susanna said, cupping her chin in her hand. "You won't be able to speak clearly around this, though you are free to scream and cry if you feel the need."

"Yes, Mistress," Amber managed, before the rubber bar was placed between her teeth and gently, but firmly pushed back into her mouth. Amber could tell that drooling was going to be a bit of a problem for her and that didn't help her sense of humiliation one bit as Susanna fastened the leather straps behind her head and adjusted the buckles until it was firmly in place. Then she attached the reins and experimentally tugged them, turning Amber's head to the left and right.

"Turn to the left. Turn to the right. Left. Right. Pulling up on both means stop. This flick of the reins, means go," Susanna explained.

Mistress Chevalier withdrew the three fingers she'd been working in and out of Amber's arsehole, and presented the well-lubricated butt plug instead, firmly pushing it inside her. It stopped, obstructed by the tight ring of muscle, and was withdrawn, only to be worked forward again.

The sensation was uncomfortable, humiliating and Amber knew, was making her sopping wet. As she grew more aroused, and more used to the wide intrusion, she imagined the plug was opening her up and being admitted further into her bottom. Then, with a squelch and a quite glorious sensation from her rosebud, it passed the widest point and her ring closed around the tapered section.

Mistress Chevalier mumbled something that sounded positive, then tugged it back and forth a few times to make sure it was properly in place. "I don't think that's coming out by accident, Mistress Susanna," she reported.

"As long as it comes out when we want it to, that's fine," Susanna replied.

"I find a wand against the clit for half an hour, tends to loosen them up a bit if they have trouble letting go," Mistress Chevalier said dismissing the problem. Amber gulped. A half hour of such play would leave her shattered and broken, those things were so intense. Amber wasn't sure if she should be terrified at the prospect or if she should hope she wouldn't be able to let go of the plug when the time came.

"Perhaps we should experiment one day? We have four ponygirls at the moment, if we count our new trainee that is," Mistress Susanna said.

"Oh yes, there's nothing more erotic than the scientific method being applied to a sexy young woman's bottom," Mistress Chevalier said with a filthy chuckle.

"I think Ginger would take the biggest one," Susanna remarked.

"Yes, but perhaps Vicky could hold on to one the longest. She's got muscles everywhere you know," Jade replied.

"I know they say it's important not to miss any muscle groups, big or small," Susanna said.

"As far as I've discovered, she doesn't."

Amber turned her head to the side where Vicky was waiting patiently, nude aside from her own harness, with Ginger and Pepper. All three ponygirls were in their full gear and had been getting the full show as Amber was dressed and penetrated. They seemed quite animated at the prospect of a butt plug competition, but in a way that suggested to Amber that they were looking forward to it, rather than dreading it. *They're all just as slutty as me, she thought to herself as her arousal ran down her thigh.*

Mistress Susanna interrupted her thoughts by taking a firm grip of a large brass ring that linked the straps of her harness between her shoulder-blades and hauling her upright bodily. With a moment or two to balance on the high platforms of the hoof boots, Amber found the butt plug was firmly in place and the tail swishing against her thighs.

"Walk on," Susanna ordered with a flick of the reins and slowly guided her out into the yard in front of the stables. Amber was grateful that the estate was so secluded. The front gate had to be at least half a mile from the front of the house, and the grounds were extensive. Amber felt a frisson of pleasure at the thought of being spied by someone out for a country walk, if they went to the edges of the estate, but there was no real risk this close to the house. Perhaps a naughty ponygirl might run off and visit the edges of the grounds, where the public footpaths might be found?

In the meantime, Amber had to walk around the yard, performing wheels and turns as instructed. Susanna began to teach her the basics of the gaits she was expected to use. Walking, trotting and cantering. Galloping wasn't something she wanted to get into on the first day.

After lunch, Mistress Chevalier, who had been observing during the morning, helped Mistress Susanna harness Amber to a small trap. It wasn't the same as the ones that Amber and Susanna had used for their race.

"Is this a different model, Mistress," Amber asked, grateful that the bit hadn't been replaced after lunch.

"Well spotted. It's a training model, lighter and flimsier than the ones the other day. It makes it easier for you to learn, and you'll use it the first time you try moving and pulling a passenger in the trap, or running at a good racing trot," Mistress Susanna said.

"Yes, there's no hurry, you'll get used to the various vehicles one at a time, with and without the weight of the passengers," Mistress Chevalier added. "Then you get to try it with a rider. That way, you don't get anyone injured, including yourself. Safety first!"

Amber had thought that would have been secondary, but since coming to know Mistress Susanna, she had been educated in the rigorous standards that BDSM players adhered to. Safewords were familiar to her already, from various books and films, but it wasn't until she began to serve Susanna that she'd understood.

Play was always to be safe, sane and consensual, Susanna had told her one night, early in their relationship. Whatever was to be done, the submissive must have consented, and precautions had to be taken to ensure their safety. Even simple bondage with rope could cause nerve damage, if the players were amateurish about it.

Plenty of videos she'd seen or books she'd read had featured subs and slaves being suspended from frames and ceilings with complete ease, but Susanna had laughed at such questions. Rope bondage took practice and time, and suspension was perfectly safe, but only if done correctly.

As Susanna had an impatient streak, she preferred padded leather cuffs and the like for bondage, and was more inclined to put Amber in a sex swing, than suspend her by her restraints.

The idea that safety came first, when she was likely to be disciplined with a cane or paddle later, and caused significant pain, would have seemed incongruous to Amber just a few short weeks ago. But now she had come to know that each implement required knowledge and skill to inflict pain, while minimising injury. A bruise healed well, but a split in the skin was a different matter.

Now, Mistress Chevalier's assertion that safety with the traps and carts in the stables was important, even though the abundance of whips and crops suggested a ponygirl would be regularly subjected to painful stimulus. Amber could expect that her bottom would be turned quite pink from a cropping or paddling if she misbehaved, but having a trap collide with a pony was something to be avoided. Deliberate punishment versus accidental injury.

"Yes, Mistresses, thank you for explaining."

Mistress Susanna had Amber walk around the yard pulling the light training trap behind her as she talked to her Stable Mistress. Every few laps, the order would go out for Amber to change gait or walk in a figure of eight rather than a circle, practicing manoeuvres.

Although the trap was very light and on good quality wheels, which appeared to be made from bicycle wheels, it was still quite a lot more exercise than Amber was used to doing. She was no gym bunny, by any means, and it was easy to see why Mistress Chevalier and the other dommes were so excited by the prospect of Vicky as a ponygirl.

Amber could well imagine the Amazonian competing on a TV game show about the hyper-fit, and crushing her enemies, seeing them driven from the field, and hearing the crying of their women, or men. Like a 1930s barbarian heroine.

As Amber practiced her gaits, the two dominants sat at a table that was sheltered from the bright sunshine by a large umbrella sticking up from the middle.

Susanna called for refreshments from the kitchen.

CHAPTER 3

"I'm surprised they got all that work done so quickly," Mistress Chevalier said.

"It doesn't hurt to have a good recommendation from a friend."

"They did an excellent job. I haven't found anything that doesn't work or fit or wasn't finished properly. Which is a far cry from every other time I've had to have a bathroom replaced or new light fittings, I can tell you," Jade said.

"I'm glad to hear it. It's worth paying for the best, but I don't know how I'd have found them without a referral."

"It was the Baroness who suggested the firm, yes? I should send her a thank you note."

"Yes, it was. I'm sure she'll be happy to be thanked at the next get together, but Amber can put a letter in the post for you if you want to write one," Susanna replied.

"That must be nice, having a personal assistant to take care of administrative work."

"Yes, I highly recommend it. I hope you can grow your business in your new workshop and then perhaps we can find you an Amber of your own?" Susanna replied.

Mistress Chevalier chuckled at that, “I love the sound of that. What type of girl should we look for?”

“How about a fashion student, who has just completed a degree in Leather for Fashion, at the University of Northam?”

“That's a thing, is it?”

“Yes, an absolutely genuine qualification.”

“Now, how would you know that? I’ve been marking tack and harness for, well, some time now,” Jade demurred, “and I didn’t know there were fashion degrees based on leather.”

Susanna answered coyly, “I may have done some research.”

“Have you now?” Jade chuckled.

“Yes, there are all sorts of relevant qualifications, from the trades guilds in London and the various arts and fashion courses. To me it seems obvious that there are two types you might consider,” Susanna opined.

“Do go on.”

“Well, there are you art and craft types of people, who have studied the skills of working with leather for tack and harnesses and the like, perhaps for horses or more for human fashion. Then there are ones who’ve done metalwork or woodwork for other toys or for the metal parts of your gear,” Susanna answered.

“That would definitely be helpful. It would save me a lot of time if the basic tasks could be handed off to an apprentice who already had skills,” Jade agreed.

“The second type is those with more of a design and fashion background. They may have less in the way of practical skills at manufacturing your goods, but might be great at realising the designs you describe in the way the rest of the industry does. Either way, many of the higher level degrees and craft courses contain some basic level of business skills as well. What you need is a good all-rounder who can help with your website, sending out orders, construction of garments. Honestly, it doesn’t matter which elements that you do, that your first employee takes off your hands. Your time is currently the most important asset you have,” Susanna advised.

“I must say, we’ve only been moved in a few days, the flat still smells of fresh paint. But coming up to the main house for meals, and Sugar and Candy helping with the laundry has been invaluable," Jade said. "I suppose any hours I was spending doing something that I can put elsewhere are a massive boon."

"Exactly. People always assume it's the thing that only they can do that is most important. The computer coding, the artisan level craftwork, the generation of business ideas. In fact, it's the paperwork, stationery orders, responding to simple emails and the like, that takes up your bandwidth," Susanna said.

"It's going to be hard to find someone suitable, in any case, given my industry," Jade said.

"Not as hard as you think, but don't let Sugar and Candy take credit for the laundry. It all goes out to a very efficient service in the local village. They just gather it all up and take care of the simple things like towels. Nothing that requires ironing. I lost a number of good blouses to gardening duty that way. For the sake of your wardrobe and the environment, don't try to get them to deal with anything that requires a crease," Susanna said.

Jade laughed heartily at that. "The cheeky minxes didn't even hint at that. I thought they were the youngest people I'd ever met who knew how to use an ironing board properly."

"We'll add a few marks to their punishment tally then, because they definitely can't iron clothes properly," Susanna said. "The service will deal with dry cleaning items too, by the way, but nothing kinky. They're strictly vanilla."

"Noted. No peephole bras and the like," Jade giggled.

Susanna's nose wrinkled up at that, "Ew. Please tell me you don't have any of those. I've never seen one that wasn't tacky."

"No, I don't. Most of my obviously kinky items are leather so they're not going in a washing machine, don't worry," Jade said cheerfully. "It was the only thing I could think of, but I second your opinion. But you mentioned it might not be hard to find someone suitable, why not?"

"I have a good working system in place. You have to, in my position," Susanna said.

"I assume your HR department takes care of things like recruitment," Jade said.

"For the businesses I don't actually run myself, certainly," Susanna said. "But not for positions in my household. I have specialists for that."

"How do you mean?" Jade said, taking a sip of the freshly made lemonade that Candy and Sugar had brought out from the kitchen for them. The two maids were now helping Amber take a few sips with a long straw and giggling as she dribbled some past her bit.

"Finding someone like Amber, to work so closely with me, takes far more scrutiny than employing a night watchman for one of the factories," Susanna pointed out. "My specialists conduct more rigorous screening to ensure that I get the most likely candidates, and I never interview anyone who doesn't meet my requirements. I have to think they have a reasonable chance of fitting in for it to be worth my time."

Jade looked Susanna's latest employee up and down. Amber was pretty, beautiful even and given that the only clothing she currently wore consisted of thin straps of leather and kinky boots, and that she was being given a drink by two young women dressed as French maids, it seemed unlikely all that had been on the job advert.

"So Amber had been vetted somehow, before you met her?"

"Yes. I prefer to headhunt, because it gives me more time for checks to be done. But there are a series of steps we use. Firstly, we identify a broad pool of candidates who can do the work. In Amber's case, it was easy to find women who could do well as a personal assistant. It's a pretty board church and her duties are minimal," Susanna said.

"You must have a lot of people you have to reject. Men, for starters."

"I employ men, just not for personal service positions, for obvious reasons," Susanna replied. "In any case, most people don't know they're being vetted by a headhunter. Don't look at me like that. It's all above board and perfectly legal, we aren't breaching privacy, legally speaking. Believe me, the expensive kink friendly barristers I've had to employ have ensured that. Of course, if it's a job we are advertising, we get lots of applicants who aren't ever going to be ideal."

"Men?"

"Yes, men or people who have archaic views on human sexuality but might be excellent at the actual job. In which case, we do everything to find them a job somewhere in one of my companies that I don't ever actually have to meet them," Susanna explained. "I can't exclude a man from being my gardener, but I'm not required to employ sexists or homophobes. And the man has to be the most qualified candidate. Women's shelters don't have to employ men, for instance, and I don't object to male accountants. My driver is a woman because she's been diplomatic protection and was the most qualified driver I could find."

"Ok, ok. I get the point, you've dotted the i's and crossed the t's of equality law and you're not investigating people beyond the bounds of privacy laws either," Jade conceded.

"No, it's alright. It's an absolute minefield. But the short of it is that a few jobs where a woman, or a man, might be preferred, are permissible. A bra-fitter can be a woman, an actor for a female role can be, a man four counselling young boys who are traumatised, a gay man for talking to teenagers about coming out. That's all fine. But a cashier in a supermarket, that can be done by anyone. It's much more reasonable than you might think," Susanna said.

"Better than it used to be, though."

"Agreed. But regardless, positions in my household are reviewed by friendly legal experts before I try to fill them. Amber, for instance, is employed as a personal assistant," Susanna said. "If she turned out not to fulfil all the criteria, she would be working from an office in London and any visit she absolutely had to make here, would be fully managed."

"I see. How did you establish that she was suitable in all the ways you hope for, then?" Jade enquired.

"There are extensive psychometric tests that can reveal bad attitudes towards some groups, so that weeds people out. Then we look at legally available information. Like if they're married, part of a group that might give a clue and so on. We also ask people to volunteer their orientation on applications. All that can be done before the interview with me and I'm the last of several interviews," Susanna said.

"You can ask their sexuality? I honestly didn't know that," Jade replied.

"Yes, but they don't have to answer. We have excellent policies for supporting couples of all sexualities, and lots of people want their employer and colleagues to know these days," Susanna confirmed.

"That's so much better than the last time I had to apply for a job. It was very much don't ask, don't tell then."

"Anyway, that's it, basically. Before my team interview them, I discard any candidates that don't seem right, then they interview them and show my their shortlist. I might still discard someone then, when they've got more information to show me. After that, full background checks are done, and hopefully anyone I meet for an interview is suitable," Susanna said.

"Amber must have been," Jade said, curiously.

"Yes, that was a tricky one. There was nothing so blatant as being in the LGBT society at university, but there were some public social media posts, a few titbits here and there, that made us think she might have a healthy interest that was unexplored," Susanna winked.

"It seems like a fine line to walk though," Jade said.

"Let's just say that Amber's interview convinced me that we had correctly judged her, shall we?"

"Your silver tongue got the response that you needed to confirm your suspicions, then?"

"What a particularly apt way to put it," Susanna replied, provocatively licking her lips. "As for my silver tongue, it wasn't just my skills of persuasion that sealed the deal. One lick of a nipple, and I knew she was game for more."

"Susanna, you are so wicked!"

"You have to take the odd risk in life, now and then and Amber seemed like a worthwhile gamble, given all our preparation. You know, Jade, she barely hesitated to strip off in the napping room at my office so I could change her outfit," Susanna said. "That and the glances she'd been throwing me as I changed, were enough to make me throw caution to the wind and test her."

"I know I might seem bold, sometimes, but that's at nightclubs and such, where I know my targets are suitable. I don't think I could ever take a chance like that," Jade breathed.

"I don't think you'll have to; with the potential candidates you'd be looking for."

"What do you think that might be?"

"As I said, fashion graduates with an interest in leather," Susanna said coyly.

"The way you specified a university and a course earlier, I thought you had someone in mind already," Jade laughed.

"No, don't be silly."

"Of course not."

"I have five candidates for you look at," Susanna replied.

Mistress Chevalier's mouth dropped open at that.

"Amber, come here so we can get you unhitched. I want you to fetch a file from the office and bring it back for Mistress Chevalier," Susanna ordered.

"Yes, Mistress," Amber said.

CHAPTER 4

After the evening meal, Amber found herself being interviewed in Ginger and Pepper's flat. She'd been allowed to get out of her ponygirl harness and other gear, and was now more comfortably attired in a plaid micro-skirt, knee length white socks, and a tie up white crop top. No girl she'd ever been to school with dressed like that, but it was clearly the aim of the costume.

Amber had to keep her knees together to keep from flashing Mistress Susanna and Mistress Chevalier across the coffee table, as bra and panties weren't part of the outfit she'd been given. The ponygirls had been put to work moving some more of the equipment back down to the tack room. The flat had been full of dismantled benches, pillories, impact toys and the like, while the contractors were on site, on Mistress Susanna's orders.

The contractors were quite professional, polite and diligent and a surprising number employed by the firm, were women and at least a couple of the men were openly gay, which was a refreshing change from Amber's limited experience of builders and tradespeople.

They weren't to be exposed to anything in the slightest bit kinky though, not even the one or two who were quite likely lesbians themselves. "Just because they might be lesbians or gay, doesn't mean they're kinky, and even if they are, everything we do here is private," Mistress Susanna had explained. That was a perfectly reasonable point, Amber supposed. *Not everyone wanted to be exposed to sexuality at work, just because Amber was enjoying that, she thought.*

So, Amber sipped her tea delicately while the two dominants talked to her about her first day trying to play as a ponygirl. She confirmed that she had enjoyed it so far and found it interesting.

"Would you like to continue training then?" Susanna asked.

"Yes, please, Mistress."

"Good. We have talked and have a plan we'd like you to consent too. I have some business dealings coming up in London which will require me to be away for a week or so. During that time, we propose that Mistress Chevalier train you," Susanna said, holding up her hand to forestall questions. "Jade is, after all, the acknowledge expert here. If you agree, you will stay here for the full week."

"Yes. During that time, I will train you properly in all the basics, far beyond what you've learned during the introductory session today. By the time Susanna comes back, you'll be able to serve her as a ponygirl and she'll test your skills to see how you've taken to it," Mistress Chevalier continued.

"What would the training be, Mistress?"

"I will leave the specifics up to Mistress Chevalier of course, but you'll be taught about the equipment, racing traps, the common instructions and you'll practice everything until it's second nature," Susanna said.

"Yes, that's it. I will go through it with you in detail, of course."

"While I'm away, I would expect you to submit to Mistress Chevalier just as you do to me," Mistress Susanna said. "Just as you did at the party. I assume that won't be a problem for you?"

"You want me to please her sexually, Mistress?" Amber asked.

"Naturally. If Mistress Chevalier tells you to kneel, you will do so with good grace. If she tells you to bend over for a caning, you will do so gratefully. If she tells you to put your tongue to work on her pussy, you will do so with just as much diligence as I would expect where it me, demanding that you provide pleasure," Mistress Susanna said. "Again, is that an issue?"

Amber shook her head, "No, Mistress. I just wanted to be sure I understood correctly. I would be happy to stay here and learn about being a ponygirl and serve Mistress Chevalier for you."

"I'm glad to hear that. When I'm back, I will test your skills and see if you have the aptitude to be a ponygirl for me, like Ginger and Pepper. Are there any more questions?"

"What if I fail, Mistress? Will I lose my position here if I'm not a good ponygirl? I don't want to disappoint you, but what if I can't do it?" Amber asked nervously.

"Don't worry about that. I want you to try it. If you don't pass my tests though, you won't be dismissed. You'll still be my personal assistant and still be my submissive. I don't expect Sugar and Candy, or Pudding or Roxy to play this way, do I?" Susanna replied. "You will still be my girl. Now, do you want to play our games for the next week?"

"Please say yes, Amber. I guarantee I'll have a lot of fun with you," Mistress Chevalier said with a grin.

"Don't you mean, that I'll have a lot of fun, Mistress Chevalier?"

"Oh, possibly. I'll be exercising you hard though, every day, and you'll be disciplined for any misbehaviour or failure," Mistress Chevalier replied. "I'm sure some of it will be fun for you, but training you properly for your Mistress, and enjoying myself are my real concerns."

"Well, in that case, I can hardly say no, can I?" Amber said. "I consent to the training program."

"You can, but for forgetting to address us properly, you're going to get a spanking, young lady," Mistress Susanna snapped. "Over my knee, now."

"Yes, Mistress."

CHAPTER 5

By the time that Amber had received the dozen hard smacks on her bottom, that Mistress Susanna decided would be her punishment, she could tell her cheeks were glowing. She tried to look over her shoulder but couldn't see the resulting colour.

"Stand up and go to the mirror. See what you made me do to you, Amber," Mistress Susanna ordered. Amber complied, loving that her domme played into what she was trying to do.

Presenting her bottom to the full-length mirror that Ginger and Pepper had in their living room, she was able to see the effect the spanking had had on her pert cheeks. They were indeed glowing a most attractive shade of deep pink.

"What do you say after a spanking, Amber?"

"Thank you, Mistress, for correcting my behaviour."

"Good girl. Now, come back and wait here," Mistress Susanna said, pointing to a spot in front of the sofa that she and Mistress Chevalier were sitting on, before she stood herself and opened a cabinet next to the mirror.

Amber waited patiently as Mistress Chevalier looked her up and down, not bothering to conceal her appreciation of Amber's young, curvaceous body in the slightest. The Stable Mistress licked her lips as she admired the submissive before her. Amber could hear her Mistress getting ready with some kind of toy behind her, and she thought she knew what it was.

A few moments later, Mistress Susanna put a firm hand on Amber's shoulder. "On your knees, slut," she ordered, applying insistent pressure until Amber dropped to the floor, "now put your cheeky tongue to work for Mistress Chevalier. Show her how much your pussy eating has improved."

Mistress Chevalier smiled as she raised her bottom from the sofa cushion so she could hitch up her skirt, lowering herself at the edge of the seat to make her pussy available. Amber's tongue was soon slipping between her lips, and Mistress Chevalier's fingers twined into her hair, forcefully taking control of her. Having the older woman directing her attention as she wanted sent a thrill of pleasure down Amber's spine, raising goose bumps on her flesh.

Behind her, Amber heard Mistress Susanna drop a cushion on the floor and kneel down. The bulbous head of a dildo pressed against her wet lips, and her Mistress took a grip on Amber's hips, before slowly thrusting the strap-on into her submissive's pussy.

Amber moaned into Mistress Chevalier's pussy, enjoying the sensations of her pussy being filled as she tasted the older woman's lips. The way that the domme twisted her hair, tugged at her scalp just hard enough to make it clear who was in charge and be a little uncomfortable, which Amber found intoxicating.

"I think she's loving this, Susanna," Mistress Chevalier said, her voice thick with lust.

"I'll have to remember to pull her hair more often."

"Yes, it seems to be motivating her well. Her skills are certainly coming along nicely, aren't they?"

"I'm happy to say she's a quick learner, she's taking this cock well," Mistress Susanna agreed. "Her participation is much better than her first tries, she's pushing back properly and getting her hips where I need them, aren't you dear?"

Amber replied, but her words were muffled because Mistress Chevalier had no intention of letting her tongue leave her clit, just to let her speak clearly. "I think that was a yes. Lick me harder, slut, I want to come on that pretty face," Mistress Chevalier urged.

Complying wasn't a chore by any means, Amber was happy to do as instructed, revelling in the effect her tongue and lips were having on the older woman. Being able to please a domme who had doubtless had dozens of submissives bring her pleasure, and be complimented for her skills, was truly gratifying for her.

Amber's whole world was still in flux, all this was still new to her. Submitting to the whims of a lover, being disciplined with pain, restrained and shared with others were all revelatory experiences to her. Everything had happened so fast, and less than six months ago, she could never have imagined being in this situation.

Being on her knees between two lovers was certainly a fantasy that she'd had, but the Amber of six-months ago, couldn't have imagined that she would actually do that one day soon. Nor could she have honestly said that she might be in this position, between two women.

Her first proper lesbian experiences had been with or under the instruction of Susanna. Amber knew that Mistress Chevalier had had her first experiences before she was even born, and to be able to bring her to orgasm was a delight.

True to her word, when Mistress Chevalier began to come, Amber's face was made as wet as her she could feel her pussy was. The older woman ground her wet pussy into Amber's mouth, and when her spasms subsided, she rolled her hips. Mistress Chevalier rubbed Amber's face against her hot, wet pussy, smearing her juices all over the young submissive's chin, lips and nose. Amber was left gasping and struggling desperately, trying to get her tongue back to work.

Mistress Chevalier's hand pushed her away from her sensitive nub, "Enough, slut. You've had more than enough."

"If she wants more pussy, shall we swap places?" Mistress Susanna suggested.

"More than happy to, though I'm a bit weak at the knees, I'm sure I'll recover in a minute or two," Mistress Chevalier said, pushing Amber aside and standing unsteadily.

Mistress Susanna pulled back, withdrawing the long, thick silicone cock from her submissive's aching pussy, then unstrapping it and passing it to her friend.

Amber's tongue was soon lapping at the eager pussy of her own Mistress, who took a firm grip of her hair too, and played into her appreciation of hair pulling. To have Susanna tugging at her, pulling her face in and demanding that Amber pleasure her, was wonderfully relaxing. Amber felt so comfortable, it felt so right that she should be on her knees, worshipping her Mistress, submitting to her body and soul.

It was truly her rightful place in the world, to be wherever Susanna needed her, to be her pet, her pony, her loyal assistant, her playful slut. The party a few weeks ago, had driven it all home to her, when her Mistress had shared her quite freely with her friends. Being publicly used, teased, punished and fucked had put Amber's feelings of submission into a whole new context for her.

Now, she was to be given over for a week to the control of another domme, who was currently fucking her vigorously with a strap-on cock. Amber was going to be trained in new skills in order to pleasure her own Mistress and be expected to pleasure her trainer and be disciplined by her.

The way that Mistress Chevalier was fucking her, was distinctive from the way Mistress Susanna had. It was more aggressive, rougher and felt more like she was being taken for Mistress Chevalier's pleasure, rather than sensually fucked.

Amber hadn't been nosy enough to find out Mistress Susanna's age, but while she was older, she would guess that her Mistress was in her late thirties, not much more than ten years older than her. Mistress Chevalier on the other hand, was more likely in her fifties, just over twice her age.

Mistress Chevalier wasn't slender and graceful in the way that Susanna was. A cruel person might have called her stout or stocky but she wasn't greatly overweight or truly unfit. In fact, while she was curvaceous, the way she was pounding Amber's pussy gave good evidence of how fit the older woman was.

It was strangely arousing to be used by an older woman who could have been one of her mother's friends or one of her professors. To know that soon Mistress Susanna would leave for London and she would be left entirely at the mercy of Mistress Chevalier. The domme was charged with training her as a ponygirl, which Amber was willing to try if it pleased Mistress Susanna, but was still unsure if she would take to it as Ginger and the others did.

Amber imagined that the training would be reinforced with spanking, caning, floggers and whips. Given the events at the party, Amber had no doubt that Mistress Chevalier would use her sexually, just as much as Mistress Susanna did and that she would enjoy every second of that. Even the corporal punishment she would be subjected to would make her aroused, and her pussy wet.

The combination of fucking, the taste and feel of her Mistress's pussy, the fingers in her hair and the thoughts of what the next week would be like, brought her to a rousing climax. Amber found herself moaning loudly into Mistress Susanna's sex as her body shuddered with wave after wave of pleasure.

Mistress Chevalier was relentless, calling her a good girl and complimenting her on coming like the slut she was, but not stopping her thrusting motions for a heartbeat. Amber's pussy was sensitive from her climax but she wasn't allowed any respite.

"You can have a break when you make your Mistress come, slut," Mistress Chevalier said, as if Amber's every shudder, moan and movement, where an open book to her. Amber wondered how many girls she'd fucked like this to be able to read her so easily.

Regardless, Amber dug deep within herself and found a reservoir of untapped talent, revitalising her efforts and forcing herself to concentrate on the increasingly rapid breathing of her Mistress. Anything was better than thinking about the wildly sensitive folds of her pussy which Mistress Chevalier continued to stimulate.

Mistress Chevalier was proved a liar, as she didn't stop when Mistress Susanna had screamed her way through an impressive orgasm. It wasn't until Mistress Susanna finally came back to her senses, and Amber had been cruelly forced to a second orgasm that left her pussy aching and tears in her eyes, that she waved the other domme away.

"Well done, Amber. You handled that fucking quite impressively," Mistress Chevalier said.

"Thank you, Mistress Chevalier," Amber gasped panting.

Mistress Chevalier smacked her bottom hard, making Amber yelp in shock, before she pulled back and the large silicone dildo plopped out of her.

Mistress Susanna smiled down at her, "Amber, clean that off like a good slut."

Mistress Chevalier didn't wait for Amber to turn around, she reached down and grabbed her hair, pulling her roughly into position. Amber was turned around and pushed against the seat next to Mistress Chevalier. Still sitting on the floor, her back arched and her head, just touching the cushion.

Mistress Chevalier crouched, and, still holding Amber's head by the hair, pushed the silicone into her mouth deep enough to come close to choking her, "Suck it, you filthy slut!"

Amber heard her Mistress chuckling as she was forced to suck the dildo and clean it with her tongue, the process leaving her gasping for air and her eyes watering.

When Mistress Chevalier was satisfied and backed off, Amber collapsed back against the firm cushion behind her, turning her head to look up at Mistress Susanna. Her domme had an almost demonic look of lust on her face and the fingers idly strumming her clit, bore witness to how much she'd enjoyed watching Amber subjugated by her friend.

Mistress Susanna reached out her spare hand and stroked the back of Amber's head, as she licked her lips in a manner that Amber could only see as predatory.

"Thank you for a lovely day, Jade," Mistress Susanna said.

"No, thank you, and your wonderful slut. I'm looking forward to training her for you. I do hope you enjoy the results."

"I'm sure I will, but this is my last night at the house for a while, so I think I'm going to take Amber back to my room and ravish her to say goodbye," Mistress Susanna replied.

"I think that's a good idea. I should probably spend some time with Vicky before she starts pinning anyway," Mistress Chevalier said, absent-mindedly stroking the length of silicone which still hung between her legs.

"From tomorrow, you'll have complete access to Amber to help you keep Vicky happy," Mistress Susanna replied. "You'll like that, won't you, Amber?"

"Yes, Mistress."

CHAPTER 6

"Now, Amber, I'm going to ask you some questions so that you can demonstrate that you understand the standard signals. One stamp for yes, two stamps for no, three if you need to use your safeword," Mistress Chevalier said. "Understood?"

Amber stomped her foot, not too hard, just firmly enough for a clear clopping sound to ring out across the concrete of the yard. It wasn't quite like the sound of a real pony's hoof, but it was close enough for roleplaying. The thick rod of rubber that was clenched between her back teeth left her unable to speak clearly.

"Good girl," Mistress Chevalier said. "Would you like me to give you a dozen hard strokes of the cane?"

Two stamps answered that question.

"Very well. Are you sure?"

Amber stamped once.

Mistress Chevalier reached out, stroking the back of her fingers against Amber's cheek. It was the lightest of touches, just barely enough for Amber to feel the line the older woman was tracing. Her temporary Mistress turned her hand over, running the very tips of her fingers down Amber's neck, skipping lightly over the leather straps of her harness, and ghosting over the swell of her breast.

Amber shivered in anticipation, the hairs on the back of her neck standing up. She had been ordered to stand up straight, shoulders back and keep her breasts pushed forward to display herself well for her trainer. *Would Mistress touch her more intimately, Amber wondered?*

"You have such soft, beautiful skin, Amber," Mistress whispered, "do you moisturise?"

One stamp.

"This nipple," Mistress started as her finger traced a wide circle around the compact areola that cover the tip of Amber's left breast, "seems stiff. Swollen. Firm. Would you like me to touch it?"

One stamp. The gentle fingers alighted on the puckered flesh, with the merest hint of pressure. "You like that, don't you, being teased? Does my ponygirl like being teased?"

Amber clomped her foot again, her voice breaking into her first attempt at a whinny.

"Oh, my! That is simply adorable, Vicky. Did you hear, Amber gave her first whinny."

Of course, Vicky was also dressed in character as a ponygirl, so she too gave a foot stomp and an encouraging whinny.

"Amber, I am tempted to lick and suck and tease these nipples of yours, until you are quite wet," Mistress Chevalier suggested. "Would you enjoy that?" she asked, receiving a single stomp and a look that implored her to act. Mistress Chevalier gave a somewhat filthy laugh at that.

"I would far rather take each of your beautiful nubbins between my thumb and forefinger, and pinch them hard, twisting them until tears come to your eyes, though. Does that also meet with your approval?" Mistress Chevalier asked, as she moved to stand directly in front of Amber, both hands now tantalisingly fluttering over the submissive's breasts and erect nipples.

Amber stomped her foot twice, vigorously rejecting the idea.

"No? You don't want me to use your nipples to bring you pain?" Mistress Chevalier said, her heavily overacted shock, entirely feigned. Amber stamped her foot twice once more.

"You really don't, do you?" Mistress Chevalier said, with a pout and a flutter of her eyelashes. "If I do it anyway, because it pleases me to hurt you, will you let me do it, anyway?"

Amber swallowed, nodding as she stomped her foot once.

"Even though you don't want to feel such pain?"

Another affirmative.

"Will it make that sweet quim of yours, flood with arousal? Amber, will it make you wet?" Mistress Chevalier asked.

Amber knew that it would, knew that the pain that was coming would be more than she could bear to receive, less just enough for Mistress Chevalier to retain control of her body and mind. Enough to make Amber's tears run freely with tears and a whisker less than would have her ending play by using her safeword.

There was no doubt in her mind, that with all Mistress Chevalier's years of experience, she had played this sort of game to perfection many times. The pain she would experience would balance on the knife edge of her limit and leave her on the verge of what she still saw as defeat.

Mistress Susanna had counselled her that the safeword was neither to be used lightly, for that would spoil the fun of both Mistress and submissive, nor was it to be avoided at all costs, risking physical harm or mental anguish to the sub.

Amber swallowed, took a deep breath, and stomped her foot once.

Mistress Chevalier gave her a peck on the cheek, then her fingers tightened like hot vices on Amber's nipples, cruelly tugging and twisting at them. Amber's eyes did indeed fill with tears, she stomped her foot twice, but struggled against the impulse to put it down a third time.

The older woman's eyes were alive with sadistic glee as Amber's gagged mouth gurgled out half a scream of pain at the rough treatment.

When Amber sucked in a breath to begin screaming again, as cumbersome as it was around the bit gag in her mouth, Mistress Chevalier dipped her right hand between Amber's creamy thighs. Her fingers found the submissive's lips, quickly parting them and rubbing at her aching clit roughly. Amber was positively gushing, her arousal far beyond the ability to deny it.

Two fingers, wet with Amber's juices were slid between her lips, under the bar of the gag, allowing her to taste her own sex.

Then the sharp pain in her nipples again, as Mistress Chevalier, with a cruel laugh, twisted them in the reverse direction. This fresh version elicited the arousal response, but the pain felt somehow different, perhaps because Amber's nipples were already bruised or perhaps it was psychological.

Whatever the cause, Amber began to weep softly, actual tears dripping down her cheeks, even as trails of liquid streaked the inside of her thighs and betrayed her pleasure.

"How beautiful you are, Amber. It's a delight to enjoy your suffering," Mistress Chevalier complimented her.

When the bit was unbuckled from one side of her face, Amber thought she might be granted leave to speak, something which Mistress Chevalier had said was strictly forbidden for an in character ponygirl. Stomps of the foot, head shakes, whinnying and neighing, were all permitted. Only human speech and sounds were restricted.

If the feet or legs were restrained, bound or in use in a way that prevented the expression of yes, no or the safeword through stomps, slaps against the leg with the palm of the hand would be used.

It was not to permit speech that the pressure on her cheeks was relieved, it was to permit Mistress Chevalier to access and possess Amber's mouth with her hot tongue. Amber found herself in a hungry kiss, being taken and used by her trainer, her mouth dominated by the questing muscle. It did nothing to reduce her level of arousal of course, it merely heightened it.

Not that Amber would have objected to such a passionate kiss, in any case. Her nipples were sore, even as Mistress more gently fondled her breasts while they kissed, but the kiss itself was divine and Amber lost herself to it for as long as Mistress Chevalier chose to draw it out.

"How delightful you are, Pony Amber," Mistress Chevalier said, looking at her expectantly.

Amber returned the look and took a deep breath. The look on the older woman's face betrayed an expectation and Amber hesitated, before happily whinnying her response.

Mistress Chevalier cracked a half smile at that, proud that her lessons were being absorbed.

"Good pony," she said, offering the flat of her palm.

Amber blushed when she saw the sugar lump treat that was being offered.

The embarrassment at being treated like this, didn't stop her dipping her head and scooping it up with her tongue, of course.

Even human ponies liked sugar cubes.

CHAPTER 7

It took a few hours for Mistress Chevalier to go through the process of putting the ponygirl harness and tack on another girl and then herself. Vicky was Amber's practice partner, which Mistress Chevalier explained in terms of rope bunnies. Amber didn't like to admit that she had no idea what a rope bunny was and made a mental note to look it up later.

At every stage, the importance of a good fit and checking things thoroughly was stressed. The harnesses for pulling a cart were quite different to those that were purely fetish costumes to create an appearance and once she was shown, the padding and attachment points made the separation obvious. A costume harness would break or risk injuring the pony girl if you tried to pull on it and looked less stylish at an indoor party.

The saddles were quite different. Some were intended to be used for a pony on all fours, so their dominant could sit directly on their back, but some were for a pony to be ridden while they were upright. It was like carrying someone on your back with their legs around your waist and your arms under their knees.

Amber didn't think she'd be able to do that at all, and she certainly wouldn't be able to carry Vicky, but they put a saddle on the muscular ponygirl and Amber got to ride her around briefly.

When Mistress Chevalier put Amber on all fours, saddled her and rode her around the tack room, that was relatively easy. Amber didn't have to bear the full weight of another person on her arms and the rider could easily put their feet down.

It was very slow to get about though and easy to see why pulling the traps and chariots was so popular and outdoor play was such a key part of the ponygirls repertoire. Mistress Chevalier explained that playing outdoors had a host of problems, mostly to do with privacy and the weather, but the sheer expense was off-putting too many people.

"You're lucky to have met Susanna so you can try this out in such excellent facilities, Amber. I'm really very grateful that you suggested that she refurbish more of the stables and let me run my workshop here. I think this is going to be a fantastic year," Mistress Chevalier said while they took Vicky's outfit off again so that Amber could give it another go.

"There, all done. Over to you. Do you think you can get it all on, in the correct order, without prompting?" Mistress Chevalier asked. "There's a treat in store for you if you do."

"Yes, Mistress," Amber replied. "I think I have it."

"Very well, I'll only chip in if you are doing anything truly bad. It's a dozen strokes if you miss anything or get it out of sequence. Proceed," Mistress Chevalier instructed.

"Yes, Mistress."

Amber set about getting the harness, bit and bridle, hoof boots and so on, correctly fitted to Vicky, trying hard to make sure she got them on in the correct order that Mistress Chevalier had laid out.

There were some items that were easier to put on first for instance, the bridle could be fitted and the bit put in place later so that the pony could still give verbal responses while you checked the fit.

The last thing that Amber had to fit was the pony tail that all the girls wore some version of. There were quite a few spare ones available, and some novelty options like a rainbow coloured one for unicorns, as well as some other types of tails for piggy play or puppy play. But each girl also had her own labelled butt plugs with tails for pony play.

Vicky's seemed quite large to Amber but wasn't grossly outsized. It was made of shining steel and the tail hair itself was quite realistic, at least, to Amber's far from expert eye.

Fitting the pony girls with their butt plug tails was Amber's favourite part of this process so far. Coating two fingers of her right hand with liberal helpings of lubricant, she instructed Vicky to bend over and assume the position. It would be easy as this wasn't their first time today but Mistress Chevalier had made it clear she was to go through all the stages each time for practice, even though Vicky was used to having toys inserted between her firm buttocks.

Amber gently probed Vicky's welcoming ring of muscle, as if it weren't already prepared and quite well lubricated. She teased the rosebud of flesh, listening for Vicky's reaction, every gasp and murmur as she slowly worked a finger knuckle deep into the body-builder.

"Good girl, Vicky," Amber said, "can you take more?"

Vicky stomped one foot, though her bit was free at this point and Amber grinned, licking her lips as she leaned down to see what she was doing in detail. She watched as Vicky's tight, glistening ring of flesh comfortably swallowed her second finger. The ponygirl gasped with pleasure as Amber began to thrust her fingers slowly in and out of her.

Not wanting to get the dozen strokes though, Amber couldn't push her luck and soon had to lubricate the butt plug with a light coating of liquid and slowly fill the space her fingers had vacated with it. She wiped her fingers on some antibacterial wipes and dried her hands on a towel, before putting Vicky's bit gag in place and checking all the straps for a final time.

"I think this is correct, Mistress," Amber said, trying to sound calm.

Mistress Chevalier nodded, "Very well, take a seat while I inspect your work."

The older woman ran her finger under straps that needed to have some give and tugged gently at the points where a cart would be attached to check everything was properly fitted. She pressed and tugged at the butt plug as well, but Amber got the impression part of her motivation for that was to torment her ponygirl, Vicky, not just check Amber's work.

Finally Mistress Chevalier pronounced the work to be good and congratulated Amber on a job well done.

"I think it's time you have a reward for your hard work and concentration, don't you, Amber?"

"Thank you, Mistress," Amber said.

"Get Vicky out of that harness, and then both of you can join me in our lovely new flat," Mistress Chevalier ordered.

"Yes, Mistress," Amber said for them both, as Vicky was still gagged.

CHAPTER 8

Mistress Chevalier was quite naked when the girls had put away the ponygirl gear and was reclining on the four poster bed that she had brought to the flat with her. A long rattan school cane lay ominously on the mattress beside her and she smiled as the two submissives, so very different in appearance, entered the bedroom.

"Amber, help Vicky put on that strap-on, there's a dear," she ordered with a wicked gleam in her eyes.

At the foot of the bed, a purple leather harness and dildo lay waiting for them. Amber knelt before Vicky and held the harness open for her to step into, Jiggling it up her thighs and slowly tightening and adjusting the straps until the fit was secure but so tight it would be uncomfortable.

The dildo itself was also purple, to match the colour of the harness and it didn't get any more realistic when it came to the shape of the thing either. It had a bit of a curve to it, small nodules along the length in a spiral pattern around it, and it was if it was a series of balls squashed together, rather than a rod. It would open someone wider, let them close, then open them up again, as you thrust it home, rather like anal beads.

The head of the thing was a comically proportioned mushroom head, with a rounded tip and an exaggerated flair around the base. Amber wondered how Mistress Chevalier took such an intrusion, as the head of the dildo widened at its base, protruding like the brim of a big, purple hat. Pushing that through any opening would force it wide, before it was inside and the entrance could close around the thick shaft.

Amber had seen much larger toys, although not in use but this one would force the recipient to open and close as each new ball was slid into them. A part of her wondered if Mistress Chevalier had ever used it on some poor girls bottom, or if it was only used for more usual intercourse.

Vicky gave her hips an experimental jiggle left and right, and then a few thrusts which came perilously close to Amber's face. She flinched back, not wanting to get a black eye from the monstrous purple silicone cock.

"Amber, you may get up here now and please me with your tongue. On all fours so that Vicky can fuck your sweet pussy with her toy," Mistress Chevalier said, with a casual tone that didn't seem to suit the immensity of the words. When Amber had seen the harness and dildo, she had imagined, perhaps naively, that she would not be the one receiving it.

Taking her time, Amber slowly got on the bed, and crawled forward, kissing Mistress Chevalier's calves, her knees, and her inner thighs as she advanced on her. She was playing for time, trying to get the picture of the enormous tool out of her mind.

When the mattress sunk behind her legs at the additional weight of Vicky kneeling on it, Amber knew she didn't have much longer before she would be impaled on the thing. Refusing to be subjected to it was an option, and a request for something smaller might be received well. Knowing, intellectually, that her anatomy was capable of taking larger things, didn't mean she wanted to find out what giving birth was like in reverse.

Amber smiled, teasing Mistress Chevalier, edging slowly forward, as the domme rolled her hips invitingly, waiting for the young submissive to apply her tongue where it was needed.

"Come to me, pet, stop teasing and show me what you've learned," Mistress Chevalier growled lustily, beckoning to Amber.

Steeling herself for what was to come, Amber finally moved forward, and dipped her head between the dominant woman's thighs, her tongue soon questing for its target in the curved join between Mistress Chevalier's lips.

"Yes, that's where you are best employed, you saucy wench. Just like that," Mistress Chevalier encouraged. The domme's hands stroked and squeezed her own breasts, playing with her nipples as Amber began to suck and lick at her lips and clit.

For a few delicious moments, Amber forgot about her impending appointment with Vicky's strap-on. Then the time was upon her and she had to struggle to keep the reasoning side of her mind in action, concentrating on pleasuring Mistress Chevalier rather than what was going on behind her.

A bottle of lubricant made an obscene spurting noise as it was aimed directly at her lower back. The cool liquid pooled in the small of her back and Vicky dipped her fingers in, using Amber's curves as a palette to work from. Amber could hear the slippery fluid squelching as Vicky rubbed her hand up and down the dildo giving it a thorough covering.

Then Vicky's big, gym fit fingers slapped a big dollop against Amber's already wet pussy, smearing the cold fluid all over her, before she began to work first one, then two fingers inside. Amber squirmed in anticipation. Extra lubrication wasn't something she usually needed, after all she was still only in her early to mid-twenties and it wasn't as if the humiliating, wicked and sometimes painful games she'd been subjected to since joining Mistress Susanna's household, didn't turn her on. In fact, she'd never been so regularly and thoroughly turned on, even as a horny first-year student, since Susanna had introduced her to Sapphic pleasures.

No, Amber didn't normally require additional lubrication, unless her bottom was the target and her arsehole needed to admit fingers or a butt plug. This wasn't the first time Vicky had played with her, so if she was adding lube she must expect it was needed. That toy had seemed big, but perhaps Vicky's huge frame made it seem smaller than it was. She must be expecting Amber to struggle with additional help. Just how big was it, really? Or was it partly the undulating bulbs that required the extra lube so that Vicky could fuck her rapidly and roughly, with the whole length of the exotically designed shaft.

Vicky didn't stop at thrusting 3 fingers into Amber's pussy to open her up, she added a fourth and used them like a spike to widen the young submissive's hungry pussy. Each powerful stroke forward distended Amber in a way that approached being uncomfortable, while feeling utterly filthy and desirable at the same time. Vicky's hands were on the large side, but she nevertheless kept going until Amber was so opened up, that her lips stretched out to admit Vicky's hand past the third knuckle.

Amber fairly howled into Mistress Chevalier's pussy as Vicky drove her wild with lust as her hand was swallowed to the wrist. Vicky grunted in surprise, "I didn't think she was going to take it all, but the greedy little harlot practically swallowed me when I gave her enough to think about it. Look, Mistress, she's got my whole hand in her."

"She has, hasn't she," Mistress Chevalier agreed. "What a greedy little slut you are, Amber? Vicky has such big hands and you're taking her fist like a champion filly, aren't you?"

Amber's tongue was still lapping at Mistress Chevalier's lips as she strove to remain focused but with Vicky's whole hand buried in her cunt it was almost impossible.

Mistress Chevalier took a firm grip on her head with both hands and tilted her face up so she could look down her body into Amber's eyes. "Is that what you are, Amber? A greedy little slut who loves to be filled up and fucked hard?"

Amber gasped as Vicky's hand withdrew, perfectly timed with the demand from their dominant, her big knuckles opening her to her widest as they were dragged out past her soaking entrance and her pussy contracted as the width of the intrusion lessened.

"Yes, Mistress!" she yelped. "I'm a filthy whore and I love being filled up with Vicky's hand."

"Do you like being fisted by Vicky?"

"I love it, Mistress. I love having her big hand buried in my pussy."

"You are such a bad girl, Amber," Mistress Chevalier said, picking up the cane with a menacing look. Amber groaned as Vicky's hand pushed in past the knuckles again.

Her eyes were still locked to Mistress Chevalier's who tutted as Amber groaned her pleasure at being fisted. With a scowl that could have been genuine or expert roleplaying for all Amber could tell in her current state, she brought the cane whistling down across Amber's buttocks with a crack that filled the room.

Amber screamed and cursed, calling Mistress Chevalier a rude name that she felt sure would anger the domme and result in more severe chastisement.

Mistress Chevalier was far from upset, the vulgarity seemed to inflame her passion if anything. She became more exuberant, as she striped Amber's bottom. "Yes, let it all out, Amber. Curse at me all you want while I punish you for being a filthy slut," the domme laughed, counting each stroke out as she delivered a dozen hard whacks, even as Amber reached a massive climax.

Amber's body shuddered as Vicky's fist pumped back and forth throughout her orgasm, and their domme continued to thrash her with the cane. It was only when she stopped shaking from her climax that Mistress Chevalier ordered Vicky to pull out, which she did to the accompaniment of a wet sound.

"Excellent. Vicky, fuck her now, while Amber puts her sweet mouth back to work for me," Mistress ordered as she grabbed Amber's head and pushed it back down to her waiting lips.

Vicky wasted no time in positioning the big, undulating cock and impaling Amber with it. It was done with skill but with no finesse or subtlety. The strap-on replaced the big woman's hand and slid inside her, without opposition. Vicky was an expert with the toy and soon built up a fast paced rhythm that set Amber on a path straight back up the peak she had only just descended.

"Keep going Vicky, Amber is loving every minute of you fucking her, aren't you slut?" Mistress Chevalier asked. Amber mumbled into the delicious meal she was consuming but wasn't allowed a breath to respond audibly so she lifted one hand and gave a big thumbs up signal. That drew a chuckle from Mistress Chevalier and a noticeable tightening of the grip on Amber's hair.

"As you command, Mistress," Vicky rumbled, not sounding like she was unhappy in the slightest. Judging by the way she alternately slapped Amber's sore bottom and gripped her hips tightly to fuck her even harder, Vicky was thoroughly enjoying herself.

Amber wondered if Vicky was really a submissive at all, or just a filthy bitch who loved to fuck women and be fucked. If she could have spoken, she might very well have asked the same question, in just as rude a manner, and been duly punished for her vulgarity. Amber knew that that prospect would only encourage her to be rude though, not put her off.

"The little trollop is coming, Mistress," Vicky said, as if this was a terrible infringement of the rules somehow, although it did not go unnoticed by Amber that the big woman didn't slow her pace or cease slapping and fondling her sensitive bum cheeks.

"You're not to come without my permission, Amber. That's very naughty of you. You'll have to make Vicky come twice with your tongue now, as punishment. And me three times," Mistress Chevalier warned. The domme pulled Amber's head up so she could speak, "What do you say to that, my girl?"

"Yes, Mistress."

CHAPTER 9

"No, no, no! Knees up higher!" Mistress Chevalier ordered.

Amber was parading around the yard, performing steps for her domme like an army recruit being shouted at by her drill instructor. Of course, when the army broke down a raw recruit, the seemingly harsh treatment was to ensure they could take orders in battle.

A ponygirl had no such life-saving motivation. Amber's reason for doing all this was to try this out for her beloved Mistress Susanna and discover if a life of sexual roleplaying as a human pony appealed to her. If she had as much of a thing for it as Pepper or Ginger, she might be offered a new role instead of being Susanna's personal assistant.

The addition of a colleague walking behind her with a riding crop, and delivering three firm swats with it when she made an error, was another deviation from the way the armed forces did things. Vicky wasn't sparing the rod either, each blow caused Amber to whimper around the bit gag in her mouth. Mistress Chevalier had ordered her not to try to run away or dodge Vicky's inducements, or else she'd let the big ponygirl chase her down and invent her own punishments.

Amber had already determined that Vicky was a filthy pervert who delighted in making the other submissives suffer. Any chance to inflict corporal punishment on the other girls was taken without hesitation or guilt. Her sadism and cruelty were different to that of Mistress Chevalier or Mistress Susanna as well. Vicky didn't hold back because she was a submissive herself, not even a little.

"Stop. Give me six jumping jacks," Mistress Chevalier ordered. The training sessions weren't just about her physical form and ability to follow instructions, Amber's temporary domme liked to include plenty of calisthenic exercise as well. The domme claimed this was to ensure the ponygirls were fit and healthy and could perform their duties.

Amber rather thought it was also because she enjoyed their humiliation as their bare breasts bounced up and down in the harnesses which surrounded and accentuated them, but offered nothing in the way of support. None of Mistress Susanna's girl had anything to be ashamed of in the health or looks department, they were all in fairly good shape, well-groomed and naturally pretty. But it wasn't about looks, so much as the feeling they were not meeting some standard or the pressure they felt to be normal girls. Modest girls. Chaste girls.

There was no real room for modesty and certainly not chastity, on Mistress Susanna's estate, but the feeling that she should not be nude, being paraded for the pleasure of other women, or publicly flogged and caned, felt real all the same. Only it didn't make Amber want to give in. It just made her more aroused, knowing there was something somehow naughty about what they were doing. Submitting to the hedonistic pleasures of the older women who held sway on the estate from day to day, or during Mistress's infrequent parties, was humbling but also thrilling.

The sense of mortification was accompanied by a bravado that made Amber feel like quite the exhibitionist, even though everyone who could see her without a telescope or satellite, was in on the events. Being watched by all those lascivious women at the party had been a complete thrill.

After the jumping jacks it was press-ups and then jogging on the spot until Amber thought her legs would turn to rubbery stalks and collapse under her.

Eventually, she was sent back to the tack room at a gallop, with

Vicky chasing after her, swatting her across the buttocks with her crop every time she caught up. Amber went as fast as she could, and Vicky could clearly have outpaced her but held back. There was just enough crop to keep Amber motivated and heated, and not so much that she completely lost balance.

Amber had only a few moments of breathing space to calm down before Mistress Chevalier had strode across the yard from the fence she usually perched on while instructing the girls, and joined them in the tack room. The domme took up a seat on a thickly padded bench and clicked her fingers, indicating that Amber should approach.

"Turn away from me. Good, now straddle my legs and sit down," Mistress Chevalier ordered. Amber did as she was told, still in her harness. The bit and bridle were removed, and Vicky was told to take off the hoof boots as well. Amber could have got them off but having help was so much quicker. She wiggled her toes as they were freed from the demanding footwear.

Mistress Chevalier parted her knees and took a firm grip on Amber's upper thighs, "Lean forward until your palms are on the floor."

Although Amber wasn't a gymnast by any means, she was able to perform the manoeuvre without help from Vicky, which was comforting and less embarrassing than having to ask for assistance from the giantess. The dominant woman repositioned her until she was satisfied and then dipped her head.

Upside down and face flushed with blood, Amber was surprised when the agile tongue of the Stable Mistress, delved between her lips and sought out her engorged nubbin. Mistress Chevalier was even better at eating pussy than Sugar or Candy, whose cunnilingus skills were considered the most expert of the women who lived on the estate.

Years of practice, serving older dominant women at first, and later as a dominant lesbian herself, had taught Mistress Chevalier every trick in the book. Despite being dominant, she had no hesitation about using her tongue to pleasure her submissives.

A part of Amber's mind was surprised that the outwardly entirely dominant woman should be happy to eat pussy, because it seemed like it should be a submissive act. Another part said the pussy belonged to Mistress Chevalier, and she could eat it, fuck it, or torment it as she chose.

It was the second part that won out, because it was so very, very delightful to have her cunt worshipped by an avoid connoisseur of the art form. Amber had rapidly grown accustomed to performing cunnilingus on whom ever Mistress Susanna ordered and had developed quite the taste for it, she thought. Her enjoyment was nothing quite like the gusto with which Mistress Chevalier faced the challenge though.

To delay her own orgasm, which Amber knew was rising fast, she concentrated on identifying the motions and techniques Mistress Chevalier was using against her wet lips and clit. Trying to evaluate them and memorise them, but being upside down was making it hard to concentrate, not to mention the rising tide of pleasure which threatened to flood the play zone any moment.

"Come for me, slut," Mistress Chevalier ordered. The degrading terms that the dominant women frequently used for Amber, might once have offended her, but now she savoured the coarse, humiliating language. The demeaning language simply aroused her, and she took pride in being a slut, a trollop, a whore or a filthy little bitch.

Amber was in service to a great woman, who looked after her and brought her both pleasure and pain, beyond her wildest fantasies. If being subjected to words, some might find dehumanising was part of the game, Amber wasn't going to stop playing.

It wasn't long before she had an explosive orgasm, as ordered. Mistress Chevalier's greedy tongue plunged between her moist lips as if she was in a frenzy to consume every ounce of her submissive's pussy. Pursed around Amber's clit, the lips allowed the domme to apply strong suction as the tip of her tongue teased the nubbin.

There was no hope of resisting the rising wave of her orgasm and Amber screamed in delight as she came hard. Her dominant did not stop licking and sucking at her sensitive slickness until Amber's thighs stopped trembling. Then she was indelicately flipped up the right way, her eyes swimming as her head rushed with the roar of shifting blood.

"Explain why I did that, Amber," Mistress Chevalier ordered, licking her lips free of her submissive's juices as she waited for an answer.

Amber swallowed hard while she formulated her answer as quickly as she could. "You did it because you reward ponygirls who are good and punish ponygirls who are bad, Mistress."

"And how do I punish bad ponygirls, Amber?"

"You enjoy all sorts of punishments and discipline, Mistress but I think you favour the cane."

"Correct. Now, on your knees girl, I want your tongue on my clit while Vicky cane's your beautifully pert bottom until you make me come twice," Mistress Chevalier said, leaning back on the bench as Amber dismounted and got to her knees at the end of it.

"Begin," Mistress Chevalier ordered as Amber's head dipped between her legs.

Vicky's cane landed the first blow even as Amber's lips emulated her Mistress's technique and pursed around the dominant woman's clit so she could suck on it and run the tip of her tongue across it.

"Make that three times, Amber," Mistress Chevalier said with a yelp as Amber's wicked tongue really got to work. "Make me come three times, and Vicky will stop caning you."

"Yes, Mistress."

CHAPTER 10

The following morning Amber spent the whole time learning how to pull a larger trap than she'd used for racing. It was really more of an open topped carriage than a trap, with four wheels and enough space for several passengers. Mistress Chevalier was the only one today, and Vicky, Ginger and Pepper were pulling alongside Amber.

It looked quite similar to the racing traps that Mistress Susanna owned, and the ones that Mistress Chevalier had brought with her, at least in the style of components and manufacturing. The carriage was built to be as light as possible but with just a few more creature comforts for the passengers.

Being harnessed to the carriage was also quite different, as the girls were in two pairs side by side like real horses pulling a coach. Pulling and handling the carriage involved the same commands for turning, stopping and accelerating, and required the same responses to the reins but Amber had to learn to work with the team.

It was important that the ponygirls work together and not pull against each other or move too fast or too slowly, lest they cause an accident. If they didn't pull together someone would end up stumbling, and they'd have to stop. If they went too fast, again, someone would stumble or wear themselves out and stopping was a team effort too.

Mistress Chevalier explained that the lightweight of the carriage was more about being able to stop it easily, than the girls ability to pull it. Since bodybuilders could pull huge delivery trucks on their own, there was ample proof that the weight wasn't much of an issue in getting going. Since they wanted to travel at a faster than walking pace though, lightweight construction let them accelerate more easily and meant they could slow down safely too.

There was an unexpected benefit to the girls that Amber welcomed - the inability for the driver to whip them all. The two lead ponies were protected by the two rear ponies, so any whipping was restricted to their unfortunate buttocks. But Mistress Chevalier cracked the whip above their heads instead of applying lashes to their bodies and that gave them the emphatic guidance they needed, just as well as a stripe across their bottom would.

At the end of the morning, Amber and the team had got a good rhythm going and Mistress Chevalier took them out for a lap of the lake, driving them progressively faster as they rounded the end and started on the home stretch.

By the time the ponygirls drew to a stop in the yard outside the stables, all four were drenched in sweat and breathing hard, gulping in big lungful's of air. Amber would have sworn she could hear her heart pounding in her chest and the rush of blood in her ears.

No time was wasted on their recovery though. Mistress Chevalier had them walk the carriage close to the coach house set aside for storing the various conveyances the ponygirls pulled and then began getting them out of their harness. Amber was freed first so that she could release Vicky behind her, then they pulled and pushed the carriage into the coach house and shut it up.

After that, Mistress Chevalier took them to the tack room, where they stripped each other of their harness and cleaned everything off properly. They used anti-bacterial toy wipes for the butt plugs which supported their tails. Each toy and bit of leather was cleaned appropriately, inspected for damage or wear and returned to its allocated storage space.

"Off to the showers!" Mistress Chevalier barked when they were all done, marching them to the changing area which was dominated by a large, white-tiled shower space with a dozen or so shower heads fixed to the wall. There were a few cubicles, but those were reserved for the dominants, while the open shower area was for the submissives.

They were already naked as they filed into the shower room under the stern gaze of the Stable Mistress. Amber saw that Mistress Chevalier was holding the garden hose with the spray attachment and her shoulders slumped. That meant cold water first.

"Line up, face the wall," Mistress Chevalier said, flicking the trigger on the spray and spattering them with cold water, making them all squeal in shock.

Once they were lined up, Mistress Chevalier went after each of them in turn, soaking them thoroughly and getting the mud and sweat of their backs. Then they turned around, screwed their eyes shut and were given the same treatment again.

Amber knew this wasn't about cleanliness, this was about the older woman enjoying seeing the girls reactions as the cold water covered their skin in goose-bumps and turned their nipples to stiff nubs. Mistress Chevalier had done this to them before, only letting them shower with soap after she'd had her sadistic fun with them and the hose.

"Turn around and bend over, feet shoulder width apart," Mistress Chevalier ordered.

This was new, thought Amber. Mistress Chevalier had stopped by now, on the days where she'd used this particular torment.

"Put your hands behind you, grasp your cheeks firmly and pull them apart. Make sure I can see everything you sluts have on offer," their domme ordered.

Amber did as she was told, feeling butterflies of anticipation inside her as she exposed her puckered hole and the lips of her sex to the older woman's lingering glances. She felt her cheeks flush red as a blush rose from her neck up to her ears. Mistress Chevalier could surely see how aroused she was by the state of her lips which were not just wet because of the hose. She wondered how the other girls looked. Were they equally aroused? It was almost a given, and she surely wasn't any more of a slut than any of them.

Then came the hose. Icy water set to a thin high pressure jet smacked against Amber's bottom and she yelped. The spray was powerful and she could feel it dimpling her flesh as it was played across each bottom in turn a few times, before coming back to be directed at the top of Amber's cleft.

The water hammered against her sensitive skin as it probed her tight ring of muscle, like an undulating finger, then down over her lips. Amber whimpered as her most intimate parts were cooled right down. It was truly perverted to be used like this, aroused by the attentions of an older woman and then cooled off so mechanically.

Had the water been warm, Amber had no doubt she could have come from the way it pounded on her arsehole and pussy alone. But the water was not warm, and that was quite deliberate. There was a mixer tap in the room that the hose could be attached to that would provide hot or warm water quite readily but Mistress Chevalier always used the one on the outside wall of the stables which only provided cold water.

It was her sadistic side that led to such torments, and it wasn't necessary for the ponygirls to come from this game, in order for Mistress Chevalier to receive pleasure. Amber heard each girl give voice to her frustration and the impact of the cold water as their domme tormented their tight bum holes and aching pussies with the water.

Finally the water was switched off, and Mistress Chevalier gave her next instruction. "Pair up and get each other lathered up head to toe, I want you so clean you sparkle."

Amber was claimed by Vicky who pulled her to one of the soap dispensers mounted on the shower wall and put wastefully large handfuls of lemon scented shower gel all over her chest and shoulders. Then the big woman set to work on Amber's cold flesh, rubbing the shower gel all over her to build up a lather and then working at each nook and cranny with methodical attention to detail.

Vicky pinched and rolled Amber's nipples between thumb and forefinger, rubbed at her pussy and slipped fingers inside her covered with the strong citrus gel as well as between her cheeks. When she was done, not an inch of Amber's body remained untouched, though her face had been washed down with a flannel wash cloth and rinsed off immediately to avoid getting soap in her eyes. That was considerate of Vicky who had a sadistic streak that Amber found terrifying and delightful in equal measure, which was borne out by a second round of attention to her breasts once her face was clean. Vicky didn't spend long but her powerful fingers inflicted pressure that had Amber's eyes welling up with tears.

Amber was able to return the favour, starting with the big woman's strong calves and thighs, before burying three soapy fingers in her cunt as she looked up Vicky's body to hold her gaze. The Amazonian looked a little cross but felt aroused as Amber rapidly frigged her, before moving around behind her to work on her powerful buttocks.

Again, Amber used her soapy fingers to penetrate, hearing a grunt of lust from Vicky but no protest from Mistress Chevalier who was leaning against the half-height wall which enclosed the shower space, watching with evident glee. Amber had two fingers in Vicky's arsehole and dripped more soap onto them to ensure she was thoroughly cleaned. Vicky ground back on her intruding digits in a way that suggested she was a little angry with her but badly wanted such treatment all the same. Amber chuckled as she withdrew her fingers and lathered up the rest of Vicky's body.

Having delved so deep in both Vicky's holes, she had to use the secondary shower head on a hose to rinse her out front and back, requiring more penetration to ensure the soap was gone. Vicky growled and gasped as she cleaned her but didn't complain with intelligible words.

"Vicky, Ginger, lean up against the wall. Pepper and Amber, get on your knees and lick their pussies until they cover your pretty faces in their cum," Mistress Chevalier ordered.

Amber and Pepper did as they were told, with excited looks on their faces, worshipping their assigned submissives with all their skill. Given the treatment they'd been having, Amber wasn't surprised when Vicky and Ginger easily reached their peaks and she got her reward of tasting Vicky's orgasm as her juice splashed over Amber's face. A few minutes later they were rinsed off and waiting patiently as Mistress Chevalier removed her thigh length leather boots and stripped off her jodhpurs and blouse before joining them.

Together the four ponygirls worshipfully soaped and rinsed Mistress Chevalier down. The domme took hold of Vicky and Ginger by their heads and guided their mouths to her stiff nipples so they could suckle at her. Looking down at Amber and Pepper she asked, "Pussy or arse, Amber?"

Amber swallowed. "I haven't had the pleasure of worshipping Mistress Susanna's arse yet, Mistress Chevalier," she pointed out.

Mistress Chevalier grunted, "I won't deny her your first time then, so put your tongue between my lips and do a good job, or it's the carpet beater for you, my girl."

Pepper seemed positively thrilled to be the one left with the task of burying her tongue in Mistress Chevalier recently cleaned arsehole. Amber shuddered at the indecency of such an act, finding it quite off-putting. At the same time, she struggled with the thrill it gave her to hear Peppers sloppy noises of delight as she tongued at Mistress Chevalier, rimming her for all she was worth. It was a massive turn on.

"You may all touch yourselves while you pleasure," Mistress Chevalier generously said before warning them, "but do not dare come before I do!"

Amber slipped fingers inside herself, even as she used her other hand to penetrate Mistress Chevalier's defences as her tongue and lips worked magic on the dominant woman's clit.

With four tongues and Amber's fingers working on her at once,

Mistress Chevalier came twice before she decided to take a moment to catch her breath.

The ponygirls quickly washed her down under orders and then lovingly dried their Mistress with large fluffy towels, before they retired for a late lunch.

Mistress Chevalier gathered them all around the table for fresh baguettes and brie, followed by high quality yoghurts as a treat.

Amber's first course was not bread and cheese, but the honour of pleasuring Mistress Chevalier again, kneeling under the table and licking her pussy to another orgasm as the domme chatted calmly to the other ponygirls.

"Good girl, that was a lovely accompaniment to my lunch. You may get up now, and eat your meal," Mistress Chevalier said.

"Yes, Mistress."

CHAPTER 11

"Come, join us in bed, Amber," Mistress Chevalier offered, pointing at the open space between her and her personal submissive, Vicky.

"Should I put my harness on, Mistress?" Amber asked, slightly puzzled as she was currently just wearing a babydoll nightdress she'd been told to put on for the evening meal.

The afternoon had been spent assembling some gym equipment that Mistress Susanna had had delivered, and then being instructed how to use it by the resident expert, Vicky.

All the while, Mistress Chevalier looked on, relaxing on a chaise longue they'd brought in for her to use while they put the new gym together.

Each time Vicky showed the first girl how to use a particular machine, that girl had been summoned, and put to work between Mistress Chevalier's legs. She had told them about the new regimen that would arise from the installation of the gym as well.

"You'll get used to this on a daily basis girls. Mistress Susanna agreed with me that you should all be much fitter than you are and Vicky is going to take charge of your exercise, as Pudding tries to control your diet to keep you healthy. Any girl found shirking her exercise plan will receive personal attention from Vicky and by attention, I mean severe punishment of her choosing, do I make myself clear?"

"Yes, Mistress," the girls had all chorused, although Vicky had been smirking at the other girls with obvious glee at the prospect of punishing them.

Vicky had used powerful pinches and twists of their nipples to emphasise how much faster they should cycle during their cardio routines and Amber's sensitive breasts still ached quite delightfully as a result. Each movement of the sheer negligee against her erect nipples brought both pleasure and pain and her pussy remained wet enough to leave trails of her juices down her inner thighs.

After exercise and a shower was, thankfully, conducted without the accompaniment of a hose, they had all put on various types of nightdress and had a light evening meal together, of salad followed by various fruits.

Mistress Chevalier had played with Pepper at the head of the table, sitting the girl on the table in front of her, and running grapes down the length of her slit before eating them. The other ponygirls had looked on enviously as their domme buried her face in Pepper's sex and brought her to one explosive orgasm after another. Ginger had been allowed to sit on her flatmates mouth, covering it with her sex because of all the noise she was making, after her second orgasm.

Vicky and Amber meanwhile, had been ordered to watch and not touch themselves which had left both of them unutterably horny.

Mistress Chevalier had them all retire to the living room to watch a documentary on ancient lesbian sex cults, which Amber wasn't sure was based on much historical evidence, before announcing it was bedtime.

Now Amber was about to join the older lesbian couple in their bed. Pepper and Ginger had been sent to their own flat with orders to sixty-nine each other until, "your jaws ache and you can't go on", as Mistress Chevalier had put it. Neither had seemed upset by the command, Amber recalled.

"No, I don't need you in harness, Amber. Just take off that babydoll and come and lie down between us," Mistress Chevalier said kindly.

Amber carefully placed the expensive sheer material over the back of a chair and crawled up the bed to lie between the two women. One small and powerful in ways that belied her outward appearance, the other as large and muscular as any woman Amber had ever met with her own power on obvious display in the form of strong thighs and biceps.

Immediately, Vicky pressed her stiff nipples into Amber's back, her leg curling over Amber's and her foot slipping between the smaller woman's calves. With a simple twist of her left leg, Vicky prised Amber's legs apart, trapping Amber's left leg with hers, like a wrestling champion.

"Mistress," Amber began as Vicky's mouth descended possessively on her neck and began passionately laying kisses on her. Mistress Chevalier shushed her, reaching out and placing a silencing finger on Amber's lips.

"No. No format titles tonight my sweet. Tonight, you may call me Jade, provided you remember that you are still here to do as I need."

"Yes, Mis… I mean, yes, Jade," Amber replied. Jade smiled and drew in close, her lips pressing against Amber's mouth and her hand gently cupping her breast.

The kiss was a work of art, conducted on the raw clay of Amber's young, lesbian body by a maestro who had been learning new skills for as long as the younger woman had been alive.

Vicky's hungry mouth against her neck and shoulder was soon matched by the proprietorial fingers which claimed Amber's sex, pushing insistently inside her and thrusting to claim her, as a powerful thumb worked in circles on her aching clit.

Amber gasped into Jade's mouth as her clit was stimulated and then pinched hard by the sadistic older submissive. When Jade's mouth dropped to suck and lick at the nipple she had been lightly fondling with her hand, it all became too much and Amber reached the first of many orgasms.

Jade looked up at her young student, her eyes locking with

Amber's as she hungrily chewed and sucked at the succulent treat between her lips. Amber gasped and bucked on Vicky's strong fingers as both women continued to assault her senses with measured control.

It was mere moments later that their practice movements forced a second orgasm from her willing body and Amber felt her head flush with the intense rush of her climax, it was as if she might faint for a moment but she rode it all the way home.

"Good girl," Jade murmured, pausing from stimulating Amber's engorged nipple for a moment. "Would you like me to eat your pussy, darling?" she asked, a note of playful desire in her voice, as if she was genuinely worried the answer might be in the negative.

"Mmm. Please. Please Jade, lick my cunt, she needs you," Amber begged, putting a hand boldly on the older woman's head and pushing gently toward her crotch.

The thrill of the mighty Mistress Chevalier taking the forceful guidance and descending rapidly down Amber's body, laying a trail of kisses until her tongue finally plunged between Amber's pussy lips, was intense. It felt almost as if she was the one in charge.

Vicky's hand was displaced and reached up to take possession of her left breast, as her other hand snaked under Amber's ribs and grasped her right breast roughly squeezing it before withdrawing as she changed their position..

Vicky rolled Amber onto her back, twisting her until she, still on her side, could lock lips with the younger woman, as their domme began to worship her pussy. The muscular subs tongue thrust into Amber's mouth and claimed her entirely for the whole time it took Jade to bring Amber to another orgasm, which she did far more slowly than Amber imagined she was capable of.

Jade was a self-described connoisseur of pussy and enjoyed savouring such moments, as she'd told Amber several times. Taking her time was her right as a dominant of course, and Amber hardly resented the slow build to such a powerful orgasm as she ended up having, although if it had gone on much longer, she might have changed her tune and begun begging for relief.

As it was, she almost dislodged Jade's hungry mouth as it licked and sucked on her swollen nub, when the orgasm the older woman had drawn from her, made her hips shudder violently and her scream out, "Jade! Oh, Jade!"

But Jade did not stop, did not relent, did not give her any ease for her sensitive pussy, she just kept on tormenting her with the ease of many years of practice. It was as if Amber's pussy was laid out like a grand piano and Jade was a concert pianist who could bring forth Rachmaninov from any keyboard she was presented with, no matter the subtle differences it might have.

Jade may have told Amber to drop her nom de guerre of Mistress Chevalier but she was still firmly in charge of their play tonight. She was an experienced lesbian who had a couple of decades or more of practice at bringing eager sluts like Amber to the brink of ruin with her tongue. Every ounce of that skill was brought to bear on Amber's pussy forcing orgasms from her with a seeming lack of effort.

The grip on Amber's thighs was vice-like in intensity, as Jade's powerful arms denied Amber any chance of escaping her agile tongue. Amber's clit was on fire, her lips swollen and puffy from nibbling, sucking and just plain arousal. She whimpered and cried out, "Please, no more." Still, Jade did not relent. Amber knew there was no reason for her to do so, and her safeword was there for a reason. It had almost begun to bubble from her lips when what could have been her fourth orgasm tore from her aching cunt.

Jade laughed, despite the gush of Amber's first ejaculation, the liquid splashed over her domme's face as she completely lost control. Jade reached out and took hold of Vicky's hair, bringing her close. The athletic submissive knew what was needed of her and began to lick her domme's face clean of Amber's juices. The two women kissed and fondled each other until Jade was satisfied.

Jade stood up and smiled down at Amber, "You've made such a mess of me, Amber, even Vicky's tongue hasn't been able to clean me up. I'm going to wash up. Vicky, get over her face."

Their domme watched as Vicky rose up and squatted over Amber's face, "Yes, now Amber, you have until I come back from freshening up to give Vicky a nice big orgasm. If you don't, I'm going to spank your pussy, understood."

"Yes, Jade," Amber breathed, as Vicky's inviting sex came down to meet her welcoming lips.

Amber worked as hard and fast as she could, and Vicky was thoroughly excited by all the play beforehand, so she felt she might have a chance to avoid an intimate spanking, if Jade's wash was anything more than cursory.

Vicky wasn't making it hard, letting Amber have access to every part of her sex, and before the taps in the en-suite bathroom turned off, she had quietly gushed her orgasm all over Amber's face. It wasn't as explosive as Amber's had been but it was undeniable that Vicky had reached a climax.

Jade emerged from the bathroom, while Vicky was still riding Amber's face. They had not been told to stop if Vicky orgasmed so they had continued. "Well, did she make you come yet, slut?"

Vicky's powerful thighs twitched momentarily and Amber thought she'd lift herself up, but then they clamped on her head, her pussy pressing down hard on her mouth, pausing her ability to breathe and muffling her voice.

"No, Mistress," Vicky said with a shake of her head Amber could feel from beneath her. "I didn't come."

"I'm disappointed, Amber, so disappointed you couldn't be bothered to work your tongue hard enough. I simply must spank your naughty little cunt now. I like to stick to my promises," Jade explained, before kneeling between Amber's widespread legs.

The first smack landed on Amber's pussy without warning as Vicky's powerful frame and tight grip obstructed her vision. Amber howled into Vicky's pussy. Jade laughed loudly at the muffled noise.

"Goodness, Vicky, how tightly have you got hold of her? The poor girl can barely breathe."

"I want my orgasm, Mistress," Vicky growled, grinding her hips into Amber's face.

"You'd better give it to her, Amber, or you'll pass out from lack of oxygen," Jade warned. "I'll speed up your punishment to incentivise you," she added generously.

Counting out each blow, as Amber furiously licked at Vicky's pussy trying to get her to come again, Jade delivered five more hard smacks on Amber's sensitive sex. Each cupped her pussy perfectly, spreading the impact across the mound of wet flesh and making a tremendously satisfying noise.

It was pure agony, but Amber wasn't going to use her safe signal to avoid it. It wasn't for this. Her thighs were soaked with her own arousal and her mind was concentrating hard on bringing Vicky off so she could just about cope with it, though it was going to sting like the blazes for hours.

Amber felt she was almost blue in the face by the time she forced Vicky to come in front of Jade. When Vicky rolled off to one side, shuddering with exhaustion, Amber tried to suck in deep lungfuls of air as quickly as possible. Jade lunged forward and purred, "I want to taste her on you, slut."

Then Amber's airway was restricted again as Jade's lips pressed to hers and their tongues intertwined. Breathing through her nose calmed the panic she'd been feeling as Vicky rode her face in that suffocating style and Jade made appreciative noises as if she was enjoying a delightful new dessert.

Finally, Jade sat back, "That was fun."

"She cheated, Jade. I made her come before you got out here," Amber finally protested, cross to have been punished for Vicky's lie.

"Is that true, Vicky?"

"Yes, it is true, Mistress," Vicky confirmed without apparent shame. "I wanted to come twice and see this beautiful sluts pussy turn bright pink from being spanked."

"I can hardly blame you for that, but you must still be punished of course. Amber, how do you want to do it?" Jade asked.

"Me?"

"Yes, you, have you been squeezed so hard you went deaf?" Jade said, rolling her eyes.

"I think you should spank her pussy too, Jade," Amber said, feeling emboldened.

"No. Not to the pussy spanking, but I want to watch you give out this punishment. I'm supposed to be training you for Susanna. This is a chance for you to learn a pussy torture she might have use for," Jade explained, motioning for Vicky to lie back.

The big submissive did as she was told, lying back and spread her legs wide, putting a pillow under her bottom to lift her hips up and expose her shaven pussy even more. Vicky didn't seem in the slightest concerned about the punishment she was about to receive at the hands of her victim, if anything Amber thought she seemed excited.

"No, no, no! That's not nearly hard enough. You need to bring tears to her eyes, girl," Jade said after Amber had delivered three rather feeble smacks which didn't even make Vicky flinch, let alone wince or cry out.

"Watch me do it," Jade ordered, bringing her hand down with a resounding echo of flesh meeting flesh. Vicky whimpered. "Like that, see?"

"Yes, Jade," Amber said.

Jade nodded and took hold of her hand, showing hers alongside it. "Shape your hand like this, now, feel how it cups her pussy? It's like clapping your hands. Flat together there's barely any noise, and it can hurt you. But cup them, and you can make much louder noises, which for our purposes can be exhilarating in itself, and hit harder without injuring yourself. Just like this," Jade said, bringing her slightly cupped hand down viciously on Vicky's pussy.

Vicky squealed in pain, mixed with thick lust. She was utterly at Amber's mercy as Jade lined up her hand like a golf pro teaching how to hit a ball properly. Jade swung her hand up and down a couple of times and then gave her the nod. "Now, you try again and put some effort into it!"

Amber licked her lips nervously and brought her hand down, almost wincing herself before it connected. There was an echoing slap and Vicky cried out. It felt less painful to her hand and when she lifted her hand away, Amber was pleased to see Vicky's skin flushing pink.

"Yes. Now eleven more like that. Quick as you can," Jade instructed.

"Eleven! She only got six!" Vicky protested.

"Because Amber is a good girl, not a naughty orgasm thief like you, Vicky," Jade chided her. She threw a stern glance at Amber and motioned for her to continue.

As Amber's hand descended time after time, Jade counted out each stroke, docking a couple as mis-hits that didn't land properly which caused further mumbled complaints from Vicky.

"That's better. I think we should practise this again tomorrow at some point. You'd like that, wouldn't you, Vicky," Jade said with a grin.

"Yes, Mistress Chevalier," Vicky said.

"Now, while Vicky is taking a richly deserved punishment, how much nipple torture have you tried, Amber? Would you like to learn how to torment a nipple properly?" Jade asked with a suggestive wiggle of her eyebrows which made Amber giggle.

"Yes, please, Jade. I'd like that very much," Amber finally managed to blurt out between fits of laughter.

"I bloody wouldn't," Vicky protested.

"Then you should be a good girl, Vicky," Jade said, shuffling up the bed, and slinging her leg over Vicky's head so she could press her pussy to her submissive's mouth, as she faced back down the bed at Amber, beckoning her forward.

"Eat me, slut," Jade ordered casually, as she guided Amber's hand to Vicky's nipple. "Now, pinch it, as hard as you can."

Amber did her best but even after several practices it wasn't hard enough for Jade's liking.

"Right, you're doing this all wrong, Amber. Vicky is really much too experienced to respond the way we want if you are so gentle with her."

"I'm squeezing really hard," Amber protested.

Jade shook her head as she rolled her hips over Vicky's wicked tongue. "No, you just think you are because your nipples are more sensitive. You need to learn to judge your partners better. Vicky is a vicious sadist, but she's also a masochist which is why she loves to be on her knees for me. She loves the way I hurt her and make her serve me. But she's tough as old nails to go with it, so what might make Sugar or Candy howl, or you use your safeword won't put a dent in her, do you understand?"

"Yes, Jade," Amber said, trying to comprehend the lesson.

"Pinch her hard then and hold it. Hard as you like," Jade suggested.

Amber reached out and took Vicky's nipple between her thumb and the knuckle of her forefinger, pinching really hard. Vicky did not cry out.

"Good now hold it and watch me," Jade said. "This is what you're doing," she said, demonstrating on Vicky's other nipple.

"Yes, Jade."

"Whereas this is what I'm doing," Jade said, pinching harder, which caused Vicky to shudder. Amber felt the woman's hips, which she was straddling to get access to her big breasts, buck slightly under her. A clear reaction to the infliction of pain by Jade. "See how her nipple is squeezed more in my hand? Tighten your grip so they match," Jade prompted.

Amber did as she was told, applying more pressure than she was comfortable with, trying to get the nipple she was pinching into the same distorted shape as the one Jade had taken control of. A shudder running through Vicky's body between Amber's thighs told her she was onto something.

"Yes, like that," Jade said. "Now, tug it upwards like this. A bit more, that's better. Now, turn your hand clockwise and twist it. Twist it like you're going to pull it off!"

Amber swallowed hard and copied Jade's motions. When they both did it at once, Vicky's muffled cries could be heard blasting into Jade's pussy as it ground against her mouth.

"I did it!" Amber blurted out excitedly.

"Yes you did," Jade said, leaning forward and pulling Amber into a passionate kiss which she kept going until Vicky finally brought her to her orgasm.

Jade broke the kiss to gasp for air as she rode the waves of her climax. Amber hugged her tightly, stroking her hair and kissing her neck as she came down from the rush.

"Is she still licking you, Jade?" Amber asked. Jade pulled back from their embrace and smiled.

"Of course," Jade said. "Vicky is a good girl and never stops licking until she's told to. Are you ready for another lesson?"

Amber nodded. "Yes."

"Good girl," Jade said with a wicked grin. "Slap her tits then."

Amber looked down at Vicky's already tormented breasts. "Slap them?"

"Yes. Swat them and see how she responds. Go on," Jade urged.

Amber looked down and bit her lip for a moment, hesitating. Jade waved her hand in a rolling motion indicating she should press on and Amber slapped her hand against Vicky's breast.

"Again," Jade urged her on. "Again. Harder."

Amber slapped her again and Jade sighed in exasperation.

"I don't want to hurt her too badly," Amber whined.

Jade lifted her pussy from her submissive's face for a moment and asked, "Vicky, is Amber slapping your tits too hard?"

"Is she slapping them, I hadn't noticed, Mistress," Vicky said.

Jade gave Amber a look that firmly said, 'I told you so!' and parked her pussy on Vicky's tongue again.

Amber took a deep breath and slapped again.

"Better, but I want her tits to go the same pink as your bottom does when you get a good, hard spanking from Pudding or Susanna," Jade clarified. "Keep going.

Amber slapped Vicky's breasts a few more times each side. Then Jade lashed her hand out, slapping Amber's left breast hard. Amber squealed in shock and pain. "Ow, what was that for?" she asked, plaintively.

"To teach you an object lesson. At least that hard please," Jade said.

Amber frowned and let rip. There was a much louder sound this time and Vicky's hip bucked under her.

"Much better. Six like that to each of her tits, quick as you can, Amber!" Jade ordered.

Amber complied, much more readily this time and had to switch hands to get the right motion in. By the end of it, her palms were stinging and Vicky was writhing under her like a horse trying to buck a rider. But she didn't use her safe signal or cry out a safeword, despite the shade of hot pink that her breasts were rapidly going.

"Wasn't that fun, Amber?" Jade grinned as she rode Vicky's face to another orgasm of the back of watching Amber inflict the kind of pain she enjoyed doling out herself. The domme panted heavily as she came down from her climax.

"Yes, Jade."

"You can call me Mistress again now," Jade said as she dismounted Vicky's face.

"Yes, Mistress," Amber said.

"Now, get between my legs and lick me until I fall asleep," Jade ordered.

"Yes, Mistress Chevalier," Amber said as she dipped her head to comply.

"Vicky, fuck her from behind with a strap-on, there's a dear," Mistress Chevalier ordered.

"Yes, Mistress," came the cheerful response.

CHAPTER 12

"This morning," Mistress Chevalier told the assembled staff of the estate, "and this afternoon, we will be holding a series of races. This is the final stage of Amber's ponygirl bootcamp week, and will test her new skills."

Amber caught Candy giving her a big wink on the other side of the circle, behind Mistress Chevalier's back. The other women, were concentrating on the Stable Mistress, who had been left in charge while Mistress Susanna was away on business. Amber smiled, but didn't dare wink back or respond to Candy when she should be listening to Mistress Chevalier's speech.

"Each race will award four points for the winner, three for second place and so on down to last place. You will stay in the same teams for the day. The winner will be the ponygirl with the most points at the end of the day," Mistress Chevalier said. "Vicky will be driven by Pudding and I will drive Amber. Ginger will be paired with Sugar and Pepper with Candy. Roxy will be our referee and her decision on points scored and rule infringements will be final. Any questions?"

"Is there a prize, Mistress?" Candy asked.

"For the winning ponygirl, yes. The driver's rewards are built into the format of the races. The winning ponygirl will be allowed to invite anyone here to their bed for the evening, as well as choose who is in charge. Vicky is excluded from winning the grand prize, since she outclasses the other ponygirls in raw power it wouldn't be a fair contest. I still expect everyone to race fairly and attempt to stay as close to Vicky as you can," Mistress Chevalier replied. "There is a treat planned for second place too, the nature of which I will reveal later."

Her answer caused a stir among the teams, as each ponygirl sized up the others, wondering who they could beat and what the second place prize might be. If the winning prize was to fuck whoever they wanted for the night and choose if they were submitting to their choice or vice versa, the second prize could be well worth it too.

"What reward do the drivers get, Mistress Chevalier?" Roxy asked.

"Oh yes, I'm glad you asked. There's not much point trying to race each ponygirl dozens of times, they need to recover after each race or the whole thing will grind to an unbearable mess of glacial speed laps around the lake, like PonyFest 2015. That was a disaster and demonstrated that exhausted ponygirls are far less enjoyable," Mistress Chevalier explained. "To avoid such disappointing events, after each race, the ponygirls will be watered and then will be available for 45 minutes to their drivers. Drivers, you may discipline the ponygirls, use them sexually whatever pleases you, just please keep to the spirit of the event and don't tire them out too much. A tired slut is a boring slut," Mistress Chevalier said. Her last comment caused a small round of laughter.

"You heard Mistress Chevalier, teams! I expect you all ready to race at the starting line by 9am. That means you have," Roxy said, glancing at her fitness band, "twelve minutes, to get in harness and get your traps to the starting line."

Since the girls were already in partial harness and they had already taken the traps out of the coach house, there was plenty of time but Roxy kept in her role as referee and marched around making sure the teams were hustling. She slapped a riding crop against the calf of her thigh-length leather boots, looking for all the world like a posh equestrian girl, out for a day of riding and champagne.

The crack of the crop against the leather of the boot was sharp enough to make Amber flinch every time she heard it, as Mistress Chevalier checked her straps and bit gag, tightening buckles here and there and checking a finger could fit between Amber's skin and the leather of the restraints. Amber knew that was important to prevent loss of blood flow, which could be uncomfortable at best, and caused serious injury at worst.

Once the bit gag was in place, Mistress Chevalier produced a short chain linking two nipple clamps, and attached them to Amber's breasts, causing her eyes to tear up in surprise. Leaning in the domme whispered in Amber's ear, "Just a little something to make sure you remember who is in charge, slut."

The domme reached down between Amber's legs and slipped two fingers between her slick lips, pressing her thumb to Amber's clit. "I knew you'd be wet, you dirty little bitch. Don't forget, the prize you can win if you do well today. If you come last, I'll punish you after each race, understood?"

Amber whinnied and stamped her foot once to indicate she knew very well what was at stake. A full 45 minutes of Mistress Chevalier's cruel punishments would leave her in ruins. She hoped that the alternative if she won was more pleasure than pain, or at least the opportunity to worship her domme rather than be chastised.

"What a good pony. Now, let's see if you can come close to Vicky's pace, shall we?" Mistress Chevalier said as she got in the trap behind Amber and flicked the reins, guiding her to the start line.

The first race got off to a good start, Amber let Pepper and Ginger take off ahead of her and Mistress Chevalier gave her the leeway to choose her own way of racing. Once they passed the first third of the track, Amber increased her pace and used the slight advantage of the shallow incline to overtake both of the more inexperienced ponygirls.

"Well played, Amber," Mistress Chevalier called out as they passed Ginger and Pepper on the left, as they were going clockwise around the lake as usual. Amber wasn't sure if the girls had recognised the terrain changed at this point and became easier, but she was hoping their legs were a little tired from trying to stay far ahead of her. They were huffing and puffing as they tried to catch up with her, but Amber felt fresh enough to keep going and she was gaining ground.

Of course, Vicky was out in front, but Amber didn't let herself worry about that too much. Her first goal was to get more points than Pepper and Ginger, so she could win the prize. She didn't want to burn herself out trying to catch up with Vicky on the first race.

Mistress Chevalier let her set the pace all the way around the end of the lake, then cried out, "Come on Amber, show me you can put in a good finish!"

Amber was planning to move up to a faster gait as she came into the home straight so she kept to her plan as long as she could, almost stumbling when her driver intervened by flicking the carriage whip sharply across her buttocks. The whip cracked, and pain seared Amber's cheeks, "Faster, pony. Faster!"

There was no choice but to do as Mistress Chevalier demanded and try and speed up. Amber was convinced she could not make it and could tell she was going to slow down as her lungs tried hard to provide her with oxygen to keep up her fastest pace. She would be overtaken by one or both of the other ponygirls and come last.

Already, her legs were flagging and Amber, healthy but no athlete, knew she had no reserves to call on for a last burst of speed. Was that the end of her race, she wondered. Then the whip cracked expertly on each buttocks, a split-second apart.

The stinging sensation gave Amber something else to concentrate on and invigorated her with fresh energy, which she put to work in service of her Mistress and drive, Mistress Chevalier.

Amber crossed the line a full hundred yards ahead of Pepper and Ginger's teams.

Mistress Chevalier was already out of the trap and leading her back to the yard when they crossed the finishing line. "Vicky is the winner!" Roxy declared. "Second place goes to Amber, third to Ginger and fourth to Pepper," she called out.

Once the trap was parked, Amber was detached from the rig, and Mistress Chevalier led her into the tack come play room in the stable block. There was no preamble, she unbuttoned her jodhpurs and sat down on a throne-like, well-padded wooden chair before she barked a command at Amber, "Take my boots off."

Amber worked as quickly as possible to get the long boots off so she could remove Mistress Chevalier's riding trousers properly. Without waiting for an order, she got on her knees directly in front of the chair and looked up at Mistress Chevalier, who smiled, pleased that Amber knew her role. The older women shifted forward in the chair, so that her buttocks were balanced on the very edge, making her easy to reach.

"Begin," was the only thing Amber's domme needed to say.

Amber reached out with both hands, teasing aside the lacey scarlet lingerie that concealed Mistress Chevalier's already moist lips with her left hand, and using the fingers of her right to slip between the lips before her and begin fingering her domme. Her tongue followed up immediately, searching for the swollen clit that crowned the delicious pussy of the Stable Mistress.

"Yes, there's a good girl," Mistress Chevalier sighed, as Amber applied her tongue to what had become one of her favourite activities. Behind her, she could hear the other teams following suit.

"Over my knee please, Vicky," Pudding said. Amber knew what that meant. Pudding's world revolved around cooking delicious food and looking after the diet of the staff and guests at Susanna's mansion and spanking women. The cook loved to turn a girl's bottom rosy pink and was so expert, that she could make some girls come just from the way she spanked them. Indeed, it wasn't long before Vicky was moaning and breathing hard, just like Ginger was.

While Pudding's hand descended time after time on Vicky's bottom, Amber had heard Sugar order Ginger to help her into a strap-on harness and begin fucking the ponygirl. She wished that she could see the maid fucking her pony, but the sounds that filled the room were still quite arousing. Mistress Chevalier was adding her own appreciative noises to the atmosphere.

Candy meanwhile, had different ideas, "I'm going to make you come so hard, Pepper and you're going to beat Amber in the next race for me, aren't you?" Amber could hear Pepper's familiar moans as Candy got work licking the lucky ponygirl's pussy.

"Yes, Candy, I can beat her. Oh, that's good. Thank you Mistress," Candy moaned.

Mistress Chevalier was completely relaxed, her eyes closed and her hands stroking her breasts through her blouse, as Amber hungrily tongued and sucked at her clit. "Do you hear that, Amber? Candy thinks she can beat you. You're not going to let her, are you?"

"No, Mistress," Amber replied, taking just a second to speak before going back to worshipping the ponygirl trainer's pussy.

"I hope not, I want to come before Pepper, and I want to win the next race too," Mistress Chevalier said.

The cry that came from Pepper's lips confirmed that Candy had heard that challenge and was redoubling her effort. Amber did too, plunging her fingers into her domme's hungry pussy and finding her g-spot, as she concentrated on her clit with her tongue.

If Amber had to choose, Candy was probably the submissive who was beast at eating pussy, that Mistress Susanna had in service to her, although Mistress Chevalier was amazing as well. The domme had the unfair advantage of having been practicing the most delightful art since before some of them were born.

There was no circumstance under which Amber would have given anything but her all to try and beat Candy. She was determined to be the first to give her partner an orgasm. It wasn't a surprise when Pepper began to scream her way through an epic orgasm, a full minute before Amber got the same from Mistress Chevalier.

The reaction to the climax that Mistress Chevalier experienced still made Amber proud. She didn't expect to beat Candy at pussy eating, or Vicky at racing yet but she was pleased with her progress. Everyone else in the room had been having sex with other women far longer than she had, after all.

Mistress Chevalier however, wasn't going to leave it at Amber having been defeated. When she was done, she reached for a wet wipe and made herself decent, pulling up her trousers and having Amber help her get her riding boots on.

Then she bent Amber over a spanking bench and thrashed her a dozen times with a flogger. With expert aim, she made it sting just the right amount to discipline her submissive, but not enough that Amber couldn't go through the rest of the day. Already, Amber could tell she wouldn't be able to see evidence of the pain she'd just suffered if she looked in the mirror.

Amber wanted to come so badly then, but Mistress Chevalier wasn't looking to please the sub, she was keen to get on with the day of racing.

Pepper had obviously been encouraged by the orgasmic bribe that Candy gave her, and she beat Amber and Ginger in the next race. Although Amber's trick from the first race wasn't going to work again, she found that an even pace, and paying attention to Mistress Chevaliers commands, both verbal and with the reins, worked well.

By the end of the day, Vicky had comfortably won each race, winning sixteen points. Pepper won the second round but lost the third and only beat Ginger in the fourth race earning eight points in total. Ginger was last with only seven points.

"Amber wins second place, with ten points overall," shouted Roxy at the end of the last race.

The ponygirls were all good sports and cheered her on.

Mistress Chevalier pulled her in for a long kiss, and fondled Amber's bottom while she claimed her trainee's mouth for some long, passionate moments.

"Good girl," she said, "now, you are due a prize. Who do you wish to take to bed tonight?" Mistress Chevalier waved her hand to indicate the assembled women that Amber could choose from.

"Can I pick more than one?" Amber asked, fluttering her eyelashes at the Stable Mistress.

"I suppose you can, you naughty minx, I didn't say it had to be just one girl, so it's not against the rules."

"I'd like all the ponygirls to join me in bed then, so we can please each other all night long. And you, of course, Mistress."

"Well, of course. How thoroughly greedy of you, Amber," Mistress Chevalier said with a sly smile.

"Yes, Mistress. I am a very greedy girl I've discovered since coming here. I love to eat as often as I can," Amber replied.

"What about Pudding and Sugar and Candy?"

"Would it be alright if they stayed to watch? I'm sure Sugar and Candy have done something naughty that requires Pudding to punish them," Amber suggested.

"Have they done anything requiring punishment, Pudding? Anything naughty?" Mistress Chevalier asked the cook.

"They've always got a black mark against their name. They're a lot of trouble you know, Mistress?" Pudding replied. "I have a list, if you wish to see it."

Mistress Chevalier laughed heartily, "No, but make sure you make them squeal, won't you? It wouldn't do for them to think they can have too many punishments without crying some cathartic tears, wouldn't you agree?"

"Of course, Mistress. The maids need to be kept firmly in their place at the bottom of our social ladder. You can't give them an inch or they'll take a mile," Pudding agreed. "I'll be sure to leave them tear-streaked and with blushing bottoms."

"Good then, it's settled. Ladies, to bed," Mistress Chevalier ordered. "Roxy, you too."

"Yes, Mistress," the seven submissive women chorused.

CHAPTER 13

"Congratulations, Amber, you did so well," Candy said.

"Yes, well done," Sugar said, giving her a big hug.

"You need to do more squats, short stuff," Vicky said before pulling her in for a bear hug that Amber thought might crush her.

"I'm sure Mistress Susanna will offer you a stall of your own, Amber," Pepper whispered in her ear as she and Ginger enveloped her in a shared hug.

"I bet you're right, Pepper," Ginger agreed.

"Thanks ladies," Amber said when everyone finally stopped congratulating her for passing Mistress Susanna's battery of tests. It felt good to have mastered the skills that Mistress Chevalier had spent many long hours teaching her, at least well enough to be considered competent. It was like passing a driving test or getting a swimming certificate that proved you were a good enough swimmer to be safe on your own.

The difference was that Amber was torn up inside. She'd had a certain amount of fun, but she was worried about what would happen next. As they worked on putting away all the traps and harnesses properly and all got showered together, Amber mulled things over in her mind.

What was it that she wanted from Mistress Susanna, now that she was back?

When Susanna had seduced her just a few short weeks ago, Amber's life had gone from what could only be described as rather uneventful, to a thrilling sequence of incredible sexual and romantic adventures.

For all intents and purposes she was the girlfriend of a wealthy business woman now, and even the thought of being a lesbian was new to her. Amber's inexperience with women before she met Susanna wasn't just due to a lack of opportunity, it was something she'd never quite settled in her mind, until that fateful moment in her boss's office, during the final interview.

Now she had a new job which had not been taxing so far but could well be quite enjoyable and would certainly offer opportunities that she'd be unlikely to get elsewhere. It wasn't just the sex and the kinky games, but potentially learning a lot about business matters that she couldn't learn elsewhere.

It had been Amber's idea to bring Mistress Chevalier to the estate to run the ponygirl stables, operate her business as a leatherworker there and renovate more of the outbuildings to accomplish that. Amber had expected the idea to be rejected outright, but Susanna gave her the responsibility of overseeing the whole thing.

Certainly, she hadn't had to do anything alone and had required lots of help, but Susanna had let her remain in charge and instead of dictating how it would go, had offered suggestions along the way. Amber had learned a lot about property investment, bookkeeping, project management and a host of other valuable business skills.

Most employers and managers, wouldn't be given so much rope to an employee at such a young age. If she hadn't also been her boss's lover, her self-doubting said from one shoulder, perhaps it wouldn't have gone the same way. Her confidence shouted from the other shoulder, that she was still learning a lot, even if it was only because she was sleeping with Susanna.

Was it a tick in the pro column or the con column that Amber's boss was an older woman who had quite deliberately headhunted a beautiful young woman, to be her personal assistant, in the hopes that she'd also fit in with her hedonistic lifestyle?

Did it matter if Amber's employment opportunities were in part coming to her because Susanna enjoyed dominating her, disciplining her rosy cheeked bottom, and riding her face to orgasm? If it wasn't all about Amber's abilities as an employee, was that a point of principal that should cause Amber to reject the marvellous opportunities that Susanna offered. Doing so would probably mean rejecting the older woman romantically as well.

It just didn't feel to Amber that she was doing anything wrong. Her feelings for Susanna were new, but genuine. Although she'd never been past the fantasy stage of thinking about sex with another woman, there wasn't a shred of doubt that she was attracted to them.

The sex was amazing and Amber was coming to terms with how much she enjoyed being submissive to Susanna, Mistress Chevalier and anyone they told her to. The kinky games and BDSM that they indulged in were sometimes humiliating, sometimes painful but always arousing and ultimately fulfilling.

The orgies that Amber had now been a part of, were so decadent that she felt she should somehow feel guilty about being so sexually open and giving. And yet, Amber experienced nothing she could identify as a guilty thought for more than a second or two. Each hint of another event where Amber might enjoy group sex or get shared with Mistress Susanna's friends, left her wet with anticipation, not scared or disgusted.

Amber had been hoping that when Susanna got back, another project would come up that would allow her to prove her worth to her Mistress in the business, and not just the bedroom. Did Susanna really respect her opinions or was she simply indulging her pet's interest to keep her happy?

A nagging doubt remained, though Amber felt that it was entirely rational to think Susanna really did want to listen to her ideas. It was unlike any management style Amber had experienced herself and more the stuff of books about entrepreneurs and the opportunities their boss's had given them.

While her mind raced with the complexities of her current situation she and the other ladies had all got dressed and were heading toward the house for dinner. A part of Amber hoped it would devolve into another lesbian orgy of the senses, a hedonistic night of pleasure, pain and laughter. If not, perhaps she would be able to grab a moment to speak to Susanna about her future.

"Come on Amber, keep up!" Candy urged.

"I'm right behind you," Amber said, though she could feel herself hesitating, her anxiety about her life going forward was distracting her. She shook her head and took a deep breath.

Amber stepped through the door into the rest of her life.

CHAPTER 14

"Ladies, a moment of your time. Ladies, your attention please!" Susanna said, tapping a knife on the side of her glass to get their attention.

The chatter around the dining table finished and everyone turned their eyes toward their employer and Mistress.

"Thank you."

Mistress Susanna smiled at them all and put the knife down, lifting her glass of wine.

"Please raise your glasses for a toast," Susanna asked, "To Amber, our new friend, colleague and filthy slut!"

"To Amber," the ladies laughed.

"I know that you've all enjoyed having Amber her at the estate and you've all felt the pleasure of her tongue on your pussies. I'm sure you agree that she's come along nicely so far and of course, today, she passed her final exam from the Mistress Chevalier school of teaching dirty girls to be good ponygirls," Susanna continued to politely laughter.

"In other news, we may need to have a brainstorming session for a better name for the school," Mistress Susanna said, and had to wait for the laughter to quiet down.

"Amber, when I first interviewed you, which seems like it was only last week, I was pleased to offer you a job as my personal assistant. You've performed your duties admirably and learned so much about yourself since you came to live here. I'm immensely proud of you, as I am of all the wonderful ladies around this table. We are a team bonded on so many levels," Mistress Susanna said.

"Hear, hear!" agreed Mistress Chevalier boisterously.

"You passed the exams Mistress Chevalier, and I set, proving that you paid attention during her lessons and have demonstrated you have the capability to make a good ponygirl. I would like to offer you the position of ponygirl alongside Pepper and Ginger in my stables, as I feel you've earned it. What do you say?"

Amber's eyes flew wide, and she glanced around the table at all the women smiling at her. Her heart beat furiously in her chest and she could feel them staring at her, all at once.

Mistress Susanna was smiling at her waiting for a response, but as the seconds ticked by without Amber replying, her smile began to crack at the corners. Amber swallowed and licked her lips. She knew she had to say something and didn't think her answer was going to please her Mistress. There was no choice though.

"Thank you, Mistress. That's a kind offer, but I will have to decline I'm afraid."

The room erupted with gasps of shock, hands flew to mouths and murmurs grew loud around her. Amber felt herself shrinking into her seat as oddly loud whispered conversations took place.

"Calm down! Calm down! Please be quiet so I can ask Amber about this," Mistress Susanna called out over the gossipers. "Amber, you have taken to being a ponygirl rather well, and by all accounts you had an enjoyable week of roleplaying and fun. Therefore, I must ask why you would turn this down. Do we need to discuss this in private?"

Amber nodded, "Yes, please, Mistress."

Susanna sighed, "Then please, join me in the drawing room. Ladies, please amuse yourselves while I talk to Amber."

The chattering started up again and gained full throated involvement by the time Mistress Susanna closed the door behind them.

Mistress Susanna sat down on a leather Chesterfield, and motioned for Amber to come forward and sit astride her, her knees sinking into the soft, burgundy leather, as she kneeled in her Mistress's lap. Susanna's eyes roved appreciatively up and down Amber's nubile body, drinking in her shapely form.

Reaching out, Mistress Susanna slipped the thin straps of Amber's dress off her shoulders and revealed her breasts. Amber took a deep breath as her lover began to stroke her breasts and tease her nipples. It was several minutes before Mistress Susanna deigned to speak to her, but her domme did not stop fondling her breasts.

"I'm not going to make this easy on you, Amber. You can explain your rejection of my offer but I haven't seen you in so long, I have no intention of not enjoying your lovely breasts while you do so," Mistress Susanna purred. "Please, enlighten me."

The damp patch in Amber's lacy panties wasn't helping her concentrate, but she managed to pull together her thoughts sufficiently to respond without resorting to lust induced gibberish.

"I did my best to be a good ponygirl, Mistress, and it's true, I had a fun week in some regards. I just can't see myself living like Pepper and Ginger do long term," Amber explained whimpering slightly as Mistress Susanna pinched her nipples most cruelly. When she'd recovered she went on, "I don't want to be your ponygirl, Mistress."

"No? Then what do you want, Amber?"

"I want to be you, Mistress."

"You want to be me? Figuratively, I hope, otherwise you'll have a difficult road ahead of you."

"I want to be a strong, independent business woman, like you, Mistress. I want to learn how to grow a business and shape some portion of the world the way you have. I could do so much good in the world, if I take this wonderful opportunity to learn everything you have to teach. One day, I could own my own company or run a foundation or make a contribution to the world. With your guidance, with you as my mentor, I think I can do it."

Mistress Susanna's hands dropped away from Amber's breasts and she looked upset.

"I see. You want to end our relationship and go into business for yourself? It makes sense I suppose, you got a taste of it with the renovation project and now you want more. I can hardly criticise you for that," Mistress Susanna said, sounding as dejected as if someone had just told her that her favourite restaurants had all closed shop permanently.

"No!" Amber protested.

"No? Is that all I'll get from you now, a negative response to everything?" Mistress Susanna grumbled.

"No, Mistress. I mean, I don't want to end our relationship. I don't want that at all. I want to be your personal assistant and learn about business at your side. But I still want you, I want to serve you. I just don't want to do it as a ponygirl or have it be so much of every day of my life."

"So you just want to share my bed, as long as there's some kind of business coaching for you?"

Amber shook her head. "I want to share your bed because I want to worship you, for the goddess you are to me, Mistress Susanna."

Mistress Susanna was still frowning, her arms crossed defensively in front of her.

Amber reached out her hand and tilted her dommes chin up, forcing her to look her in the eye. It was a bold move, and Amber could already picture being bent over and thrashed soundly for daring to be so forward.

"Mistress. I..." Amber trailed off.

"You what?" Mistress Susanna said, glaring into Amber's very soul.

"Mistress, you know that I love you, don't you? You know that every moment apart this week has been agony for me, far beyond the torments that Mistress Chevalier inflicted. I don't want to be in the stables. I want to be in your bed. I want to wake up next to you. When you invite Candy to your bed and have her lick your delicious pussy, I want to be beside you, watching my love receive her pleasure."

"You love me? Really, truly, love me?"

"Yes, Mistress. Haven't I shown that?"

"But you won't be my ponygirl?"

"Susannna, do you really need another ponygirl? Honestly?"

"I don't need one," Susanna said, almost whining and placing greater emphasis on the penultimate word. "I don't see why I can't have another one.

Amber rolled her eyes and giggled. "Very well, Mistress. As soon as I get the chance, I shall set myself a project, 'Find greedy Mistress Susanna a third ponygirl. Must have big boobs, pierced nipples and a craving for more discipline in her life.' How's that?"

Mistress Susanna laughed. "It'd be nice if she had some tattoos, and tongue and clit piercings too," she joked.

"I'll make a note of it. 'Pierced everywhere. Only genuine sluts need apply.'" Amber replied solemnly.

"Perfect. You know, you'd probably make a good personal assistant, Amber," Susanna said with a wink.

"That's what I've been saying!" Amber giggled. Susanna's hands found her breasts again and Amber's nipples were soon as stiff as bullets, or at least, as she imagined bullets must be, not that she'd ever held one. "Oh, Mistress. That feels wonderful."

"I love you too, Amber."

"I know."

"You did not," Susanna said, looking faintly scandalised

"I think I did."

"Did you just quote that scruffy scoundrel?" Susanna said, shaking her head softly as Amber's hands reached out and gently stroked her breasts through her dress.

"You know I did." Amber replied, rubbing her thumbs over her domme's hardening nipples.

"I happen to like nice girls," Susanna said, emphasising her words with a cruel, twisting pinch of Amber's nipples.

"No, you don't," Amber gasped, her eyes watering as she leaned in to claim her Mistress's mouth with a passionate kiss, as her fingers played down her stomach and slid into her panties. Susanna did not protest Amber contradicting her.

The wet lips her fingers slipped between would have borne out her statement, regardless. Mistress Susanna tipped her head back and moaned her confession.

"Yes, Amber."

CHAPTER 15

Amber had wanted to ravish Susanna right there and then, but her Mistress and boss would not allow her to take it quite that far. She insisted they tidy themselves up and get back to the dinner party. Amber tried pouting, but it simply earned her a rather casual smack across the rump and a stern look which further dampened her panties but didn't lead to any more fooling around.

Mistress Susanna did lift Amber's fingers to her lips and suck them clean of her own juices, winking lasciviously at Amber as she did so. "Mmm. I do taste good, don't I?"

"Yes, Mistress," Amber breathed, utterly enraptured by the horny display.

"Now, we must go back to the others, I want to speak to them about what we've discussed."

"You do?"

"I do, come along now," Mistress Susanna said, taking Amber's hand in hers and leading her back to the formal dining room with its large banquet table surrounded by all the household staff, from Roxy and Pudding to the ponygirls and Mistress Chevalier and the maids.

Normally they did not all eat together, and the maids ate with the cook, but Amber passing her exams was a major event and Mistress

Susanna had decreed it a celebration. Pudding had cooked an amazing meal and once it was served, the cook and maids had joined the rest of the household.

The room was full of conversation when the doors opened and quieted down quickly when Mistress Susanna strode in with Amber in tow.

"Ladies, I have an announcement to make, Amber has decided against the life of a ponygirl and I was surprised, but I fully support her reasoning. I'm pleased to say that she will continue to serve as my personal assistant and live here with us," Mistress Susanna said.

The assembled ladies clapped and cheered happily.

"I know that some of you probably hoped Amber would want to play as a pony with you, but I'm sure you'll have plenty of fun with her regardless of that," Susanna said. Mistress Chevalier agreed loudly.

"I'd like you all to follow me to the sitting room," Susanna said, striding from the dining room into a nearby room which was set up with lots of comfy chairs and chaise longue, a baby grand piano in one corner. It was a grandly appointed room and one of the main rooms used during the orgy a few weeks previously.

Susanna had them clear the coffee tables and Ottomans from the middle of the room, and stand around in a semi-circle while she stood in front of the fireplace with Amber.

"Sugar, please remove Amber's dress and hang it up somewhere neatly," Susanna said calmly as if it were the most natural thing in the world.

"Candy, fetch me the rosewood box in the writing bureau would, my dear?" Susanna said, as Sugar slipped the straps of Amber's elegant dress off her shoulders, and brought it down her body, to puddle around her ankles. Amber stepped out of it and Sugar took the dress away.

Candy had found the expensive looking box, which looked like the type used for expensive diamond jewellery, only that it was an expensive work of art in itself. It was probably an antique, Amber thought.

"Sugar, take her panties too, they're pretty but I think everyone would rather see Amber full nude, am I right, ladies?"

The assembled ladies gave a resounding confirmation and Amber couldn't help but blush, despite the encounters she'd had with each of them, her sense of mild embarrassment at being exhibited for their enjoyment remained. Stepping out of the panties as Sugar worked them down her legs, left her utterly exposed, her neatly shaven pussy on display for all to see.

"Much better," Mistress Susanna said. "I have asked you in here, to bear witness to this moment. Amber, please kneel."

A little murmuring rose up among the ladies but a sharp glance from Susanna brought silence as Amber dropped to the rug on her knees. Amber kept her back straight, and shoulders back, filling her lungs and making sure she was displayed well for her Mistress, and the audience.

"Amber, it is perhaps premature to suggest this, but I would like you to consider doing me the honour of accepting this token," Mistress Susanna said, opening the box and presenting the contents for all, including Amber, to see.

"This is merely a placeholder, a play item I had made for you, in anticipation of this happy moment," Mistress Susanna said. "The real one would be somewhat different and more symbolic," she explained.

Inside the box, on a velvet cushion, lay a beautiful leather collar. It was a deep burgundy, with fine stitching and stamped with beautiful patterns. At the throat there was a silver nameplate that read, "Amber" above a thick half-moon hoop for a leash or restraint. It was very tall, almost neck height. It was a posture collar, she realised, one that would keep the submissives head in a particular position and restrict movement.

"Amber, will you accept my collar, and the commitment that it represents?"

As Susanna had said, this collar was an item for play but collaring a sub was a huge step, tantamount to a proposal of marriage, Amber well knew. None of Susanna's many submissives had been blessed in this way, although they all had a great deal of commitment from Susanna. This was special, unique.

The room was utterly silent, everyone waiting with bated breath on Amber's answer.

Amber felt tears well in her eyes, overwhelmed with the emotional weight of the response she had to give.

"Yes, Mistress."

AUTHOR'S NOTE

Thank you for reading Her Lesbian Boss: The Complete Series - Books 1-6 of The Submissive Lesbian Personal Assistant series.

If you enjoyed this six book omnibus of the series, and can spare the time to leave a review on Amazon or Goodreads, I would greatly appreciate it.

Positive and constructive feedback and comments, even a simple star rating, are a great way to let me know that you want to read more about these characters.

This is the second omnibus edition I've done, the first being of my paranormal romance series The Consort of the Werewolf King, which follows Will and his alpha, Brian.

I hope you'll check out some of my other books.

Thanks, K.F. Jones

News and Updates - April 2020

Below you'll find some information about this series and the projects

I'm working on next. You don't need to read this, but it's here for those who are interested.

Her Lesbian Boss - Completing the Series

If this edition is your first time reading the Submissive Lesbian Personal Assistant series, I really hope you enjoyed it and found that the story flowed well.

Between finishing the last book and publishing this omnibus edition of the complete series, I did an extensive editing pass on books 1-4. The primary reason was to polish the story so that it could be at its absolute best for this omnibus.

A few more typos and punctuation issues were eliminated but most of what I ended up doing was polishing language for clarity and improving the overall story.

I ended up increasing the length of the series from about 107,000 words to 122,000. The shortest book is now 15,000. Most of the extra content is in the first three books but all books got tweaks and improvements.

I feel confident that the additional text consists of You'll find out a bit more about the characters, a little more back story and probably a fair bit more to some sex scenes.

The same updates are being uploaded to the individual books as well. A slight oddity of Amazon's system is that if you download a book that has been updated, you'll still get your old file.

If you're reading this version, it will be the up to date text. But unless you enable an update, and Amazon agree to make it available, you don't get updated copies of your old books.

This is for your benefit - any notes that you attach in the Kindle app, would be lost if the author updates the file for the book.

It's all managed through Manage Content and Devices on the Amazon website so if you go there and look at your books, you'll be able to see any updates that are available to you.

As I mentioned in my last couple of author notes, I had planned to release this omnibus at at the £9.99/$9.99 price point, bought separately in ebook format, all six books would cost £17.94/$17.94. It's a bargain for people who buy directly, and Kindle Unlimited readers can access the book for free anyway.

Instead, I'm going to target the £0.99/$0.99 price point for launch and I may keep it at that low price.

Most of my income from these books comes from Kindle Unlimited subscribers, borrowing and reading them. I'm paid per page read for those readers.

Selling a large omnibus edition at a huge discount, will hopefully allow me to reach more readers, push the book higher up the charts and I can then reach more KU readers as a result.

If not, a lot of people will get a very cheap book and I'll raise the price later.

Launching books is a lot of trial and error and the same techniques don't always work.

If price is an issue, the most cost effective way to read my books is to subscribe to Kindle Unlimited (if you read a few a month). That's how I read so much, I could simply never afford to read everything I do, if it I had to buy each book, rather than borrow it.

As I mentioned last time, I really enjoy writing about Amber and Susanna, and I have plenty of ideas as to what they will get up to as their relationship develops. If there is sufficient demand, I'll write another series about their ongoing spankings. I mean, adventures.

Do I hear the cry of tropical birds on an island retreat for kinky lesbians? Perhaps the sound of bells, which could either signal a wedding, or a thoroughly deviant surprise some of our dominants have for their subs?

Remember, let me know what you want, because I promise, I will pay close attention to requests.

You can follow me on Twitter if you want to see every panicked post I make about a new story idea I've had, that I have outlined but don't have time to write.

This happens to me a lot when what I'm really trying to do is get a nice lather of my favourite Tea Tree oil soap all over me in the shower.

One day, I will write some of them.

Amber's Culinary Adventures

I am going to continue writing a series of short stories, Amber's Culinary Adventures, when I have spare moments.

Don't worry, they're not actually about cooking. Here's some title ideas - see if they whet your appetite:

- A Dash of Pepper (available now)
- A Sprinkling of Sugar
- A Taste of Pudding
- A Filling of Ginger

The Culinary Adventures will be single scene, erotic shorts about an encounter Amber has with one or more of her friends.

As with A Dash of Pepper, I will release them all as individual works, at the lowest price point Amazon allows, £0.99/$0.99. They will also be available in Kindle Unlimited.

When I have enough, I will release an omnibus which will be the most cost effective way to read the stories if you don't subscribe to Kindle Unlimited.

If you prefer not to buy erotica short stories (this series is made up of novelettes and novellas for anyone who is curious) that's perfectly understandable.

At that price point, they're kind of loss leaders for me anyway due to the way Amazon's royalty structure works (that's not a complaint just something we consider when pricing).

What I expect is for readers to prefer to buy the omnibus edition of short stories instead, but I'll publish them individually too, rather than wait based on that assumption. In any case, the Kindle Unlimited readers can download them one at a time if they exist as individual books.

Here's a summary:

- A series of erotic stories about Amber
- Short, one or two scenes, 5K words

- $0.99/£0.99 individually
- Omnibus to follow
- Seven outlined so far!

One advantage these shorts have, is that I can fit them in as palate cleansers (for me) between other writing projects.

Enchanted - Paranormal Academy Series

Carlotta and I will be starting our outlining next week for the revamped Hellcats series, if all goes according to plan at least. We had a virtual (social distancing friendly) meeting the same night that I launched Driven by Her Lesbian Boss, to discuss our plans.

Since then, we've started having a meeting most nights to talk over some aspect of the world building.

We've picked a new location, a new name for the Academy and thus the series, and we're working on fleshing out the outline for all five books.

What's the new name for the series? We'll announce that at a later date. Probably when we relaunch Enchanted in the new format.

Our plan will be much stronger this time around so we're really looking forward to getting the series rebooted.

Though we're changing the background a little, the first book will still be called Enchanted. The story will be stronger and it will still be be sexy paranormal academy reverse harem romance (or whychoose)
.

I can't put a precise timescale on when you'll see the new book but it will be my primary project for a while. In fact, I expect to be on another long call about the world building tonight which happens to be April 1st.

If you want to follow my Twitter that's a great place to get updates and ask questions.

The account is not for the faint hearted though, as there's a fair bit of NSFW (Not Safe For Work) content so don't follow me on Twitter if that would be problematic for you.

I'm afraid I follow and retweet all sorts of erotica authors, artists, photographers and naughtiness, so you have been warned.

My Facebook is much tamer, aside from the covers which aren't all that risqué anyway.

Let Me Know What You Think

For those of you who have Kindle Unlimited, you can borrow all my books and, if you want to read them again at some point, you'll be able to borrow the omnibus editions so they don't use up lots of slots in your Kindle library.

Don't forget to let me know if you want me to prioritise writing more of the Lesbian Boss series, over say, finishing the Sexy Student Lessons series or adding another quartet to my Consort of the Werewolf King series.

I'm quite active on Twitter at the moment though it's NSFW (not safe for work), so be warned.

It's a pretty good place to reach me as I write this (March 2020) if you want to support me, talk about the books, or let me know which of my series I should concentrate on next.

Thanks for your support, and for buying the book or borrowing it through Kindle Unlimited.

Yours steamily,
K.F. Jones

A NOTE ON KINDLE UNLIMITED

Or: Why KU is great for authors.

I have recently seen a few social media comments from Kindle Unlimited (KU) subscribers who are worried that borrowing a book doesn't help the author they want to support.

I'd like to take a moment to explain why you needn't worry about this. The TLDR (too long, didn't read) version of this is, "Please borrow and read as many books as you want in KU. Don't feel you have to buy them outright to support your favourite authors."

For anyone who wants a bit more details, I'll try and explain this as briefly as possible. Because a KU subscription lets you borrow a book for 'free' I think some readers think the author is not paid at all.

Actually, we get paid per page that you read. Longer books thus earn more for us in KU than shorter ones, and may even earn more from KU reads than the cover price we've set.

Many new authors think that that's a bad deal for us, but if that were true, why are so many great authors putting books in KU?

There are more benefits to us than just the payment per book. Each sale of a book improves our ranking on Amazon. But a borrow is equivalent to a sale.

Rising in the charts, especially into the top 100 for a genre, means our book is seen by more readers. Everything else being equal, if more people see our books, more will buy them or borrow them.

Making a living as an author is simply about having enough readers who regularly choose your books. It doesn't take all that many readers to support the equivalent income of a full-time job.

Speaking only for myself I worry about my readers, my friends and family and their finances. I'm a frugal person, with relatively minimal living expenses. I have a lot of debt and I'm not wealthy, but the future I can see for me, is wonderful. Many people are not so fortunate.

I write full-time (in other genres as well) and my only income is from selling my books.

I would still much rather have someone borrow my book in KU than buy it outright, unless that's their preference. Some of my readers purchase my erotica in paperback format and that's great.

I like paperback books too, but I no longer have to carry them on a train or a plane. My ideal home would essentially be a library with a kitchen and a bathroom, and a big armchair for falling asleep in while reading.

Whether you want to read my books in KU, buy the Kindle, or the paperback, I'm happy to have you as a reader.

I run sales on my books and sometimes put the first in a series up free. Every series I complete will be available in a box set/omnibus, which will be cheaper for those not using KU.

I do that, because smarter authors than me, have proven it is worthwhile to offer discounts to attract readers.

I just want lots of people to read my books. I'd like to reach the point where I have paid off my debts, have a mortgage and can donate some of my excess income to charities.

It's really touching to me that people are thinking about the authors and other artists they support, and are keen to support us. But don't go hungry or miss a bill doing it, and don't feel bad about being a KU user.

Now, if you recently won an enormous lottery and want to read in

KU, then buy the Kindle and the paperback, none of us are going to object. I just don't want to think that someone might spend money they shouldn't for my benefit.

If you want to help more, a **review** on **Amazon** or **Goodreads** is enormously helpful. Not many readers review erotica and I get why but it would be wonderful to have more reviews as it helps other readers choose the right books.

I figure if you're reading my really long author notes, you might be amenable to say something nice, or at least constructive.

I love a glowing review as much as the next author but honesty and constructive criticism are better than flattery.*

If there are any of readers who have been worrying about whether Kindle Unlimited is fair on authors because they get the books 'free' just remember, you pay a subscription, and that's where Amazon gets money to pay us.

If the business model didn't work for readers, Amazon and authors, it would shut down.

With love,

K.F. Jones.

*I am so down for being flattered though.

ALSO BY K.F. JONES

The Consort of the Werewolf King is the first series by K.F. Jones and follows a young English biology student, who is bitten by a wild wolf.

His friends and colleagues insist that there are no wolves in the UK. William's hunt to prove he was not imagining things leads him to meet, Brian, a local landowner who may be more than he seems.

Consort of the Werewolf King (series page)

Bitten by the Alpha - Book 1

Claimed by the Alpha - Book 2

Trained by the Alpha - Book 3

Initiated by the Pack - Book 4

Consort of the Werewolf King Omnibus - 1-4

Other work by K.F. Jones

Dawn and the Galvanic Capacitor

Dawn and The Pilferer's Punishment

Dawn and the London Society

Dawn is a bounty hunter, bodyguard and private detective in a steampunk world full of adventure, excitement and lusty antics.

The Tribulations of Dawn will follow our heroine as she tries to reclaim a stolen item for her employer. The Professor is at the forefront of research into advanced steam technology, and his invention could change the world for good or ill.

Dawn has a wandering, and somewhat lascivious eye, to match her quick wit and mean right hook. Woe betide the thieves when she catches them.

But can she be well-behaved for long enough to safely return the gizmo to the

Professor? Or will it slip through her fingers and send her off on the chase again?

Submissive Lesbian Personal Assistant

Amber, a young woman who is seduced by her new employer, a dominant and wealthy lesbian.

It is now complete, with a HEA but I may write another follow on if there is demand.

If you're reading this book, you've already got this series!

Punished by Her Lesbian Boss

Seduced by Her Lesbian Boss

Trained by Her Lesbian Boss

Raced by Her Lesbian Boss

Shared by Her Lesbian Boss

Driven by Her Lesbian Boss

Her Lesbian Boss: The Complete Box Set

ABOUT THE AUTHOR

K.F. Jones writes erotica and romance books in a range of genres, with the first series, The Consort of the Werewolf King being a paranormal erotic romance.

CotWK is about a young man, Will, who finds love in the arms of Brian, a mature alpha older werewolf with a kinky streak, and a shocking secret. Brian teaches his new cub everything he needs to know to complete his initiation ritual with the pack.

The steampunk world of Dawn, a bold and lusty heroine on a mission to recover a dangerous stolen invention, is an ideal setting for all sorts of sexy, funny, adventures. When time permits, you'll see far more books in this series.

The next project is a refreshed version of Enchanted, the first book in our paranormal romance series.

If you'd like to find out when new books are released, join the mailing list at the website. **http://kfjones.net/**

twitter.com/kfjonesauthor
facebook.com/KFJonesbooks
pinterest.com/kfjonesauthor
goodreads.com/kfjones
amazon.com/author/kfjonesbooks